HERITAGE OF THE XANDIM

FUREY, Maggie

Heritage of the Xandim

CHRONICLES OF THE XANDIM
~ VOLUME I ~

HERITAGE
OF THE
XANDIM

MAGGIE FUREY

GOLLANCZ
LONDON

The right of Maggie Furey to be identified as the author of
this work has been asserted by her in accordance with the
Copyright, Designs and Patents Act 1988.

First published in Great Britain in 2009 by Gollancz
An imprint of the Orion Publishing Group
Orion House, 5 Upper St Martin's Lane, London WC2H 9EA
An Hachette UK Company

A CIP catalogue record for this book is
available from the British Library

ISBN 978 0 575 07665 5 (Cased)
ISBN 978 0 575 07662 4 (Trade Paperback)

1 3 5 7 9 10 8 6 4 2

Typeset by Deltatype Ltd, Birkenhead, Merseyside
Printed in Great Britain by CPI Mackays, Chatham, Kent

www.orionbooks.co.uk

The Orion Publishing Group's policy is to use papers that are natural,
renewable and recyclable products and made from wood grown in sustainable
forests. The logging and manufacturing processes are expected to conform
to the environmental regulations of the country of origin.

This book is dedicated, with the utmost gratitude, to
Professor Ciaran Bolger,
Consultant Neurosurgeon, Wizard and Genius.
You gave me back my life. I can never thank you enough.

WITH GRATITUDE

During the last few years of illness and a nightmare of pain, it sometimes seemed impossible that I would ever make it through. The fact that I finally did is due in no small part to a number of very special people, and I would like to take this opportunity to thank them all.

First and foremost, my everlasting thanks go to Professor Ciaran Bolger, Neurosurgeon, who performed delicate, intricate and risky spinal surgery with inspiring confidence and skill.

Thank you, Dr Raymond Victory, Consultant in Pain Management, whose very name made me feel better, and whose nerve blocks helped keep me going.

Thanks to Dr Ian Bothwell, my GP, whose kindness, help and understanding got me through a horrible time, not to mention his wife Edel, receptionist, and Practice Nurse June Darcy, who were so supportive.

Thank you, Patricia Swords, Reiki and Amatsu Practitioner, whose hands, and whose friendship, had a positively magical way of easing the pain.

Many thanks to Mary Varilly for being such a kind and wonderful friend, and helping me so much in every way she could; and to her daughter Claire, who has inherited her mother's compassion.

Thanks to my neighbour Linda Moore, who was always just a phone call away.

Thank you, John Meaney, for the Tapping.

Thanks to my sister, Lin Stockley, for flying over from Edinburgh and back in a day to feed my cats while Eric had to be away.

Thanks to Paddy Sheridan and Ken Carrington, for being, as always, charming, delightful and kind friends who were on hand to provide good company and some lovely evenings out.

Many thanks to my Dad, Jim Armstrong, for all the hours of worrying he put in on my behalf, and to my mother, Margaret, who came over from England on several occasions to take care of a post-operative daughter who was helpless in a full-body brace while her husband was working at the other end of the country.

I can't leave out my cats Merlin and Sunshine in the thanks. They somehow knew that all was not well, and one or the other, if not both, stayed at my side at all times.

I would like to thank my agent, John Parker, who kept the lines of communication open even when I couldn't face talking to anyone, and who worked so hard to make sure I had a career to come back to.

A multitude of thanks go to Simon Spanton of Orion Books, with whom I had recently signed when all the trouble started. I'm tremendously thankful for his patience and understanding in being willing to wait so long. Thanks also to Jo Fletcher of Orion, whose own experiences gave her such an insight into my difficulties.

Thanks to John Jarrold, for his wonderful editorial insights into the manuscript of this book. As always, John, it's a tremendous pleasure to work with you.

Most of all, I would like to thank my husband Eric, who has stuck with me through thick and thin, and patiently nursed a wife who for weeks after her surgery couldn't even make a cup of tea or take a shower without assistance. I love you so much. You are the best thing in my life.

And finally, to all the readers who have waited through this lengthy and mysterious absence: thank you. You're what it's all about.

THE CAILLEACH

The omens brought the Lady of the Mists down to the shores of the Timeless Lake. They came to the Cailleach in the midst of her waking dreams, disturbing the tranquillity of her eternal meditations. In this Place Beyond the World, there was no day or night or passing of the seasons; there was no hunger, thirst, loneliness – or change. There was only the Lady, one of the powerful, ancient Guardians who had been present at the world's creation and who would be there at its end. Only the Lady, and her endlessly-spun web of contemplation. Until the omens came, like a stone thrown into the tranquil waters of the Timeless Lake, casting ripples of disquiet through her thoughts.

The sense of unease that awoke the Cailleach from her reverie drove her out of her resting place in the great Tree that lay at the Centre of all things, beneath the Timeless Lake. Quitting her softly glowing chamber in the Tree's hollow heart, she passed down the steps that were natural formations in the stonelike bark, crossed the floor of the vast cavern in which the behemoth was rooted and passed into the extraordinary woodland that edged the clearing. It was a forest carved from stone: every detail was perfect, from the trees with their leaves of jade and finely wrought blossoms of translucent quartz, right down to the flowers made of coloured gems, the insects with bejewelled wings and the delicate stone birds, so realistic that they might burst into flight or song at any moment.

Beyond the forest of stone lay the spiral of basalt steps that took the Cailleach out of the cavern. Climbing up and up, driven by anxiety, driven by need, she finally emerged through a portal in the rock, high up on the pinnacle of the island at the centre of the Timeless Lake. The only light came from the stars scattered across a sky that was the clear royal blue of a sapphire. Constellations were reflected in the smooth lake waters, but, strangely, the stars that shone there came from a different sky from that above. Treading the spiral path of shining stone with care, the ancient Guardian made her way to the foot of the pinnacle and knelt down on a tongue of rock that protruded into the still, dark lake with its glittering reflections from some unknown sky. Looking into the infinite depths, she waited to see what had called her here.

A film of silvery vapour drifted across the surface of the water. It swirled, dissolved, coalesced, then parted again, revealing and obscuring a succession of vivid images. Forming and dissolving, they flickered through the depths, giving the Lady a window into the future. The world she had helped to create spun before her in all its complexity – then her eyes were drawn to one continent in particular.

In its northlands, she saw Eliorand, city of the Phaerie, shrouded by the cloak of glamourie which gave it the appearance of a forested hill. Further south, beyond the Phaerie realm ruled by Hellorin the Forest Lord, dwelt the four races of Magefolk, wielders of elemental magic. The Cailleach caught glimpses of the Winged Folk, masters of the element of Air, in their peak-top city of Aerillia; the Dragonfolk, Masters of Fire, in their jewelled realm of Dhiammara; the Leviathan and their partners in magic the Merfolk, who roamed the ocean depths to wield the power of the element of Water, returning from time to time to the coral city of Amauin, where their wise ones dwelt. Finally there were the wizards, human in form and skilled in Earth Magic, who dwelt in beautiful Tyrineld, their seat of lore and learning, on the wild, rocky coastline of the western ocean.

Also scattered throughout the continent were the lowly slave race of mortals who, with no powers of their own, existed to serve both Phaerie and Magefolk. All the races, Magical and mortal, were still dwelling side by side as they had done for many a long age, in varying degrees of harmony and discord, but without overt conflict. The Lady of the Mists, however, had an uneasy premonition that this fragile peace was about to be shattered.

Suddenly a dark, spreading stain the colour of blood obscured the visions in the water. It cleared to reveal a series of images that chilled the Cailleach's heart. Her unease turned to dread as she watched the Magefolk fashioning four mighty magical artefacts; weapons of extraordinary power, using elemental forces that were too intense by far for the mundane world. The Cailleach gave a low cry, her horror vying with sheer anger at such folly. The Mages had taken too much upon themselves – could they not *see* that their actions were certain to end in catastrophe?

Images followed one upon the other in swift succession now, showing the Phaerie and the four races of Magefolk ripped apart by war. The force of their magic devastated the land with fire and ice, flood and tempest, earthquake and plague. A crazed colossus threatened to shatter the very bones of the earth in his madness. A beautiful and ancient city vanished forever. Entire races were brought to the very brink of extinction, and it seemed inevitable that some of these must perish utterly, leaving great tracts of the ruined lands devoid of life.

The visions faded into darkness, leaving only the enigmatic waters of the Timeless Lake. Slowly, the Cailleach rose to her feet, her heart dark with foreboding. Was there to be no future for the Magefolk, for the Phaerie – for the world?

She was about to turn away when a ripple passed across the surface of the lake, sending wavelets lapping at her feet. Away from the island, at the point where the lake was deepest, a patch of water began to glow with a crimson light that appeared to be rising slowly from the very depths. The Lady of the Mists froze, forgetting even to breathe. She had dwelt in this place beyond the very beginnings of the world, and she had never seen anything like this.

As it rose towards the surface the light grew brighter, changing colour as it gained in brilliance, moving up through the spectrum to a violet so intense that the Cailleach's eyes could scarcely focus on it. The water began to bubble and boil – then suddenly the light changed to the blue-white dazzle of a lightning bolt as three stars erupted from the lake in a fountain of silver spray and hurtled towards the heavens, rising to take their place in the skies above, changing the face of the constellations forever.

And in that moment, the Lady knew. She no longer needed to look into the lake, for the visions came clearly and directly into her mind. Three women, all born when the moon was concealed by the shadow of the sun, would hold the future of the world in their hands, determining whether it would be lost or saved. Three children of a red moon, a blood moon, born when the sky was dark and full of violent portents: one a Wizard, one Phaerie-born, and the other ...

The Cailleach paused and blinked, as if by doing so she could clear her inner vision. Try as she would to see this woman – and she knew in her heart that it *was* a woman – all that would come into her mind was the image of a grey horse; running, running ...

As the vision faded, the Lady of the Mists clenched her fists in frustration. Who was that last woman? *What* was she? Why couldn't the Cailleach see her? For she knew, without a doubt, that this last star, this last child, this last, enigmatic woman, would prove to be the most important of all.

PART I

~

ELIORAND

THE WILD HUNT

On a winter's night when frost made the city of Eliorand glitter like a jewel-box, and the air was so cold that it splintered on the tongue, the Hunt made ready for its first great ride of the season. An air of frantic activity permeated the stables of Hellorin, Lord of the Phaerie. Lamplight blazed in the vast complex of paddocks, boxes and barns that took up much of the northern face of the eminence on which the city was built. The stables housed not only the horses belonging to the Forest Lord's courtiers, but also those of most of the other Phaerie in the city, for the rest of the hill was taken up with beautiful houses, gardens, gracious parks and public buildings, with little provision for livestock. Everyone gained from the arrangement. The Phaerie could keep their magnificent animals in the best possible facilities with little inconvenience to themselves, the horses benefited from the most skilled of attendants and, in addition to the levies which increased the royal coffers, it pleased Hellorin's sense of power to have the unique breed of Phaerie steeds under his control.

The grooms – mostly human slaves who, due to their hard work and expertise, occupied a privileged position in the royal household – were bustling to and fro: some grooming, some checking hooves, while others saddled the horses, decking them in caparisons made from fabric that glowed with coloured radiance. Orders flew back and forth, but there was no time for the banter that was permitted on a normal day. Aelwen, Mistress of the Royal Horses, stalked back and forth along the aisles between the boxes, her eyes seemingly everywhere at once, making sure that nothing was neglected or skimped, and that everything was done to her usual exacting standards.

A current of restless excitement was sweeping through the horses. All but the very youngest beasts had hunted before, and knew exactly what was happening. Corisand, in her stall at the end of the row, fidgeted and snorted, striking with a forefoot at the door of the box. She laid her ears back at the stable lad who was trying unsuccessfully to make her keep still so that he could saddle her, and the young groom cursed and yanked roughly at her bridle.

'Here now, enough of that. Stop wrenching her around, you halfwit, and leave her to me.' Kelon, Aelwen's head groom, entered the box, leaving room for the lad to scurry out. 'You go and finish getting Maiglan ready for the Lady Tiolani, and I'll see to this fractious little girl myself.'

'Little girl, my backside,' the lad muttered sullenly. 'She's as big as any of the others, and twice as bloody awkward. What she wants is a—'

'What she wants is someone with a bit of common sense, instead of an idle, thoughtless fool.' Kelon's voice had taken on an icy bite that had even the mare turning her head in surprise. 'And I've told you before, Horsemistress Aelwen will have no swearing in her stable. Now get about your work.'

Scowling, the youth stamped off, and Kelon, the smile back on his face, turned to Corisand. 'Now then, little one, let's get you settled down and looking beautiful. You'll be carrying the Lord of the Phaerie, remember, and you have to look the part.' His hands were gentle and, unlike the other groom, his voice was soothing and soft. Also, there was a sense of presence and strength about him that made Corisand cease her antics immediately.

Kelon never raised his voice to any of the horses – he didn't have to. He was a horseman to the bone, and in his presence the most recalcitrant of animals suddenly found itself behaving exactly as he would wish. Now he was putting on the saddle with deft expertise, talking softly to her all the while in a low, crooning voice. 'There now. That's better, isn't it? And you won't have to worry about that young idiot any more. I'll have a word with Mistress Aelwen, and by tomorrow he'll be back among the field labourers hoeing cabbages. Serve him right, too. Some folk just aren't fit to work in a stable.'

Corisand was a horse, and her thoughts were not like those of a human. But she knew what it meant when all this bustle happened, and every horse was prepared. She knew that soon she'd be out and free: running, flying through the frosty night air, hurtling with her companions across forest clearings in a shower of mud and leaves, and leaping over fallen trees. That feeling of freedom, illusory though it was, was what she lived for. The urge had been in her blood ever since her birth: an independence of spirit that had almost cost her her life when she had seemingly proved unrideable; the only horse ever to defeat the skills of Aelwen and

Kelon. It had been the Forest Lord's inability to resist a challenge that had saved her, and even he had needed to use magic in the beginning, to control her and override her will. So now she'd become Hellorin's horse, replacing his ageing grey mare Maiglan, who was getting too old for the Hunt. The compromise had not come without a bitter inward struggle, but the Wild Hunt was the only thing that came close to the perfect freedom that Corisand craved.

The horses were not the only ones to be excited by the prospect of the coming Hunt. All the men and women of the Phaerie Court, their eyes ablaze with a fierce excitement, streamed out of the Forest Lord's palace and hurried down the flight of steps that led to the courtyard, where they gathered in laughing, chattering groups, waiting for the grooms to bring their mounts to them. The Phaerie hunters were a glorious sight, their faces exquisite with a timeless beauty, and their hair spangled with gems. Their clothes, made of a flexible, silken material spun from the cocoons of luminous moonmoths, fitted them as closely as a second skin. The fabric was light as spider silk but warmer than wool, and it glistened in a multitude of hues, for each thread had been magically imbued with its own inner radiance, so that their garments glowed brightly in the starlight.

In a corner of the courtyard the pack of fellhounds – great silver-grey dogs with eyes of golden fire – milled about restlessly, kept under control by Gwylan the Huntsman and his assistants. The fellhounds yelped and snarled, catching their masters' excitement. They knew what lay ahead: soon they would be released upon their quarry, to run their victims down, and tear, and kill.

A silvery fanfare of trumpets marked the arrival of the Forest Lord. Hellorin appeared in the torchlit doorway, cloaked in his customary green and silver, his long, dark hair touched with starlight, his tall form powerful and muscular, his shoulders broad beneath his cloak. He wore a golden crown of oak leaves, above which could be seen the shadowy form of a stag's branching antlers. At his side stood Arvain, his son and heir, who, with his tawny curls and lively golden eyes, was the image of his mother.

Hellorin looked fondly at his son, his eyes brightening at the memory of the beloved soulmate he had lost. Estrelle, the Lady of the Forest, had been beautiful indeed. Her hair, the colour of autumn leaves, had reached almost to the ground. Her eyes were golden, and her complexion, so unlike the translucent pallor of most Phaerie ladies, looked as though her skin had been kissed by the sun. Frank, fearless and fair, with a merry smile and sparkling eyes, she had been a perfect foil for her royal consort, adored by her people almost as much as she was loved by Hellorin himself. She had died twenty years ago, just a year after giving birth to Arvain's sister, Tiolani. Hellorin and his subjects still mourned her passing.

The Phaerie were Immortal, and did not pass from the mundane world unless they chose to do so, or were killed by an accident or an act of violence. Arvain, therefore, was unlikely ever to succeed to the leadership of his people, but he appeared not to mind. Possessing his mother's sunny nature, he was content to study magic, to perfect his martial skills with sword and bow, to enjoy his many friendships – and to take part in the Hunt. Sharing his father's passion for the extraordinary Phaerie horses, he took a great interest in the improvement of the breed.

'Ho, Ferimon, there you are.' Arvain descended the staircase a step or two to talk to his friend. 'Looks like a good night for hunting.'

'Not for me.' Ferimon grimaced. 'I lost at dice with Jeryla, and she's making me ride with her and the rest of the net-casters tonight.' As tall as Arvain, he was more than a match in looks for his high-born companion, with his sun-gold hair and his blue eyes that were most unusual in one of the pure-blooded Phaerie. A cluster of young women hovered around them, all hoping for a golden glance from the bright eyes of Hellorin's heir, or the flash of a charming white grin from Ferimon.

Hellorin, seeing that smile, felt his stomach tighten.

When he smiles like that, he is the image of his father.

For an instant, Estrelle's face flashed before him, not lively and laughing as he remembered it best, but pale and spattered with dirt and blood, a gash across the temple and an ugly bruise darkening all down one side, while her golden eyes, their splendour dimmed in death, stared up blankly at the forest canopy above.

With a shudder, the Forest Lord thrust the dreadful memory away. This would be Tiolani's first Hunt, not a night for bad memories, and he had always sworn that he would never blame the son for the transgressions of the father.

Arvain was laughing at his friend. 'That'll teach you to wager with Jeryla. She's the most skilful cheat at dice I ever came across.' Suddenly remembering his proper place, he ran back up the steps to his father. 'How the court love their little amusements,' he remarked to Hellorin, gesturing at the bright-eyed throng below. 'They are as eager as the hounds to be off. See? They can scarcely wait.'

And neither can you, the Forest Lord thought, his stern mouth softening into a smile. 'Speaking of waiting, where is that sister of yours? She had better hurry.'

'Ah, let her be, my Lord. Tonight is special.' Arvain laughed. 'I recall my first Hunt. I spent an age getting ready, as vain as any girl. It's the same for us all. I will call her.' For a moment he was silent, his golden gaze opaque and inward-looking. 'She comes.'

'Are you *sure* I look all right?' Tiolani turned this way and that in front of the mirror, scanning her reflection with a critical eye

Varna, her lady-in-waiting, two years older and Ferimon's sister, cast her eyes up to the ceiling. 'For the thousandth time, you look perfect. Now, can we *please* go? It will not do to keep the Lord of the Phaerie waiting, even if he is your father.' Grabbing Tiolani's hand, she tugged her determinedly towards the door.

Tiolani glanced back for one last look in the mirror. She was always concerned about her appearance – that was all part of being the Forest Lord's only daughter – but tonight was different. Now that she had reached her twenty-first year, she was about to join the other members of her father's court in one of their best-loved and exciting pastimes, but this would be about more than just thrills and sport. Her first Hunt was a rite of passage which all Phaerie must undergo. Only when she had killed her first human would she truly be accepted as an adult, and a member of the Phaerie Court.

Will I like it? Will I really like hunting mortals – all the bloodshed and the slaughter?

Of course she would. Tiolani dealt firmly with that small quiver of doubt. She was Phaerie, and Hellorin's daughter. The Hunt was part of her heritage. It was in her blood. Why should she not come to love it as Arvain had?

As Varna hurried her out of the room, the image in the mirror lingered in her mind. Could she compete with the slender lady-in-waiting, as dark as her brother was fair, and one of the greatest beauties of the court? She decided that she could. Like Arvain, she had inherited her looks from her mother, though the copper in her tawny hair was a shade or two deeper. Her eyes, however, instead of being golden, were dark grey; uncannily like those of her father but lacking, as yet, the mastery of Hellorin's piercing gaze. Tonight they sparkled in a face that was pale with excitement. Her long red-gold hair normally hung loose down her back in rippled waves, but tonight, under Varna's skilful hands, it had been threaded with gems and looped back in an intricate arrangement of braids. After much deliberation, she had settled on shining gold for her costume, and the result was dazzling. She might be a newcomer to the

Hunt, but she was damned if she would let any of the hard-riding females in the Court outshine her when it came to looks.

At that moment, Arvain's call, spoken directly from one mind to the other, broke into her thoughts. 'Tiolani, are you not ready yet? Hurry up, you little monster. Do you want to keep the entire court waiting all night?'

Tiolani gasped in dismay. 'Tell Father I'm sorry,' she called back. 'Varna and I are on our way right now.'

Hearing the sound of hoofbeats, Hellorin turned towards the entrance of the long, echoing tunnel that curved through the depths of the hill, even passing beneath the palace itself, to emerge in the courtyard before the great doors. This permitted the Phaerie steeds to be brought with ease from the north-facing stables at the bottom of the hill to the palace high on the southern slopes, without having to thread a long and tortuous way through the crowded streets above ground. The passageway had been cunningly wrought by magic, and lit all along its length by crystal globes filled with tamed lightning that crackled and hummed and gave out a tingling ozone smell.

A procession of grooms was leading the horses into the courtyard up the gentle ramp at the tunnel's entrance. Hellorin looked at the animals with pride. The mounts of the Phaerie could rival and in some respects even surpass their masters in splendour. Their necks arched proudly, their great muscles moved smoothly under shining coats and their long manes and tails swept down in waves of gleaming silk. In appearance, speed, stamina and every other respect, they were far superior to the horses of the Wizardfolk – as well they might be. They were different. Special. They were bred only here in the royal stables, and they were never traded or sold to people of other races. Their origins were a mystery known solely to the Phaerie.

The Phaerie loved secrets, and it pleased the Forest Lord inordinately that his Wizardly rivals had never guessed the origins of the Xandim breed: that these splendid creatures had once been shapeshifters, capable of switching at will between human and equine form. Hellorin smiled. The subjugation of the Xandim race had been one of his greatest triumphs. His people had discovered the tribe of metamorphs in the mountains that formed the northern boundaries of their own realm. The Xandim were a primitive people by the standards of the Phaerie and Magefolk civilis- ations, and it had been no great task to subdue them. Their human aspect had been of little interest to the Forest Lord – he already possessed mortal slaves aplenty. He had been stunned, however, by the magnificence of their equine forms, and it had been a simple enough matter to formulate the spells which trapped them in that shape forever.

Arvain ran back down the steps and took the reins of his magnificent chestnut stallion from the groom. 'It's a good thing,' he said to his father, 'that none of the Magefolk know that the Xandim ever existed – otherwise, no doubt, they would be raising their usual bleeding-heart outcry at what we've done.'

Hellorin shrugged. 'After this long age, there is no way in which they could discover the truth. No living soul outside the Phaerie can remember the origins of these animals, and after so many generations have come and gone, even the Xandim themselves must have forgotten that they were ever human.'

You are almost right, Hellorin – but one of us remembers. One single Xandim holds the memories of a race long gone.

The chestnut stallion Valir, Arvain's mount, eyed the Forest Lord coldly. No one, not even his own people, suspected that he possessed an intelligence and intellect far beyond that of an ordinary beast. Of them all, only he remembered that the Phaerie horses had come from very different beginnings. He was the Windeye, or Shaman, of the Xandim race – a role which had originated in the time before the tribe had been enslaved and trapped in their equine shapes, and which had been passed down through his bloodline during all the countless generations in captivity. Only the Windeye possessed powers of the Old Magic, which stemmed from the same ancient roots as the arcane abilities of the Phaerie. And though he was unable to access this magic whilst in his equine shape, at least it allowed him to think and reason in a human way – and, more importantly, to remember his origins and those of his people.

It wasn't easy. To become Windeye was to be born into a life of frustration and loneliness. The other Xandim could neither think nor communicate in the complex manner of the Phaerie. They had few actual words – such as 'food', 'run', 'come', 'go' and 'danger' – and these could be expressed through a change in stance, the roll of an eye or the tilt of an ear, as well as through vocal sounds. Their thoughts were also simple, and based on emotion, cause and effect, or instinct. Much worse, they could neither remember nor understand what they had lost. What could a Windeye – one solitary individual – do to change all that? Valir was trapped: without magic he stood no chance of fighting the Phaerie and regaining his humanity, yet until he could take on human form, his powers would be lost to him, and he could do nothing to help his people.

Standing there in the crowded courtyard, the stallion wondered which of his many sons and daughters would inherit his mantle when he was gone. Only one in every generation had the seeds of the Windeye's powers lying dormant within, which would burst into life following the current Shaman's death. *So I'll never find out which of them it will be,* Valir thought. *If only there was some way of knowing. Then at least I could warn them, prepare them, try to explain ...*

Even if he could discover the identity of his successor, there was no way he could make an equine mind understand what lay in store. *Maybe they are better off not knowing,* he thought grimly. There would be time enough, once they had assumed the mantle of Windeye, for them to be tortured by the memory of what they had lost, and were powerless to regain. Time enough to know frustration and despair because they were unable to help their people. Time enough to be revolted by the savage slaughter of the Hunt. Time enough to loathe and abominate the Phaerie for what they had done.

All too aware that they were keeping Hellorin and the Phaerie Court waiting, Tiolani and Varna had raced down corridors and flights of stairs, but when they reached the lower levels of the palace, their progress was slowed by knots of courtiers who were all heading in the same direction for the self-same purpose.

Why, we're not so late after all, Tiolani thought indignantly. *From what Arvain told me, I thought everyone would be standing around in the courtyard, waiting for us – though, if they had been outside, at least there would not be all these crowds to delay us.*

She had no intention, however, of letting the crowds obstruct her. 'Make way,' she called out in imperious tones. 'Make way, there.' Reluctantly, the members of the court – a bunch of empty-headed idiots in the candid opinion of Hellorin's daughter, and they didn't like her any better – moved aside to let the girls through. They hurried between the massive carven doors of the palace, and went out into the courtyard.

The Lord of the Phaerie, who still stood at the top of the steps, turned to greet his daughter. 'I'm so sorry I'm late,' Tiolani said, curtseying low. Her contrite tone and expression notwithstanding, she was confident that her father would forgive her. He always did.

Hellorin smiled. 'It was worth the wait. You look lovely, my dear. Absolutely radiant. All this excitement has you shining like a jewel. Ah, to be taking part in my first Hunt again.'

Though Tiolani smiled at him, warm with such praise, her attention was already wandering, her eyes moving, seemingly of their own volition, to seek out Ferimon in the crowd. Surely tonight, *her* night, he would look at her a little differently? Maybe realise that she had grown into more than just his friend's bothersome little sister? But his shining blond head was turned away from her as he talked and laughed with the usual crowd of young women who were always around him, hanging on his every word, and he was paying no attention to her at all. Not even tonight.

Tiolani's glow of pleasure died, and the temper that she had never really learned to control rose up in its place. What was the point of stupid compliments from her father? She could get them any time. Gritting her teeth with frustration, she turned away from Ferimon and his collection of fawning females. She was damned if she would let anybody see the jealousy that always overwhelmed her at the sight of that coterie of giggling fools, and she had no intention of joining their ranks. She was Hellorin's daughter. She could never demean herself in such a way. And she had far more important things to think about tonight than Ferimon.

Her brother slung an affectionate arm around her shoulders. 'Worried about the Hunt, Monster? Stick close to me. I'll show you how it's done.'

Forgetting, for a moment, that they were under public scrutiny, and therefore she ought to be on her best behaviour, Tiolani glared at him. 'Will you, indeed? Well, for your information, I'm not the least bit worried. I'm as good a rider as you are, any day.'

The Huntsman, Gwylan, came up the staircase and bowed low to Hellorin. 'All is ready, my Lord. My scouts have found our quarry for tonight – a nest of feral humans living in the forest to the south.'

'Excellent,' Hellorin said. 'Have the horses brought immediately.' He turned to his assembled subjects. 'Come, my children. Our sport awaits us.'

Tiolani was very proud of her own horse. He was a recent acquisition – a birthday gift from her brother – and the fastest, most spirited mount she had ever ridden. His coat was dark bay in colour: a deep, burnished reddish-brown, with a black mane and tail, and legs black to the knees, as though he had been wading in midnight. He moved like a dancing flame. His eyes were bright and brimming with curiosity and mischief, and a white star blazed on his forehead. She called him Asharal. Spirited and fiery, he was not the easiest of rides, but to Tiolani's prejudiced eyes he was utterly perfect. She was very surprised, therefore, when there was no sign of him among the horses being led out. Instead, Aelwen approached her, leading Maiglan, her father's old mare.

There was no mistake. The Horsemistress stopped in front of her and smiled. 'Here we are, my Lady. Your mount awaits.'

'What are you talking about?' Tiolani demanded. 'That's not my horse. Where is Asharal?'

Aelwen was unfazed by the girl's imperious manner. Such was Hellorin's love of the unique Phaerie steeds that he considered his Horsemistress the most important member of his court, after his family. Furthermore, she had been not only Estrelle's best friend, but also her half-sister. Aelwen was a Hemifae, one of the many Phaerie with human blood in her veins, sharing the same father as Hellorin's consort but borne by a mortal mother. Phaerie women found it difficult and dangerous to give birth, and sometimes a couple, unable or unwilling to take the risk, would use a mortal woman to bear children for them. Though these half-bloods were accepted as Phaerie in almost every way, everyone was tacitly aware of the difference.

Over the ages, the Hemifae had tended to become the travellers, the traders, the innovators and the artisans, who were prepared to journey to the world outside to expand their knowledge or improve their fortunes. In the meantime, the full-blooded members of Hellorin's race had become an aristocracy, devoting their time to magic, to their martial skills, to their pleasures – and, of course, to the Hunt. Only they could become members of Hellorin's court. Though Aelwen had been nominally admitted to that select body long ago, she had used the concession little since her beloved sister's death, despising the formality, the ridiculous, overly elaborate fashions and the sneering asides of the courtiers towards the half-breed in their midst. The dubious privilege had been granted her partly due to her skill with Hellorin's precious horses, but mainly because of her close kinship with Estrelle. The two of them had even looked similar – or so most folk said. Aelwen had glowing copper hair, a much darker shade than that of Estrelle, but her eyes were that same glorious gold. She still looked young and beautiful, as did all the immortal Phaerie-folk, but her face had that indefinable cast that denoted maturity, and the expression in her eyes was kindly, shrewd and wise as she addressed the scowling girl. 'I'm afraid you won't be riding Asharal tonight, my dear.'

'Why? What's wrong?' Tiolani demanded. 'Is he lame? What have those idiot grooms of yours done to him?'

A stab of anger wiped the pleasant expression from Aelwen's face. *How dare Hellorin's pampered brat of a daughter criticise the running of my stable,* she thought. *I've devoted my life to these animals. What she knows about their care wouldn't fill a thimble.* 'There is nothing wrong with him,' she replied. 'Asharal is in my charge, and as you are well aware, he receives the best of care. Or were you implying otherwise?'

Tiolani had the grace to blush. 'No, no, of course not,' she said hastily. 'But why have you not brought him out?'

'I am acting on your father's orders,' Aelwen told her. 'He says you'll have enough to cope with on your first Hunt without trying to ride a horse as untried as yourself. Instead, he's lending you his own horse, Maiglan.'

'What? That old thing? Well, I won't do it. I refuse to have all the members of this court sniggering up their sleeves at me.'

Aelwen shrugged. 'Suit yourself.' She called to one of her grooms, who had just left his charge with its owner. 'Siglon, will you take Maiglan back to the stable, please? The Lady Tiolani won't be riding tonight.' From the corner of her eye she saw Hellorin, alerted by the commotion, looking their way, and smiled to herself.

Evidently Tiolani had noticed her father, too. 'No, wait. Stop.' Clearly determined to make one last effort, she turned pleading eyes on her aunt. 'Aelwen, please?' she wheedled. 'You know how Father respects your judgement. Surely if *you* said it was all right for me to ride Asharal, he'd reconsider—'

'Tiolani, forget it. You're about to embark on a very risky undertaking. Your safety is Hellorin's primary concern, and he's right. On your first Hunt it would be madness to ride such an inexperienced, hot-blooded animal. Take it as an honour that your father trusts you with his precious Maiglan, and let her look after you on your first few Hunts. After that, you'll have the experience to teach Asharal all *he* needs to know.'

Tiolani sighed. 'All right,' she grumbled. 'Arvain will never stop teasing me, but if it's the only way I can join the Hunt, I suppose I'll have to ride father's decrepit cast-off.'

'Your brother won't tease you. He learned to hunt on an experienced old horse just as you are doing.' Aelwen smiled to herself, and stroked the mare's bowed neck. 'As for Maiglan, I think she may surprise you.'

'And those stupid humans will sprout wings and fly,' Tiolani muttered ungraciously as she mounted the mare and, without a word of thanks to Aelwen, rode off to join her father and brother.

The Horsemistress looked around the gathering, checking that all was well with her precious charges. Everything was going smoothly. The throngs of brightly clad Phaerie were all mounted now, and drinking stirrup-cups of mulled wine served by slaves in the palace livery. As a Hemifae, Aelwen was not permitted to join the Hunt, though she owned a splendid black stallion from Hellorin's best stock, and her happiest hours were spent on horseback. Yet she had never had the slightest urge to join the hunters – perhaps because of what had happened to Estrelle?

Or because of the unwelcome, uncomfortable knowledge that the blood of their victims also ran in her veins?

Tonight, however, she wished that just this once she could have gone with Tiolani. In the excitement of the Hunt, there was no way that the girl's father and brother, despite their best intentions, would be able to keep an eye on her. It needed someone with a clear head to do that, someone who was not participating in the Hunt. Someone whose thoughts were not fogged by excitement and bloodlust. In other words, herself. Though Tiolani was so spoilt that sometimes Aelwen itched to slap her, she was still Estrelle's daughter, and as such the Horsemistress felt a deep sense of responsibility that would have been most unwelcome to the recipient, had she known about it.

Aelwen's common sense, however, would not let her indulge in mis-placed concern for long. *You fool*, she told herself. *An accident like the one that killed Estrelle is a rare occurrence, and Maiglan is an old hand at this business. She'll keep Tiolani out of trouble, and the girl will be fine, as well you know. It's high time she started taking some responsibility, even if it* is *just for herself and her own safety.* She knew it was true. In reality, she was far more concerned that Hellorin's daughter was living a life in which she was constantly pampered, protected and indulged. All of Tiolani's potential was going to waste. The girl should be allowed a chance to develop some backbone, or she'd be nothing but a useless, self-centred, feather-headed ornament to Hellorin's court for the rest of her life. That was no exist-ence, Aelwen thought, for the daughter of Estrelle, who had been such a competent, capable, generous and intelligent woman. *Am I failing the girl in some way?* she wondered. Yet what could she do when Tiolani's father and brother spoilt and cosseted her to such an extent?

Tiolani, despite being mounted on the despised Maiglan, was stand-ing beside Hellorin and Arvain. Her face was flushed, her eyes were sparkling, and her sulks had clearly been forgotten in the excitement of the moment. Aelwen loved her with all her heart, and would never wish any harm to her, and yet ... 'If only something would happen to throw a few challenges into the girl's life,' she murmured to herself. 'That's the only way Tiolani will ever develop the strength of character that she so badly needs.'

She had no idea, then, that before the sun came up she would bitterly regret those words.

2

~

INITIATION

Though Tiolani was disappointed about Asharal, she tried to do as Aelwen said, and appreciate that her father was doing her an honour in letting her ride his own horse. The silver-white mare bore her years lightly, and still had more than sufficient stamina, speed and spirit to serve a novice huntress well on her first Wild Hunt. From her pricked ears and the brightness of her eyes, it was plain that she was delighted to be hunting again. She snorted and stamped as they waited in the courtyard, as impatient to be off as any of the younger animals. Hellorin, in the meantime, had mounted his new mare, Maiglan's daughter; a much darker, dappled grey with a black mane and tail. The creature was far more fiery and wilful than Asharal, Tiolani thought with a tinge of resentment. He had called her Corisand, an ancient Phaerie word for a tempest, and ever since she'd been a foal, she had lived up to the name.

The Forest Lord blew on a silver horn, and suddenly the courtyard fell silent save for the baying of the great grey fellhounds. He flung up his arm in a skyward gesture, and the magic of his flying spell streamed from his fingers in glittering trails that drifted down like snow to cover the riders of the Hunt, their mounts and the pack of hounds in a cloak of scintillating light.

Gwylan gave the signal to loose the fellhounds. The pack leapt forward as one, streaming across the courtyard, but before they reached the gates they were in the air and climbing fast, the shimmer of the flying spell leaving a trail of sparks beneath their feet. Hellorin's dappled mare bounded forward, diamond starbursts appearing beneath her hooves as the spell took hold. She sprang into the air and simply kept on going, running easily as though ascending a gentle slope, with every stride taking her further aloft. Arvain, holding in his own chestnut stallion with difficulty, turned to Tiolani. 'Come on, Monster. Follow me.'

Tiolani gathered her reins and urged Maiglan on. She felt the lurch as the mare leapt forward and they took off in their skyward leap just a stride behind Arvain. As she climbed, the frosty night air swept past her, burning chill against her face and hands, and whipping away the crystalline clouds of her breath. Beneath her, she glimpsed a dizzying whirl of rooftops; then, as she gained more height, the entire city stretched out beneath her. At the top of the eminence on which Eliorand stood was Hellorin's palace, a cluster of elegant towers with a complex of other buildings grouped round them that contained everything from banqueting halls and state chambers right down to the palace kitchens, and the workshops and living quarters of those whose sole work it was to maintain the royal abode in all its beauty and splendour. Like all structures in Eliorand, the buildings were fashioned from polished wood and stone with the flowing, organic lines that the Phaerie loved so well, so that they seemed to spring naturally out of the hillside. Close to the palace in magnificent dwellings lived the true Phaerie, the members of Hellorin's court. On the lower slopes were the homes of the Hemifae, as well as markets, workshops and beautiful gardens and parks.

'Watch where you're going, you stupid little ...'

Tiolani, whose attention had all been on the city below instead of on her fellow members of the Hunt, wrenched her horse out of the impending collision almost by instinct. The other rider did the same and veered away, cursing all idiots who didn't know enough to keep their wits about them in the sky. In the heat of the moment, he had never even noticed who had so nearly run into him, and Tiolani was glad of that. She had been gawking like some mooncalf at the view, while so many other horses were moving at speed in the sky around her. Her heart hammered at the thought of what would have happened if she or the other rider had been unseated in a collision. A fall from this height meant certain death. How could she have been so inattentive, knowing as she did that Ferimon's father, drunk and careless, had caused just such an accident which had taken the life of her mother?

The entire court was now in motion, rising into the night skies to add their glittering presence to the glory of the stars. They were an awe-inspiring sight, terrifying in their splendour, their robes of shimmering, many-hued luminescence trailing behind them in sparkling drifts like comet-tails. The horses were caparisoned in the same glistening fabric, and their reins gleamed with pure white light. As the riders swept low above the treetops, following the baying hounds, everything that their trailing vestments touched took on the mysterious radiance, to be limned in frosty rainbow sparkles that spread from branch to branch, outlining the boughs and leaves in delicate traceries of lustre.

When Tiolani looked down at herself, she saw the visual component of her father's spell glittering on her own skin and clothing. The gold she had chosen for her costume not only suited her colouring and looked suitably regal for her rank, it would make her easily visible to Hellorin who, annoyingly but not unnaturally, wanted to keep an eye on her this first time. Though the Phaerie seemed to approach it in a light-hearted spirit, the Hunt was dangerous. With horses plunging down from the skies and hurtling through the forest in pursuit of their quarry, collisions could, and occasionally did, happen: with trees and other obstacles, or between the horses themselves. Sometimes the prey would fight back, and the thrust of a well-aimed weapon could slay one of the Phaerie as easily as it could kill one of their slaves.

At the thought of these dangers, Tiolani felt a hollow sensation in her stomach. 'It's nothing but excitement,' she told herself firmly. 'I'm an excellent rider, I know how to use a weapon. Nothing can possibly go wrong.' She flexed her shoulders against the comforting weight of the bow that was slung across her back. She could have used a sword with equal facility; indeed she carried one and had been well trained in the use of both weapons. Tonight, however, she had decided that it would be better to keep a certain distance between herself and her quarry. Though she had been sparring for years with her tutors and various opponents, she had never actually killed a living creature with her sword. Somehow, she was reluctant to see the spurt of blood as blade bit into flesh, and hear the crunch of metal biting through bone. Not this first time. She would have enough to think about, without that.

Hellorin laughed aloud for sheer joy and urged his mount higher, and Corisand, for once, did not resist him. Viewed through a horse's eyes, the Phaerie did not present such a brave and beautiful sight, for they could clearly be seen as the predators they were. Feral, cold and pitiless, their eyes glittered with a savage light, and the miasma of blood-lust hung around them like a dark and reeking cloud. On this special night, however, Corisand was untroubled by the ruthless and barbaric side of her masters' nature. She too was caught up in the exhilaration of the soaring climb towards the stars, and the thrill of the wild chase through the crisp night air. Unlike Tiolani, she was not looking forward to the sport the night might bring, or concerned about the dangers involved. She only knew that for once she was free to run, and to revel in the smooth play of healthy muscles as they bunched and stretched in powerful motion. The vision of an equine, with her eyes set to the sides of her head, meant that she could see almost all the way around herself, so she was aware of her fellow horses on every side, before and behind, and could lose herself in the elation of running with the herd.

Tiolani, in the meantime, was following her father and brother, her heart beating fast with excitement, the icy wind stinging her face and pulling her long hair out of its braids to unravel into a wild banner that streamed out behind her. The lights of Eliorand, twinkling like earthbound stars on their hill, fell away quickly, to be replaced by the dark, mysterious tangle of the forest, with here and there the shining line of a stream or river threading its way through the gloom. Tiolani wished she could silence all the sounds around her and lose herself in the wonder of the night. Yet the huffing exhalations of the horses, the wild music of the horns, the baying of fellhounds and the excited voices of the Phaerie Court, calling to one another as they raced across the void, were so much a part of the night's magic that it would be wrong, somehow, to lose them.

The Hunt galloped on, streaking across the skies, eating up the miles as the forest sped by below them, sounding their silver horns and singing songs of bloodshed and slaughter. When they reached the broad river that marked the border between their own realm and the lands of the Wizards, they ignored the treaty that existed between themselves and the Wizardfolk and continued onwards as before – but now Gwylan the Huntsman led the fellhounds spiralling down among the trees, bringing them back to earth to seek the scent of humans.

There were two sorts of humans at large in the forest. The first had been seeded there by Hellorin himself in previous centuries, so that they could breed in the wildwood to provide his hunters with a ready quarry. The remainder had escaped from servitude, either to the Phaerie or the Wizards. Though the mortal servants of both Wizards and Phaerie were bred to be nothing but slaves, it was only natural that some would grow weary of their lot, and escapes were inevitable. Most of the fleeing slaves were rounded up quickly as their masters used the powers of scrying to learn of their whereabouts, but others had survived over the years to breed, and now groups of wild or feral humans were scattered throughout the forest. The little band that were to be hunted tonight were slaves; escaped from the Wizards, they had fled far indeed from their masters, taking shelter many miles to the north of Nexis, the settlement that lay closest to the border of Hellorin's kingdom. So far, no one had bothered to come looking for them and against all odds, they were managing to survive the winter. A pitiful encampment of roughly built huts, their roofs white with frost, were clustered in a forest clearing as if seeking protection in numbers from the terrors that lurked in the dark and the wilderness – but there was no protection from the predators that sought the humans this time.

A horn rang out, and the deep baying of hounds echoed through the trees. The pack had found their quarry. Like falling stars, the Hunt came hurtling down out of the sky, and Tiolani heard the sudden thunder of hooves as the horses' feet hit the ground and galloped on without breaking stride, throwing up clots of mud and dead leaves as they ran. Maiglan landed in the midst of the others with a jolt that rattled her rider's teeth, then the mare was bounding forward. Tiolani held on tightly, flinging an arm up to protect her face as they went crashing through bushes and dodging between tree trunks at breakneck speed. At first she was in terror of slamming into an obstacle or another rider, but presently she realised that Maiglan, despite her speed, was sure-footed, alert for any hazards and careful to avoid them. Suddenly she was fervently glad that her father had insisted she ride an experienced horse. But where, in all this confusion, was the quarry? Up ahead she could hear yells and screams and the clamour of the dogs, but at first her view was obstructed by the other riders. These soon began to scatter, however, peeling away to pursue their individual victims, and Tiolani finally caught her first sight of her prey.

The Phaerie whooped with excitement and howled with bloodlust as they hunted their victims down one by one with the huge grey dogs, closing on the helpless humans who darted this way and that between the trees in a futile attempt to escape. Great teeth seized and tore, scattering bloody chunks of flesh. Blades glittered in the starlight, whining as they clove the air, shearing through muscle and sinew, crunching into bone. The frosty leaves that coated the forest floor were darkened with spreading pools of gore, and the screams of the dying rent the night.

Her palms slippery with sweat, Tiolani took a tighter grip on the reins and swallowed hard, forcing back the nausea that was rising in her throat. She was Hellorin's daughter – she was damned if she'd disgrace herself in front of the entire court. 'Get hold of yourself,' she muttered. It helped to remember what her father always said about these particular mortals. Feral humans were vermin, no better than rats. They bred like rats too, and if left unchecked would outnumber Phaerie and Magefolk in no time. Their extermination did the world a favour.

Tiolani felt better at the thought, and ashamed of her squeamishness. *Never mind*, she told herself. *Many people feel that way on their first Hunt.*

Just concentrate on getting one of these humans. Then the worst will be over, and your honour will be satisfied.

The Hunt had drifted away from her through the forest. It wasn't far – she only had to follow the sound of the Phaerie crying out to one another, and the screams of the mortals. Coming upon a knot of hunters and hunted in a clearing, she singled out a victim, a short stocky male with greying hair. He was clad, like the others, in nothing but dirt and a tatter of rags and animal skins that made him look bestial indeed: a far cry from the clean and neatly turned-out slaves in her father's palace. Somehow, that made it easier for Tiolani to see him as prey. He darted to one side, and the experienced Maiglan turned to follow the fleeing figure as it dodged between the trees. Looping her reins around the pommel of the saddle, Tiolani reached for her bow and, within an instant, had an arrow in place. She had been hitting moving targets from horseback since she was ten, so this should present no great challenge. She sighted, fired – and in that very instant another rider darted out from between the trees and took the quarry's head off with a single swiping sword-blow. Tiolani's arrow flew over the top of the victim and embedded itself in a tree. The body stumbled on for a step or two, then fell to the ground, twitching and spraying blood, while the head bounced and rolled right under the feet of Maiglan, who snorted and sidestepped, causing her rider to lurch in the saddle.

'Hey,' Tiolani yelled. 'How dare you take my—' She faltered into silence as the other rider turned, and she recognised Varna – but a Varna she had never seen before. In place of the amusing, deferential lady-in-waiting she had always known, there was a wild-haired demon whose eyes blazed with a savage light in a blood-spattered face. '*My* quarry,' Varna snarled. 'Find your own.' She wheeled her horse and was gone.

Shocked, Tiolani hesitated for a moment – then she realised that the Hunt was leaving her behind once more. Muttering a curse, she swung Maiglan around and set off in pursuit. By all Creation, this was more difficult than it looked.

Dael would have given anything to be able to change places with one of his hunters. He was an outcast among outcasts, and death surrounded him on all sides. He ran through the forest, praying he could keep one step ahead of the Phaerie; hoping he would not run into one of his fellow human escapees, who would think nothing of betraying his whereabouts to save their own hides. If he should be caught, he could expect little quarter from either race. His father, Lamus, had been the leader of the outcasts until, sick of his evil temper, brutality and violence, the others had banded together and clubbed him to death only a few days ago. Though Dael had been just as much a victim of his father's bullying as the others, and bore the scars and bruises to prove it, his blood had been tainted in their eyes. They had spared his life, but banished him from their little community and driven him away into the forest, where he had been facing the prospect of slow death by cold and starvation, before the Forest Lord's hunters had arrived to alter his fate.

Somehow, he had never expected the sight of the Wild Hunt to be so terrifying. Throughout his life, Dael had heard all the tales. 'Be a good child, or the Phaerie will come for you,' was a ploy used frequently by human mothers. But no matter how bloodcurdling the stories had been, nothing could have prepared him for the real thing. His only warning had been the distant belling of hounds, then the flame-eyed pack came streaming through the skies, with the Phaerie following in their wake like a shower of shooting stars: a heart-stopping sight in their glowing robes. Dael gave a moan of terror. It was just his luck that it had to happen now, when he was frozen, half-starved and all alone in the world without a soul to care whether he lived or died.

There had been little time to act. The best he could manage was to push himself into some bushes, in the hope that he would not be seen, and the fellhounds would find other victims. But one of the hunters, a girl about his own age, had spotted him and fired at him with her bow. Luckily for him, she had turned out to be an awful shot and the arrow had thudded into the ground just beside him. Dael hadn't given her time for a second attempt. Springing to his feet, he ran blindly through the trees, finding strength and speed from sheer desperation, even in his cold and starving state. But it had all been pointless. Behind him he heard the crack of breaking twigs and the crunch of fallen leaves being crushed under heavy hooves. A quick glance over his shoulder showed him that another group of Phaerie were after him.

As hard as Dael could run, his pursuers could close the distance faster. A blast of magic hit him, knocking him off his feet. Even as he stumbled and rolled, he felt the spell penetrating deeper into his body to freeze his nerves and liquefy his muscles. He hit the ground hard, stark-eyed, terrified and gasping for breath. There was a blur of movement at the edge of his vision, then a shadow engulfed him and a horrible, clinging weight fell on him, wrapping itself around his body. For an instant, blinded by sheer panic, he did not understand what had happened – then he realised that he was buried beneath the silvery meshes of a net, and could only lie there, helpless, and wait for them to come.

Would the cold-eyed hunters finish him with an arrow or a sword? Or would he be torn to pieces in the jaws of the ravening hounds? It flashed through his mind that twenty years of slavery wasn't much to call a life, and for an instant his fear was lost in anger at the sheer unfairness of it all. Then the Phaerie were upon him, and his fear returned tenfold as he waited for the blow to fall. Instead he heard laughter. 'Call that a cast, Ferimon?' a female voice said. 'You're supposed to net them *then* bespell them, you fool.'

Three Phaerie, two men and a woman, stood over him. 'He took me by surprise,' Ferimon protested. 'What is he doing here, so far from the others? Anyway, how could I have made a decent cast when the wretched trees were in my way? *You* take the net next time, if you're so clever.'

'Never mind.' Clearly the third hunter was set on keeping the peace. 'It doesn't really matter as long as we have him. He looks like a nice, sturdy young specimen, and capable of a good day's work. Come on, roll him over and wrap him properly, and we'll take him back.'

Take him back? Dael's first sensation was one of overwhelming relief. They weren't going to kill him. The close proximity of death proved how precious even a life of slavery could be.

Working together, the Phaerie bundled him securely into the net, then fastened it to the saddles of all three horses, taking the weight between them. For a moment, as the horses started to move, Dael was bounced and dragged through mud and rotting leaves. Then suddenly he was airborne, his stomach lurching as the net swung far above the ground, and his body in its thin tatters of clothing was pierced by the cold night air.

By now, the initial relief of his reprieve was fading, leaving behind a sinking sense of dread as he thought of the future. He looked up at his Phaerie captors, laughing and bickering good-naturedly as they rode home in triumph. They wouldn't be so cheerful and confident if they knew what he knew about the madness his fellow escapees were planning. Mortals would not be the only ones to die in the forest tonight. Then would come the vengeance of the Phaerie. Despite the fact that Dael had escaped death in the Wild Hunt itself, he knew that, before the night was done, not a single one of the slaves who had taken refuge in the forest would be left alive.

Tiolani was wondering just how a bunch of runaway slaves could manage to make themselves scarce. She urged Maiglan into a gallop and sped through the trees with reckless speed, hoping to catch up with the rest of the Hunt before it was too late. This time, she came upon a different group of her fellows, and discovered to her surprise that not all of the Phaerie were there to kill. She watched the net-casters, open-mouthed.

Why had no one ever told her about this? Then the answer came to her. It was of great importance that Hellorin's daughter should kill on her first Wild Hunt. Until she had done that, she had no business getting distracted by any other possibilities. Still, this sort of hunting looked like more fun than the carnage Tiolani had witnessed, but she could see that it must take a great deal of skill and practice. Tomorrow, when she got home, she might ask her father if she could look for a group to join, but tonight she still had her first Hunt to get through.

She rode on through the trees, looking anxiously about her, hoping to catch a glimpse of a fleeing human figure. Was she too late? Had the Hunt already run out of victims? Then ahead she saw someone making a pitiful attempt to hide in a clump of scrubby bushes. A young man, probably a little younger than herself, she thought. He huddled down low, shaking with terror, his eyes closed tightly. Tiolani grinned. Why, surely she couldn't miss *this* one. He hadn't even seen her. Raising her bow, she took careful aim. There would be no failure this time – but as she loosed the arrow her arm seemed to jerk of its own volition, sending the shot wide. The arrow thudded into the ground within inches of the young man's leg. He leapt up with a howl and ran off between the trees – only to be captured by a group of net-bearers, who felled him with a blast of magic and scooped him neatly from the ground, carrying him away between them over the treetops.

Tiolani slammed her fist into her thigh, disgusted with herself. What in Creation had happened? She'd had the shot perfectly lined up: how could she possibly have missed? To make matters worse, it wouldn't take the Hunt long to deal with one small colony of feral humans. As time went on, her chances of making a kill were growing less and less, and how would she bear the humiliation if she failed?

Hearing voices and the baying of fellhounds to her left, she set off in that direction. All at once, a figure came swerving out of the under-growth, almost beneath her horse's hooves. Without thinking, she raised her bow and fired, and this time there was no mistake. The figure jerked, staggered and collapsed as the arrow thudded into its back. Punching her fist into the air, Tiolani gave a cry of triumph. 'I did it, I did it!' As she dismounted for a closer look at her prey, the hound that had been in pursuit burst out of the bushes and seized the twitching body by one arm, worrying and jerking at it, and pulling it over onto its back. Tiolani saw the face of a girl no older than herself. Her pretty features were contorted in agony; stained with the blood that had gushed from her nose and mouth. Her blue eyes stared, wide and unseeing, at her killer.

Tiolani bolted into the bushes and was violently sick. As she emerged, wiping her mouth on her kerchief, she came face to face with Arvain. 'Well done, little sister.' His face glowed with pride. 'That was a superb shot.'

Unhooking her water flask from her saddle, Tiolani rinsed out her mouth. 'You saw me,' she said, when she could speak again.

'From the other side of the clearing,' her brother told her. 'Your first kill. How proud Father will be. I called to him in mindspeech and told him: he is on his way.'

'Arvain, you won't tell anyone I—'

'Never fear, a lot of folk throw up the first time – myself included.' He grinned. 'Your secret is safe with me.'

Then, almost before she knew what was happening, her father was there, with Varna and a crowd of others, all thronging around to congratulate her. Her father, beaming with pride, dipped his fingers in the blood of the dead human and marked Tiolani's cheeks and forehead. 'All praise to my daughter, the Lady Tiolani,' he announced. 'On this night she has killed her first quarry and thereby reached her maturity. She now belongs fully to the Wild Hunt of the Phaerie Court.'

Tiolani tried not to shudder at the touch of the sticky gore on her face. She longed to rub it off, but that would have to wait until she got home. Instead she forced a smile, and accepted the cheers and compliments with good grace. Soon, having entered into the spirit of the occasion, she found that she actually *did* feel proud of her achievement. Just so long as she didn't have to look into those dead, blue eyes, everything was fine.

3
~

POINT OF NO RETURN

The horses were the first to sense that something was wrong. Corisand, standing together with Maiglan and Valir, pricked up her ears at the muted hiss of whispers and the scuffling of furtive movement in the surrounding bushes. The reek of anger and fear came to her, strongly overlaid by the smell of humans. She threw up her head and stamped restlessly, aware that the other horses were also fidgeting as the current of unease flowed through their ranks.

The Phaerie were crammed into the clearing; talking, laughing, completely unaware that anything was wrong as they clustered around Hellorin's daughter to congratulate her on her success. The attack came without warning. Suddenly the air was thick with arrows. Screams echoed as Phaerie and horses alike were mown down by the deadly rain. Arvain, standing next to his sister, was hurled backwards by the force of the arrow that pierced his throat. As he fell, he grabbed Tiolani and pulled her down with him. He was dead before he hit the ground, but his corpse was sprawled half on top of her, and his fingers, constricting in a rictus of death, remained tightly locked around her arm, preventing her from rising. A number of shafts pierced Hellorin's body, followed by another hail as the bowmen reloaded. Clearly, he was their chief target. He staggered and sank to his knees, and at the fall of their Lord, the Phaerie still standing were overcome with confusion and dismay. Only a handful seemed able to put up any coherent defence. Though a few of their attackers had fallen to their bows, the renegade slaves were picking the others off one by one.

Many of the horses were running, terrified by the arrows, the screams and the stench of blood and death, only to be shot or captured. Just as Corisand turned to flee, an arrow whistled past her, missing her by a hair's breadth, and buried itself in Valir. The chestnut stallion went down, thrashing in agony. Before she could move, he had drawn his last breath.

Nothing could have prepared her for what happened next. As Valir died, knowledge exploded through Corisand's mind. In one astounding instant she knew her people's history and her own identity. Her world, her life, her reality were all smashed into a million pieces, and reassembled in an entirely new pattern. Shock turned her muscles to water, and before she knew what was happening, she too was down on the muddy, bloody ground beside her dead companion. All this time, he had been Windeye of the Xandim – and now his mantle had passed to her.

But there was no time for Corisand to come to terms with her new identity. The humans had brought off their attack with such speed and unexpectedness that it might have succeeded, save for one thing. These slaves were runaways from the Wizards. They did not understand that Phaerie magic was different from that of their former masters, and they had no idea of the awesome powers they were about to unleash. Corisand, still blinded by shock, did not see Hellorin stagger to his feet. Despite his terrible wounds, he was drawing on every last scrap of his immense vitality and force of will to keep going, just a little longer. In a voice like a thunderclap, he roared out a word as old as time, and the surrounding woodland came to life. The earth shook, and a sinister wind moaned through the branches as the trees awoke. Then, across the chaos, the Forest Lord struck back.

His inarticulate bellow of rage and grief broke through Corisand's absorption in her own plight, and she opened her eyes to a sight that would burn itself upon her memory to the end of her days. In an eyeblink Hellorin grew from normal size into a towering colossus who blotted out the stars. A blast of magic exploded through the clearing, radiating outward from the immense form of the Phaerie Lord, its force enough to uproot bushes and tear the branches from trees. Even the surviving Phaerie were knocked off their feet by the force of the onslaught, and the humans at whom it was aimed stood no chance. Now it was their turn to cry out, as each one found themselves encased in a column of vivid green radiance that seemed to rise up out of the ground.

The emerald light flared – and all at once the undergrowth where a pack of wild humans had lurked was filled with statues, as each and every one of the rebels was encased within a sheath of stone. Every last detail was clearly etched, including their faces, which bore expressions of such agonised horror and fear that Corisand was certain they must have had time to realise exactly what was happening to them. Were they still alive, encased in their prisons of stone? She had a feeling that it was so, and though she did not feel like wasting pity on them, she could not help but shudder at the cruelty of such a fate.

Hellorin's eyes flashed beneath his lowering brows. Clearly, he was not finished yet. Clouds rolled up, mountainous, black and menacing, and blotted out the stars. Thunder reverberated through the treetops. Lightning splintered in a searing arc from sky to ground; sizzling blue-white bolts that leapt from one petrified human to the next, linking them all, for one blinding instant, in a net of fearsome elemental energy. One by one, the stony figures exploded in a cloud of dust that blew away on the shrieking wind, leaving not a single trace of their passing.

The wind dropped, as suddenly as it had risen. With it went the massive bank of darkest cloud, rolling the storm away to the south until the sky was clear and the stars shone forth once more. Hellorin dwindled back to normal size. As his wounds finally overcame him, he swayed and toppled like a mighty tree, his hand reaching out across the intervening distance, towards the body of his son.

With a desperate effort, Tiolani wrenched herself loose from the grasp of her brother's dead hand. She averted her eyes from Arvain's face. She couldn't look at him, because if she saw him lying there, pale and still, not breathing, she would have to face the fact that he was dead, and she just couldn't do that. Not yet. With a gargantuan effort, she managed to haul herself out from under his heavy body, but when she tried to get to her feet, her legs would not support her. Instead she crawled across on her hands and knees to where her father lay, all the while muttering to herself in a low voice. 'No, he can't be, it can't be true, he isn't dead, he can't be dead too, he can't be ...' It was like a charm, or a spell to make Hellorin hold on to life. He would have to be alive. She wouldn't accept any other alternative.

Events seemed to happening so slowly, with the smallest thought, the slightest movement stretching out into hours. Only now was she aware, at the edge of her vision, of the other Phaerie who had survived the massacre. They were just beginning to move and struggle to their feet, as though time was being drawn out for them in the same unnatural way. Nevertheless, Tiolani was the first to reach her father.

So many shafts had pierced him – how could he still be alive? Yet, as she lifted his head, Hellorin coughed, and drew a rasping breath, and suddenly time snapped back to its normal course. She became aware that other Phaerie were arriving, older and more experienced in such emergencies than she, surrounding her, kneeling by her side, and by that of her father. The Tiolani who had set out on the Hunt that evening would have been content to take a step backwards and let the others deal with the situation; to surrender to her grief and let herself be comforted. But in a few short moments, everything had changed. Her mother had died many years ago, her brother had perished tonight, and Hellorin was badly, perhaps mortally, wounded. She alone was left of the Forest Lord's line.

There was no time to waste. Each shuddering gasp her father gave sounded as though it might be his last. Tiolani took a deep breath and cast quickly back in her mind to her lessons in magical lore, so recently ended. Finding the spell she needed, she raised her hand and let the power channel through her mind. A silvery-blue light shimmered into existence around Hellorin's body as she activated the spell that would take him out of time. Blocking out all distractions, she poured every ounce of herself, every bit of strength and will and determination she could muster, into the magic to boost her power, adding some of her own life force into the spell to bolster the fading vital spark of father's being.

Only when he was completely surrounded in the magical light, and the spell was sealed in place, did Tiolani allow herself to slump, exhausted, over Hellorin's body, taking great, ragged gulps of air which made her realise that she had forgotten to breathe while casting the spell. But it would be all right now. Her father was safe for the moment, taken out of time, his life preserved until he could be returned to the city and tended by the most skilled of healers.

Tiolani had forgotten the presence of the others until she felt a hand on her shoulder. The dark-eyed, gaunt-faced Phaerie with the saturnine expression was Cordain, her father's Chief Counsellor and oldest friend. 'Well done, Lady,' he said. 'Your swift action may have saved his life.'

The Forest Lord's daughter shrugged the hand away and got to her feet, looking at Cordain with eyes as bleak and cold as winter. 'Don't just stand there. Have my father borne back to Eliorand with all speed.' For a moment her voice faltered, but she took a deep breath and hardened her heart. 'And find others to bring my brother and the remainder of the fallen home. We will not send them to their rest in this wild and dismal place.'

She took a deep breath. 'My father's flying spell is powerful, and it will linger a few hours more, even though he is supporting it no longer. Nevertheless, we must move swiftly. Search for any other wounded, take them out of time and have them conveyed to the healers as quickly as possible. Find any missing horses and hounds.' She looked for the first time at her brother, and her voice grew hard as steel. 'And search the woods for any surviving humans. There are likely to be others hidden away, the older and weaker of them, and the women and children. I want every one of them found, do you hear me?'

'And what shall we do with them when we have found them?' Cordain's voice held a new respect.

'Kill them. Every last one. By the end of the night, before the flying spell fades, I want every last accursed human in this part of the forest dead.'

High above the forest, Dael was carried northward by his captors. The journey in the net was a nightmare: as well as immobility, the Phaerie spell had afflicted him with dizziness and an unpleasant prickling throughout his entire body that was painful in its intensity. The wind flayed his flesh with knives of ice. His cheek was pressed hard into the twisted meshes of the net, so that he had no other choice but to look down at the forest, which seemed to wheel and lurch as the net swung and swayed beneath the swift Phaerie horses. He could not be sure whether the nausea that gripped him was due to the unaccustomed motion, or to the magic that had struck him down.

Dreadful though his situation might be, it was better than staying down below to be slaughtered. The other fugitives had been so carried away by the daring of their plan that they had seemed unaware of the risks that were all too obvious to the outcast. Reabal, the successor to Dael's father, was a man of more courage than sense, and had inflamed them with his stirring speeches. Despite all the evidence to the contrary, he had persuaded them that a handful of hungry, ill-clad humans with makeshift weapons could defeat the might of the Phaerie.

The entire insane scheme had been the result of desperation; of men with nowhere left to go turning on their oppressors like cornered rats. But they had failed to take into account that, even in the near-impossible event that they managed to kill every single one of the hunters, there would still be a multitude of others dwelling in their northern city of Eliorand. Fear gripped Dael with claws of ice and steel. What was to become of him? When the remaining Phaerie discovered the massacre of their brethren by the humans, their vengeance would be beyond imagining.

Despite their burden, Dael's captors were travelling at a tremendous speed. Again and again, he tried to turn his head to see what lay ahead of him, and what his captors were doing above him, but to no avail. The Phaerie magic still held him in helpless thrall.

Finally his efforts paid off, though he thought he was imagining things at first. Had his head moved, maybe? Just a fraction of an inch? Or was he being deceived by false hope? But no: once again he felt movement, slightly stronger this time, and better still, his fingers gave a little twitch.

From the careless way his captors were handling him, Dael felt sure they weren't expecting their magic to wear off so soon. They had been in such a hurry to bundle him up, and so confident of their spell, that they had never even bothered to search him for weapons. Though the temptation to move was overwhelming, especially when a painful tingling began to signal the return to life in all his limbs, Dael forced himself to remain limp and motionless. He thought of the small knife – all he'd had with him when his fellow slaves had driven him away – concealed in a pocket in his ragged pants, and dared to hope a little, though for what, he couldn't say.

The riders seemed to be heading for a steep hill rising out of the forest, which proved to be much further away than he had first thought, for when they finally reached the tree-covered eminence, its sheer size astonished him. The riders flew over the summit, and began to slow their speed and lose height, approaching the level of the treetops. Dael was baffled. When he'd been a slave among the Magefolk, he had always been told that the Phaerie dwelt in a great city – so why did they seem to be planning to put him down in the middle of nowhere?

Over his head the conversation between his captors had been going on throughout the journey. Dael, preoccupied with his troubles, had paid little heed to the talk, but now his ears caught the words 'slave' and 'captive'. Suddenly he was all attention.

'Why bother, Jeryla?' one of the male Phaerie was saying. 'Leave it to the keepers of the slave pens. It's their job.'

'Don't be mean, Ferimon,' the woman replied. 'It'll cost me no effort, and the poor thing may as well see where he's being taken.'

See? Dael was puzzled. What did she mean? The Phaerie must have known his eyes were open when they bundled him into their net.

'You're too soft on them,' Ferimon complained. 'When all's said and done, they're only animals.'

Jeryla shrugged. 'A little kindness never hurt anybody. If you two can manage the net, it will be but the work of a moment to take care of him.'

Dael felt the net lurch and sway as, with much grumbling on Ferimon's part, the two male Phaerie took the weight between them. The temptation to turn his head to see what was happening was overwhelming, but while Dael was fighting for self-control, the female came riding into his field of vision, her elegant bay horse pacing the air and her pale, gem-studded hair streaming in the wind. She gave him a mocking smile.

'Now, little human, open your eyes to the truth.' Lifting her hand, she cast a ball of rippling blue light at his head. He screamed as it splattered against him, covering his shrinking face with glittering sapphire sparks that sank into his skin with a mild burning sensation. He could feel them penetrating his skull and concentrating around his eyes, with a warmth that would almost have been welcome, were it not so uncanny.

The Phaerie woman laughed, and disappeared from his sight as she rode back to her companions. Once more the lurching began as she took her share of the burden, and the net began to turn slowly, back and forth. As the green eminence spun back into view, Dael stifled a gasp of shock. Before him, instead of the steep, tree-covered slopes of the great hill, was a beautiful, shining city of elegant buildings and many soaring towers.

So that was it. The city had been disguised by a spell. A chill ran through Dael at this further evidence of the power of the Phaerie. In attempting to combat the Wild Hunt, his fellow escapees had failed to understand the risk they were running. He had little doubt that those who'd remained in the forest were doomed – but what of those who had been captured already? Dael was certain that the vengeance of his captors would extend beyond those who had been personally involved in the attack, including himself. One thing was patently clear: if he allowed the Phaerie to take him to the city, he was as good as dead.

Already they were flying over the stretch of forest lying directly south of the city. There was no time to waste. Better to risk a fall from this height than face who knew what kind of terrible fate at the hands of the Phaerie. Surreptitiously Dael groped for his knife – and a sudden chorus of shouts and curses broke out from the Phaerie above. For a blood-freezing instant he thought they had caught him – then he realised what they were saying. It had happened. The attack was taking place right now. 'Come on,' he heard Ferimon shout. We've got to go back and help them.'

Jeryla hesitated. 'But what about—'

'Who cares? There's plenty more where he came from.'

The blade of a long silver knife glittered in the starlight as it sliced easily through the meshes – then the net gaped open and the Phaerie were already turning, speeding back the way they had come. Dael caught a single glimpse of them as he twisted in the air and began to fall.

All around the clearing, the survivors of the Wild Hunt were picking themselves up, ministering to the wounded, or searching frantically among the fallen for missing friends and family. Though Gwylan the Huntsman had been killed, Darillan, his apprentice, gathered together a small group of helpers and set off in search of the missing fellhounds, while others searched for straying horses. The Phaerie mounts who had remained in the clearing were caught and tended by willing volunteers, and a trembling Corisand found herself being helped to her feet and checked for wounds, before she was tethered with the group of horses who had remained unscathed.

Unscathed in body, at least, she thought. She knew that in her mind and heart and spirit, she would never be the same again. Nor would her Phaerie masters – or the humans of this world. Once word leaked out and spread though their ranks, as it inevitably would, that such an attack had taken place and come so close to succeeding, would fear of what had happened to these rebels be enough to discourage others from trying the same thing? What would happen if it did not? And how would tonight's happenings affect the human slaves already belonging to the Phaerie? The Forest Lord – if he lived, for his wounds had looked grave indeed – had lost his only son. Would he be content with the vengeance he had exacted upon the ferals? Or, in his grief, would he extend his revenge to all humans alike?

Corisand never knew what made her turn her head at that moment and look at Tiolani. The young woman was standing in the middle of the clearing as though overseeing the efforts of the Phaerie to recover themselves, but her gaze was turned inward. In the course of but a few moments, she seemed to have aged a dozen years. Her face, which so recently had been alight with girlish excitement, was now pale, cold and hard as marble, and her eyes were filled with a bleak, implacable hatred that chilled the Windeye to her very soul.

Suddenly Corisand realised that this girl would be the sovereign of the Phaerie until Hellorin recovered, if he ever did recover. If he should die, then Tiolani would be crowned as Lady of the Forest, and the prospects for the humans looked bleak indeed. But that was not Corisand's only concern. Most important of all, how would the repercussions of the attack affect the well-being of the Xandim? She had a foreboding that after the events of this night, the world would never be the same for anyone.

Corisand shook her head. She was unaccustomed to thinking like this. It was difficult and it *hurt*. It opened up whole new concepts of past and future, cause and effect, conjecture, concern and a sense of responsibility she had never experienced before. Until a few moments ago, she had never even known that such a thing as a Windeye existed. Not for the last time, she wished that she could have remained in blissful ignorance for ever.

She watched in horror as the remnants of the Hunt were sent out again until, one by one, any remaining humans were rounded up or hunted down. The Phaerie, damaged and distraught though they might be, were not permitted to rest until all the vermin had been accounted for. Corisand was concerned to see that Tiolani had elected to ride out with the huntsmen, instead of returning home with the wounded Hellorin, in order to make absolutely certain that not a single human remained alive in the woods. Her hatred was so intense that it had overcome even her deep love for her father. With newfound understanding, the Windeye shivered at the thought of what this might portend. Tiolani's rage at the mortals was uncontainable, and she had even vowed that all those human slaves who had been captured alive and taken away before the ambush had happened would share the death of their brethren before the night was out. A number of the Phaerie had been slain, which was crime enough – but it was clear that for the wounding of her father and the murder of her brother, she could not make the humans pay sufficiently dearly.

Corisand was spared any part in that final slaughter. Along with several other horses, she was in no fit state to be ridden. To her relief, she was left in the clearing with the wounded, their helpers and some vigilant guards. If Tiolani seemed to have aged a dozen years, Corisand herself felt as if she had aged a century in the course of this night, and was longing with all her heart to go home to the comfort and security of her own roomy box in Hellorin's stable.

At last that interminable night drew to a close, bringing the return of the bone-tired hunters who, under Tiolani's goad, had slaughtered every human they could find for miles around. Darillan and the other huntsmen collected together the hounds, and the Phaerie, weary, shocked and grieving, took to the skies and headed for home. With their departure, the forest fell into a wary and watchful silence. The cluster of primitive dwellings, which had once represented independence, pride and hope for a handful of rebels, stood dark and abandoned in its woodland clearing. Gradually it would fall prey to the elements, and the relentless overgrowth of brambles, weeds and saplings would blot out every trace.

It was almost daylight when the stunned and battered remnants of the Phaerie Hunt got back to Eliorand. The clear night skies had paled sufficiently to quench the glitter of the stars, and a crimson streak showed low on the horizon in the east. Corisand looked away from it quickly. It only reminded her of the blood that had been spilt that night. Instead she turned her gaze longingly towards the city and home – and was startled and confused to see the change that had taken place in her absence. As the light grew, the city of tall, slender towers, blooming gardens and leaping waterfalls took on the form of a forested eminence that stood high above the surrounding woodland. It almost seemed that the two images of woodland and city had been overlaid, so that the eye perceived first one and then the other.

Corisand was rescued from confusion by the new way of thinking that had come to her that night when the old Windeye had died. She realised that this strange glamourie, this shifting and changing, must be part of a Phaerie spell: a carefully crafted illusion to conceal their city from hostile or unwelcome gazes. As the light grew, the magic that disguised the city would become stronger, probably reaching its peak when the sun was highest in the sky. The spell must not work on animals, she supposed, or she would have seen it before; but now that Corisand had been catapulted into the role of Windeye, she was finally able to perceive both the illusion and the reality.

Illusions, however, were the least of Corisand's concerns on that night of terror and loss. Her mind had still been reeling from the revelations that had swept through her like a spring flood, changing the entire landscape of her mind and washing away so much of her previous, simple life. With Valir's death had come the realisation that she and the other Xandim were captives, slaves, robbed of their birthright and trapped in this equine shape – though that had not always been the case. Long ago, there had been a choice. The fact that in the past, her people could take the same form as their captors had stunned her deeply – but less so than the knowledge that she and she alone now bore the responsibility of restoring them to what they once had been.

When it had been time to leave the forest, her body felt sodden with exhaustion, and she was shaking from the aftermath of her experiences. At least, because Hellorin had been wounded, Corisand would be led home with the other injured horses instead of ridden, and she'd been glad of the respite. Her mind had been opened to the inner world of the mental gestalt that enabled not only mindspeech, but also the ability to see into another's mind, to sense their thoughts and feel their emotions. This was the wellspring from which all magic stemmed, though the new Windeye was far too stunned to understand the implications immediately.

At first, it was all she could do to keep functioning amid the storm of Phaerie emotions that raged around her. Horror, pain, anxiety, grief; shocked disbelief that the human vermin could have turned on them with such devastating consequences – and, overriding all else, Tiolani's terrible rage. In addition, she could feel the terror and agony of her equine companions, which came to her in primitive bursts of raw emotion that assaulted her senses like physical blows; all the worse because they had few words with which to express their feelings.

Never in her life had she been so glad to return to her cosy stable; to be fed and watered, to have the mud and the spatters of gore washed from her dappled hide, to have her aching limbs rubbed and her small hurts tended, to be groomed and cosseted and wrapped in her own warm woollen rug, and left in a bed of thick, soft, fragrant straw to rest. As the human grooms worked on her, she found herself puzzling, for the first time, over the chasm which existed between those who tended her and the ferals the Phaerie had pursued that night, who had fought back with such unexpected savagery.

No one would ever hunt *these* humans. Clean, hard-working, valued and cared for by their masters, they were an essential part of Phaerie society, keeping it running with their menial labour and leaving Hellorin's folk free for other, more enjoyable pursuits. How great a difference lay between these mortal slaves and the quarry of the Wild Hunt, who had been viewed and treated as nothing more than animals. Yet they were exactly the same species. She was still trying to puzzle out the difference as she fell asleep. And surprisingly, sleep came very swiftly, as if her weary body and overburdened mind could scarcely wait to escape from the fears and memories and revelations of that night.

In the morning, of course, it was all still there. Corisand awakened to find that she was Windeye of the Xandim and, with no one to teach or guide or help her, she was going to have to make a start at sorting out the confused mass of memory, knowledge and emotion that churned in her mind. Somehow, she must learn to think clearly in words and images, to reason, conjecture and organise her thoughts. Somehow, she would have to find a way to shield herself from the mental emanations of others which assaulted her unceasingly. Somehow, she'd have to learn the extent of her new powers and abilities – for she understood in her deepest heart that these existed, though she could not say how she knew.

4

~

THE FIRST STEP

At first, Tiolani could barely grasp the fact that Hellorin's mantle had landed on her shoulders. Though the Forest Lord's life had been preserved by her swift actions, he had been hovering on the threshold of death when the Phaerie brought him home. Two cadres of skilled healers had been forced to work on him in tandem; one holding him to life while the others fought to repair the horrific damage that the arrows had wreaked deep within his body. Because any one of Hellorin's injuries would have been enough to kill him, the healers could only work very slowly, and it took so much power to maintain his hold on life, and so much concentration to perform the difficult, delicate and extensive amounts of healing, that the process would be extremely protracted – at least so Tiolani had been told. And in the meantime, due to Arvain's death, the reins of power had been thrust into her unready hands.

Tiolani's grief at the loss of her brother was so acute that she simply wanted to crawl into bed, pull the bedclothes over her head and never get up again. What did she care for power? What did she care that the realm of the Phaerie needed a ruler? She didn't give a damn for the Phaerie. Arvain was dead; her father could be dying, and nothing else mattered.

It took the Hunt to change her mind. Nothing could bring back her brother, but at least she could avenge his death, and she gained a little surcease at the thought of making the accursed feral humans of the forest suffer as he had suffered. Even on the first night following the ambush, with Hellorin hovering on the brink of death and Arvain not yet sent to his rest, she ordered the Wild Hunt out again, though she herself had kept to her chamber all day, seeing no one but Varna; she had no plans to leave it any time soon, not even to ride out in the cause of revenge. Unfortunately, she had forgotten one important detail. Though she had

40

demanded to be left alone, Varna brought someone to see her: Darillan, Gwylan's former apprentice, now promoted to Huntsman. Taking in his flustered expression, Tiolani realised that he looked about as ready for his new responsibilities as she was for hers, and that small insight of fellow feeling was enough to prevent her from sending him away.

Darillan bowed low. 'Lady Tiolani, I beg pardon for intruding on your grief like this, but if the Hunt is to ride out tonight as you instructed, then we must have your help.'

'Why me?' Tiolani replied listlessly. 'Whatever it is, get someone else to do it.'

'But, Lady, you are the only one who *can* do it.' Darillan looked agitated. 'Without the flying magic the Hunt cannot ride out, and the spell can only be performed by one of the Forest Lord's line.'

'Oh.' For a moment, Tiolani could think of nothing more intelligent to say. Embarrassment made her as flustered as the young Huntsman himself. How could she have forgotten such a detail? What a fool she must look. Then dismay overwhelmed her embarrassment. She had never attempted the flying magic before. There had been no reason. She had only accomplished her first Hunt the previous day. Whenever possible, Hellorin had performed the spell himself, and if he could not be present, Arvain had been there to take his place. And though her brother had explained to her how the magic was done, she'd never had the chance to try it for herself. Well, she would get her chance now, and she'd better do it right. If she failed, there was no one else who could work the magic, and if Hellorin did not recover, the Wild Hunt would be finished. For a panic-stricken moment she had thought of putting off the entire business until she felt better able to cope, but the craving for revenge was too strong. 'Very well,' she said to Darillan. 'I'll come at once.'

Then another idea occurred to her. If she had to face the Phaerie courtiers in any case, she might as well ride out with the Hunt, and wreak some vengeance on the humans in person. She called back the Huntsman, who was already on his way out of the door. 'Wait, Darillan. I've decided to join the Hunt tonight after all. I'll just need a few minutes to change clothes. Send a message to Aelwen immediately, and have her get Asharal ready. You can tell the others I'll be with them shortly.' With that, she turned to her lady-in-waiting, who had been hovering warily by the door. 'Varna, tell the maid I'll need my riding clothes immediately.'

When Tiolani emerged from the palace, she found that the number of hunters in the courtyard was seriously depleted. Some, it was true, had been killed or wounded the previous night, but it was patently clear that the heart had gone out of Hellorin's Wild Hunt. Many had been deeply shaken by the ambush, and many more were downright afraid to enter the forest again. No one had ever expected the prey to fight back. Those who had joined the Hunt this evening consisted mainly of those who, like herself, had lost loved ones in the ambush, and were riding out for revenge. There was no pomp and splendour tonight; no gaiety or chatter or brightly coloured clothes, for all the Phaerie were in mourning. This sombre band of riders, all that remained of the Wild Hunt, were there for one reason only: to kill as many humans as they could find.

As she walked down the steps into the courtyard, Tiolani could feel every eye upon her. For a moment her courage failed her, but she knew that if she retreated now, she would never have the courage to try again. While she'd been dressing she had hastily run through all the details of the spell in her mind, and she could only hope that she remembered everything correctly.

Praying that her nervousness did not show, Tiolani walked across the courtyard with her head held high. When she approached Asharal, he was plunging and sidestepping, despite the best efforts of Aelwen who held him, her brows together and her lips pressed tight in an expression of profound disapproval. Tiolani met her eye coldly, daring her to comment and refusing to feel guilty. Her father may have forbidden her to hunt with her new horse, but Hellorin wasn't here now, and it was up to her to make her own decisions. Without a word to the Horsemistress, she mounted and rode into the centre of the courtyard, her stomach churning. 'Are you ready, Darillan?' she called.

'I'm ready, Lady Tiolani.'

With a sweep of her arm she included all of the hunters in the courtyard. 'Then let's ride!'

Tiolani took a deep breath and closed her eyes, trying to concentrate on the spell. It wasn't easy when she was the focus of every eye in the place. To make matters worse, Asharal was shifting and fidgeting beneath her, interrupting her train of thought every time she tried to gather her will. Tiolani knew an instant of doubt. Had it been a mistake after all, to ride the excitable young horse? Had Aelwen been right? The very idea of having to admit to the Horsemistress that she had been wrong was enough to sting her into action. Aelwen didn't know everything. Sharply, she pulled Asharal back under control, holding him in tightly, and reining in her wandering concentration at the same time.

Reaching deep inside, she focused on the elements of the conjuration, building an image in her mind of the Wild Hunt climbing up through the air and riding the skies over the forest. The more detailed and vivid her image, she knew, the stronger the magic would be. Once she had it clear in her mind, she drew on the Old Magic and accessed the elemental powers of Air, letting the forces build up and up within her. When she felt that the magic was strong enough, she poured it into her image of the Hunt in flight, and then let it go, feeling it flowing out through her fingers to cover the riders, their horses and the hounds.

She did her best with the spell, though she knew it wasn't the same as her father's flamboyant magic. Lacking the glittering splendour of Hellorin's conjuration, Tiolani's effort only summoned a sickly greenish luminescence that gave the Wild Hunt a grim spectral appearance. Good enough, she decided. It matched her mood entirely. When she took off, followed by Darillan and the pack, then the rest of the Hunt, the horses lumbered into the air with some effort. Nevertheless, she had done it, and she would certainly improve with time. Tiolani felt a warm glow of triumph within her. At least she had made a start on fulfilling her new responsibilities. For a moment she thought of Hellorin, who still lay on the brink of death with the healers doing their utmost to keep him alive, and her resolve hardened. She wouldn't let him down. She would take the best possible care of his realm, and in doing so she would honour the memory and avenge the death of the brother who was no longer there to take his rightful place.

The Hunt was a bloodbath. This time, Darillan took his hounds to the south-eastern reaches of the forest, where the scouts had previously spotted signs of another band of ferals. These were wild humans bred for the Hunt and, though they were more primitive and less intelligent than their slave counterparts, they were much more crafty and wise in the ways of the forest than the escaped slaves. Nevertheless, it didn't take the hounds long to track them down.

Tiolani was not the only one out for revenge that night. There was no suggestion of capturing any of the prey alive, and every member of the Wild Hunt set about the killing with grim purpose. In the ensuing carnage she acquitted herself well, not only managing to control her difficult horse through sheer force of will, but also bringing down a number of mortals on her own account, slaying them with both sword and bow. Men, women and even children – it made no difference to her. The crunch of bone, the spurting blood and the cries of agony and terror all served to assuage her grief a little, and by the time there was nothing left of the human colony but piles of slaughtered corpses on the blood-soaked forest floor, she felt calmer and more at peace than she had done since her father's fall and Arvain's death.

She rode home with the gore cooling on her body. It reddened her arms and chest, and covered her face in a stiff, stinking mask, plastering her hair down to her skull. Tiolani smiled grimly to herself. She had waded in so much human blood that night that it had soaked her garments – and it felt wonderful. And she had only just started. She knew that now. For killing her brother, she would visit death upon the humans a thousandfold.

Tiolani had been in control while she was out with the Hunt and there was killing to be done. When she returned to Eliorand, however, all her fears and worries surfaced once again, and her grief returned with overwhelming force. She realised, then, that there would be nothing for it but to ride out with the Hunt each night like a driven creature, for only in the killing could she forget her troubles for a while. It would be much more difficult, however, to get through the days, with so much to learn about ruling, the additional burden of new responsibilities, and long, wretched hours spent sitting by Hellorin's bed, talking to her father in the hope that one day he would open his eyes and respond to her. And how could she face day after day of this grief? The Phaerie were unaccustomed to the death of their own, for it happened so seldom. How could she bear the loss of her beloved Arvain? Things might have gone ill for her indeed, save for the discovery that she was not alone in her sorrow.

Ferimon had been her brother's best friend, and the object of Tiolani's girlhood dreams and fantasies for several years. Unfortunately, Arvain had discovered her infatuation for the handsome blond courtier, and his merciless teasing had eventually been enough to put her off the whole idea. She could never be sure that he hadn't told his companion about her feelings, and the idea of them laughing behind her back made her want to die of humiliation. Ever since then she had avoided Ferimon, just in case. Her pride would never allow her to risk putting herself in such an embarrassing position. Doing without him had been difficult at first, but as time went by she had tried to avoid his company, and if she still looked for him around every corner – well, only she would ever know.

In her own grief following her brother's death, she forgot how deeply Ferimon would also be affected, until he came to her two days after Arvain had been sent to his rest. The funeral had been very hard on Tiolani. Robed in red, the colour of death and mourning among the Phaerie, she had led the procession of mourners out from the palace to the massive amphitheatre, its basis a natural hollow in the land, which had been constructed on the northern side of the hill, facing the fertile vale of the Phaerie heartlands and the soaring peaks beyond. There her brother's body was incinerated in a single flash of magic, and the remains taken aloft on horseback to be broadcast to the winds. As Arvain's sister, it had been her duty to perform the ceremony and scatter the ashes, riding aloft over Eliorand with an honour-guard of Phaerie in the sky behind her.

It was the most terrible thing Tiolani had ever been obliged to do, but somehow, for the sake of her brother, she had managed at least to maintain the appearance of being strong and brave throughout the proceedings, though she had not been able to eat a single morsel of the feast afterwards, and had only choked down a cup of strong wine, in a toast to Arvain's memory. Though she had gone through the day with jaws clenched and her hands knotted into white-knuckled fists, at least she had comported herself with dignity right to the very end, but when she finally regained the sanctuary of her chambers, she collapsed on the bed as though she had been clubbed, and made herself so ill with weeping that Varna had been forced to send for the physicians.

Ferimon was her first visitor after the funeral. At the time, she had no wish to see him or anyone else, but Varna nagged and nagged until she'd persuaded Tiolani that she couldn't shut herself away forever – and besides, how could she refuse her brother's best friend? When he arrived, she was sitting in the window embrasure, looking out at the city and the forest beyond as they slowly faded in the gathering dusk. It was as though all the colour had been leached out of the world, leaving only stark black, chill white and sombre shades of grey. Snow had begun to fall thickly out of a bleak sky and was already lying on the iron-hard ground, the roofs of the buildings and the skeletal branches of the trees.

The evening was a perfect foil for Tiolani's mood. Everything seemed desolate and dead, as though the whole of nature shared her loss of Arvain. Ferimon's appearance, however, was enough to jolt her out of her preoccupation. One look at his face told her that she was not the only one who had suffered deeply over her brother's death. At least she'd had Varna to take care of her while she had been laid low by grief, but she could see at a glance that Ferimon had allowed no one near him since Arvain's funeral rites. He was still wearing the same red robes, now wrinkled and stained, and his normally immaculate blond curls were matted and uncombed. By the looks of the deep, black hollows beneath his tear-swollen eyes, he hadn't slept, and judging from his white, drawn face and his shaking hands, she suspected that he hadn't eaten, either.

Tiolani's heart went out to him. She had barely tasted food herself since she had sent Arvain to his rest, but Varna had managed to coax the odd morsel into her despite her resistance. (She guiltily glanced at the scars on her door and the stains on the blue carpet, mute evidence of the bowl of soup she had thrown at her lady-in-waiting the previous day.) Stoically, Varna had borne the brunt of her anger at the unfairness of it all; had bathed her sore red eyes with cold water; had brushed her hair and, only that morning, had coaxed, badgered and finally ordered her into a bath and some clean, fresh clothes. And though, at the time, Tiolani had wished her a million miles away, she now felt a rush of gratitude towards her patient companion. Without Varna and her pestering, she, too, would have been in the same dreadful state as Ferimon.

Varna hadn't managed to improve Tiolani's manners, however. With a stab of remorse, she realised that Ferimon was still kneeling in front of her, waiting, as protocol demanded, for his ruler to speak first. She summoned him to sit with her in the window embrasure, and poured him a goblet of wine. 'My dear Ferimon,' she began, 'please forgive my abstraction. These last few days have been difficult for us all, but as my brother's best friend, you deserve better from me. What can I do for you?'

'My thanks for your courtesy, Lady Tiolani,' he replied, 'but in truth, I came to do something for you. On the day before your first Wild Hunt, Arvain asked me to perform an errand for him. He had commissioned a special gift for you to mark the occasion, and he asked me to go down into the city and collect it for him, as he was busy with your father, and had no time to go himself.' In a shaking voice he went on: 'He died before I had a chance to give it to him. Please forgive me for not bringing it to you sooner, but my own grief …' He swallowed hard and began again. 'Arvain would be angry if he knew how long I had delayed. I know how much he wanted you to have this.'

He handed her a small golden box with her name inlaid on the lid in tiny, coloured gems. 'Oh,' she gasped. 'It's beautiful.'

'Your pardon, Lady, but the box itself is not the gift. Look inside.'

With fumbling fingers, she found the catch and opened the little box. Inside, nestling on a bed of white velvet, was a single pale-green gem cut in the shape of a faceted teardrop that hung from a simple chain of white gold. Tiolani's eyes blurred with tears. 'It's perfect,' she whispered.

Ferimon nodded. 'How like Arvain, to find exactly the right thing. He loved you very deeply.' Now both of them were weeping. Afterwards, Tiolani never remembered how they came to be sharing an embrace – it seemed to flow naturally out of their mutual grief and love for her brother. Certainly, at that point, they were simply comforting one another, and when the comforting turned into something deeper, it felt like the most natural thing in the world. And as Ferimon swept her up in his arms and carried her away from her cold window embrasure and into the glowing warmth of the lamplit bedchamber, she suddenly found her grief a little easier to bear.

Firmly, Tiolani pushed away the thought of her father's disapproval.

He need never know. How could he? Frozen outside time, stranded in unconsciousness as he was, he might as well be in another world. Wrapped in Ferimon's embrace, she was unaware of just how close she had come to the truth. A mortal, or even a Wizard taken out of time as Hellorin had been, would truly be lost in oblivion. For a Phaerie with the Forest Lord's vast powers, there was another option.

When Hellorin fell, the last thing in his darkening vision had been the face of his dead son. When he opened his eyes again, Arvain's features were still before him. Seared into his memory, they seemed to fill his world as far as the horizon. Grief and pain struck at him like cold serpents, wrapping him in coils of agony and rage that constricted his breathing and sent his blood hammering through his head until he cried aloud and pounded his fists on the uncaring ground. But it was as though that cry had roused him from confusion. Suddenly it came to him that Arvain's beloved face had only been etched upon his mind's eye. It was no longer there in actuality.

The reality was far different. Though he was still sprawled in the same unnatural position in which he had fallen, he no longer lay on the damp, muddy leaves of the forest clearing. Silence had replaced the harrowing sounds of battle, and there was no sign of friends or foes, living or dead. The dreadful pain of his wounds had vanished, and his body had been made whole once more.

He was lying in a vast chamber on a shining floor that possessed the blue-white smoothness of a frozen lake. The distant walls and ceiling, elegantly carved and supported by slender pillars and graceful, springing buttresses, were constructed from a similar material. The roof was so high that wisps and skeins of cloud had gathered, drifting lazily between the pillars and spreading like veils across the open stretches. Far, far above, snow appeared to be falling from the ceiling: a fine, crystallised shower that drifted gently down, glittering as it fell and vanishing just before it reached the ground.

A clawed fist of ice, which had nothing to do with the frigid air of the chamber, clenched itself around Hellorin's guts. He was no stranger to this place. He had been here before. And he had never expected to be back. There was a world, a dimension, another reality beyond the boundaries of the mundane world which the Magefolk and mortals – and now the Phaerie – inhabited. A mysterious Elsewhere governed by the Old Magic, where elemental beings of great power held sway, and nothing was as it seemed. They had dwelt here, once, he and his people. The Phaerie had been denizens of this land for an eternity, until Hellorin had decided that the mundane world held richer pickings. It had been a long and difficult struggle to release the Phaerie from the bonds of the Elsewhere, and to do so he had been forced to give up one of the greatest heirlooms of his race. So why had he been pulled back into this place? Who had brought him here? His heart plummeted at the thought of being trapped here once again.

'Hail, O Lord of the Phaerie. I little thought to see you within my walls again.' The voice, though female in tone, thundered through the immense hall, as loud and overwhelming as an avalanche, so that Hellorin felt physically battered by the sheer intensity of the sound.

The Forest Lord rolled over and sprang to his feet, spinning around towards the source of that monumental voice. Far away, at the furthest end of the hall, was a towering throne of ice that was bigger than his entire palace. There sat a gigantic woman, of a scale to match the vast surroundings. Her grey robes swept down around her feet, and her long mane of white hair fell across her breasts and shoulders, reaching all the way to the floor. Her face was rough-hewn and craggy, made up of sharp planes and angles, and her dark eyes were cold, hard and inscrutable, holding an awesome power in their depths.

Hellorin concentrated all his magic, feeling his body expand to make him an equivalent size to the giantess. It would have been a grave mistake to let her look down upon him as though he were some insignificant insect. Then he walked up to the throne and bowed low. 'Madam, I greet you,' he said. 'It is a joy to see you again, after so long a time.'

Her frosty expression did not alter. 'Liar. You spurned this place, and risked everything to take your people to another world.'

'A world which *you* were never denied,' Hellorin flashed. 'Where was the justice in that? You have no right to sit in judgement on me and mine.'

'Just or not, that world was my birthright. It was never yours. And, unlike you, neither I nor the others of my race sought power or conquest. Know this, Forest Lord: your departure unbalanced massive energies that should never have been disturbed. Would never have been disturbed, but for your treachery, your attempt to go back on your sworn word. You and your folk may have escaped this place, but you caused terrible destruction in doing so. In your absence you have made many enemies, O ruler of the Phaerie.'

Hellorin lifted his head and locked eyes with her. 'And must I count you among those enemies, Madam?' he said quietly.

She laughed, a harsh sound like the grinding scrape of a rockslide. 'Nay, Forest Lord. After all, your attempt to steal what belonged to us was doomed to failure. And since you caused considerable damage to certain of my foes, I owe you my gratitude.' Her eyes flashed. 'But only to a point. You have too much arrogance and power to be trusted.'

Hellorin's gaze remained steady. 'The same could be said of us all.'

She shrugged. 'We Moldai are what we are. But most of us, no matter how proud or ambitious, would have had more discernment than to involve ourselves with your plans, and aid you in your perilous experiments with the Fialan, the Stone of Fate. Only Ghabal was rash enough to risk such a thing.' A flicker of pain crossed her face. 'He paid.'

'Paid? What happened to him?'

'What do you care? You got what you wanted, Hellorin. When you planned to quit this world, you never considered that there might be a cost to those who remained here. Even if you had, I doubt you would have let such a small consideration deter you.'

The Forest Lord knew that he could not deny her accusation. 'Tell me what happened to Ghabal,' he repeated.

'It took both your combined wills and all of your joint powers to work upon the Fialan, in order to open a portal between the worlds for you and your people. But you failed to consider a fundamental law. When such a vast amount of energy has been harnessed, there must always be an equivalent recoil.'

She shook her head. 'The results were devastating. You know, of course, that the Moldai are the only race to exist simultaneously in both worlds. That is why you needed one of us to help you form your portal. In the mundane world, we take the aspect of mountains of intelligent, living stone. Here in the Elsewhere, we can alter our forms as we choose. The backlash from your portal was so extensive that it hit Ghabal in both realities. In the world to which you journeyed, Ghabal's mountain peak was riven and shattered by the titanic forces that were unleashed. He can no longer dwell there now. In this world, those same physical forces could have no impact, but ...' She spread her hands. 'The mundane half of Ghabal was now missing, twisted, deformed beyond all hope of redemption. The shock, the agony, drove him insane. Everyone fears him now. Everyone avoids him, for there is no telling what may provoke him, and what he might do if he is angered. His first actions in his madness were to attack the Evanesar, the Elementals of the Old Magic, wreaking great havoc and destruction. That is why I said that you have many enemies here, Hellorin. Your rash actions affected not just the Moldai, but all the denizens of this world. All of them know that you precipitated the disaster.'

The Forest Lord concealed his dismay behind a nonchalant shrug.

49

'The misfortunes of the Evanesar trouble me not at all. They were never friends of the Phaerie in any case. But tell me, Madam, if you will – does Ghabal still have the Stone?'

'You gave it to him. The most powerful heirloom of your house in exchange for his assistance in creating the portal. That was the bargain, was it not? And now that he has it, who would dare try to take it away from him? You fool, Hellorin. Thanks to you, a mad, twisted, unpredictable creature possesses an artefact capable of causing untold damage, not only in our world but also the other, and we have no means of removing it from him. Can you wonder that you are detested and despised by so many?'

Hellorin took a deep breath. His entire future now hung in the balance. 'And you, Madam? You were my friend and ally down many a long age. Has your friendship also turned to hatred?'

'You asked me that already.' Again, she gave a harsh laugh. 'Is my friendship so very important to you now? But you may rest easy. The Moldan of Aerillia does not alter her allegiance so lightly. What care I for the misfortunes of the Elementals and their ilk? I am willing to stand by our old friendship – for now, at least.'

'For now?'

'Indeed. Who do you think brought you here? I sensed your spirit wandering, lost in oblivion beyond the boundaries of Time, and recovered it, though I was unable to reach your corporeal form. That must remain in the other world, who knows where? But I did not bring you here out of kindness. You must make reparation for what you have done, Forest Lord. Your rash actions have loosed a grave peril upon this world, and you must put right your error. Retrieve the Stone of Fate. Make this world safe once more.'

'And if I cannot recover the Fialan?'

The Moldan's eyes flashed. 'Cannot? Or *will* not?' Then she shrugged. 'It makes no difference. Without the Stone, how can you return to your own world? You must be in your current plight because someone took you out of time. Have you made enemies there, as well as here? If you fail to take back the Stone, your corporeal form is at the mercy of others, Hellorin – and what will become of you and your people then?'

5
~

TＡKU

What have I become? What is to become of me?

In the pastures on the outskirts of the city, Corisand looked out of the window of her stable at the snow falling thickly in the night and wished, for once, that she had some of the other horses there to keep her company. Following the ambush in the forest, the stables had been in a state of chaos, with many horses injured, some of them very badly. As she had been unscathed, they had put her here in the far paddock, which boasted its own little stable, and had left her alone. Just now she presented a problem that Aelwen did not need, for she could only be ridden by Hellorin, and it would be a long time indeed before he was in any state to ride her – if, indeed, he survived at all.

Corisand listened to the gossip of the grooms and riders whenever she could, with her new understanding, and gathered that the Forest Lord was still locked in a timeless state by the healers. By rights he should have been dead. Only Tiolani's intervention had held him to life for long enough to take him out of time and bring him home, and everyone was remarking, with a mixture of surprise and admiration, that Hellorin's new heir had inherited a will every bit as strong as that of her father.

With her only rider close to death, Corisand had been turned out into the wintry pasture during the day, and only brought in at night. And already, during these last three dark days, she had discovered what it meant to be truly forsaken and alone. Now she could think in the same way as the two-legged ones: the Phaerie, Wizards and mortals. For the first time, she could feel as they felt: loneliness, worry, frustration and grief.

Several horses had been lost during the slaves' attack. One of them had been Valir; lordly, magnificent – and her sire. Maiglan, her dam, had raced across the clearing and into the forest in her panic, and there she had caught her foot on a root and fallen, breaking her leg. When the Phaerie found her, there had been no option but to destroy her. Their deaths, and those of the others, filled Corisand with renewed anger against the Phaerie. The Xandim were her people, her responsibility. How dare that accursed Hellorin and his subjects use them as simple animals? How dare they ride them into risk and danger? She rejoiced that Hellorin, the oppressor of her people, had fallen. She hoped he had suffered. She wished fervently that he would die. If she was ever to free the Xandim, Corisand reckoned that Tiolani would prove much less of an obstacle to her plans.

If she ever came up with any plans. First of all, she had to acquaint herself with her new role, its advantages, its burdens and its limitations. Little by little, during the lonely hours in her isolated pasture, Corisand had begun to make sense of it all. She had found a way to shield herself from the thoughts and emotions of others by taking her mind to a place she'd loved ever since she was a foal: a secluded valley in the mountains, with a waterfall and a crystal-clear lake, where groups of the Phaerie horses were pastured in turn for a good long rest in the summer. Having discovered this mental refuge into which the emanations of others could not intrude, she found that she could begin to organise her own thoughts. Gradually she sifted through her new legacy of knowledge, until a complete history of her people emerged.

The Xandim were not the same as other horses. Their physical make-up was slightly different, in that they could run faster and jump higher than their ordinary equine brethren, and they had more stamina. They could also see clearly in colour, as the Phaerie, Wizards and humans could, and could utilise the magic of the flying spell, whereas the average horse could not.

They were an ancient race, though not as old as the Magefolk or the Phaerie. The mechanism by which they changed shape drew upon the Old Magic, but the Windeye was the only one with the ability to access and use its powers for other reasons. To her surprise, Corisand discovered that, in ages long past, all the Xandim had been adept in the use of magic, but a religious movement had sprung up which denounced its use as evil and unnatural. The cult had swept like wildfire though the Horsefolk, creating a schism between those in favour of using the abilities with which they had been born, and those who rejected the arcane force of the Old Magic. After a long struggle, the cultists had triumphed, and the last of their opponents were hunted down and slain, or forced into a life of subterfuge and concealment. The use of magic had dwindled from generation to generation, and much valuable knowledge of their civilisation was lost to the Xandim. Only the line of the Shamans had kept the flame alive, persisting through all the years of danger and doubt, and finding ways to pass information, memories and powers from one Windeye to the next – until eventually, everything had come to Corisand.

Had the Xandim only been aware of what they had lost, they would have regretted throwing their powers away as they had done, for when their race had been attacked by the Phaerie, they had been easily overcome and enslaved, trapped in their horse forms by Hellorin because they no longer had any magical gifts through which they could change back. And what was worse, the race had stagnated in this shape for so long that even Corisand, the new Windeye, was unable to access the magic – not until she changed back into human form. And how could she do that? All too soon she had discovered the bitter dilemma that had tormented her predecessors, and it seemed that she was no closer to reaching a solution than they had been.

Corisand stirred restlessly, desperately seeking a way to distract herself from her gloomy thoughts. A change of light in the stable window drew her attention, and she saw that the night had taken on a peculiar, luminous glow that turned the falling snowflakes into a glittering veil. *How very odd*, she thought. And, since anything was better than staying where she was, bored out of her mind and sinking deeper into despondency, she decided to go out and discover the source of the weird glow.

Now that she was the Windeye of the Xandim, bolted doors were the least of her problems, and the door of her box soon swung open as she carefully worked the bolt loose with her lips and teeth and slid it back. Now, if only they hadn't actually locked the outside door of the stable … Manipulating the catch turned out to be a little more tricky, but after a while she worked it out and pushed the door open. A blast of chilly air came whistling in, but Corisand ignored it and stepped out into the snow.

The night was filled with magic. The snow fell thickly from the low clouds overhead, but far away over the treetops a break had appeared in the cloud cover and the moon, just past full, was shining through the gap, illuminating the millions of tumbling snowflakes as they fell, and filling the night with that mysterious, pearly glow. Utterly entranced, Corisand forgot her problems. Tentatively at first, but with increasing skill and confidence, she began to prance and whirl, dancing with her shadow in the moonlight and weaving hoofprint patterns on the soft white ground, while the falling snow turned her dappled coat to glimmering silver and decked her dark mane and tail with sparkling diamonds. Tomorrow, she told herself, she would once again take up the burdens of the Windeye and, as winter turned to spring and then summer, she would get used to her new role, and begin to learn the things she needed to know. But that was for the future. Tonight, there was only the moonlight, the snow and the dance.

Entranced and transported by the moonlight and the whirling snow, Corisand circled and pirouetted, carving her complex patterns in the thick white covering on the ground, until she was too weary to dance any more. Weary, but for once relaxed and at peace, she returned to the stable, carefully closing the doors behind her, so that the Phaerie would not know she had been out. The snow showed no sign of stopping. By morning, it would have filled in the tracks she had made and obliterated all signs of her presence outside, and none of her captors would be any the wiser. Feeling ready to sleep at last, she lay down on her thick, soft bed of straw, closed her eyes and was lost to the world.

Lost to one world, at least. As she drifted away into slumber, Corisand felt an odd little sideways jolt, and a peculiar, twisting sensation deep within her that had her opening her eyes in surprise.

And the stable had vanished.

The snow and the moonlight had vanished, leaving her standing in a soft, all-encompassing mist that glowed from within with a dim amber light.

Her body had vanished – as she discovered when she tried to take a step forward, and fell flat on her face. It was only then that she saw the arms that she had automatically thrown out in front of her to save herself from the worst of the impact. Smooth-skinned arms, and strong, sturdy hands. Like the Phaerie. Like the humans. Corisand let out a low, strangled cry compounded of astonishment, shock and joy. How could this be? Somehow, she had managed to release herself from her equine form at last, and take on her alternative shape.

For a moment, Corisand stayed where she was on the ground, resting on soft, black moss, her mind awhirl with possibilities and questions. She looked at her hands, outstretched in front of her, and realised that her vision had altered radically. Instead of the all-round viewpoint of a horse, she could only see in front of her, but the vision of each eye overlapped, giving her an unprecedented perception of depth and distance. Slightly unfocused at the inner corner of each eye was a triangular, flesh-coloured object which she realised must be her nose. Marvelling, she lifted her hand and touched the contours of her face and, lifting a strand of long, glossy, dark-brown hair, felt the silken texture, giving it a slight, experimental tug. 'Ouch!' She decided not to do that again, but the sharp little pain was lost in wonder. Why, she had a voice; a mouth that could form words, could articulate her thoughts. This was incredible.

She ran her hand down the soft, velvety skin of her arm, and turning her left hand over, examined it closely: the delicate whorls of skin on her fingertips; the fingernails, translucent as a shell; the mysterious map of crossing and interconnecting lines on her palm; the graceful wrist with its network of blue veining on the inner side. And most important of all, the thumb, opposed for grasping. Joy surged through her. This was where the true control and power lay. This was what had given the two-legged ones such mastery over the other inhabitants of the world. The ability to use tools, build cities, wield weapons. To forge slave-chains for their fellow creatures.

Well, now she could compete with them on their own terms. But where was she? How had she come here? Corisand remembered falling asleep, and considered the possibility that she might be dreaming, but the reality of becoming a biped was far beyond anything she had ever imagined. These new sights and sensations simply could not be originating in her own mind. True, since she'd become Windeye she'd had visions of the Xandim in their alternative form, but never from the viewpoint of *inhabiting* such a body.

What was this mysterious, miraculous place that had allowed her to shed her equine shape at last? She could see nothing all around but the weird, glowing mist, and a shiver ran through her as she wondered what it might conceal. Were the dangers commensurate with the wonders? She was willing to wager that they were, and she had a feeling that by lying on the ground she was putting herself at risk. Better to discover how to use this body while she had the chance, then go and confront whatever might be lurking in the mist.

But first, she'd have to get to her feet, and that turned out to be enough of a challenge to be going on with. Corisand scrambled onto all fours, then considered her next move. Rising up as high as she could on her knees, she put her right leg out in front of her. Now what? If she put her weight on the right leg, maybe the left would help to push her up ...

Good thing this moss stuff is soft, she thought a moment later, as she pulled herself out of the sprawl into which she had fallen. *Still, I think I was working along the right lines. Let's try it again.* Another three attempts found her standing, precariously balanced on two feet instead of four, and she was sure that if only there had been something in that infernal mist to hold on to, she would have done it in less. It took a while longer and a few additional tumbles before she mastered the art of walking and, until she got used to the unfamiliar form of locomotion, she would just have to hope she didn't meet anything that she needed to run away from.

Although Corisand had been preoccupied with discovering the advantages and limitations of this new and unfamiliar body, she had not lost sight of her main objective: to find out where she was, and what had finally freed her from the prison of her equine form. She wished that she had a weapon of some kind, but that could not be helped. Naked and alone, she set off bravely into the enclosing mist.

Corisand walked for a time in an unchanging landscape, in the strange, glowing amber light, with misty vapour still blocking her vision, and the thick, black moss soft beneath her bare feet. There were no sounds or scents to give her any clue as to her whereabouts, and she had no idea of the direction in which she was moving. She had no sense of time passing in that changeless place – she could have been there for hours or minutes.

At length, however, the surface beneath her changed from moss to grass, and the mist began to swirl away in one direction, leaving an aperture through which she could see a strip of green turf with the inviting glint of water beyond. Quickly, Corisand stepped through the hole before it began to close again, and immediately swung around in a circle, to make sure there were no enemies nearby. She could not see another living creature, but to her surprise the uncanny mist had vanished without trace. Behind her was a forest of pine, spruce and hemlock trees that towered to an incredible height. The little grassy swathe on which she stood thrust back in a tongue-shape, bounded by the dark wall of the magnificent forest, beyond which she could glimpse the snowy peaks of mountains. As she whirled, completing the circle, she discovered that she was standing on the shore of a lake.

The temptation was overwhelming. Hurrying to the lakeside, she bent down on one knee and looked into the mirror of still water. Then Corisand saw the new form that she'd assumed for the first time. A cloud of tangled dark-brown hair, framing a rather rounded face with dark eyes and a small, straight nose. A mouth that dimpled on either side as she broke into a sudden smile at the delight and wonder of it all. A strong, sturdy, compact body, with full, rounded breasts that made her eyes open wide in surprise. As she had never seen the Phaerie or their human slaves unclothed, she found one or two more surprises on the way down to her feet, but all in all, she decided she liked what she saw.

Now that her curiosity had been satisfied, she scrambled to her feet again – she found it easier this time, now that she was getting the measure of her new body – and took a proper look at her surroundings. The calm waters of the lake were the extraordinary, clouded blue of moonstones, and wound away into snow-streaked mountains on her right, so that she could not see where it ended in that direction. On her left, seemingly not more than a mile or two away, was ...

The Windeye's jaw dropped in amazement. At that end of the lake, descending into the water like a towering white wall, was a glacier. The river of ice, its upper surface ridged and jagged, went curving away as it sloped upwards out of sight, to be lost among the peaks beyond. She knew exactly what it was, though she had never seen one before. She could feel a new force tingling through her mind and body, thrilling her with an energy that was as potent, formidable and uncanny as the glacier itself. Corisand laughed aloud. In this otherworldly place, in this unfamiliar two-legged body, her Windeye's powers had come blindingly alive, filling her mind with new and complex thoughts and providing her with all the knowledge and insights she needed to survive here. She did not know how to wield the magic yet, but that would come. She had a feeling that she was here to learn. But where was this place? Why, despite all this new knowledge in her head, did she not recognise it?

Corisand felt as if she could not take in enough of the glacier. She had never seen anything so awe-inspiring. This titanic flow of ice took her breath away. Its sheer immensity was difficult to encompass, for there was no way in which to gauge perspective. The whiteness of its rough, ridged surface was streaked and stained with grey, consisting of rock that had once been huge boulders before being pulverised into the finest of powders by the mighty forces within the ice. In its heart, however, the glacier held a magical surprise – drifts and patches of pure and stunning turquoise blue; clear and radiant as a jewel and heartbreaking in their intensity and perfection. Here, so close to the vast work of nature, she could feel the chill from it on her hands and face. The air was utterly still; filled with a silence so vast and profound that it could be felt like a pressure on the skin.

Shock ran through the Windeye as she realised that the landscape was alive. The glacier was a sentient being with a vast, overwhelming aura of power and presence. And then it spoke. Shattering the silence, sounds came from the ice: creaking and grinding and a peculiar popping noise, with every now and then a loud, explosive crack. Corisand could not understand the language, but she had a feeling that she'd be able to learn. Above all things, she wanted to communicate with this entity.

Determinedly, she set off around the lakeside towards the towering frozen wall – and then suddenly, it came to her that she was wasting time. With the burgeoning powers of a Windeye, she should be able to do much better than this, and her instincts told her that the best way to impress this formidable being would be through magic. But how? Looking out across the lake, Corisand relaxed her mind and let the answers come to her. She knew that the knowledge lay within her: concealed, instinctive, waiting to be unearthed and unleashed. Closing her eyes, she let herself sink down through her consciousness, emptying her mind to allow the wisdom that lay buried beneath the surface come rising up and flooding in. Around her, the landscape held its breath. Even the mighty glacier fell silent, as if waiting to see what she might accomplish. She reached down into the very core of her being to the star of shining light that was the dormant seed of her power. And as she touched it, the magic flared up in an incandescent burst of radiance that flooded her heart and mind, tingling through her hands and blazing out through her eyes. The reflection in the lake of her astonished face showed that her pupils had turned a bright, reflective silver. Seen through those silver eyes, the world had changed.

Othersight. The word leapt into her mind. The magical vision of a Windeye that showed her the world in an entirely different way. The waters of the lake gleamed with a crystalline light, and the mountains beyond had become prisms, brilliant with iridescent hues. The trees and grass around her were glittering like jewels. On the glacier itself, the dingy grey streaks of pulverised rock had become drifts of sparkling diamonds, and the patches of that thrilling, incandescent blue had spread to encompass the entire entity, and had taken on a new, almost unbearable intensity.

Most incredible of all, Corisand could see the wind: all the eddies and currents of moving air that swooped and swirled above the surface of the lake and the glacier like glowing rivers. In a flash of revelation, she comprehended at last why the Windeye was so named. But the new understanding went much further than that. All at once, she realised that the winds were her weapons and her tools, a link from the heartspring of her magic to the outer world. In conjunction with her Othersight, she could shape miracles – she was sure of it. Now was the time to put that certainty to the test.

She snatched at the long strands of air as they swirled past, grabbing a handful and twisting them round her fingers. They were fluid to her touch, with a cool, silken feel. Concentrating hard, she poured her Othersight into them, igniting them into streams of blazing silver radiance. These she spun out to form a bridge, which she cast towards the glacier, creating a glowing arc through the air that reached from her feet to the intense blue entity of ice.

A grin spread across the Windeye's face and a warm glow of pride ignited within her. *Not bad for a first attempt*, she told herself, although she knew that the true test of her magic was still to come. The graceful arch of her gleaming silver bridge was beautiful indeed, but could she trust it with her life? It was time to find out.

In her heart, Corisand was certain that confidence would count for everything in achieving her objective. Firmly closing her mind to any doubts, she lifted her chin and stepped firmly onto her first creation. The bridge remained firm and steady beneath her feet. The structure she had spun out of nothing more than empty air and a Windeye's magic looked as fragile and ethereal as moonbeams, but was as firm beneath her feet as any ancient bridge of stone. She took another step forward, noticing as she did so that her feet almost adhered to the surface. This was her own magic, and it seemed that her creation was determined to keep her safe. As the gleaming span took her far out above the cold lake water, she was more than grateful for that.

As the Windeye drew gradually closer to the glacier, the mysterious noises within the ice became louder. Strange as it might seem, she was certain that they held a great deal more meaning than mere random bursts of sound, and as she continued to listen with all her concentration, they began to reverberate through her head and resolve themselves into words whose meaning she could almost grasp, and which became increasingly clear as she drew near to the far side of the lake. She was wondering what she should do when she reached it when the matter was taken out of her hands.

From the top of the glacier where the wall of ice met the lake, the head of a gigantic serpent reared slowly into the sky. Its colossal form, white as the glacier ice, towered high above the stunned Windeye, and it looked down at her through eyes of the same vibrant, translucent blue as the glacier's heart. 'I am Taku, Serpent of Ice, Spirit of the Glacier and Master of the Cold Magic.'

6
~

KINDNESS OF A STRANGER

Tiolani and Corisand were not the only ones who were finding that their circumstances had been radically altered on the night of the ambush. When the Phaerie cut him free of their net, Dael plummeted like a stone into the forest below. His life would have been over had he not fallen into the thick canopy of a huge old chestnut tree. He crashed through the slender upper branches and the sturdier boughs below, and eventually thudded to a halt in a fork between two of the tree's great limbs, battered, bruised and breathless, in a shower of twigs and bark. Winded, he lay still as a number of prickly green seed cases that had been stubbornly clinging to the tree throughout the winter came bouncing down around him. Everything settled at last and he realised, with a great deal of astonishment, that he was still alive.

It was still a long way to the ground, however. Moving carefully on his precarious perch, he took stock of the damage. His clothes, already in tatters before he'd been captured, were in a worse state than ever, with the bitter wind finding its way through every hole and rent. Violent pain stabbed through his chest when he breathed in – he had at least one broken rib. Blood was running down his face from a deep cut that was perilously close to his eye, and seeping into his pants from a gash in his left thigh. The left sleeve of his shirt had been practically torn off to expose a badly abraded shoulder and an arm bent at an odd angle. When he tried to move it, he felt the grate of broken bone, and was so overwhelmed by pain that it made him nauseous and faint. There was a tender lump on the side of his aching head and, judging by all the other lesser aches and pains, his body must be a mass of bruises and smaller cuts.

He couldn't believe he had survived.

From the way his captors had been reacting, he knew that the attack on the Forest Lord must have taken place, but what had happened then? And after it was all over, would the Phaerie come back with their terrifying hounds to look for him? Or would they simply assume that the fall had killed him? He had no way of knowing, and he supposed that there was no point in worrying about something he couldn't affect. He would just have to hope for the best, and get on with the business of trying to survive. Right now, the Phaerie were the least of his problems.

First, then, the arm. Working clumsily, one-handed, he untied the frayed old piece of rope he used as a belt and bound the injured limb to his aching side. It was the best he could do to keep it immobilised. Using strips from his torn shirtsleeve, he bandaged the cut in his leg as tightly as he could manage. As for the rest of his hurts – well, they would just have to take care of themselves. Until he could find some water, there was little more he could do for them.

The first difficulty lay in actually getting down from the tree in one piece. He knew he'd do better to wait until the sky grew lighter, but he was afraid that if he tried to stay up there for the rest of the night he would drift off to sleep and fall to the ground. It felt like an awfully long way to climb down, especially with only one arm and an injured leg. He was only able to take shallow breaths, due to the pain that knifed through his ribs with every inhalation. Shaking all over, partly with fear and partly from the reaction to his fall, he began to descend, selecting his route with care. He got stuck a couple of times, in places where there was nothing he could do but scramble and slither and eventually let himself drop, trying to protect his broken arm as best he could and praying that the boughs below would be strong enough to catch him. Somehow, his luck held. He finally made it down. As his feet touched the ground he felt his knees give way, and he slumped, exhausted, against the tree's massive bole.

When Dael awakened he was aching, chilled to the bone and furious with himself for falling asleep in the open. What if a wild animal had come along? Or worse still, one of the accursed Phaerie? Might-have-beens, however, were the last of his worries. So far, he had been fortunate indeed, but he had a suspicion that his luck had finally run out. His injuries alone were probably enough to condemn him to a lingering, painful death, especially if the cuts and lacerations should fester. Alone in the forest in winter, he was hopelessly ill-equipped to survive. He had no means of making a fire, he didn't have a cloak or blanket, and his clothing was hopelessly inadequate for the freezing weather. His only way of keeping warm at night would be to heap dead leaves around him. With no tools or weapons apart from his useless knife, he couldn't hunt animals for food, and there was nothing growing in the forest to eat at this time of year: it was a long way from the nesting season for birds, and there were no mushrooms, nuts or berries.

Dael rubbed his hand across his face. He had tried to keep going, but the odds had been stacked so high against him it was hardly surprising that nothing ever went right. He closed his eyes, sunk in dark despair, too weary and desolate even to weep. What was the point? There was no chance of him living through this mess. Why put himself through any more misery and pain? He had his knife. He might not be able to kill an animal with it, but he could easily open one of his own veins.

The handle of the knife, usually so familiar in shape and texture that he never gave it a moment's thought, felt different today. The smooth, carved bone seemed alien and heavy in his trembling hand, and the blade gleamed with cold menace in the grey morning light. He tried to find the right place on the wrist of the broken arm – awkwardly, since it was still bound to his side – once again feeling that shock of agony as bone scraped against bone. Pressing the keen edge of the knife against his flesh, he braced himself to slash deeply. How long did it take to bleed to death? Hopefully, it would be over quickly, and then ...

And then what? Some slaves believed that they would go to some kind of ease-filled paradise – well, Dael would believe *that* when he saw it. Some were sure that they would be reborn into a better life. But how could such a thing be possible? They would still be humans, wouldn't they? Still be slaves. Dael had always suspected that such notions could be nothing more than wishful thinking – and that being the case, did he really want to throw away the only life he had? Though it was unlikely that he would find another group of ferals or escapees to help him this close to the Phaerie city, it wasn't absolutely impossible, was it? His life was all he had. The only thing they had not been able to take from him. How could he throw it away as if it were worthless? The Mages and the Phaerie might think mortals were little more than animals, counting for nothing, but Dael would never let himself sink so low as to believe that. When the Phaerie had cast him so carelessly from the skies, they had believed he would die. Why go out of his way to prove them right? If he ended his life now, they would have won. And he had been through so much already and survived. Why not wait a little longer? After all, he thought bleakly, what was the hurry? He could kill himself any time.

Survival in the forest proved to be even more of an ordeal than Dael had expected: an unending struggle against pain, cold and hunger. Try as he might, dragging himself over the uneven ground with the aid of a staff he had made, he could find nothing to eat. Even animals were few and far between in this cold weather – not that he'd have been able to kill them, even if he had managed to find them. After a fruitless day's searching, he curled up in the hollow core of a dead tree, taking his roughly made staff, a stout fallen branch, with him as his only means of defence, and shivered through the hours of darkness.

On the second miserable day he was lucky enough to come across a squirrel's winter cache of nuts, which he smashed open with a rock, devouring the fragments greedily. On the third day, however, he found nothing but the rigid body of a crow lying beneath a tree. It had been dead for so long that even a single mouthful of the raw and stinking flesh made him too sick even to attempt any more.

That was the day it started to snow. When he'd awakened that morning, he had felt colder than ever, and there had been a thin sprinkling of white over his leaf-pile. Later, as the day drew on towards evening, the snow began to fall in earnest, filling the air with fat, swirling white flakes as he staggered onward, growing colder and weaker with every hour that passed.

As dusk was deepening the shadows, he stumbled across the settlement. He emerged into a clearing to see a cluster of rough shelters: vague shapes in the swirling snow, much like the one from which he had been banished. Dael's heart leapt. Another colony of humans. These folk didn't know he had been cast out. Surely they would help him. With a cry of joy he lurched forward across the rough, hummocky ground of the clearing. As if in answer to his cry, lights appeared as people bearing torches emerged from the doorways of the dwellings, and a group of men, women and children stepped out to greet him.

All at once, Dael knew that something was very wrong. Surely he should be able to smell the smoke from the settlement's fires? And why were these people approaching in such eerie silence? Surely they should be calling to him, asking him who he was, speaking to one another, making some sound?

Just as the moon rose above the trees, a swirl of snowflakes blew across the clearing and obliterated the figures. Dael's feet caught on one of the hummocks and he went down hard, screaming with agony as he jarred his broken arm. Measuring his length in the snow, he came face to face with a little girl. She lay sprawled on the frozen ground with her skewed limbs half-buried, her ice-encrusted skin the same colour as the drifting snow. She seemed to be looking up into the sky – save that one eye had been picked out by the crows, and the other was obliterated completely, for the entire left side of her face had been sheared away by what looked like one enormous bite.

The bite of a fellhound.

The Hunt had been there before him.

He hurled himself backwards, gagging and retching, his empty stomach trying to empty itself still further. His out-thrust hand landed on a hard, icy form with familiar contours … Looking around, he saw another face, that of a man this time, whose head had been shorn away from his body. With a shriek, Dael leapt to his feet. All those hummocks scattered across the clearing must be corpses! The snow had obliterated the blood and stench, but here and there he could see that what he had taken, in the shadowy dusk, to be a branch with a cluster of twigs at the end was actually an arm. A thicker bough could only be a leg, though it was not attached to a body. Now that he understood what he was seeing, some of the shadows on the ground resolved themselves into faces that were mauled like that of the child, or twisted with fear and torment.

Snatching up his fallen staff, Dael scrambled to his feet, heart hammering. He looked across at the shelters, but found nothing there but blackened, burned-out wreckage. For an instant he thought he could still see the tenebrous forms of the ghosts – then they too had vanished into the snow and the night.

Before he had time to assimilate what had just happened, Dael heard the sound of snarling behind him. Now that night had fallen, the forest's predators were coming to feast upon the bodies of the dead. Wolves loped through the trees, running low to the ground, and he caught the moon-like reflection from the jewelled eyes of a lynx. All around him, animals were holding their grisly feast, gnawing, and ravening as they quarrelled over the lumps of frozen meat that they tore loose from the scattered bodies. So far, with so much easy food available, they had ignored the human interloper in their midst – but how long would that last? What if a bear should come? It was doubtful that he'd be able to defend himself against a smaller creature like a wolf or a lynx, but against one of the gigantic forest bears, he would certainly stand no chance. Impelled by terror, Dael scrambled out of the clearing and fled the dreadful scene of carnage as fast as his weak and weary body would take him.

On he went, staggering blindly through the dark woods and the snow. Only his stubborn will kept him going: a flat refusal to surrender his life. He had survived his father's brutality, his compatriots hadn't succeeded in killing him when they'd exiled him, and the Phaerie hadn't accomplished his death, even though they had dropped him out of the skies from their net. He had even survived his own sense of hopelessness. After coming through all that, he was *damned* if he was just going to lie down and die because he was cold and hungry and snow was falling on him. Somehow, come what may, he would get through this, if only to spite his former captors.

At last the ground began to slope upwards, becoming increasingly steep, and he hesitated for a moment, wondering if it was worth the effort it would cost him to keep going in this direction. Yet maybe, if he could climb above the general level of the forest, he might be able to spot another settlement of feral humans like the one he had already found. At the very least, he might be able to see somewhere to shelter.

Dael did his best to keep moving throughout that night, knowing that if he lay down he would have neither the strength nor the will to get up again. Dawn would soon be breaking, he kept telling himself. With the daylight would come fresh hope. Scarcely aware of his surroundings, he wandered aimlessly beneath the trees in a darkening dream – until abruptly he was shocked back into awareness as his stumbling foot encountered nothing but empty space. He lost his balance and fell forward, rolling and tumbling down a steep, stony slope, bounding and sliding and turning head over heels, faster and faster – until a large boulder came looming out of the night. Helpless to avoid it, he collided with the huge stone, crashing into it and hitting it hard. There was a bright flash of pain, then Dael's world went dark.

The Cailleach was sitting by the fireside, enjoying the random flickering of the golden flames, the comfort of the warmth washing over her skin, the spicy tang of mulled wine. It was strange to be back in the world again. Strange, but very good. Too good, if truth were told. Sometimes, she wondered if she had been wise to come here. But her vision had shown her the risks of destruction for so many of the wonders she had helped to create, and somehow she just couldn't sit back as a dispassionate spectator and watch all her hard work pulled down. Such direct intervention was against the Laws of the Cosmos, and if the other Guardians ever found out, the retribution would be grave indeed: she would certainly be banished from this world she loved so much, and her brethren might even take her powers from her. Even so, having located the pivotal time when events might be steered in one direction or another, she had come anyway. Not to interfere, she kept assuring herself. Certainly not. Just to be on hand in case she should be needed. However, though she had been willing to risk the penalties for defying Cosmic Law, she had never for one moment considered the other, more insidious dangers to an Immortal who had long dwelt on a higher, more ethereal plane.

It was a tremendous leap from the changeless tranquillity of the Timeless Lake. Here she could feel the beat of the passing seasons in

65

her blood; the world turning beneath her feet. Here, time flowed like a golden river against her skin. The contrasts of this mundane world were unsettling: day and night, sun and moon, the warmth of her tower room and the chill of the snow outside. She had to get used to an overload of information from her senses: the colours of the sky and the landscape, the joyous sounds of birdsong and the sigh of the wind in the trees, the icy little kisses of snow against her skin and the taste and texture of food. Now that she had come into the world, she must perforce share all the sensations that the beings who dwelt here must suffer and enjoy. She needed to eat and drink; she needed clothing and sleep. Though she used magical means to provide herself with these everyday necessities, it still galled her, on occasion, that she could not do without them.

Her powers, the fundamental, creative force of Gramarye, the High Magic, furnished the Cailleach with most of her requirements, but sleep was more difficult to come by. She was accustomed to being in control of her own awareness, and the idea of falling into unconsciousness for a number of hours filled her with a strange, nameless fear. At night she would keep herself awake, only to find herself drowsing unexpectedly through the day, and losing large chunks of time thereby. Nevertheless, she still paced the high chamber of her tower in the hours of darkness, or sat before her fire as she was doing tonight, trying to think of ways in which she could prevent the world of her creation, that she loved so dearly, from being destroyed through the folly of its inhabitants.

Right now, she could do nothing but wait for the three women of her vision to appear. Her Seeings in this earthly dimension were vague, uncertain and undependable, yet the Cailleach was convinced that these unknown females who would hold the key to the future of the world were not far away, and must surely reveal themselves soon. Or so she hoped. Every day she spent enjoying the sensual wonders of this rich and beautiful world would make it all the more difficult for her ever to return to her own unchanging realm.

The Lady of the Mists walked across to the window of her high tower and looked out. Beyond the dim reflection of her face, with its long white hair and pale moonstone eyes, dawn was breaking over the wintry landscape, and she looked out with pleasure at the valley, the lake and the trees. Here, at least, she could feel as much at home as it was possible for her to be in the mundane world that had been spun out of her dreaming, and the dreams of the other Guardians.

This world had been her own conception for the most part, which was why she had remained responsible for watching over its fate. While it was being created, she had devised a special, magical valley that reminded her of her own Timeless Lake. In this world it took the form of a steep-sided bowl in the midst of the great forest. In the centre was a tranquil lake with an island of dark stone that almost seemed to float upon the surface of the water. And on the island was a tower that took the form of a gigantic tree, the twin of the Cailleach's home in the Timeless Lake.

This secret vale was sacred and steeped in magic. It was the living heart of the world she had created with her brothers and sisters. It would never change significantly down all the long ages because, no matter what should befall it, this place would always find a way to return to the original pattern: the tree-lined bowl, the lake, the isle, the tower. In this era, the Cailleach had given the tower the form of her own beloved Tree at the Heart of the World, but she knew from her Seeings that in the future, it was destined to rise and fall; to be destroyed and rebuilt a number of times and in a variety of designs – and yet, in its fundamental essence, it would always remain the Tower.

The Cailleach was snatched out of her reflections by a warning tingle that passed right through her body. Someone had entered the Vale. Furthermore, she was certain to the very core of her being that it was someone who would play a significant part in the crisis the world was facing. Was it one of the three unknown women? Had fate brought her to the Lady's very doorstep?

On the table stood a silver bowl of crystal-clear water from the lake, and the Cailleach stooped over it eagerly, willing an image of the intruder to form. To her disappointment she could see very little detail: rocks, a few sparse and broken trees, and a still, dark figure lying on its face beside a large boulder. Alive? Dead? It was impossible to tell. Stifling a curse, she threw her thick cloak of black feathers, cowled and fringed with white, around her shoulders and stepped out onto the high platform at the top of the external staircase that curled around the trunk of the tower's treelike walls. Taking a deep breath, she lifted her arms – and the shape of a woman shimmered into the form of a great eagle. She soared upwards from the ledge, revelling in the uplift as she spurned the ground; enjoying the rush of wintry air through her feathers. With her raptor's keen vision she scanned the landscape, circling the vale until she had found the place she sought. The area was easy to recognise. A landslide had wiped the trees from a section of the valley wall, leaving a long scar of rough and stony ground in its place.

Close to the bottom of the slide, the accumulation of tumbled boulders was piled together with the splintered remnants of the trees that had been lost in the disaster. At the foot of the snowy mound, the Cailleach saw the dark blot that she sought. Landing quickly, she shimmered back into her human shape and ran towards the still form that lay sprawled in the lee of the boulder. She turned the body over carefully, and her spirits fell in disappointment. This was not one of the women she had been seeking. It was a young man, and one of the wretched slave race of humans, at that. He appeared to be on the very brink of death. How could *he* affect anything in the future? And yet the urgent feeling that the poor wretch would be important to her plans would not go away. Though she had no idea why, it was vital that she save his life. Casting her cloak about him, she took him up in her arms and apported him back to her tower.

The Cailleach was moved to a depth of feeling unusual for her at the sight of the pale, thin form that lay so still on the comfortable bed she had created with a careless wave of her hand. As a rule she remained aloof from the individual creatures who inhabited the world she had created, for what would be the point of involving herself with lives that sparked so briefly down the long ages? She had never bothered to study the slave race before – there had been no need – but now she decided it was time she started. When the coming upheavals took place, it looked as though the influence of the humans on the world's future could be far greater than any of the Guardians could possibly have expected.

Furthermore, she still couldn't shake the feeling that this particular human would be important. What she had not counted on, however, were the emotions he engendered. In the changeless Otherworld of the Timeless Lake, she had little need of such feelings, which interfered with the stillness of her meditations, so the strong sense of sympathy and concern that came over her at the sight of this pitiful, injured, helpless creature took her by surprise. So preoccupied was she with the slave, it failed to occur to her that her sojourn in this world was affecting her emotions, making them increase in strength.

Having rescued the human from the brink of death and brought him home with her to her tower, it was but a short step to convince herself that healing the pathetic creature did not *really* count as interfering in the events of the mundane world. If she didn't intervene, he would perish from his injuries, and having gone to all the trouble of rescuing him, she decided that it would be ridiculous to let him die.

When it came to taking care of this new responsibility, the Cailleach, with her powers of Gramarye, had considerable advantages over a worldly rescuer, whatever their race. While he remained unconscious, she used her powers to cleanse his filthy, lice-ridden body, thinking, as she did so, that her recently acquired sense of smell was not necessarily a good thing in this case. It took her quite some time and effort to heal all his injuries: the broken bones, wrenched muscles and the skin covered in bruises and abrasions, but finally, with a sense of tremendous satisfaction, she could declare herself content with her work, and clothe her patient in a clean, white robe.

Only when these basic needs had been attended to did she start to wonder how she would manage when he awoke. No one must ever learn that a Guardian had crossed the invisible boundary into this reality, as her presence could interfere with all sorts of imponderable factors connected with the fate, self-determinism and philosophies of the indigenous races – not to mention bringing down the wrath of the other Guardians on her head. For everyone's sake, she must persuade this young man whose life she had saved that she belonged to his world.

The Cailleach decided to present herself as a Wizard, for that would give her the widest opportunities to use her powers. To maintain the disguise, however, she would have to make some very sweeping alterations. Her tower, like her home in her Tree at the Heart of the World, consisted of one spacious, circular chamber set high above the ground. She had needed no lamps or fire, for warmth and light emanated from the very walls, and there were no furnishings save a table, a chair and a bed. So far, she had obtained all her worldly needs such as food and clothing through magic. The tower was singularly uncluttered, for whatever she needed she could simply materialise out of thin air. That would have to change.

Leaving her wanderer to the long, profound sleep of healing, the Cailleach bent all her energies to the task before her. Standing in the midst of the great, circular chamber, she pictured in her mind the changes she wished to make. There could be two sleeping chambers up here, with a general living area and a study in which she could work and meditate on the floor below. Finally, she would divide the ground floor into a large, cosy kitchen and a smaller store room for foodstuffs and other supplies, which she would have to apport in by magic before her stray awoke. The stairs should be inside, rather than around the exterior of the tower, and she would need an additional entrance at ground level. On the snowy island outside her tower, she created a garden which, though dormant at present beneath its cold, white covering, would one day have fruit trees and beehives, rows of thriving vegetables and curving beds filled with many-hued flowers. Oh, and the shape of the tower itself should change. She envisioned a tapering, elegant form, instead of the tree shape to which she was accustomed ...

To her surprise, the Cailleach found herself smiling. Maybe it would be a good thing to escape for a while from the unvarying existence of a Guardian. There had been very little change in her life down the long aeons since she and her siblings had created this world. She had forgotten how invigorating it could be.

Dael woke up to utter confusion. With a shudder, he remembered that dreadful fall; remembered his arm snapping like a twig beneath him; remembered the agony that knifed through his chest as he hit a rock and his ribs broke; recalled the rough stones tearing at his skin as he plunged wildly downhill.

So where was the pain? Gingerly he moved his arms and his legs, poked at his ribs and felt his skin for scrapes and tender bruising. There was nothing. He was ravenously hungry and he felt a little weak and shaky, but otherwise he was absolutely fine. He simply couldn't understand it. By rights, he shouldn't even be alive.

Abandoning the puzzle, Dael turned his attention to his surroundings. In his early life in the Wizardly fishing settlement on the western coast, before his father had led the group of slaves to escape, he'd had a bed of sorts, a simple, narrow affair with a thin mattress supported by rope netting on a wooden framework, and a ragged blanket to cover him. In his life of so-called freedom in the forest he had slept on the ground. Now he found himself in a bed that was warm and comfortable beyond his wildest dreams, with clean, white linen, soft pillows and a quilt stuffed thickly with feathers.

The bed was the main feature of a chamber that was clearly a section of some bigger, circular structure, for it had one long straight wall and another that curved round in a sweeping arc to form a semicircle. The walls of this unusual room were made of a strange amber-coloured stone that Dael had never seen before, which was so translucent that the light from outside actually shone through the curving wall in a warm, golden glow. At one end of the straight wall was the door, whilst the bed was against the other. On the curving wall a fireplace had been built on the side of the curve nearest the bed, with a generous fire that was just burning down from a blaze to a great bank of glowing embers. On the side closer to the door was a window, with a table and two chairs set beside it. The floor was covered with woven rush matting of a pale straw colour, and the other furnishings of the room consisted of a large wooden chest covered in intricate carvings and, beside the fire, a wooden rocking chair with cheerful crimson cushions.

When he had first awakened, Dael was feeling dreamy and comfortable, but now, as he became more alert, he began to feel increasingly afraid. Where was he? How had his hurts miraculously vanished? Who owned this place, and why had they rescued him? Who would bother to give such comforts to a lowly slave?

Dael stiffened in his bed at the sound of footsteps outside the room. The door glided soundlessly open. Quickly he feigned sleep, squinting out through lowered eyelashes at the dark-robed figure who was approaching the bed – until his gasp of surprise gave the game away.

He had never seen anyone like her. She was neither tall nor tiny, but her presence was overwhelming. She certainly wasn't human, but was she Phaerie or Wizard? Somehow, she didn't quite look as if she belonged to either race, though he thought he could detect faint traces of both. Her hair was long and a shimmering silver-white in colour, giving the initial perception that she was an old woman – an impression belied by her face, which was neither old nor young, but changed subtly each time he blinked, so that he could never register a definite image. Yet overall, his impression was one of a luminous, transcendent beauty that filled him with awe. Her pale, silvery eyes, glowing like moonstones, held him in thrall for some unguessable period of time, so that when she spoke, her low, melodious voice seemed to come from a land far away.

'You're awake at last, I see.' Her smile took his breath away. No one had ever looked on him so kindly before. 'Now, before we go any further, there are three things you need to know,' she said briskly. 'One: you're safe. Two: you're quite well. You only need to rest for a day or two to complete the healing. Three: you're not a prisoner. If you are stupid enough to want to go back to starving in the forest, then you've no business here.' She smiled again. 'I might add that you're a very fortunate young man indeed, but I expect you know that already.'

'Who – who are you?' Dael whispered.

'You can call me Athina,' the mysterious woman answered, 'and you are in my tower in the very heart of the wildwood. Wherever you came from, you almost blundered right onto my doorstep.'

'I never heard that anyone lived all the way out here,' Dael said in surprise.

For a moment, her smile vanished, and her face darkened. A shiver of fear went through him. It was as though someone had switched off the sun. 'And of course, *you* would know,' she snapped.

'I'm sorry, my Lady,' he said humbly.

The smile returned. 'Of course you are.' From somewhere out of his sight she produced another pillow and propped him into a sitting position. 'Here, drink. You'll be fiendishly thirsty, I expect. You've been asleep for a very long time.'

Obediently he drank the water, which was cool and tingling, and the most delicious thing he had ever tasted. When he had finished it all, he lay back with a sigh of satisfaction. 'Thank you,' he said.

'If you feel hungry, there's food on the table beside your bed,' she said. 'I will leave you in peace to eat. Then you should sleep a little longer. When you wake again, we'll talk properly. I have a great many questions for you, and I expect you also have a few to ask me.'

He didn't see her leave, yet suddenly, Dael found himself alone once more. And as soon as his mysterious benefactress had gone, the feelings of fear that had been removed by her presence came rushing back, followed by – just as she had predicted – a whole cartload of questions. Who was she? What did she want with him? Why was she going to all this trouble for an insignificant human slave?

All such thoughts were driven from his head by a wonderful, savoury aroma. Dael's stomach began to growl. Food. The woman had mentioned food and sure enough, when he turned, there was a little table at the side of his bed with a tray containing a bowl of steaming soup, and a plate of bread and cheese. He fell on them ravenously, though his stomach was so shrunken from starvation that he found he could eat far less than he'd expected: only half of the thick bean soup and a single piece of bread. With a sigh he returned the food to the table and lay back on the pillows – and it was only then, when his immediate needs had been satisfied, that he realised something strange was going on. Thirsty after his meal, he had absent-mindedly reached for the goblet, remembering, too late, that he had emptied it earlier. But to his surprise, it felt heavy in his hand, and when he looked, it was full again, and though the room was warm, the water was as cool and fresh as if it had just been drawn from a well.

Dael blinked in confusion. How had *that* happened? He knew very well that the strange woman had not refilled the goblet before she'd left the room. Come to think of it, he'd never seen her bring the goblet in anyway, nor the food. And now that he cast his mind back, on his first, cautious survey of the room, he was positive there had been no table beside the bed, with or without the food. So where in all Creation had it come from? And why, though the soup had been standing there for at least half an hour, was it still piping hot when he ate it? Despite the warmth of the room, Dael felt a shiver of fear run through him. His head was awhirl with questions, none of which he could even begin to answer; the most pressing of these being: what did this mysterious and very powerful woman plan to do with him?

Then, just as he felt panic beginning to overtake him, he had a clear memory of the woman standing before him in her dark robes, emphasising what she was saying by counting the points off on her fingers. He re-membered her words:

'*One: you're safe. Two: you're quite well now. You only need to rest for a day or two to complete the healing. Three: you're not a prisoner.*'

Suddenly, Dael felt better. For the first time in his life, someone was taking care of him and treating him with kindness. Never before had he been given his own room with a fireplace – *a fireplace* – a soft, comfortable bed and plentiful food. And no one had ever smiled at him the way this mysterious Lady had done.

Even if she turns me into a frog or a monster later on, even if I have to work from dawn till dusk, it'll have been worth it, just for this, he thought. *Even if she* kills *me, it will have been worthwhile. But I don't think she will. She said I'm safe, and that I'm not a prisoner.*

He felt his eyelids beginning to close but, just as he was on the edge of sleep, he heard a small, warning voice in the back of his mind:

You'd better hope she was telling you the truth.

Dael ignored it, turned over, and went back to sleep.

7
~

THE EVANESAR

The grinding, creaking, rumbling voice of Taku was the sound of the glacier. 'Who comes here, where no stranger has dared to tread for many a long age?'

Corisand staggered and almost fell, her mind blank with shock. All her equine instincts were screaming at her to flee, while the reasoning, human side of her was determined to stand its ground. This awesome being might look terrifying, but so far it had made no move to hurt her. How could she ever hope to save her people if she ran away from every challenge?

She took a deep breath and tried to control the knocking of her knees. 'My name is Corisand,' she said in a loud, clear voice, 'and I am the Windeye, Shaman of the lost race of the Xandim, and Seeker of the Truth.'

Though the serpent's expression did not alter, its voice took on a more kindly note. 'I judge that you are also a speaker of the truth, O Corisand. I already knew you were the Windeye of the Xandim, for it was I who sensed your presence in the mundane world, and brought you here. It came as a great revelation, not to mention something of a shock, to discover that the Xandim race, despite all my fears, was still in existence. What is this truth that you seek, Shaman? The accursed Phaerie Lord—' His voice sank to a menacing growl. 'Has he finally loosed his tyrant's grasp upon your kind?'

Now it was Corisand's turn to be astounded. 'You know about that?' she gasped. 'But how?'

The glittering blue stare of the serpent fixed upon her greedily. 'There was a time when I was known to each Windeye, through all the generations. They were welcomed among myself and my fellow Elementals, granted access to this world through our powers, and honoured by us for their wisdom and their skills. Then Hellorin subjugated the Xandim, and without their magic, we were unable to connect with your Shamans.'

'You say "we",' Corisand interrupted. 'So there are more of you?'

'Indeed there are.' Light flooded the sky from horizon to horizon. Rippling veils and bands of colour drifted, a jewel-box of hues all pulsing, streaming and mingling in wild and spectacular abandon; green bleeding into pink, spun with blue and lavender and gold. The air hummed and crackled with energy, a roaring whisper right on the edge of hearing. And in that sound was a voice. As the Windeye watched, open-mouthed, the form of an eagle emerged within the drifts of liquid light, its vast, glimmering wings of drifting colour spreading across the sky. Fierce golden eyes transfixed her with their piercing gaze.

'What in the name of all Creation do you think you're doing, Taku, bringing her here? She has no business in this world.'

The great serpent reared up to face the eagle's glare. 'She is the first Windeye in many generations who has been able to venture here, and I brought her because she does have business in this world. The Lord of the Phaerie is here, Aurora. Did you not know?'

'What?' Corisand gasped. 'But that can't be. His Wild Hunt was ambushed in the forest by a pack of feral mortals. He was wounded, almost dead, and to preserve his life, his daughter took him out of time.'

'And left his spirit in oblivion, lost and disembodied. The Moldan Aerillia, an ancient ally of the Forest Lord, sensed his presence and succeeded in bringing him here. He still holds Corisand's people in slavery. This world is the only place she can fight him.'

'That has nothing to do with the Evanesar.'

'How can you say that? The Windeyes of the Xandim have been our friends and allies down all the long ages, just as Hellorin has been our foe.'

'*Your* friends and allies, you mean.' There was an edge of mockery in her voice. 'Most of us outgrew the need for pets long ago. What use could she possibly be against a being with the powers of the Forest Lord? What use were any of them? They couldn't even protect their own people.'

'This one may surprise you.'

Corisand, who had been listening with mounting annoyance to the argument going back and forth over her head, decided she'd had enough. Gathering a double handful of glimmering air, she moulded it into a missile and hurled it down with all her force. As it struck the magic that held up her bridge, it exploded with a resounding bang, and a fountain of light shot up into the sky, spreading out in a canopy far above and raining down again in sizzling spatters of silver.

Taku and Aurora shut up abruptly. Two pairs of fearsome eyes, one blue and one gold, pinned her, but the Windeye was too angry to be cowed. 'I'll thank you to talk to me, not over the top of my head,' she snapped. 'You may be ancient and powerful, but that's no excuse for rank discourtesy. And as for protecting my people, I'll cherish and defend them to my last dying breath. Why do you think I'm here? And Taku: you may have brought me here for your own reasons, but if I can use this place to free my race, I won't let anything get in my way.'

There was a protracted moment of silence – then, just as Corisand was having serious doubts about the wisdom of her outburst, Aurora began to laugh, sending waves of rose-coloured light flickering across the sky. 'You may be right,' she said to Taku. 'She has already surprised me. And she does not lack for courage.' She turned to fix the Windeye with her glittering gaze. 'Very well, little sister. Let us talk.'

'Thank you,' said Corisand. 'When you came, Taku was just telling me about the Elementals.'

'As you should already know,' said Aurora severely, 'there are four Elementals of the Old Magic dwelling in this world. Taku, Elemental of Water and Master of the Cold Magic; myself, Aurora, Elemental of Air and Mistress of the Wild Magic; Katmai, Elemental of Fire and Master of the Death Magic; Denali, the Mother, the Great One, Elemental of Earth and Mistress of the Old Magic. In the Elsewhere, we are known as the Evanesar.'

'But I didn't know any of that,' Corisand replied. 'That's why I need answers. Where am I? What is this Elsewhere that you mentioned?'

'It is, if you like, a sister world to your own,' Taku replied. 'An alternative realm in which the Old Magic reigns supreme.'

'But how did I get here?'

'I brought you,' he answered brusquely. 'And now it is time for you to answer some of *my* questions. I will repeat what I asked you before. Has Hellorin released your people from their bondage?'

Corisand sighed. 'No, that has not changed. I have only recently come into my powers, and because we have been trapped as horses, my predecessor was unable to explain anything to me; nor could I access my magic. I have no idea how or why you brought me here, but I count it the greatest stroke of good fortune. Surely this could not have happened by chance. I'm hoping desperately that it means I might be the one Windeye, out of so many lost generations, who could save her people.'

Taku regarded her thoughtfully. 'It would certainly explain why, after such a lengthy absence, I was able to call a Shaman of the Xandim back to this place. Perhaps you are right, Corisand. Your coming here can be no coincidence. This realm, like your own, is governed by a number of natural laws. In your mundane world, the laws are mainly physical, dealing with the forces and energies of objects interacting upon one another. Here, however, those natural laws are mainly magical. Before today, I would have been unable to bring you here, for in your equine form you lacked the magic to make that initial connection with me. But now something has changed. When Hellorin was brought through from your own world by Aerilia, one of the Moldai, that created the portal through which I could reach you.'

The Windeye frowned. 'But who is Aerillia? And you mentioned the Moldai before. Who or what are they?' she asked.

Aurora sighed pointedly at a further interruption.

'It's not my fault,' Corisand protested. 'This is all new to me, remember? It seems that I can draw upon the knowledge of my predecessors to give me an understanding of my own world, so I knew what a glacier was, for instance, though I have never seen one. But when it comes to this place, I have not the scantest knowledge about anything. So far, I have just been going on my instincts.'

'And very good instincts they are,' said Taku. 'I imagine that the wisdom of your predecessors regarding this place is no use to you because such a tremendous length of time has passed since your forebears were able to access their powers and come here. The knowledge, useless to the Windeyes in their equine state, must have been lost during the intervening years.'

'Will you help me reclaim it, Taku? I must learn to understand these things. As Windeye, the knowledge is my birthright, but it goes much deeper than that. If I am to free my people, I will need every advantage I can find.'

The serpent dipped his head. 'Very well. Ask. I will do what I can.'

'Why ask only him?' There was an edge to Aurora's voice.

A number of excuses raced through Corisand's mind. Then she decided to stick with honesty. 'Taku brought me here,' she said, 'and so far, he has been much more friendly.'

A flash of red lit up the sky. 'I give my trust and friendship where and when they are merited. But I am willing to help you for now. Who knows? Trust and friendship may follow. I certainly would not be offering my assistance if I did not believe that.'

Corisand smiled. 'I also believe that we could become friends, and I am glad of it.' Addressing both now, she added, 'You said Hellorin's spirit was brought here. Does that mean I am only here as a spirit, too?' She ran a hand down her body. 'This certainly feels like solid flesh and bone to me.'

'To all intents and purposes, it is solid flesh and bone,' Taku told her. 'Conditions in this world are formed by our powers and will and imagination, and can even extend to our physical forms. Here magic rules, and only those possessing magic can come here. Things are less rigid, less certain, more malleable. But though the body you are wearing now is a reality in this world, I was only able to bring your spirit here, Windeye. Your true physical form is back in the mundane world, in a semblance of sleep.'

Corisand felt crushing disappointment. 'Then this human form – it isn't even real.'

'No.' This time, Aurora answered. 'There you are mistaken. It is real, and it belongs to you. If you finally succeed in freeing yourself and your people, and regain your human aspect in your own world, you will find it to be just as it is here and now.'

'But what happens if the Horsemistress, or one of the other Phaerie, comes along while my spirit is here? Surely they'll try to awaken me. What will become of me when they cannot? Or would their attempts to wake my body drag my spirit back there?'

'Be easy,' Taku said. 'Time here runs very differently, relative to the world in which you live. We can return you very shortly after you left, so that there will be no opportunity for the Phaerie to be suspicious.'

'Well, that's a relief. But why did I assume this shape in the first place? Why not take the one to which I'm most accustomed?'

'Ever since you became Windeye, and learned what you could be, your mind has yearned after this alternative form.' Taku's voice was kind and patient, as though he could sense just how much this meant to her. 'Also, you have all the courage and wisdom of your forebears, Corisand. It was only natural that you would choose the more powerful aspect of your being – the one in which you could think and communicate clearly. The one in which you would be most useful to your people. The one in which you could fulfil your dreams, and access your true powers at long last.'

All at once, the serpent's voice turned grave. 'But I give you warning, Corisand. Heed me well. Other beings dwell here. Their will, their thoughts, their magic can influence and mould reality just as well as your own, and if it comes to a clash of wills, the most powerful will prevail. So a conflict here will not be won by physical strength, but by the power of magic and imagination. Always keep that in mind. One day it may save your life.'

A chill crawled up her spine. 'And if I were to die here?' she asked quietly. 'What would happen to the Corisand of the mundane world?'

'If you die here, you die in all realities.'

Aurora's stark words were as shocking as a physical slap. The dream-like sense of unreality that had beset her since her arrival in this strange new world burst like a bubble. She knew, however, that she could not afford to let herself be daunted. This miraculous opportunity had some-how been granted her, and she could not afford to let it go to waste. She straightened her shoulders and lifted her chin. 'In that case, it is all the more important that you teach me what I need to know.'

'Indeed.' There was new respect in the serpent's mien. 'Then let us return to the association between the Moldai and the Forest Lord. The Moldai are an ancient, elemental race who dwell simultaneously in this realm and the mundane world. Here, they usually take the form of giants, and though they can change their shape as they choose, they are inevitably very large in scale. In the mundane world, their aspect is tre-mendous mountains of living stone. Originally, they were the offspring of Denali— '

'Who can't say that the rest of us didn't warn her,' Aurora interrupted in acid tones.

'Be that as it may,' Taku said, and resumed his tale. 'The Moldai belonged solely here in this Elsewhere, but as they grew in power they became ambitious and, like the Forest Lord, desired the conquest of other realms. However, unlike Hellorin, who quit one place for the other, the Moldai wished for a foothold in both worlds, and in order to achieve this, they were prepared to stop at nothing.

'They discovered that they would need a tremendous amount of power to achieve their ends. Something that could both store magic and magnify it. But they lacked sufficient lore to complete the task. For that, they needed the help of the Phaerie, a different race with a different form of magic. Hellorin agreed, and so, between the two ancient races, the Fialan, the Stone of Fate, was created.'

Corisand discovered that she had been listening with such attention that she'd been holding her breath. 'What did it look like?' she asked.

'What a very female sort of question,' Taku scoffed, ignoring the red flare that emanated from Aurora, and flashed across the sky. 'Considering its vast power, the Fialan was small, and quite innocuous-looking. I expect, however, that *you* would have thought it very pretty. It was simply a glit-tering green crystal, about the size of your circled finger and thumb, but it was one of the most powerful implements in this world, and Hellorin's price for his assistance in its creation was very high. After they had used the Fialan to gain their footholds in both worlds, the Moldai had to give custody of the Stone over to the Phaerie.'

'Give such tremendous power into Hellorin's hands?' Corisand gasped. 'They would be mad to do such a thing.'

'Nevertheless,' said Aurora, 'that is exactly what they did. The Moldai had no choice, and in truth, they had little need for the Fialan once they had achieved their ends. But it rankled that the Phaerie should possess this priceless artefact that was partly their handiwork. So, before they gave up the Stone, they put an additional charm of their own into it, without the knowledge of the Phaerie. It was half a spell: in order for the Stone to be used, the spell must be completed – and only the Moldai knew how.'

'But surely Hellorin would have found that out straight away?'

'Why would he? They had designed the Stone to create a portal between the worlds, and at first the Phaerie were content here in the Elsewhere. But as their race grew and prospered, we Evanesar decided to set curbs on their ambition. At that point, Hellorin decided that he too wished to take his people to the mundane world, so that he would be free of us, and his ambition could no longer be shackled.'

'He tried to use the Stone and failed? He must have been absolutely livid.' Corisand's eyes sparkled. 'Oh, how I wish I could have seen that.'

Taku's eyes glittered with amusement. 'As you say. And worse was to come for the Forest Lord. The Moldai knew that the opportunity for which they had waited so long had finally come to pass. They withheld the spell of completion until the Lord of the Phaerie had met their price – the return of the Stone of Fate into their custody. He agreed, seemingly readily enough, though inside he was raging. The Stone was given back to the Moldai and placed in the custody of Ghabal, one of their most powerful magicians, also known as Steelclaw in the mundane world. He had been nominated as the one who would act as focus for the spell of completion; the one who would combine his magic with that of Hellorin in order to allow the portal to form.'

'But Hellorin had a treacherous plan to take back the Fialan.' Aurora's voice grew harsh with anger. 'Even as the portal opened and his people passed through, he tried one last, desperate act of magic to wrest back the crystal from the Moldai. The result was catastrophic. The portal spell required tremendous amounts of two differing sorts of magic – that of the Phaerie and that of the Moldai – all bound together in a delicate and precarious equilibrium of force and counter-force, and Hellorin's additional spell shattered that balance.'

Taku's voice was a growl. 'The resulting explosion almost destroyed the Elsewhere, and brought death and havoc to many of its inhabitants. The worst fate, however, befell Ghabal. Since he had been using the

Fialan to help Hellorin form the portal, he caught the direct recoil of the spell and was dreadfully injured. In the mundane world, his body was shattered, the living rock of the mountain peak riven and melted. Here in the Elsewhere, he suffered hideous disfigurement, and was driven hopelessly insane. Yet he managed to retain the Stone, and still holds it, to this day. All that power and potential is now in the hands of a violent, mad and unpredictable creature.'

Corisand's mind was racing, almost too fast for her to keep up with the welter of ideas and possibilities. 'If Ghabal has the Stone of Fate, and the Moldai can dwell in both realities, does that mean he could use it in either world?'

Taku nodded solemnly. 'I suspect that may be the case. Your own world is in danger, as well as this one.'

'That's not my consideration at present. I'm wondering...' The Windeye took a deep breath. 'I wonder if there is any way the Stone could be used to free my people? If I could only negotiate with this Ghabal, and somehow persuade him to help us. After all, his great enemy, the Forest Lord, is also my foe. Might that not be enough to convince him?'

'It would be sheer madness even to attempt such a thing,' Aurora snapped. 'Put any idea of bargaining with Ghabal out of your mind. His people made a covenant with Hellorin once, and it cost him almost everything. He will never negotiate with anyone else. Approach him with that end in mind and he will strike you down.'

Corisand scarcely knew whether to be relieved or disappointed. Though it had seemed such a simple, elegant plan, the thought of actually trying to form an alliance with the crazed Moldan had filled her with misgiving. Yet if she could not be his ally, she would have to take the Fialan away from him, and that alternative was far worse. Nevertheless, she would have to do it, and she meant to. The fact that she hadn't worked out how she could possibly achieve such a thing was simply a trifling detail. She fixed the serpent with her gaze. 'But if I possessed it, I could use the Stone?'

'I think,' said Taku cautiously, 'that with some training, you might learn to use it and bend it to your will. Hellorin and the Moldai made the Fialan for a specific reason: to use as a gateway between the worlds. But the Stone itself is not the portal. It is simply a way to store and magnify their magical power. I have the feeling, however, that other, alternative forms of magic – say the power of a Windeye or a Wizard – may achieve additional and far different ends.'

'But we do not know for certain,' Aurora added hastily, 'and you would risk a great deal in trying to master such forces single-handed – if indeed you ever got that far. If you are determined to proceed along that path, you must first take the Stone from Ghabal. How do you propose to achieve that? Others have tried before you. None have succeeded. None have survived.'

At Aurora's dark words, Corisand felt dread rising up like a dark miasma from her belly to her brain. With a struggle, she held it back. '*You* think I can do it, don't you?' she said to Taku. 'That is why you brought me here, is it not?'

'I brought you here on a gamble, nothing more,' he said, with a wary glance at Aurora. 'When I felt a Windeye abroad in the mundane world again, it seemed that there was one last chance, one faint hope, to regain the Stone. But when I brought you here, I did not know your mettle. Now that we understand one another a little better, I begin to see the faintest gleam of hope for all of us, and I am prepared to help in any way I can.'

'Taku.' Aurora sounded shocked. 'What have you done? You brought this innocent here, and I have watched as you cleverly manipulated her into thinking she could recover the Stone. This is all wrong. How dare you give her hope where none exists, only to further our ends? She has no idea what she would be facing.'

'I have simply made the most of an opportunity. She is a Windeye. Their powers are different from ours. It has been so long since Hellorin or Ghabal faced one of her kind that she might be able to take them by surprise. Some of the old Windeyes were very strong.'

'That didn't stop the Forest Lord from enslaving her race,' Aurora snapped. 'What you ask is beyond her, Taku. It is beyond any of us. How can we ask her to do what we cannot?' The clear, golden gaze of the eagle turned in Corisand's direction. 'Windeye, be warned: what Taku asks of you is not reasonable. Let me send you back to your own world.'

Corisand stretched up a hand towards the shimmering vision in the sky. 'Thank you, Aurora, for trying to protect me. I know you have my interests at heart. But can't you see that Taku is right? This is my only chance to free my people, and I can't turn away while that one small hope exists. If I succeed, then we all win, and if I fail ... Well, there will be another Windeye to follow me, and carry on in my place.'

'There.' Aurora turned on Taku. 'Now see what you've done.'

'I have done what I intended to do. What I had to do.' His voice was implacable, and his stare as level as her own. 'This meeting was no accident, sister. This was fate at work. I have no idea how we can bring such a thing about, but I have a feeling that the days of both Ghabal and Hellorin as threats to the world are numbered, and that their power is finally about to meet its match.'

'You'd risk everything on a *feeling*—' Aurora began.

Corisand cut her short. 'Please, stop this. Surely we should all be on the same side. The two of you can dispute this until the end of time, but that won't get us anywhere. Whatever Taku may have done, however he may have manipulated me, I am here now, and I want to make the most of it.' She paused. 'One thing puzzles me, however.' All at once, there was a new edge, hard and cold, to her voice. 'Why do you need to involve me in this? If you Evanesar are such an ancient, powerful race – strong enough, even, to set bounds on the ambitions of the Phaerie – why can't you take the Stone for yourselves?'

'When the Phaerie and the Moldai were creating the Fialan, the same thought occurred to them.' Taku's voice was a low, angry growl. 'No matter how they planned to cheat one another, they were absolutely united on one thing: the Evanesar must never get control of the Stone. So between them they set a ward upon it. If one of the Evanesar so much as touches the Fialan, it would not only destroy itself, but the violent implosion of forces would destroy both worlds.'

'Fools!' Aurora said. 'For their Guardian Magic cannot be undone – it is part of the very form and structure of the crystal. And now that the stone has fallen into unsafe hands, we are powerless to intervene.'

'As you will always be powerless against me and mine.'

The voice was like a blade being turned in Corisand's guts. 'Hellorin!' She spun to see the Forest Lord standing on the apex of her own bridge. Anger blazed up within her to consume the terror. How dare he set his filthy, treacherous feet on her beautiful construct? How *dare* he sully the shining purity of her first magic with his foul touch?

'So. We have a new Windeye.' His voice was soft with menace. 'I might have guessed it would be you. You were always stubborn, recalcitrant and disobedient. Always the rebel.' He smiled, and the cold, cruel contempt in his eyes sent chills crawling through her body. 'But as I am sure you recall, I mastered you then. And I can master you now.'

Corisand gritted her teeth, gladly embracing the anger that burned within her. Taking care to keep any sign of it from her face, she half-turned away with a dismissive shrug. 'That was in another time, another world. Things are different here. In your own realm, you mastered a dumb, powerless animal. Are you so proud of that? It's not much of an achievement. Not much to brag about.'

Hellorin's face paled with anger. 'You delude yourself if you think that anything has changed. Despite your current guise, you are still nothing more than an animal, spawned of a primitive, barbaric race.' His voice dropped into a snarl. 'Human or equine, when I have finished with you, your body will go to feed my hounds, and your hide will make a fetching carpet for my floor.' As the last words left his mouth he struck at her, his body suddenly towering high overhead, a bolt of dark lightning sizzling from his outstretched hand.

Everything happened at once. Taku flung a vast wall of ice between Corisand and the Forest Lord. Aurora swept down a wing, and the Windeye was shielded by a many-hued curtain of energy. And Corisand herself, acting on some bone-deep instinct, created an illusion of herself as a vast colossus and stepped into that image, so that she grew as tall as her foe. At the same time, she formed the air into a shining, mirrored shield and threw it in front of her, so that she reflected Hellorin's magic back at him. With a vicious curse, the Forest Lord vanished, and Corisand felt triumph swell within her. The first blow had gone to her.

The serpent and the eagle, however, did not drop their shields. 'It is time to send you home, little sister,' Aurora said softly. 'Hellorin will soon be back, and this time he will be prepared. You are not ready to face him yet.'

Corisand's heart plummeted. 'But I don't want to go back,' she protested. 'I can learn more, do more, help more if I stay here, in this body. I'm only just getting started.'

'You can always return,' Taku said kindly. 'We will bring you back when it is safe, and Hellorin's attention is elsewhere. Then there will be time to help and teach you.'

'But how can I come back? You said yourself it was only the coincidence of the portal opening that allowed you to bring me here in the first place.'

'Now that you are here, however,' Taku told her, 'we can create a link that will let us bring you here whenever it is safe.' With alarming speed, he struck with his fangs at the edge of the glacier. Chips and shards of the glittering blue ice flew up, and Corisand reflexively put out a hand and caught a piece. About the size of a walnut, it glistened on her palm like a jewel, and she could feel the intense cold beat against her skin.

'When you get back to your own world,' Taku told her, 'the ice will go with you. Swallow it quickly, before it melts, and that will provide the link between us. Three times you will be able to come; three times the spell will last. And remember this: time runs differently in this world, it swirls and flows like a river. At this moment we cannot say how soon we will be able to bring you back, but do not fear. As soon as it is possible, we shall send out the summons.'

The serpent dipped his head to her. 'Farewell, Windeye. Go with our blessing.'

Aurora spread wide her wings as if to embrace Corisand, sending veils of colour rippling across the sky. 'Farewell, little sister. We have faith in you.'

Then there was that sudden slippage, that same sideways jolt as before. Corisand found herself back in her stable, on four feet instead of two, the glorious fire of her magic nothing but inert ashes. Her mind was a dreamlike world of bright impressions filled with colours that were no longer clear to her eyes, and she fought in vain to recapture that clarity and complexity of thought that had come so easily to her human form. She shook her head, no longer certain whether the events of that other world had been reality or a dream.

Then her eye caught sight of something glinting, down at her feet in the straw. Her heart leapt. The ice! Taku's ice, and in this world, it was melting fast. Quickly she bent her head and licked it up, together with dust and bits of straw from the stable floor, and swallowed the cold, hard fragment.

All at once, it was as if a window had opened, and she caught a brief glimpse of Taku's glistening form, and Aurora's colours glimmering and shifting as her wings stretched out across the sky. Joy flooded her entire being with light. Not imagination, then. Not a dream. And she would see them again. She had their promise. Sooner or later, she would go back to that world of magic and miracles and deepest peril, to set about reclaiming her birthright as Windeye of the Xandim.

8
~

SIGNS OF PERIL

Hellorin lay, magnificent and motionless as the carven figure on a king's stone tomb, his strong, handsome features blurred and silvered by the eldritch glimmer of the time spell. Aelwen, to her surprise, found herself groping for Cordain's hand, in search of comfort.

'Is there no sign of improvement?' she asked. 'Surely after two months we should be seeing some sort of change?'

The Chief Counsellor shook his head. 'It is a mystery. The healers seem to be making no progress at all.'

She shuddered. 'I cannot help but be unnerved by such unnatural stillness,' she said softly – though she could have shouted at the top of her lungs for all the difference it would make to the Forest Lord. 'He has always been so vigorous, so vibrant; always moving, always doing, always in absolute command. To see him looking so diminished and vulnerable shakes me to my very bones.'

Cordain looked at her shrewdly. 'Such a reaction surprised you, did it not?'

'How well you know me.' Aelwen smiled sheepishly. 'I never found him lovable – not even particularly likeable, although he could be incredibly charming and kind when it suited him. In all the years I have known him we've knocked heads any number of times, but—'

'But it has always been about the horses,' Cordain said, 'on which subject you are the most knowledgeable, and he respects and admires your skills. You would never have dared oppose him on any other matter – but at least he possessed the redeeming quality of always being open to advice. Indeed, he valued and respected his counsellors and experts, including the two of us, and always listened carefully and courteously to their suggestions.' Cordain looked fondly down at his Lord. 'Mark you, more often than not he would go his own way in any case, but at least he would act from a foundation of knowledge and a new consideration of the long-term consequences of his actions, which often turned his judgements to a more tempered and far-sighted course.'

'Sometimes he had his secrets,' Aelwen pointed out. 'There were things he did that he would never explain even to the closest of his advisors – like never letting a single one of the Phaerie horses out of his kingdom. Merchants and couriers had their own special mounts, clearly a more ordinary breed than ours, and only they were ever permitted to pass beyond the borders, except during the Hunt, of course.'

Cordain shrugged. 'Every ruler has secrets, Aelwen.'

'Tiolani has certainly taken *that* to heart. Already she appears to have more secrets from us than Hellorin ever harboured. She has been ruling for two short months: surely this is the very time for her to turn to her father's experienced and respected counsellors, even if only to learn the day-to-day functioning of so complex an organism as our realm. But does she? She does not.'

'She has dismissed us, every one,' Cordain said. 'The only person she listens to now is that shifty-eyed Ferimon.'

'Shifty?' Aelwen raised her eyebrows. 'If only he were. Then she might notice there is something wrong. But he's always perfectly charming, sunny-faced and utterly guileless. It takes folk of our own age and experience to realise that he's *too* damned perfect – you just know that somewhere underneath the politician's smiles, a serpent lurks.'

'And we can see it, but Tiolani cannot. Aelwen, I fear for this realm, for all of us, if the Forest Lord does not recover. Tiolani has inherited his strong will without his wisdom. She seems utterly oblivious to the problems that are developing within the realm, though they are a direct result of her refusing our help on the one hand, and neglecting to act herself on the other.'

'Foolish girl.' Aelwen shook her head. 'All the years she was growing up she fancied herself in love with Ferimon, and now, when she is grieving and vulnerable, along he comes, suddenly finding her attractive even though he barely spared a glance for her before.'

'It is as if she's under his spell,' Cordain said. 'He is isolating her from all other influences. She refuses to listen to us any more – not even to me, and I am afraid to keep trying, for the more I persist, the angrier she grows. I am hoping that you can get through to her, Aelwen. If you cannot, then no one else has a hope of influencing her, and we are lost.'

'If she's alone with me, in the presence of her father, maybe I'll stand a chance,' the Horsemistress replied. 'That's why I asked her to meet me here.'

Cordain nodded. 'Then I will leave you now. May you be successful, Aelwen – for all our sakes.'

Tiolani paused outside Hellorin's chamber. 'But why did Aelwen ask to meet me here?' she repeated to Ferimon. 'Why not the stables, as usual?' She hated her father's sickroom, though she dutifully visited him for several hours every day. It hurt her to see him lying there: that helpless stillness struck Hellorin's daughter to the heart, and filled her with guilt. Full well she knew that, were he back on the throne, he would never permit her association with Ferimon. Because of this, she had not pushed as hard as she might for an answer from the healers.

Ferimon, clearly mistaking the reason for her hesitation, took her arm. 'Come, my dearest. You have nothing to fear from your father's Mistress of Horse. You are sovereign here.'

'Indeed. And if I must, I shall prove it to her before this day is out.' With no way to back down without looking weak and foolish, she took a deep breath, and nodded to the guards to open the door.

When Tiolani entered the chamber, Aelwen got to her feet and bowed respectfully, but the girl did not miss the flash of annoyance, glimpsed then swiftly veiled, at the sight of Ferimon.

'My Lady,' the Horsemistress said in a tight, controlled voice. 'I requested to meet with you alone.'

'And I decided to deny your request.' Tiolani's chin took on an arrogant tilt, and her voice was cold and hard with defiance. 'Ferimon is my most trusted and valued advisor. Anything you wish to say to me, you can say in front of him.'

'Very well.' Aelwen could be defiant too – but in her case her words emerged with the quiet force of assertion. 'Since you raise the subject, it is of your advisors that I wish to speak.' She gestured to the chair beside her. 'Come, sit by me, my dear. Let us have a comfortable talk, as I used to do so often with your mother.'

Oh, but that Mistress of Horse was cunning. Tiolani ground her teeth and strove to keep her annoyance from showing on her face. There were only two chairs in the room, and the bed was inaccessible because of the time spell, so that if she sat down with Aelwen, Ferimon would be isolated and plainly superfluous. And as for dragging her mother into this business – that was a low blow!

She answered Aelwen's blandly innocent smile with one that was barely more than a grimace. 'We will stand, Horsemistress. This will not take long.'

Without a hint of her emotions showing, Aelwen shrugged. 'As you wish.' That gambit having failed, she went straight to the attack – or that was the way it seemed to Hellorin's daughter.

'Tiolani, Cordain tells me that you have dismissed all of your father's counsellors.' She gestured at the recumbent figure of the Forest Lord. 'I have known your father well for many years – from long before you were born – and you can trust me when I say that he would be saddened and dismayed by your actions. He trusted those advisors implicitly, and with good reason. My dear girl, do you not see how much easier they could make your life? A vast responsibility has suddenly dropped upon your shoulders, but it was no different for Hellorin. Those very people whose counsel you are spurning helped to lift a good deal of his burden by taking care of so many of the small but important day-to-day details involved in governing the Phaerie realm.'

'I don't care about that. I—'

'Then you *should* care.' Anger flashed in Aelwen's voice, like the edge of a bright blade that caught the sun. 'There is more to ruling this land than spending all day mooning over a lover and all night riding out to bloody slaughter with the Hunt. Did you know that this long, cold winter has destroyed a large part of the moonmoth population, and that our silk harvest this year will be the smallest in recorded history? Did you know that dozens of disputes have arisen, both minor and major, that can only be mediated by the sovereign? Did you know that our people are becoming increasingly restive and concerned? Were you aware that your decision to close the borders is making life incredibly difficult for our merchants and traders? That we are already running out of certain goods, such as oil and wheat and herbs, that we normally obtain from outside?'

Tiolani felt her face grow hot as anger with a black and ugly twist of guilt rose up inside her, but Aelwen was still speaking.

'Tiolani, these matters can all be dealt with. *Be* Hellorin's true heir. Make him proud. Talk to Cordain and the other counsellors. Work with them to put this realm to rights, before matters deteriorate any further. Whatever you may have been led to believe—' again there was that blade-flash of anger as she flicked a glance at Ferimon '—we are all on your side, and our only wish is to help you through these difficult times. We—'

'Enough!' Tiolani was surprised to hear how like her father she sounded. To her relief, Ferimon, silken smooth, slid into the ensuing silence.

'The Lady Tiolani has noted your concerns, Horsemistress Aelwen, and you have her assurance that they will be dealt with in due course. Your advice on counsellors is well taken, however the Lady can appoint her own.'

'I will appoint my own,' Tiolani echoed, love and gratitude for his support glowing within her. Why had she not thought of that before? Ferimon was so clever. Feeling in control once more, like a ruler and not the guilty little girl that Aelwen had evoked, she waved a dismissive hand at the Horsemistress. 'You have known me since I was a child, Aelwen, and I understand that you are only trying to help, but you are interfering in matters that are beyond you. You may return to your horses, and leave the rule of this realm safely in my hands.'

As she spoke, she called in mindspeech to her new bodyguards, recently appointed at Ferimon's instigation. They had been standing just beyond the chamber doors and entered at her word, standing stiffly at attention. Their message was clear to everyone in the room. 'You are dismissed, Aelwen, with our thanks.'

The Horsemistress was still outwardly calm, still keeping her temper reined, but her anger showed in her eyes, burning darkly in a bone-white face. Without a word, she walked to the door – then turned abruptly and pointed at Hellorin. 'What will he say when he wakes, Tiolani? Will he think that you have honoured his trust? Will he be proud?' She turned her gaze from the Forest Lord to Tiolani. 'You know better,' she said quietly, and left.

Tiolani turned and pounded the wall with her fists, weeping with rage. 'How dare she? How *dare* she speak to me like that? She belongs in the stables. What does she know about ruling?'

Ferimon enfolded her in a comforting embrace. 'Never mind her,' he crooned, his voice cajoling, comforting. 'Aelwen knows nothing. She *is* nothing. She is beneath your notice. And if there is any trouble within the realm, we are more than capable of finding it out and setting it to rights without the interference of a jumped-up dung-shoveller and that coterie of feeble old fools who used to be your father's lapdogs. You have no need of them, dear one. You will be the greatest ruler the Phaerie have ever seen.'

Tiolani turned into his embrace and laid her head trustingly on his shoulder. 'Oh, Ferimon, what would I do without you? Sometimes it feels as if you are the only one who understands me. Thank all the Fates that you are here.'

PART 2
~
TYRINELD

9
~

DORTENTS

The seasons turned, in the wildwood and the lands beyond. Winter slunk away, defeated, and the warmer days returned. On the other side of the forest and far to the south of the Phaerie realm, the city of Tyrineld, jewel of the western coast and home of the Wizards, glimmered in the bright sun of early summer. In a garden in the northern sector of the city, a magpie took off from the branches of a cherry tree in a single long glide and swooped down to land on the high wall at the bottom of the lawn. There were voices coming from the lane on other side of the wall, and the bird looked down from its perch with bright, curious eyes. Two Wizards were passing by along the narrow back street: Bards, by the cut and purple colour of their robes. One of them, the woman, had fastened her robe at the neck with a glittering amethyst and silver brooch that the magpie, attracted by the flash and sparkle, eyed acquisitively.

'I thought this was a short cut,' the man was complaining. 'You haven't managed to get us lost in these back streets, have you? I haven't the faintest idea where we are.'

'Don't worry,' the woman replied. 'We're nearly there. This is the back of that blind girl's house.'

The magpie lifted off from the wall and glided down low over the couple, depositing a large splattering dropping on the woman's head with a derisive cackle. Leaving curses and howls of disgust behind it, it turned and flew back up the garden, where a young woman, with a strong-boned face and abundant dark hair that carried a smouldering crimson spark in the sunlight, was seated beneath the cherry tree.

Iriana held out a hand and let the magpie perch there as she stroked its shining, iridescent black head. 'That'll teach them, won't it?' she said, switching her vision from the bird's eyes to the eyes of the cat who sat

93

on the table beside her. There was a brief instant of darkness, then the world took on an entirely different perspective as Iriana moved from avian vision to feline. 'Blind indeed,' she snorted. 'That's all *they* know.'

The Archwizard Cyran sat in the topmost chamber of his tower, all his attention fixed on the silver mirror that rested on the table before him. The images from his scrying had faded, leaving only his own reflection: dark eyes and a bony nose in a long, mobile face lined with laughter and sorrow, all framed by his mane of silvering dark hair. The memory of the events he had just witnessed, however, was burned deep into his mind. Again! He clenched his fists until the fingernails bit into the palms. How many more times would he be tormented by the same dreadful vision? Shuddering, he rose from his chair and rubbed his eyes, as if to wipe away the lingering images he had seen in his mirror.

After a moment, the familiar room came back into focus: a spacious octagonal chamber with a floor of dark wood that had been burnished to a rich glow, and dark beams on the ceiling, carved with twining flowers and vines. The walls, painted a warm shade of cream, were obscured by bookshelves overflowing with volumes and racks of scrolls, diagrams and maps pinned in any available space, and cabinets containing all sorts of paraphernalia including a selection of wines and the ingredients for several sorts of tea, including taillin, a fragrant drink made from the leaves of a bush that grew locally, which was the staple stimulant of the Wizardfolk. There was a desk and a long table that could be used for work, or eating, or meetings and conferences, and the north-western wall had a fireplace which, during these summer days when a fire was not necessary, contained an illusion of flickering flames. Golden light flooded in through the four great floor-to-ceiling windows with their broad, balustraded stone balconies that looked out north, south, east and west over Tyrineld.

Cyran poured himself a goblet of crimson wine. Gripping the cup with both hands to offset the slight tremor in his fingers, he drank deeply, as if in hope that the welcome warmth could counteract the chill of fear that settled in his heart whenever the visions appeared. In an attempt to calm himself, he turned his back on the table with its silver mirror, walked across to the eastern window and looked out at his home.

The city hugged the coastline around two deep coves defined by three promontories, with the bay to the south encompassing both the seaport and the mouth of the Tyrin River. At various locations around the bays were the eight Luens, spacious complexes of elegant old buildings, centres of learning and excellence that covered every aspect of Wizardly life. Ariel's Tower, the soaring edifice housing the Archwizard and his administrative staff, was perched above the seaport on a high, rocky cape. Occupying a similar position on the northern promontory was the Luen of the Academics, the centre of Wizardly knowledge and learning. The Luens of the Healers and the Spellweavers were also located there, whereas the Bards, including the artists and weavers of tales, had gravitated to the long, narrow cape to the south, building their Luen there and colonising the crumbling old mansions which had once, before the district fell out of fashion, been the homes of the merchants who berthed their vessels on the opposite side of the bay.

The southern bay was thronged with ships, its extensive docks swarming with Wizards, mostly sea captains or the richly robed merchants, whose Luen was nearby. The humans were even more numerous: the fishermen, the lowly ships' crewmen and the half-naked stevedores unloading cargo. This was the commercial area of the city, with its countless shops and markets, and the Luen of Artisans was also near the centre. The Luen of Warriors, however, was set apart from the others, high on the slopes above the city's outskirts.

Around the bays, Tyrineld had expanded into a tangle of narrow streets lined with beautiful snow-white houses that embraced the tranquil blue ocean and climbed the hillsides beyond. The Wizards' homes were interspersed with trees, parks and gardens that were a mass of blooms in any season of the year. The city was old, its stones steeped in history and learning and peace. It looked as though it would last for ever. Until the dreadful day two years ago when the visions had first appeared, Cyran had always believed it would.

It had begun with such a small thing – the Archwizard had misplaced a book and, having turned his study upside down, he'd suspected that he'd left it behind when he had been reading in the garden the previous day. Too busy (or too lazy, if he was being honest) to go and hunt for it, he had prepared his silver mirror and sat down at the table to scry for the lost volume. Once he'd found it, a small apport spell would soon have it back where it belonged.

Holding the image of the book in his mind, Cyran had gazed into the shimmering glass. Sure enough, it was in the Academy gardens, lying on his favourite bench among the willows by the ornamental lake. He tutted to himself. The Great Library of Tyrineld was the most extensive collection of knowledge and wisdom in the entire civilisation of the Magefolk. Its contents were a trust handed down through each generation of Wizards, and the careless mishandling of one of the precious tomes by the Archwizard himself was hardly setting a good example. Sharalind, the Chief Archivist, tall and stern, with brown hair that was never quite tidy and an arresting, high-cheekboned face, was the most feared and formidable being in the entire city – and, incidentally, Cyran's consort. She would have his hide if she found out.

Hurriedly, Cyran had banished the scrying. With a negligent snap of his fingers, he apported the missing volume back to his desk and gave the dew-spotted leather covers a hasty wipe with his sleeve. As he did so, his eye was caught by a flash of colour in the silver mirror. He turned towards it, with a frown that was a mixture of puzzlement and irritation. He hadn't lost control of a scrying since his student days. Then he saw that the images in the glass had changed. Frozen with horror, unable to tear his eyes from the dreadful scenes before him, he watched the destruction of his beloved city, and saw the entire Magefolk civilisation tear itself apart in bloody conflict.

The visions had come to an end in profound darkness, as though night had fallen on the era of the Magefolk. For a long time, Cyran had simply sat, his face in his hands, unaware that tears were leaking between his fingers. Then suddenly he straightened, and wiped the salty drops from his face. Leaping to his feet, he hurled the mirror out of the open casement, and heard it shatter into jagged splinters on the flagstones of the courtyard below. Shuddering, he closed the window with a bang. The warning had been well taken. The catastrophe had not happened yet. Maybe it could be averted altogether. At any rate, there would be time to prepare.

And there *had* been time, Cyran thought, bringing his mind back to the present. In the two years since the first of the visions had come upon him, he had been working tirelessly to make provision for the worst. His first action had been to warn the leaders of the other Magefolk races – the Dragonfolk, the Winged Folk and the aquatic Leviathan – for the calamity he'd witnessed had threatened to destroy them all. At first they had taken him seriously, but two years later the world seemed to be continuing on its tranquil, ordered course, and Cyran could sense that doubts were beginning to creep in. Their main objection lay in the fact that so far, he had been the only one to see these visions. Surely, they argued, if he had experienced a true foretelling, then they should also have received a similar warning. Cyran hoped with all his heart that they were right. Nonetheless, he felt compelled to persist, though the other leaders had insisted that he keep the information to himself for the present, to avoid spreading unnecessary panic among the Magefolk races.

The Archwizard, however, had continued to lose sleep over the horrendous possibilities that seemed to lie in his people's future. At first the dread visions had returned every time he attempted to scry in crystal or mirror, but to his frustration they kept coming as brief, disconnected glimpses of war and terror, none of which gave him any clues as to when, why or how this cataclysm might take place. If only he could know how much time remained for his people and the other Magefolk races to prepare.

One of his main concerns was the amount of magical knowledge and lore that might be lost forever if the disaster happened, plunging Magefolk civilisation back into a primitive age of barbarism. Eventually, he had asked his fellow leaders for permission to send three of his brightest and most trusted young Wizards, one to each of the other three Magefolk races, to learn what they could of the other disciplines of magic. This had caused an uproar among the others. Nothing like it had ever been tried before, and the consensus of opinion seemed to be that it was impossible for a Mage of one race to learn the magic of another. If, however, Cyran was right, and such a thing could be accomplished after all, then they were reluctant to give away the many secrets of their lore.

Eventually, however, the Archwizard had worn them down. His three carefully selected delegates had been away for almost a year now, ostensibly just to learn and study, as none of them, and none of their hosts apart from the Archmages, had been told of Cyran's vision of the cataclysm to come. The Magefolk leaders had made the secrecy a firm condion of the plan, as they were reluctant to spread panic amonst their people on the strength of a vision – and one not even their own.

Yinze was in Aerillia, city of the Winged Folk; Ionor, using specially created spells to allow him to breathe underwater, travelled beneath the sea with the mighty Leviathan; and Chathak had gone to the far southlands, across the Jewelled Desert to the Dragonfolk in Dhiammara. So far, much to Cyran's disappointment, none of the other leaders had sent delegates to one another, or to the Wizards in Tyrineld. If only even one of them could experience the ghastly visions he had seen, it would be another matter, but until that happened, they still continued to doubt; though they were willing to go along with his wild schemes for the sake of respect and old friendship – so far, at least.

That was only the beginning. What about the lore of his own people? Would there be any way to protect the knowledge and wisdom laid down through many generations, and preserve it for any Wizards of the future who might survive the evil times ahead? He had pondered long and hard, trying to think of ways to minimise the damage, until finally he had the good, and long overdue, idea of stretching his promise to the other leaders and involving Sharalind in his deliberations. In truth, he had no choice. His consort, determined to get to the root of the sleepless nights he fondly imagined he'd been hiding from her, his constantly worried expression and his sudden attacks of absent-mindedness, had bearded him in his tower late one night, put a locking spell on the door, poured wine for them both and had refused to let him leave until he told her what was troubling him, giving him no quarter until he finally surrendered.

On hearing his tale, Sharalind had put down her cup on the overloaded desk and crossed to the fireplace, where she'd stood gazing into the flames for so long that Cyran began to be concerned. He looked at her dear face, which others seemed to find so stern, her untidy robes and the tousled brown curls escaping from their knot at the back of her head. What was she thinking? He had never managed to work that out in all their years together. All he could do was wait patiently for her response. 'I wish you'd told me this before,' she said eventually.

'I wish I had, too. And I would have, but the other Magefolk leaders made me promise not to tell anyone. Forgive me, love.'

She turned to him with a wry smile and took his hand. 'Ah, but there lies your biggest mistake: telling the other leaders before you had told me. You idiot. Think of all those sleepless nights you could have saved yourself—'

'You *knew* about those?'

'Of course I did.' She squeezed his hand. 'Anyway, thank goodness you've had the sense to confide in me at last. I hate to think of what you've been putting yourself through, trying to bear this burden alone.'

'But as Archwizard, the burden is mine to bear,' Cyran protested. 'It isn't fair of me to lay it on your shoulders too.'

'To be sure, the whole business is dreadful beyond words, and it scares the daylights out of me,' Sharalind admitted soberly. 'All the same, I would rather know what we are up against than remain in blissful ignorance until the blow falls. And at least this way, I can help you prepare for the worst.'

'As Chief Archivist, you have responsibilities enough of your own, without taking on mine.'

She cast her eyes up to the heavens. 'But Cyran, my love, as Chief Archivist I'm exactly the person you *should* be asking. I know more about the preservation of our lore than any other living Wizard. Furthermore, this should not stop at just me. Wizards cannot live on magic alone, and there are other measures we should be taking in case of war. There are several other people you should be consulting: the Heads of the Healers and Merchants, for a start, so that food and medicinal herbs can be preserved and stockpiled. What of the Artisans and Spellweavers, also? If war is coming, their contribution will be important. And what about Esmon? *He* ought to be told, if anyone is.'

'You know very well how I feel about Esmon.' There was a thin, sharp edge of anger in Cyran's voice. 'To begin with, he thinks I'm a weak Archwizard, and that he ought to take my place. And if that weren't enough, he and his self-styled Warriors are a danger to us all, with their notions of using magic for martial purposes.'

'I know, and I agree with you. Indeed, these visions you've been having prove your point that magic is far too powerful a tool ever to be used in war. But my love' – she reached out and touched his face gently with her fingertips – 'don't you see that your visions are telling you that it will happen, and probably in our lifetime? Otherwise why should you be the one to receive these warnings? Someone or something is going to set this dreadful business in motion, and magic is clearly going to be used, whether we like it or not. And if we don't reciprocate in kind, we'll be utterly overwhelmed. Also, if you take him into your confidence and include him in your plans, Esmon is far more likely to work with you, rather than against you – and we need all the help we can get. We must take this opportunity to make ourselves as ready as we can be to withstand the onslaught, and Esmon is the Head of the Warrior Wizards.'

Cyran realised that his soulmate was right. From that time onward, as well as insisting on monthly conferences for all four Magefolk leaders, he had, without telling his other three counterparts, let the Heads of all eight Luens of Tyrineld in on the secret, and had started to hold regular meetings with them to plan, as best they might, for a future that seemed to be filled with dread and doubt. One of those meetings had been scheduled for today, but Cyran had cancelled it. He had certain plans of his own that he wanted to put into action first, and he hoped to act with swiftness and secrecy so that that none of them would have a chance to argue and object – as they inevitably would.

Thoughts of meetings brought Cyran's mind back to the scheme that he was so carefully keeping secret from his deputies. Certain happenings to the north of the Wizardly realm had begun to cause him grave concern. After the attack on the Wild Hunt by renegade slaves the previous winter, the Phaerie had started to make raids further and further south to pursue their revenge. He was now receiving reports from the northern frontier town of Nexis that the Hunt had, on several occasions, crossed the border, and slain mortals who had been carrying out legitimate tasks of forestry and planting for their Wizard masters. Such depredations could not be allowed to continue, but Cyran knew he must act with great caution. Were these Phaerie raids the first skirmishes in a greater war – or had his visions caused him to exaggerate the danger in every trivial happening?

The sound of feet pounding up the stairs interrupted his deliberations and heralded the arrival of Avithan, Cyran's son, who came bursting into the room in his usual reckless fashion, giving the impression that he had too many things to do and not enough hours in which to do them. Avithan had recently succeeded to the position of Head of the Luen of Spellweavers, where he could finally indulge his passion – the invention of clever spells intended to make life easier for the Wizards in a whole variety of ways. The trouble was that the Wizardfolk in general, including Cyran himself, had little use for this very practical, unobtrusive form of magic. What was the point, he'd argued with his son, when they had mortal slaves to perform all the menial tasks?

Avithan, however, had remained undeterred. 'Most of us are becoming far too dependent on mortals,' he replied. 'How can such a thing be healthy? What would happen to the Wizards if our race were ever to be thrown onto our own devices? We should be able to take care of ourselves.'

'Oh, come now,' Cyran had scoffed. 'How likely is it that a tribe of ignorant, short-lived primitives with no magic would ever gain the power to govern themselves? Mortals were born to be slaves, and that's the end of it.' And as that was also the consensus of opinion among the other Wizardfolk, Avithan had found himself very much on his own. He didn't let that bother him in the slightest, however, and continued with his innovations undeterred by scepticism and scorn. And while people might scoff at his theories on the mortals, they were quite happy to make use of his spells when it suited them. Much as he disagreed with Avithan's unlikely notions about the slave race, Cyran had to admire his son's determination and convictions. Avithan had earned the powerful position of Head of a Luen through his own abilities and hard work, and he was determined to run things his way.

If their disagreements had been limited to such minor matters, all would have been well, but unfortunately Avithan was opposed to his father over something far more serious. When Cyran had revealed his visions to the Heads of the Luens, the result had not been what he had expected. Instead of pulling together to face the threat, as he had hoped, the Luens had become divided. Some of them backed the Archwizard in his determination to avoid such a conflict at all costs. The others had suggested: 'What if the visions show that war is inevitable? It's vital that we prepare for that contingency.' They were pressing to be permitted to fashion a weapon of power with which they could defend themselves, and there were those among the leaders of the other Magefolk races who agreed with them.

To Cyran's chagrin, Avithan had joined the opposing faction, and there was now a coldness between son and both parents that had never been there before. To make matters worse, the Archwizard knew perfectly well that the young man had inherited the tenacious stubbornness of both Sharalind and himself; though it pained him to distrust his own flesh and blood, he felt a distressing suspicion that Avithan and his Spellweavers, together with the Warrior and Artisan Luens, might actually be working in secret on the project to develop a weapon. So far, however, they had been very careful to cover any traces of such seditious activities, and Cyran was left wondering whether he was wise to harbour such doubts, or whether he was being shamefully unfair to his son.

Today Avithan erupted through the doorway as though he had a pack of fiends behind him. He looked his usual untidy self, with his long, dark hair tousled and slipping out of the thong that held it back from his face. His dark-green robes, though clean enough, were wrinkled, spelling out to the observant eye that they'd been carelessly thrown down on a chair the previous night, and put on again without a second thought this morning. 'I'm so sorry I'm late.' His smoky grey eyes took in the sight of his father all alone and widened with surprise. 'Where is everybody?'

'Well, for one thing, you must have mistaken the time. The meeting isn't due to start for an hour. But that doesn't matter in any case because I've cancelled it for today, and the others won't be coming.'

'Cancelled it? Why did you do that? Has something happened? If there's no meeting, why am I here?'

'Because I want to speak to you in private.'

Avithan made a wry face. 'All right, Father. What have I done this time?'

Cyran ignored the question. 'First of all, will you find Iriana and fetch her here? This matter concerns you both.'

'Iriana? But … Listen, if this is about what she said to you yesterday, she didn't really mean it, Father. She just gets so frustrated, that's all. She wants to travel so much, and she was desperately disappointed when you passed her over last year in favour of Yinze and the others.' Avithan gave his father a hard look. The appropriate response to Cyran's visions was not the only matter over which the two of them disagreed. 'You know,' he went on, 'this is very unfair to her. As far as we are aware, she's the only one of all the Magefolk whose powers encompass all four of the elements of magic, instead of just the one. She's certainly the only Wizard, and if the Leviathan and Dragonfolk and Skyfolk have anyone equally talented, they've never mentioned it—'

'That doesn't mean a thing,' Cyran interrupted. 'We haven't told them about Iriana, and equally, they might not have mentioned any of their own people who have been similarly blessed.'

'And you know what I think about *that*.' Avithan gave his father a reproving look. 'Considering the gravity of those visions of yours, it's sheer folly for the Magefolk leaders to go on as they have done, sitting on their little secrets like a bunch of old hens in a roost.'

Cyran shrugged. 'I'm sure the Magefolk leaders will be very sorry to hear that they have disappointed you,' he said drily. 'Stay out of matters that aren't your business, Avithan.'

'Iriana *is* my business,' Avithan replied. 'She's my friend. And stop trying to change the subject, Father. I know that under the circumstances it would be out of the question for her to join Ionor beneath the ocean, but would it really hurt to let her visit one of the others in Aerillia or Dhiammara?'

'Apart from the very practical problems she would face because of her blindness, Iriana is unique among our people because of her abilities. It would be sheer folly to risk her by sending her so far from home. Now stop trying to second-guess me, Avithan. Just go and fetch her.' Then Cyran saw the unhappy expression on his son's face, and relented a little. 'Don't worry. This has nothing to do with her little outburst yesterday, and I'm not sending for her to reprimand her, even though she may be the first person in history who has ever referred to their Archwizard as a pig-headed old nincompoop – to his face, at any rate.' He tried to look stern, then gave up the unequal battle. 'I can understand her frustration, believe me. That's why I allow her a little more leeway than I would other folk.'

'So why do you want to see her?' Avithan asked curiously.

'Mind your own business. I want to see the two of you, not just Iriana, and you'll find out the reason soon enough. Tell her I want to talk to her, and bring her back here. Go on, don't stand around. Oh, and while you're over there, will you inform your mother that the meeting is cancelled?'

'So that you don't have to?'

'Exactly,' Cyran replied. 'Tell her I'm busy just now, but I'll explain tonight.'

Avithan shrugged. 'I'll do my best, but frankly, I can't see her curiosity holding out for that length of time. May I use the bridge?'

'Of course. You don't need to ask. You may have created it for the convenience of your aged parents, but it was your invention. Be my guest.'

'Thanks.' Avithan stepped out of the tall northern windows and onto the balcony beyond, shutting the doors of glass behind him. Only when his son was safely out of sight did Cyran allow himself to smile. Ever since he had sent away Yinze, Ionor and Chathak last year, Iriana had been a thorn in his flesh with her restlessness and her longing to travel. For a number of reasons, he had been forced to deny her wishes, and watch with concern as she became increasingly frustrated and unhappy. Today, however, he had a surprise for her. Her wishes were about to be granted – but not in the way she expected. His decision had not been taken lightly, but he had been forced to overcome his misgivings because she had talents he needed at this time. He only hoped that he was doing the right thing.

10

IRIANA

Avithan stepped out onto the balcony that overlooked Dolphin Bay and the northern peninsula beyond, where the towers, domes, Library, work-rooms and other buildings of the Academy were perched on top of the tall cliffs of the headland. Drifting across on the wind came a cacophony of bird and animal voices from the ever-changing menagerie of creatures that were being studied; the discipline of Earth Magic encompassed not only minerals, gems, rocks, soils and stone, but also the plants and animals that existed in harmony with the earth in a complex web of life. Graceful, spacious aviaries stood out like black lace against the sky, and the curved structures of the massive glasshouses, big enough to take even mature trees, glittered in the sun like jewels.

Below the Academy, on the sheltered southern side of the promontory and rising up from the calm waters of the bay, was a network of twisting streets with many lovely old residences, which were mainly occupied by teachers, students and the Wizards who had elected to study the various aspects of Earth Magic in greater depth. This was where Iriana lived, along with Avithan and their other closest friends. From where he stood he could pick out her house among all the others. It didn't look so far away, yet she was separated from him by a void of air and a long reach of ocean, and, until recently, his only option would have been to leave his father's tower and either walk or ride right around the bay to the other side, or take a boat across.

He had created the bridge to help his mother, who spent her days across in the Library of the Academy. One stormy winter's evening, Sharalind had arrived home at the Archwizard's tower after a long, hard day, dripping wet, frozen to the bone and, not being one to suffer in silence, complaining bitterly. It was then that Avithan had set to work to solve a problem that must have been plaguing Archwizards for generations. After a number of false starts and failures, he had created a spell that would extend a magical bridge of light from one peninsula across to the other, stretching from the roof of the Great Library on one side to the balcony of Cyran's tower on the other.

Unlike many of his inventions, this one had met with universal excitement and acclaim (except for the boatmen who made a living by ferrying folk across the bay). Immediately plans were made to put bridges in more accessible places between all three promontories for public use. All such schemes, unfortunately, had been doomed to failure, for the spell had simply not been strong enough to take more than three people at any given time. Furthermore, after a few hours the magic began to decay, making the bridge extremely unsafe. Fortunately, it had been Avithan who had discovered the fault. Even more fortunately, he was a very good swimmer and there had been several boats on hand in the bay at the time to pick him up – and have a damn good laugh at his misfortune. So in the end, only one of the magical bridges had been created, and the spell was renewed every time it was used.

A circular plug of thick crystal had been set into the floor of the balcony to hold and focus the magic. Avithan passed his hand over the gleaming disc and put forth his power, activating the spell that slept within the stone. Out shot a great, curving rainbow of light (he had put in the colours for his own amusement and his mother's pleasure), arcing above the waters of the bay in a gentle curve and anchoring itself among the buildings on the far side. As soon as Avithan set foot on the radiant bridge, he was swept away within the rainbow and carried safely to the other side of the water, where he was gently put down on the flat roof of one of the Library's corner turrets without having stirred a single step. With a wave of his hand he banished the spell, and the rainbow vanished like a dream, leaving him standing on a crystal disc that was the twin of the one on the other side.

A small, circular observation chamber had been built at the centre of the roof, and from this a door led down into the Library itself: a vast labyrinth of halls, corridors and chambers extending for three floors above the ground and three below, carved out long ago from the living rock of the cliff. Avithan wondered where he might find his mother, but for once, it proved to be easy. As he was hurrying downstairs he ran into her – quite literally. She emerged onto a landing from one of the smaller study rooms carrying an armful of scrolls just as he was passing, and he crashed into her, sending her burden flying.

'And where do you think you're going in such a hurry?' Sharalind demanded.

'On an errand for Father.' Avithan was gathering up scrolls from the floor as fast as he could. 'He wants to see Iriana.'

'What? Before the meeting?' She frowned. 'What on earth is that man up to now?'

Avithan shrugged. 'He didn't tell me. But he did ask me to give you a message. The meeting has been cancelled for today. He says he's too busy just now to explain, but he'll tell you all about it tonight.' Forestalling the barrage of questions that he knew would be coming, he thrust the scrolls back into his mother's arms and beat a hasty retreat. He wondered what his father was hiding from his mother. Normally he told her everything. Just what scheme was Cyran hatching?

Once he had left the grounds of the Academy it was downhill all the way. He could have traced the fastest route in his sleep, threading his way through the narrow streets between the shuttered white houses with their high-walled gardens, and taking short cuts down alleyways that scarcely looked wide enough to accommodate a human being. At last he emerged in a peaceful little square with a fountain in the centre, which, in a highly unlikely flight of fancy on the part of the sculptor, had plumes of water spouting from the mouths of three dragons with extended wings. The houses, two on each side of the square, were spacious, old and grace-ful, with shutters painted green and intricate ironwork on the balconies. Creeping plants clung to the walls, laden with vivid flowers of various hues. They filled the air with perfume, and were alive with bees and iridescent hummingbirds.

This delightful place was normally Avithan's home: he dwelt in one of the two houses on the north side of the square with his friends Ionor, Chathak and Yinze. During the past year, however, they had been away in other parts of the world studying the arcane disciplines of the other races of Magefolk, and Avithan, finding the echoing house too empty and lonely, had moved back temporarily to the Archwizard's tower, with his parents. Much as he loved Cyran and Sharalind, however, he found himself regretting his loss of independence and missing the companion-ship of his friends very much. He was looking forward impatiently to their return, when everything would get back to normal.

The house adjacent to Avithan's dwelling was the home of his three female friends: Iriana, Thara and Melisanda. All seven of them had bonded while they were students at the Academy and, despite having talents that covered varying areas of Earth magic, they had been together ever since.

He used the opening spell for the front door to let himself in and stood blinking in the shadowy hallway until the sun-dazzle had faded from his eyes, and he could make out the floor laid with slabs of marble, the carvings of flowers, birds and fabulous beasts on the panelling of golden oak, the elegant wrought-iron banister on the curving staircase and the intricate moulding on the ceiling. Avithan was accustomed to such grandeur – the house he shared with his male friends was very similar – but he often wondered at the enigma that had brought a bunch of young Wizards just starting out in the world to live in dwellings that had clearly once belonged to someone very important.

The houses now belonged to Iriana: an unexpected inheritance for a girl with a mysterious past. She was a foundling, an abandoned baby discovered on the steps of the statue in the central square of the city market. At first it was thought that she must be another of the half-breed babies that cropped up occasionally, offspring of a Wizard and a mortal slave. Unlike the Phaerie, for whom the Hemifae were an integral and important part of their society, the Wizardfolk disapproved of such relationships greatly, and any resulting children were usually terminated before birth, or abandoned.

Investigations by the Healers, however, had proved Iriana to be a full-blooded Wizard, and she was adopted by Sharalind's friend Zybina, who brought the girl up with her own child, Yinze. No one had ever solved the mystery of her parents, though they were certainly not from Tyrineld itself. They might have come from another town or village – or, more likely, they may have been some of the Wizards who elected to dwell in isolation in far-flung places, in order to study their magic in solitude and peace. Whoever they were, they were certainly well off, or had wealthy connections. When Iriana had come of age, an anonymous package arrived for her containing the keys and the deeds to the two houses, legally correct and made out in her name, together with a generous sum of money in gold. Iriana took them to be some sort of guilt offering, and accepted them as such, but had refused to let Zybina and Sharalind investigate further. 'My family didn't want me as a child, and I don't want them now,' she had said coldly. 'I'll take their gift, whoever they are – it's all I've ever got from them, and probably all I'm ever likely to get – but apart from that, they can go to Perdition as far as I'm concerned.'

Without telling her, Cyran had tried to trace the previous owners of the houses, which had long stood empty, but they had covered their tracks too well. It burned Avithan's heart to think that Iriana's parents must still be out there somewhere. Did they watch her in secret? Did they ever think of her at all? If he ever discovered their identity, he would take great pleasure in telling them exactly what he thought of them.

'Why, it's Avithan. This is a pleasant surprise. What brings you here?' Thara had emerged so quietly from an adjacent room that he been unaware of her presence till the sound of her voice had made him jump. He was always amazed that she could move so quietly, because Thara was a *big* girl. She was tall even in a race of tall folk, with broad shoulders, strong, clever hands and an ample and voluptuous figure. She was skilled in working with all things that grew in the earth, so her face and arms were tanned from all the hours she spent outdoors. Her face was beautiful, and her brown eyes almost always held a sultry twinkle.

'It's nice to see you too, Thara,' he replied. 'Is Iriana here?'

'So it wasn't me you came to see, then.' Thara made a wry face. 'Story of my life.'

Avithan grinned at her teasing. 'Well, the Archwizard wants to see Iriana at once,' he answered, 'so I'm afraid I have to defer the pleasure of your company until another day. Where is she? In the garden?'

Thara nodded. 'She's watering the plants for me. Her method saves me hours of backbreaking toil. Ask her for some lemonade. It's made with lemons from *my* tree—'

'Which you grew overnight from a pip,' Avithan chanted. 'Honestly, you and your tree.'

'I'm very proud of my lemon tree,' Thara said unrepentantly. 'No one has ever managed to crack the secret of accelerated growth before, not without a lot of deformities creeping in. Personally, I think it was extremely clever of me.'

Avithan hugged her. 'It certainly was – and we're all proud of your tree.'

'Does Cyran want to see her about that business yesterday?'

Her abrupt change of subject took him off guard. 'No,' he said, 'he told me it wasn't that. He wants to see the two of us together about something, and he's acting very mysterious—' He caught himself sharply. 'Damn it, Thara, stop trying to trick information out of me.'

Her brown eyes gleamed with mischief. 'Not while I can still get away with it. Go on.' She made shooing gestures with her hands. 'Go and see Iriana.'

Avithan made his way through the house to the back door, emerging out of the shadows and into the sunlit garden. He saw Iriana sitting alone beside the pond under her favourite tree, a late-flowering cherry that had only recently dropped its bounty of blossoms to lie in snowy drifts around her feet. Her long hair looked dark in the tree's deep shade, but in sunlight it was red, although a much deeper shade than the normal bright hue that was common to the Wizards – more like wine, perhaps, than fire – and it fell around her face in gentle waves. Clad in her favourite old, darned crimson gown, which had faded with time and much washing to a soft rose, she was concentrating, hand upraised, on the pond, from which a swirling vortex of water droplets, threaded with rainbows, was spinning out across the garden, covering the plants with a silvery mist of moisture. Melik, her cat, sat on the table close at her left hand, his blue eyes, vivid in his dusky face, staring with great concentration at the spinning column of water. Avithan watched, spellbound. A combination of Air and Water magic! How fortunate she was, of all the Wizards, to be the sole possessor of such incredible abilities. Then he remembered her lack of sight. The recompense was only fair. Would he be willing to sacrifice his sight to possess such power? He knew he would not.

Iriana completed her task, dusted off her hands with the air of a job well done and bent over some papers that lay before her on the little wooden table. As he drew closer he could see that she was writing furiously, and the cat had now turned all his attention to the work in hand, his eyes fixed on the paper and the scribbling pen. A jug of lemonade was at her elbow, together with a glass, and Iriana took a sip of the cool liquid without once looking up from her work, her hand going unerringly to the glass and lifting it to her lips.

Before Avithan had time to call out to her, a colossal black dog with bright, intelligent eyes and a shaggy coat emerged from under the table and came strolling unhurriedly down the path to meet him, looking like the bear for which he had been named. At the same time, a magpie erupted out of the cherry tree with a clatter of wings and swooped down towards him in a long glide. Iriana lifted her face from her work. 'Avithan, how nice to see you. I thought you had a meeting this morning.'

'For some reason better known only to my father, it was cancelled.' As always he hid the tiny stab of pain within him at her use of the word 'see'. For Iriana had been born blind, and even the most skilled of the Healers had been unable to ameliorate the problem; it seemed certain that this was why her parents had so cruelly abandoned her. Iriana, however, let neither her lack of family nor her blindness get in her way. For she had also been born with a gift to compensate for her lack of sight: a remarkable affinity with animals that allowed her to reach into their minds and communicate with them as one of their own. And even before she could walk, her animal friends had become her eyes.

As he walked down the path towards her, with the magpie flashing ahead of him and Bear pacing gravely at his side, Avithan knew that Iriana would be picking up images of him from the eyes of the dog, the cat and the bird, and would be switching from one to the other as best suited her needs, though she neither overrode their natural behaviour nor controlled their movements in any way. She could communicate with them after a fashion, though as far as she could explain to Avithan, they used very few words, and lacked the complex sentences and concepts of human languages. Instead they used a combination of images and emotions, body language, scent and physical touch – and each of them did it differently. Iriana had mastered the art of communication on a simple level with all of the animals close to her, as well as a number of species from the Academy menagerie. The creatures with her today were only a few of her companions: she also had a huge and fearsome mountain eagle that terrified the life out of Avithan; the mate of the magpie; a hawk; a barn owl; and, stabled near the outskirts of the city, a piebald horse on which she loved to ride out, either alone (to the great disquiet of Cyran, Sharalind and Zybina) or with her friends.

Iriana's face lit up at the sight of Avithan, and she beckoned him into a chair. 'You look hot,' she said. 'Here, sit down and have some lemonade.' Without looking at her glass, she refilled it from the jug and passed it to him – a trick that always tended to unnerve strangers, who often did not notice the cat sitting beside her on the table, his round blue eyes fixed unerringly on the jug and glass as Iriana completed her manoeuvre, then switching to Avithan as she handed over the drink. He was a large and beautiful animal, long-haired, with a dark, almost black face, legs and tail, while the rest of his body was a pale cream with duskier patches on his back and flanks. He was Iriana's shadow, who was with her everywhere she went, more often than not perched on her shoulder.

Avithan drained the glass in one long swallow. 'Thanks, I needed that.'

'Good, isn't it? Thara made it fresh this morning—'

'With lemons from her very own tree,' Avithan finished for her, with a grin which she was quick to return.

As always, Iriana's smile transformed her face into a striking loveliness, though her countenance could appear stern in sorrow, reflection or repose. She had strong, rather severe Wizardly features: high brow, square jaw, well-defined cheekbones and jutting nose; but as far as Avithan was concerned, they combined in a particular and unusual harmony that made her stand out from the other young female Wizards. Though she could not see through them, her large eyes looked perfect to the casual glance. Though their unusual shade of deep, misty blue lacked the piercing intensity so characteristic of the Wizardfolk, their unfocused gaze held a sense of intriguing mystery, as though she were looking through some invisible boundary into other worlds.

'So tell me, what brought you over here in such a hurry?' Her question snapped him back to the matter in hand. Reluctantly, he tore his attention from her face, remembering the errand on which he had been sent.

'I've just come from the Archwizard,' he told her. 'My father sent me to fetch you. He said he wants to see you at once.'

'Me? Why?'

Hearing the faint note of alarm in her voice, Avithan hastened to reassure her. 'It's all right. He said it was nothing to do with that fight you had yesterday, though he wouldn't tell me the real reason.'

'Do you think he's had second thoughts, then? Oh, Avithan – has he decided to let me go after all?'

He stared at her in surprise. Such a thing had never even occurred to him. 'Iriana, you're the most single-minded female in the world. It's probably about something else entirely, so don't go getting your hopes up. It didn't sound to me as if he had changed his mind.'

Her jaw tightened. 'I don't see why not.'

Avithan gave it up. 'Well, let's go and find out, shall we? He wanted to see you as soon as possible, so we'd better not keep him waiting.'

He held out his hand to her, but Iriana the self-reliant would not take it, and he suppressed a flash of annoyance at her obduracy. Sometimes she took this business of being independent much too far. It meant that she kept everyone, even the friends who loved her, stubbornly at arm's length – where Avithan did *not* want to be. Her animals had no such difficulty. She lifted Melik to her shoulder, and Steel the magpie swooped above, spying out the path ahead. Bear came with them, even deigning to break into a lumbering run. He was a lazy creature at the best of times, and with his thick, shaggy coat he found it difficult to deal with the summer's heat in Tyrineld, normally saving most of his activity for the cooler evenings.

They retraced Avithan's steps through the city and went back into the library, which was pleasantly shady and cool on such a hot day. As they hurried down the narrow corridor, he was certain he caught a glimpse of his mother out of the corner of his eye, peering at them around a door. But when he turned his head there was no sign of anyone, and he hid a smile. Sharalind was absolutely bursting with curiosity, and he was willing to bet that when the attendees did eventually gather for Cyran's postponed meeting, she would be the first one there.

The warmth of the sunshine struck them once more as they went out onto the turret roof, where Avithan activated his bridge of light again. Melik and Bear were used to it by now, and the magpie simply ignored it and soared across the gap at their side, cackling derision at the seagulls that swooped and dived at the gallant intruder flashing past them in his livery of black and white.

As they sped over the ocean on the magic bridge, Avithan glanced at Iriana. Why did his father want her? What was she thinking? He could guess. When she had an idea in her head, she didn't give up easily. He himself was ambivalent about the whole business. On one hand, he wanted to see her happy, and fought his parents and Zybina for her independence at every opportunity. On the other, if he was honest with himself, he didn't want her to go away. It wasn't just the inescapable fact that, despite her remarkable adaptation to her blindness, the risks out there must be greater for her than for most folk. He understood that she was capable of managing most difficulties very well, and had great faith in her. No, he was ashamed to admit that his motive was pure selfishness. He didn't want to let her go because he would miss her desperately, and the light would go out of his days until she returned.

11

~

THE EMISSARIES

In times to come, history would know her as Iriana of the Beasts. But history never did tell how she had come to forge such close links with the animal world, nor did it ever explain the reason. In times to come, she would win great renown, be transformed into a mighty figure of legend and eventually be revered as a goddess – but if anyone had tried to tell her so, especially on that ordinary summer's day in Tyrineld, she would have laughed them to scorn. The last of her concerns was the future – apart, that is, from the near future in which she hoped to persuade the Archwizard to finally let her see something of the world beyond her home.

When she entered the tower with Avithan and her animals, Cyran was waiting for them. Iriana was surprised to see Esmon, the Head of the Luen of Warriors, also present. It was no secret among the wizards of Tyrineld that he and Cyran did not usually see eye to eye, so what could he be doing there? And, for that matter, why had the Archwizard summoned Iriana herself into such august company? Avithan might also be the Head of a Luen, but that was different – she had known him all her life. Remembering with horror that she was still wearing her patched old gown, she wished that she had taken the time to change. Why had she let Avithan drag her here so quickly? With Melik's vision she looked at Cyran, anxiously scanning his face for any clues as to why he had sent for her, but his expression was grave and somewhat aloof as usual, and gave nothing away.

'Ah, there you are,' he said. 'Come in and make yourself comfortable. You know Esmon, do you not?'

'Indeed,' the Warrior said with a smile. 'My younger brother Chathak is one of Iriana's best friends.' Tall even for a Wizard, with long, slanting green eyes that could glitter with a cold and merciless light, Esmon cut an imposing figure to his friends. To his enemies, he was positively intimidating. His head was bald, the hair growth suppressed by magic, but his face was his most arresting feature. The flesh was tinted in places by magical means into a dramatic mask, fashioned like the wings of a glittering, multicoloured bird that swept across his eyes and the upper parts of his face. All of the Warrior Wizards wore such winged guises by Cyran's order. They were designed to act as a warning, like the brilliant colouring of many venomous creatures. The Archwizard strongly disapproved of the use of magic to fight and kill and, though he had grudgingly accepted that the Warriors must exist, he had insisted that other Magefolk must be warned if they were in the presence of one who had mastered the killing spells.

'Now,' Cyran said, 'sit down and make yourselves comfortable. I have a matter of great importance to discuss with you.' He offered them wine, and when they were all supplied, he sat down with them at the table, Avithan and Iriana to his right and left, and Esmon beyond Avithan. Iriana settled herself and her animals quickly. Melik leapt down from her shoulder and arranged himself decorously on the table, his tail wrapped neatly around his paws, as though he too sensed the importance of the occasion, while Bear took up his usual position underneath it, and the magpie perched on the curtain rail of the northern window, his head turning this way and that as he surveyed the scene with his bright, beady eyes.

Iriana waited expectantly for the Archwizard to speak, but when he did, his opening surprised her. 'Before we begin, Iriana, there is one important condition that I must impose upon you. I must swear you to the utmost secrecy. You may not, on peril of your very life, disclose to another living soul what you will hear in this room today. I am putting colossal trust in you by letting you into our innermost counsels. Can I depend upon your discretion? Do you swear?'

Wondering what she was about to hear, Iriana put her hand to her heart. 'Upon my life, I swear never to reveal what I hear today to another living soul,' she said gravely.

Cyran nodded. 'Then all is well. Now, firstly, I would like to give you some background to the current situation. I demanded an oath of secrecy, Iriana, because what I am about to divulge is known to only a handful of people: the other leaders of the Magefolk, the Heads of the Luens in this city, and my lifemate and son. So you see that you will be joining a very small and select company – though by the time you've heard what I have to say, you'll probably wish you could go back to a state of happy ignorance. Nevertheless ...'

Iriana listened intently while the Archwizard told her of his visions, and his fears for the future of the world of the Magefolk. He explained that those fears had been the reason for Chathak, Ionor and Yinze being sent away to the other Magefolk to learn their alien magic so that, hopefully, Iriana would not be the only one to bear the responsibility of preserving such knowledge for the future if things went badly wrong. As his words unfolded, she knew that he meant the annihilation of the Magefolk, or something very close to it, and felt a chill of horror spreading to the core of her being. When he had finished, she asked, 'Why did you tell me this? What can I do to help?'

The warmth of Cyran's unexpected smile and the look of pride that shone on Avithan's face helped to dispel a little of the coldness within her. 'Bless you, my dear. I knew I could depend on you,' Cyran said. 'Now, in the light of what I have just told you, allow me to explain why I brought you here today. Lately I have been receiving messages from Nexis that have made me very uneasy. It seems that the Phaerie Hunt is getting out of hand. They have been blatantly trespassing into our lands, and have killed not only the feral humans that are their rightful quarry, but also a number of slaves belonging to the Nexian Wizardfolk, who were at work within our area of the forest.'

'What?' Esmon exclaimed. 'They've broken the treaty? Cyran, we can't let them get away with that.'

'Indeed.' The Archwizard looked around at them all. 'I hold that treaty with the Phaerie to be one of my greatest accomplishments, and it has won us years of peace — peace we should not relinquish lightly. Clearly, these encroachments cannot be permitted to continue, but we must act with the greatest caution. The last thing we want is to precipitate the hideous conflicts I witnessed in my vision. That is where you come in, Iriana and Avithan. I intend to send an official deputation to Hellorin, and I want you two to comprise the delegation, with Esmon, an experienced traveller and hunter as well as a Warrior, to take care of you both, and keep you out of trouble.' He smiled at Iriana. 'You are about to get your wish. I am sending you on a journey at last.'

Iriana gasped. For an instant all other considerations were overwhelmed by delight. 'Is it really true?' she said. 'You're going to let me go away? Oh, thank you, Archwizard, thank you a million times.' Then practicality asserted itself even in the face of such excitement. 'But why did you choose Avithan and me? Don't misunderstand me, sir – I don't want you to change your mind – but why would you not send more experienced people on such a vital mission?'

'You're right, Iriana,' Cyran replied. 'In normal circumstances that is exactly what I would have done. But as I said, I want to avoid precipitating any conflict at all costs, and you are exactly the people to allay their suspicions. Avithan is not completely inexperienced in these matters. He and Hellorin met on several occasions when the terms of the treaty were being negotiated. My son has sufficient rank to show the Phaerie we hold them in respect, but you'll be looked upon as messengers only, I hope, and will not be seen as a threat.'

'Not be seen as a threat?' Esmon growled. 'The whole point is to let them know we're a threat otherwise they'll just keep trampling all over us. And before you say it, Cyran, I understand your fears, especially after the visions you've been experiencing. But the Phaerie won't respect anything other than a show of strength. The best way to head off any conflict is to demonstrate that we're an adversary to be feared.'

Cyran shook his head. 'I won't take that risk, Esmon. Not yet. If diplomacy fails, there will be time enough to do things your way.'

'Of course it will fail. They'll laugh in your face. I'm telling you—'

'Enough.' Cyran leapt to his feet. His expression, normally so benign, was as cold and remote as the face of a mountain. 'May I remind you, Esmon, that you are not the Archwizard, much as you would like to stand in my place. And while that is the case, *I* will dictate the policy for our people, and you will carry it out. Your objections have been noted, but for now, we will proceed in accordance with my wishes.'

For a moment they remained there, eye to eye. Iriana could sense their two wills clash like swords. Through Melik's eyes, she saw Avithan tense, clearly preparing to intercede in defence of his father if necessary. Then Esmon shrugged, deliberately breaking the tension. 'On your head be it. But how do I fit in with your overtures of peace? It's plain enough that *I'm* a Warrior.' He touched the winged mask that was magically stained into his skin. 'If they don't see me as a threat, then they're fools.'

Cyran nodded. 'You're right, of course. And – I cannot believe I'm saying this, because it goes against every principle I possess, and I know I will never hear the last of it from you – but I want you to remove your mask, just for this trip. You can accompany Avithan and Iriana as guide and hunter to the party, but the Phaerie must never guess that you are a Warrior.'

Esmon laughed harshly. 'Mask or no mask, it's obvious that I'm a Warrior, but if you insist that we go through with this charade, then I'll do my part. The fact that you're prepared to abandon your precious principles in this case only serves to emphasise the danger that we all face, and it shows me how convinced you are that you're right.'

'The situation is dangerous, which is why I want you to go in disguise at this point. Though I do need you to take care of these two young travellers, there *is* a more important reason for your inclusion in the party. I want you to use your experience as a Warrior to try to discover, or at least estimate, the offensive and defensive capabilities of the Phaerie, in case it should ever come to a war.'

Esmon sat back and gave Cyran a wolfish grin. 'Well, why didn't you say that in the first place? Truly, Cyran, whatever you may believe of me, I don't want a conflict any more than you do. Because of my experience in developing magic as a weapon, I know even better than you the appalling risks we'd be running if the situation ever came to a war.'

Avithan and Iriana had listened to this exchange in silence. Though Cyran had told them of his vision, and explained his concerns to them, the actual mention of war made the danger seem far more real and im-mediate. Now, however, Avithan spoke at last. 'That explains Esmon's role,' he said, 'but what, exactly, are *we* supposed to say to them? If the peace and well-being of the entire Magefolk civilisation may be at stake here, I want to be sure we don't make any mistakes.'

Cyran gave his son a look of approval. 'I simply want you to suggest that we believe the trespass of the Phaerie took place in the heat of the chase. And as it must clearly have been an oversight on their part, we are prepared to look upon the slaughter of our slaves as a case of mistaken identity. Tell them we will make certain that our slaves carry clearer identifying marks from now on, and that we would be grateful for their assurance that such a blunder will never happen again.'

While he spoke, Iriana's mind had been racing. 'And why will we *really* be there, Archwizard?' she asked. 'As spies?'

Cyran winced. 'I wouldn't have put it so bluntly, but yes, you're right. It is important to let the Phaerie know we are aware of their encroach-ments, and that we object, but your main purpose in Eliorand will be to collect as much information as possible.'

He picked up his cup and took a sip of wine. 'We must learn what is behind these disquieting events that are taking place within the realm of the Forest Lord. The glamourie over Eliorand has been strengthened, and even our most powerful scryers cannot penetrate the veil. All con-tracts with our merchants have been cancelled and trading has ceased, as has any form of communication. Why is Hellorin isolating himself like this? Why these sudden raids? How has the situation changed? It is vital that we discover whether we can continue to coexist peacefully with the Phaerie, as soon as possible.'

He hesitated. 'You should also know … I had a spy in Eliorand. Until now I have kept him secret, his identity known only to myself. But since the winter, about the time these raids started, I have heard nothing from him.' The Archwizard shook his head. 'After all this time I fear some evil fate may have befallen him, but if he yet lives, I hope that he will find some way to contact you once you are in the city.'

'If they are so keen to isolate themselves,' Avithan said, 'are you sure they will let us into Eliorand?'

'Unless they want to risk a deadly insult to the Wizardfolk, they will not dare turn away the named representatives of the Archwizard, one of whom is my son. And once you are inside, Iriana, you will be in a position to use the unique talents that are the reason for my sending you with Avithan, rather than some other young Wizard.'

Iriana nodded. She had been wondering why he had chosen her, but had been afraid to ask.

'Surprisingly, I am not referring to your all-encompassing magical skills – in fact, I am hoping you won't need to use your powers of Fire, Water and Air at all, because the Phaerie must not find out that you possess them. The discovery might put you in the gravest of danger. You have other gifts, however, that will prove more valuable to us in these circumstances. You alone among the Wizardfolk possess certain unique abilities.'

Cyran reached out a hand to stroke the cat at Iriana's side, the bleak expression on his face softening a little as Melik began to purr. 'To compensate for the fact that you cannot see, you have developed your other senses to an extraordinary degree. You told me once that you can tell by the tone of a person's voice whether or not they are lying, and I need that talent now. The Phaerie are masters of lies and deception, but at this time it is imperative I know the truth concerning their activities and their plans. Furthermore, your blindness will make you seem less of a threat. When someone has lost the use of one sense, people often wrongly assume the same impairment in the others, so they may let things slip in front of you. And because you are engaging and kind-hearted, you may even be able to make friends among the Phaerie – and, more importantly, among their slaves. Try to get as much information as you can out of the human servants. If it is possible, I also want you to use your animal companions as spies. They can go where you cannot, especially the birds, and who would suspect a mere animal of being a threat? I wonder, do you think you can access their ears as well as their eyes?'

Iriana nodded. 'I'll need to practise a little, but I think I should be able to manage it. Was there anything else, Archwizard?'

'Yes: one more thing. The Phaerie, as you know, ride horses that can fly. They are carefully guarded and Hellorin will not permit even a single one of them to be sold. If you can do it without putting yourself in danger, Iriana, I want you to find out their secret. Do they fly through their own powers, or is it due to some Phaerie magic? And if so, could we duplicate the spells? In future, if my fears do not prove to be groundless, flying horses could be a great advantage to us in any conflict.'

Once again, Iriana felt a surge of excitement. To actually see the legendary Phaerie steeds … For a moment she wondered if she was dreaming; then she recalled Cyran's terrifying prognostications. No, this was serious business, very serious indeed, and she would be carrying a great deal of responsibility. She realised that not only Cyran but all of the Wizardfolk – indeed, all of the Magefolk – were depending on her to make a success of this mission.

Avithan, in the meantime, had been looking increasingly grave. 'And why are you sending me, Father?' he asked. 'What is my role to be?'

'Simply this. You are a personable young man, if I say so myself, and of very high rank among the Wizards. I want you to charm Tiolani, Hellorin's daughter. Do your best to win her confidence.'

'*What?* Father, surely you don't mean you want me to court this girl?'

No. He can't! With difficulty, Iriana stifled the words before they came out of her mouth. Her thoughts, however, seemed to have run away with her. What if Avithan really did fall in love with this Phaerie woman? And why was it suddenly so important to her that he did not?

Cyran looked from one of them to the other, his face unreadable. 'I want you to do whatever you must to get her on our side. Though she would hardly be allowed to wed a Wizard, an outsider—'

'It's just as well.' Avithan's eyes sparked with anger. 'Because it doesn't matter what you're hatching, *that* isn't going to happen.'

'Of course not,' Cyran said smoothly. 'But as for the rest, she has considerable influence over her father and brother. If you could somehow persuade her into convincing Hellorin to renew our friendship—'

'Father, you go too far,' Avithan said angrily. 'This is wrong, to deceive a lonely and vulnerable young girl. How can you expect it of me?'

Cyran shook his head wearily. 'Because I have no choice, my son. And neither have you.'

12

TOWARDS THE FAR HORIZON

'Merciful Creation.' Iriana stepped back, hands on hips. Through the eyes of the eagle that sat patiently on top of the wardrobe, she regarded the superabundance of belongings piled all over her bed. Tomorrow at dawn she'd be setting out on her first real journey beyond the bounds of the city, but how could she possibly manage to take everything she might need? All she'd have would be her own bedroll and saddlebags, and there would be a single packhorse that she would share with her companions.

Her mouth twisted in a wry combination of dismay and amusement. 'I think we may need another packhorse,' she said aloud.

'It looks as though you'll need a whole herd of them.' Thara stood grinning in the open doorway, with Melisanda at her side.

Melisanda, tall and willowy, with a narrow face and tumbled waves of pale-blonde hair, shook her head reprovingly, but she too had a sparkle of humour in her hazel eyes.

'You're no help,' Iriana said plaintively. 'How can I fit it all in? We're going north, and Esmon warned us it would be cold. He made me buy all this new stuff today when we were getting outfitted for the journey.'

It was true. Much earlier that day, the day after their meeting with Cyran, just as the sky was beginning to grow light, the Warrior Wizard had hauled two very bleary young people, neither of whom had closed their eyes all night, from their beds. Avithan had spent a restless, sleepless night worrying about the responsibilities his father had heaped on his head, and Iriana had lain awake through the hours of darkness, too excited about seeing the world at last to close her eyes. So it proved that the first precept of adventuring – early starts – had come as something of a shock.

When visiting the market, Iriana usually took Star, her sparrowhawk, for vision, and Bear for protection. She was disadvantaged in a crowd, for it inevitably took a second or two to get an animal's eyes to focus where she wanted. Folk tended to barge into her a lot because she couldn't move aside in time, but when the huge dog was with her, people got out of *her* way. Bear was also a defence against any thieves or pickpockets who thought a blind girl might be easy prey.

The morning air was cool and fragrant. The sun, peering over the hills behind the city, lit the colours of the flowers on vines and in window boxes. Esmon led the way, walking so fast that Iriana and Avithan found themselves scrambling to keep up. The dawn-still streets were empty of people, the silence so intense that Iriana could hear Avithan's footfalls and her own ringing out sharply, and even the clicking of Bear's claws against the paving stones was quite distinct. Only the Warrior made no sound, moving soft-footed as a leopard in his worn old boots.

The vast, open-air market was down by the harbour; a village of brightly coloured canopies and laden counters stretching along the side of the bay behind the busy area of jetties, piers and docks. A good half-mile on each side, it sold everything from fish fresh off the incoming boats to jewellery and artefacts brought by traders from afar. At one end there was a bandstand where, later in the day, music would be played to entertain those who browsed among the stalls, but at this time of the morning, the market belonged to the people with serious business.

The stalls were still setting up their wares for the day. Crustaceans, beady-eyed and wrathful, were scrabbling around in boxes as trays of silvery fish were sorted and placed on beds of ice. As Esmon purchased leathery strips of jerked salmon, Iriana examined with interest the shimmering spell that had been laid over the fish to keep them fresh and safe, while Star, on her shoulder, screamed abuse at the gulls that swooped hopefully overhead.

A man walked past, his back bent beneath the carcass of a deer. Other butchers displayed joints, hams and sausages fragrant with herbs. While the warrior was buying beef jerky and bacon, Iriana fought to keep her animals away from the nearby stalls that sold crates of live rabbits and chickens. Though she had trained Star and Bear to obedience, such a collection of live prey was irresistible. Today, however, she could allow no leniency. In a crowded place such as this she needed to be in control; able to look where *she* wanted. 'Star! Bear!' she scolded sharply. Bear sidled guiltily back to her side immediately, letting her guide his vision once more. Star, however, asserting his independence as raptors sometimes will, flew up and perched defiantly on the top of the stall.

Through Bear's eyes, she was aware that both Avithan and Esmon had turned to watch her, and knew what they were thinking. That familiar worried frown was on Avithan's face, and the warrior was watching speculatively, one eyebrow slightly raised. Out of the blue, buying supplies on a pleasant morning had become a test. If she could not control the creatures she depended upon in a simple market, how would she manage if a crisis should occur when they were out in the wilderness?

Today of all days – they *would* go and let her down. Iriana forced back mounting annoyance, because she never allowed herself to become angry with her animals. They were her helpers, her constant companions and her friends, and she loved them. Her face hot with mortification, she put her vision through the hawk's eyes and made him look at her as she stood below. Firmly and quickly, she distracted him from the temptations all around, and called him again. This time he obeyed, and Iriana was gratified to see Esmon's almost imperceptible nod of approval. Avithan, however, still had that faint line between his brows. Plague on him! Would she never prove herself to him? Would he ever come to believe in her? She turned away from him, vexed and disappointed.

The companions walked on until the smells of fish and raw meat were replaced by the sweet fragrance of brightly coloured fruits and the sharp, green tang of vegetables. In turn, this area gave way to the dairy section with its milk, butter and cheeses, then to general foodstuffs. Esmon bought dried provisions: beans, oats and a small bag of grain for the horses. Dried fruit, flour, sugar, salt and taillin.

A couple of small coins secured one of the boys who worked in the market as porters. He trotted along behind them, carrying the packages and giving the enormous Bear a wide berth as the Warrior led Avithan and Iriana away into the adjacent area of the market, where he proceeded to outfit them for their journey. A delighted Iriana found herself with a new coat of soft, flexible leather, breeches of the same material and another pair in a sturdy, hard-wearing weave, plus a thick woollen tunic, a cotton shirt and two others made, to her joy, from silken, cobweb-light moonmoth fabric.

Esmon grinned at her delight. 'Since we're visiting the Phaerie, you should be wearing one of their major exports.'

'But it costs a king's ransom.' Iriana's protest was half-hearted as she stroked the peacock-blue fabric of one of her new purchases.

'Prices have gone sky-high since supplies from Eliorand dried up,' Esmon told her. Then he chuckled. 'But Avithan's father is kindly footing the bill for this little lot, so you should make the most of it. These shirts are extremely practical – not that you care about that right now. They pack light, and you'll be thankful for an extra layer of clothing next to your skin as we head north.'

Avithan picked up one of the shirts, distaste written all over his face. 'They're all very well for Iriana, but isn't this stuff, well, a bit effeminate?'

The Warrior's mouth quirked. 'I wear them,' was all he said.

Avithan shut up abruptly.

'They come in dark colours too.' Iriana could barely suppress her laughter. 'I'm sure we can find something suited to your – er – masculine state.' She herself was covetously eyeing the beautiful gowns hanging at the rear of the stall. 'Esmon,' she wheedled, 'don't you think that since we're visiting the Phaerie Court as Cyran's emissaries, I ought to look the part? I mean—'

'I know exactly what you mean.' The Warrior shrugged. 'Go ahead and pick a couple, but don't take too long choosing. We haven't got all day.'

By this time the sun was high in the sky, throwing gleams and sparkles from the tops of the blue waves. 'By the Light,' Avithan said, 'I'm hungry as a wolf.' Esmon and Iriana were quick to agree. At the far end of the market was an abundance of stalls that sold all sorts of hot food, and they wandered through a medley of delectable aromas, trying to reach a consensus. At Avithan's suggestion, they finally decided on freshly grilled fish that had been caught that day, held between the halves of a substantial bread roll. Horn cups of tart lemonade completed their meal.

By this time everyone was laden with packages but, by a miracle, they managed to get all the food and their purchases to the harbour wall without dropping or spilling anything. On a generous impulse, Iriana had brought an extra roll and a drink for their young porter, and his face lit up like a beacon when she put it into his hands.

Freed from their burdens, their parcels piled in a heap in the shade of the wall, the Wizards sat on the rough, sun-warmed stone, resting hot, tired feet and enjoying their food. As they ate, they watched the boats with their bright sails gliding in and out of the harbour, conversing idly in mindspeech to be heard over the shrill cries of the gulls, the calling of the market hawkers and the cursing of the stevedores on the docks.

Once they had refreshed themselves, it was time to make their final purchases. The two younger wizards completed their new outfits with thick green cloaks made from the greasy wool of mountain sheep, which was renowned for its water-repellent qualities. In addition, Iriana needed a knife of her own, a practical blade that would do for anything from skinning and butchering a rabbit to shaving bark for kindling. Esmon picked one out for her, and won her everlasting gratitude for his unhesitating confidence that, blind or not, she could handle such a keen blade.

Iriana only hoped that she could prove worthy of his trust. She wasn't at her best with sharp knives. Generally the idea of adopting her animals to be her eyes had always worked well for her, but as she had seen today, their attention could be diverted at any moment by a sudden noise, a movement, the scent of another beast close by. Normally, she could cope well enough with their distraction. Today, for instance, when Star had been uncooperative, she'd had Bear to provide an alternative. It was the same when she was reading or writing, or doing any number of other tasks. But if an animal looked away, even for an instant, when she had a sharp blade in her hand, the result was usually disastrous.

At a young age, Wizards were taught such useful spells as stopping the bloodflow from a cut, closing the wound and healing it quickly, without scarring. By now, Iriana had the process off to perfection, because she'd had so much practice. Over the years, she had persuaded herself that it didn't matter. She hated cooking anyway, so what difference did it make? But in her heart, it burned her. She managed her blindness so well that she hated having to admit to any limitations.

One aspect hurt her more than any other. She hadn't been able to carve herself a beautiful staff, as all wizards should do when they grew into their magic. Some of her compatriots' staffs, finished, polished and glowing from the magic with which they were imbued, were works of art indeed. Others bore simpler designs. But because they had been made with love and care and magic, all of them were beautiful. Iriana, on the other hand, had something that might well have been a broomshank. It was ugly, plain and clumsy, she was deeply ashamed of it, and therefore used it as little as possible. For that reason, her powers had gained an unusual depth and focus of their own, but she knew that might not be enough if she and her companions ran into some sort of trouble on their journey. No, she would have to take the embarrassing thing with her, and make the best of it.

In the evening, as she was telling Thara and Melisanda about her day, the detested staff lay on the bed with the rest of the paraphernalia waiting to be packed. 'How will I fit it all in?' Iriana said again.

Thara, who often made trips beyond the city in search of rare plants and herbs, put an arm around her shoulders. 'Don't worry,' she said. 'I can show you how to fit the maximum amount of equipment into the minimum of space. You see, it's not about taking what you might need. You only have to take what you can't do without.'

'I've brought something to help the work along.' Melisanda produced a bottle of sparkling golden starwine from behind her back.

'Did someone say starwine?' Zybina, Iriana's foster mother, appeared in the doorway.

Iriana hugged the tall, stately woman whose flame-red hair was twisted around her head in a coronal of braids. 'I'm really glad you came. I've been so busy getting ready, I was afraid I wouldn't have time to come over and say goodbye.' *And I was worried that you'd make a fuss about the whole business*, she added in her most private thoughts.

Zybina, however, always had a way of knowing. 'Don't worry,' she said. 'I didn't come over to give you a lecture – I've already talked to Cyran.' She sighed. 'First Yinze going off into the blue yonder, and now you. By all Creation, I'll hate having both my chicks so far away.'

'It won't be for long,' Iriana assured her. 'I'll probably only be away for a month or two, and Yinze is due back very soon.'

'Iriana …' Zybina hesitated, glancing uncomfortably at the other two Wizards. Melisanda took the hint. 'Come on, Thara. Let's see what we can scrounge from the kitchen.'

When they were gone, Zybina turned away and looked out of the window. Iriana waited. She knew what this would be about.

'Iriana, I don't want to ask this, but … I know you'll be passing through Nexis on your way north, and I was wondering—'

'If I intend to visit Challan,' Iriana finished for her. She joined her foster-mother at the window and laid a hand on her arm.

Challan. Once, he had been her foster-father, Yinze's father and Zybina's soulmate. Gentle, studious and more than a little absent-minded, he had given every appearance of loving his family. But when Iriana had still been no more than a young girl, he had abandoned them with little explanation save that he could no longer stay. While Yinze had been bitter and angry, Zybina had been utterly bereft – and Iriana had felt guilty. Her own parents clearly hadn't wanted a blind child. What if Challan had thought the same way? Maybe it was her fault he had left, because he couldn't stand to be around her. She had never told a living soul this dark secret; not her friends, not even Avithan. All these years it had been festering deep within her soul. If she had ruined the lives of her beloved mother and brother, how could she ever live with herself?

Challan had moved to Nexis – that much they knew, though every attempt by Zybina to see or contact him had been firmly rebuffed. She was far too proud to ask anyone who had visited the frontier town, and for some reason, no one who had been there ever wanted to bring the subject up. Now, after all these years, Iriana was headed in that direction herself – and, once and for all, she had to learn the truth.

Zybina sighed. 'I wish you wouldn't,' she said. 'There's no need. Challan is part of our past now, Iriana, and we should leave him there. Leave him alone. No good will come of tearing open old wounds.'

Iriana took a deep breath – and came to a decision. She had another reason for going. For a long time, Yinze had been waiting to distinguish himself in some way, before confronting his father. Now that the Arch-wizard had entrusted such an important mission to him, he had achieved his goal – and when he returned, she knew he intended to head straight to Nexis. She wanted to spare him that; spare him the trouble it would cause if their confrontation turned to violence, as well it might. Yinze's temper tended to burn hot, especially where Challan was concerned. If she could obtain the necessary answers, maybe she could talk him out of going in person – but Zybina didn't need to know any of this. If she was concerned about the possibility of Iriana seeking out Challan, she would be far more worried about Yinze doing the same thing. To Iriana's way of thinking, her foster-father had caused quite enough worry to the woman she loved as a mother. She was determined to spare her more – and so she lied.

'I thought I would have to. But then I reflected on it some more and realised that, whatever his answers may be, I'm not going to like them.' She strove to lighten the mood. 'So you see, you have nothing to worry about. Come on, mother of my heart. Have some starwine and join the packing party.'

Between the four of them, it turned into a convivial evening, but Iriana made sure to be in bed before midnight, and was up the next morning before it grew light, eating bread and cheese and drinking cold taillin she had brewed the night before. Though apport spells were illegal within the city, except for the official launch and reception points, Esmon had assured her that in this case, Cyran would turn a blind eye. In the stables outside the city there was a special area set aside for materialising bag-gage, and Iriana sent off her bedroll, saddlebags and the stuff she planned to put on the packhorse with one mighty apport spell which took so much out of her that she had to sit down on her bed for a moment.

Once she had pulled herself together, she gathered the animals she was taking with her. Melik, a typical cat, had already sensed that some-thing unusual was happening, and had disappeared. She and Bear tracked him down beneath the bed, and Iriana lured him out with a piece of her breakfast cheese. The magnificent eagle Boreas would be travelling under his own power, and Seyka the big white owl rode in her basket slung over Iriana's shoulder.

A soft knock on the door announced Avithan, as they had planned to walk out to the stables together. They had arranged to meet Esmon at sunrise, and there was no time to lose as they needed to walk through the city to the North Gate. 'Can I take that?' He indicated the owl's basket. 'It'll leave you free to take Melik, and Boreas, I suppose, will fly.'

'Thanks.' Gratefully, Iriana handed Seyka over. 'Come on, Avithan. I can't wait to get started.' She pushed open the back door, heading for the short cut through the garden to the narrow lane behind.

'Aren't Thara and Melisanda coming to see you off?'

'No, we decided to say our farewells last night, when we had more time.' She grimaced. 'Zybina came too, but I must say, she handled the whole thing very well. By and large, she kept all her worries under wraps.'

'I said goodbye to my parents last night too, though my mother wanted to keep me up till the early hours with reams of advice.'

'No changes there, then,' Iriana said wryly.

They made their way through the sleeping streets in the mysterious, crepuscular light, sometimes silent, sometimes talking, their voices soft in the magical hush. Eventually, taking the steeply sloping road that led through the North Gate beside the turreted walls of the fortresslike Luen of Warriors, they gave their names to the warders who watched the entrance to the city, and stepped out into the world beyond just as the rising sun turned the sky inland into a sheet of gold. There stood Esmon, with all four of their horses, including Iriana's beloved piebald Dailika.

'Very punctual,' he said. 'I've packed your gear this morning to save time. If everyone is ready, shall we go?'

Iriana could hardly wait. Seyka's basket was positioned on the pack-horse and fastened securely into place. Then, letting Avithan hold Melik, she mounted Dailika and reached down for the cat, who sat in front of her. As they prepared to leave, she switched to her horse's vision, thereby losing a lot of colour and depth perception but gaining the ability to see all around, even behind.

With Esmon leading the way and Iriana and Avithan following in order, they made their way along the dusty switchback road that climbed up through the olive groves, breathing air that was already beginning to warm and take on the scents of herbs and trees. High on the hilltop, Iriana looked back at the beautiful city that curved around the sparkling blue bays. In her thoughts, Iriana sent a farewell to Tyrineld, her friends and the animals she had left behind. She wondered what she would know, what she would have learned about herself and her world by the time she came back.

'If you've any sense, you'll be wondering how you'll get back and *if* you will,' Esmon warned her in mindspeech. 'Remember, Iriana, you're not going on a picnic.'

'Yes, Esmon,' she replied obediently, inwardly indignant that he had picked up her tumultuous thoughts, and vowing to think a little less loudly in future. She was too excited, however, to feel squashed. At last. At long last she had been freed from the constraints of the city. As she looked out over the rolling hills to the far horizon, Iriana's spirits soared to meet the rising sun.

13
~

FROM THE SHADOWS

Today, for once, the scrying was going as it should. Cyran had used a crystal instead of the usual mirror, and it appeared to be working. To his relief, he saw what he'd been looking for rather than a confusing jumble of ill-omened portents. The crystal, a massive chunk of clear quartz, sat on the table in the sunlight, and within its depths he could see, small but very clear, an image of three tiny figures on horseback, leading a packhorse behind them as they cantered steadily across an expanse of un-dulating green downs. Three days had passed since the cold dawn when Avithan, Iriana and Esmon had set out. By nightfall they would reach the northern settlement of Nexis and the first leg of their journey would be safely over. The Archwizard nodded in satisfaction. Of course they were safe. How many times had he told Sharalind over the last few days (when he could get a word in edgeways) that Iriana would come to no harm?

To say that Cyran's consort had disagreed with his decision to send Avithan and Iriana to Eliorand would be putting it mildly. Sharalind's explosion of anger had broken every window in the building, and it had taken repairing spells from a squad of Wizards to put right the mess. Even now, three days later, her treatment of him was as cold as the northern mountains, and he had a feeling that he would not be back in favour until the emissaries had returned safely to Tyrineld. Archwizard or no, he was also in considerable trouble with Iriana's guardian, Zybina, and caught between the two formidable females, he was beginning to wish that he, too, could have been riding to Nexis with his son and Iriana.

Unfortunately, the Archwizard couldn't shrug off his responsibilities so easily. Cyran wrapped his crystal in a velvet cloth and put it away, then began to prepare for a meeting with the other Magefolk leaders. Taking his mirror from its cabinet, he unwrapped it carefully from its velvet covering and repeated the process with two others. Then he placed all three of them on the table and tilted them carefully to catch the morning sunlight and reflect it onto the wall. When the three patches of light were properly aligned and glimmering alongside one another, he was finally ready to begin.

He wondered why the others had called this meeting. There had not been one due for another six days, and normally all the arrangements were left to him. Could something have changed at last? Had one of them finally been given a warning, as he had? The Archwizard was torn: half-wanting to be vindicated in the eyes of his peers, but half-dreading confirmation of the horrors he had seen.

The misgivings of the other leaders had hit him hard. He had worked so laboriously and struggled for so long to be made Archwizard. Many had thought him too scholarly, not sufficiently practical, and his determination that magic should never be used for warlike purposes had made him many enemies among those who believed that the Wizardfolk should have the means to defend themselves, especially living as close as they did to the Phaerie. He had finally succeeded in his ambition, however, and during the years since he had achieved the leadership of his people, he had always been certain that he was doing a good job. Now that confidence had been shaken. Since these visions had started he had known no peace, analysing every move and decision he made for fear of where it might lead. At the back of his disquiet, there were always the insidious doubts that had made sleep a thing of the past. *What if, in trying to avoid this catastrophe, I bring it about?* In the end he had no choice but to trust his own judgement and do the best he could. If only the other leaders had shared his presentiments! Cyran hoped with all his heart that they had been wrong to doubt.

He was just about to sit down at the table when the door opened soundlessly and a figure wearing a dark cloak slipped inside. Cyran turned. 'How dare you enter my chambers without knocking—'

'I? Knock?' The intruder laughed lightly, but without mirth. 'Why get into bad habits?' His hair was dark, and tied back from his face. He had the tall, lean form of one of the Phaerie, but there was a solid muscularity to his body, and his face and jaw had strong, chiselled features that indicated otherwise.

'Taine!' The Archwizard gasped. 'May the Light be praised. You were away for so long, I was sure you had been caught.'

'I very nearly was. I had a lot of trouble getting out, now that the Phaerie have closed their borders. Also, I'm sure that Dhagon, who is still head of Hellorin's Chahiri spy network, suspects me.' He broke into a lazy smile. 'His accursed agents were snooping around all over the city, and since I had to kill several of them during my escape, he'll certainly be after my blood now.'

Cyran ignored this. *'They've closed the borders?'*

'The Phaerie realm has been isolated. No one gets in or out any more.'

'Oh, mercy, no.' Cyran felt as though he had been kicked in the guts. 'I have just sent my son and a young, blind, inexperienced girl to Eliorand as emissaries.'

Taine's eyebrows shot up. Coming from one so skilled at hiding emotions, his expression betrayed his feelings more strongly than a shout or a curse. Nonetheless, when he spoke, his voice remained mild and calm. 'Your son and a blind girl. Pardon me for being frank, Archwizard, but what in the world were you thinking?'

Temper flashed through Cyran, hot and red. Anger at himself as much as the weary spy. 'I thought you were dead. If you had even managed to get some kind of message to me it would have helped, but for months I've heard nothing. I had to do something – I have my reasons for not wanting open warfare with Hellorin's folk. I felt that by sending the most non-aggressive representatives possible, I might have a chance to treat with the Phaerie, not to mention find out what's going on up there. And Iriana might be blind, but she has special abilities, talents that might have proven very useful in finding out some of the Phaerie secrets, had she been able to gain entry to Eliorand. She might also have been able to discover what had become of you.'

'When did you send them? How fast were they planning to travel? I saw no sign of them on my way here, but that means nothing, for I seldom travel on public roads – especially when I've needed to steal myself a fresh horse.' A rare spark of humour brightened his weary eyes. 'Over the years, I've learned a lot of short cuts.'

Cyran had begun to pace. 'They left three days ago, and they were in no hurry. They planned to reach Nexis by tonight. And I had more sense than to send them alone. They have Esmon, the Head of the Luen of Warriors, with them.'

'Good. That makes me feel a little more confident about their safety. Give me a couple of good horses and I can catch them before they reach the borders of the Phaerie realm. I'll set off at once.' Taine swayed with exhaustion even as he spoke and, dangerous though the situation might be, Cyran took pity on him. 'Will an hour or two make any difference?'

The spy shook his head. 'They'll be dawdling along, no doubt, and stopping to eat and sleep. I won't. Even if I set off at nightfall, I should still catch them easily.'

'Then sit down and rest yourself. When did *you* last eat or sleep?'

Taine unslung the compact pack from his shoulders, doffed his muddy cloak and threw himself down in the nearest chair. 'I came straight here without stopping, except to steal a fresh horse in Nexis.'

'I've been scrying in that direction off and on for the last three days, keeping an eye on my son and his companions,' Cyran said. 'Why did I never see you?'

'I know a spell that screens me from observation by scrying.'

'I've never heard of such a spell.'

The spy shrugged. 'Phaerie magic, a lesser version of their glamourie spell. I did inherit some powers from my father, you know, as well as my Wizardly mother.'

The Archwizard poured taillin from the pot that always stood on his desk, kept warm by one of Avithan's useful spells, and added a generous dollop of honey. He thrust the cup into Taine's hands, and took a goblet of wine for himself. He forced himself to be calm and concentrate on the matter in hand, instead of worrying unnecessarily over Avithan and Iriana. 'What is really happening in Eliorand?' he asked. 'Why have the Phaerie closed their borders? Tell me what you've learned.'

'It's even worse than you might have imagined, Archwizard,' Taine said.

Cyran listened with growing consternation as Taine told him what had taken place during the winter. This was all wrong. There were too many questions here; too many imponderables. He and Hellorin had ruled their respective realms for so long that each could predict, within reason, what the other would do in any circumstances. But Tiolani now ruled the Phaerie, and she was an entirely unknown quantity. Hellorin and Estrelle had waited long indeed for their daughter, and the untimely death of his beloved consort had made Hellorin all the more inclined to indulge his child. Young, pampered, inexperienced, undisciplined: any of these traits spelled trouble in a ruler. Put them all together, add the fact that the girl was half-crazed with grief over the death of her brother and was being influenced by this Ferimon – another unknown and suspect quantity – and you had a recipe for certain disaster. How would she cope with the challenges of her sudden rise to power? That she had found an outlet for her grief riding with the Wild Hunt every night, exterminating every feral human she could find without regard for treaties, borders or anything else, was indicative of the grave nature of the situation.

Cyran could feel the beginnings of a headache tightening behind his eyes. What would be the best way to deal with a situation such as this?

'That's not all,' Taine said quietly, interrupting the Archwizard's racing thoughts. 'The healers could not remove the arrows from Hellorin and several other of the wounded Phaerie until they had brought them home. Most of the projectiles were destroyed during the healing process, but I finally managed to get my hands on one.' Unstrapping the pack, he reached inside and withdrew a long, thin package, well wrapped in cloth. Balancing it on his palm, he held it out to the Archwizard.

Cyran took the package and unfolded the cloth with care. The discoloured shaft had been soaked in blood, but he ignored the dark, jarring energy of pain and death carried by the stains. His eyes were riveted on the arrow itself. Contrary to his expectations, it was smooth and straight, with perfect fletching and a beautifully forged iron point. His eyes opened wide. 'This was not made by a pack of renegade slaves living wild. Were they all like this?' he demanded.

'To the best of my knowledge.'

'Then where did the humans get them?'

'I don't know,' Taine confessed. 'One thing seems certain: someone has been providing the ferals with weapons. Hellorin has an enemy – but who? Is it one of the Phaerie, or someone else? My instincts tell me it must be Ferimon, but I have no real proof, and cannot be certain.'

The Archwizard frowned. 'I must learn the identity of Hellorin's secret foe. Will they be an ally to us, or an enemy? Our entire future could depend on it.'

'Of course. I'll take a few hours' rest, and set off for Eliorand tonight. I'll send Avithan's party back and continue on alone.' Taine's face was as expressionless as stone.

'Taine, I regret the necessity for this. The situation is so serious, however, that—'

The Archwizard broke off, his reply unfinished, as a cascade of sound, a plangent fall of musical notes, echoed through the room, and the air came alive with swirling, scintillating coloured light.

In an eyeblink Taine was on his feet: tense, alert, ready to defend himself. 'What's that?'

'Nothing to worry about,' Cyran said. He gestured towards the wall behind them. There, in one of the patches of glimmering light he had created earlier, an astonishing form could be seen: a great golden Dragon. Even as a small image on the wall, the entity was vibrant with beauty and power. An elegant head, with formidable jaws, sweeping back and forth on its long, graceful neck; great eyes glowing with a deep, slumbrous garnet fire; a strong, compact body with a tapering tail – and the glorious wings, a translucent gold web with a complex network of glittering silver veining, all stretched between outspread digits of a similar construction to batwings, and spangled with the multitudes of darkly gleaming scales that were used to capture the sun's energy, on which these amazing beings fed.

Taine gasped. 'By all Creation! I always wished to see one of the Dragonfolk.' His eyes grew wider as distinct figures began to take shape within the two other areas of shimmer: the vast, dark, streamlined bulk of a Leviathan, and a stern-faced queen, her hair white except for a black streak on either side of her head. She was cloaked in a pair of dark-brown wings with white flashes, and her fierce, golden eyes had the keen, uncompromising gaze of a warrior.

The Archwizard was careful to keep his smile hidden. He never thought he'd see the day when something would take Taine by surprise. He pushed back the chair. 'I'm afraid the rest of our discussion will have to wait. As you can see, I'm late for a meeting with my fellow Magefolk leaders. Thanks to your timely news, we'll have a great deal more to discuss than we expected. Go downstairs to my apartments. Sharalind won't be there at this time of day. Refresh yourself, rest. Get a good meal inside you. I'll have food sent at once.' He touched a small, glowing crystal that stood on his desk, spoke into it briefly, then turned back to Taine. 'There you are. Make yourself comfortable, and we'll continue our conversation later.' He put his hand on the other's shoulder. 'Taine, I am more grateful than I can say for all you are doing. I swear I will find a way to repay you. If you ever need anything I can give you, you need only say the word.'

'Thank you.' For the first time, Taine's face relaxed into a genuine smile. 'Cyran, I can't tell you how good it is to be back among my mother's people. I'm happy to be of use to you, if I can.' Looking over his shoulder so that his eyes could linger on the extraordinary images on the wall, he went out of the room and, with one last, regretful look, closed the door behind him.

Cyran extended his senses beyond the chamber, just to make sure that Taine had really gone, and was not listening outside. The informant was unique: he had been born in the forest of a Wizardly mother, Cerica, who had been living there in solitude in order to perfect her magic. His father, Astreth, had been lost from the Wild Hunt when his horse bolted and threw its rider, stranding the Phaerie deep in the woods when the flying magic had expired. They had fallen in love and lived together in secret, and Cerica had borne Taine. But when the boy was five, one of the magical monsters that inhabited the side of the forest within the Phaerie realm had broken through Hellorin's wards and strayed across the border. Cerica, meditating alone in a woodland glade, had never stood a chance. The grieving father had returned with Taine to Eliorand, claiming that the boy's mother had been a human slave, for the Forest Lord, deeply suspicious of the Wizards, would never have permitted a child with their blood in his city.

Taine, therefore, grew up keeping secrets, and though his father's denial of his mother gave rise to a certain coolness between them, he had only pursued the other side of his heritage much later, when Hellorin had discovered his secret and he'd been forced to flee the Phaerie realm. But he had integrated well within the city of the Wizards, and had eventually come to Cyran and offered his services as a spy.

That night, passing a bottle between them, they had talked right through until dawn, and the Archwizard had learned something of Taine's lonely past, and begun to understand what had triggered his change of allegiance. Though aware of the risks – it was, after all, possible that Taine could have been acting for Hellorin and feeding disinformation to the Wizards – the Archwizard had been convinced of his integrity. In all the time he had been using the half-breed as a spy, he had never once had cause to regret his decision.

Taine is loyal – too loyal for his own good, Cyran thought. *In all conscience, how much longer can I continue to make use of him? Surely he has earned his place among the Wizards many times over? Each time I send him back to Eliorand, the risks are growing. Am I treating him as expendable, holding out a promise that will never materialise, until he takes one risk too many, and is killed? Yet in the current situation, what choice do I have? I can only hope that one day I will be able to hold true to my word – and that Taine will survive long enough to earn the peace and security to which his contributions to the weal of the Wizards have more than entitled him.*

After several days' hard riding, Taine appreciated the comfort of the Archwizard's luxurious quarters. Taking off his travel-soiled boots at the door, he let his feet sink into the thick, soft carpet, with its intricate patterns woven in pure, bright colours. He had been here before, and knew his way around. He went straight into the bathing room, to finally shed the dirt of the trail and get into the one change of clean clothes he had brought with him.

It did not take him long. When he emerged, the meal was ready and waiting under covered dishes, all set out on the table beneath the window. He made short work of rich fish soup, bread, cheese, cold fowl, assorted fruit and a sweet pastry to round off the meal. As usual, he ignored the pale, fragrant wine that had been provided, and helped himself to taillin instead. His life was one of concealment, of subterfuge and secrets. His sure instincts and quick reflexes had saved his life more than once, and he never dared risk dulling them with wine or spirits.

How had he come to this? Belonging nowhere, with nothing in his world but loneliness and danger. Sitting beside the sunny window, Taine closed his eyes and let the years roll back to his youth in Eliorand. Everything had seemed to be going in his favour, and the future was full of promise. He had apprenticed to a merchant, and was looking forward to his first trading journeys out of the Phaerie realm. He was in love with Aelwen, at that time the assistant to Hellorin's Horsemaster, and they were planning a life together. They had been young, and full of hope and energy, and nothing had seemed impossible – until, without warning, the shadow had fallen across his future.

The Forest Lord had discovered the real identity of his mother. His father Astreth, no real horseman, had once again been unwise enough to take part in the Wild Hunt that his son was denied through his half-blood heritage, and had sustained a bad fall. In a dying delirium, he had somehow blurted the truth to Hellorin, and at last the secret was out.

Taine remembered that night so very clearly. Because there had been a Hunt, and Aelwen was busy preparing for the return of the riders, he had been sitting alone by the window of his chambers with a glass of wine at his elbow, looking out at the towers, with all their twinkling lamps that held so many hues, on the lower slopes of the city. He had maps of the route through the forest to Tyrineld spread out on the table in front of him, together with a scholarly old tome on the history of the Wizardfolk and the Earth magic they used. He wished he could have found a treatise that was a little more recent. In a few days' time he would be making his first journey to the city of the Wizards with Ambaron, the merchant to whom he was apprenticed, and he wanted to be prepared.

All was peaceful, all was quiet. He had been looking forward to seeing Aelwen tomorrow, once her work was done. She always had a busy time when the horses returned from the Hunt. They were weary, hungry, and they and their accoutrements were stained with mud and blood. Inevitably, a number of them were lame, or had other injuries that needed tending ...

There was a sound like a thunderclap and his chair was hurled over backwards by an explosive blast of air. Heart hammering, he scrambled to his feet – and saw Aelwen herself, white-faced and gasping for breath, standing on the hearthrug. He was horrified to realise that she had apported straight into his chambers, an act that was illegal within the boundaries of the city, and highly dangerous besides. It required an immense amount of power and, if the apporter was not strong enough, it could use so much energy that there was not sufficient remaining to stay alive. Besides which, if Aelwen had materialised within a wall, or a piece of furniture – or even himself … Shudders crawled down his spine at the thought of the dreadful consequences.

Taine rushed over and took her in his arms. 'Aelwen! What in Creation do you think you're doing? You could have been killed—'

'There's no time for that.' Aelwen's hair had straggled loose from its braids, and she shook it impatiently out of her eyes. 'Taine, you've got to get out of here. Your father – I'm sorry, but he was killed during the Hunt. Estrelle has just sent a message by mindspeech to warn me. Before he died, Astreth let slip the truth about your mother to Hellorin, and he was raging at the deception. Taine, you know that *he* would never allow someone tainted with Wizard blood to survive. You've got to be safely away before he returns.'

And just like that, within the space of two breaths, his life had been shattered into shards. There was no time even to think of his father's death, or how he felt about it. Aelwen's panic leapt to Taine like a lightning bolt, and he found himself stuffing food into a bag, pulling on his boots and throwing his cloak around his shoulders, while Aelwen snatched blankets from the bed and rolled them into a bundle as she told him what she knew about his father's accident. He was only half-listening. Why should he care about the man who had just wrecked his life? He thrust his sword into its sheath, snatched his bow and quiver, then Aelwen grabbed his hand and there was a sickening, swirling sensation followed by a violent lurch as she apported them back to the stables. A horse was already saddled, waiting for him. How had she managed everything so quickly?

She must have been reading his mind. 'Kelon took care of it for me, while I was fetching you.'

I'll wager he did, Taine thought. He had noticed the wistful, hungering look in the other groom's eyes when Aelwen was about. He would be overjoyed to get rid of the competition. But why only one horse? The hollow clutch of panic twisted his stomach. 'Aelwen? You're coming too?'

'I can't.' Her eyes flooded. 'Oh, Taine, I'm sorry.' With an effort she got control of her voice. 'Estrelle is my half-sister. You know how close we are, and so does Hellorin. If I go, he'll know at once that she was the one who warned me. I can't make that kind of trouble for her.' With tears streaming freely down her face, she clasped him in one last, desperate embrace, and he crushed her in his arms, unable to bear the thought of leaving her. Firmly, she pushed him away. 'Go quickly! I'll always love you.'

'And I'll love you. To the end of my days.' Somehow he found himself in the saddle, and then Aelwen was dwindling into distance and darkness, as the forest reached out to swallow him.

Though his mix of Wizard and Phaerie blood allowed him to see the track in the blackness beneath the midnight trees, the way was slick and muddy from heavy rain the previous day. Nevertheless, Taine had little attention to spare for hazards. His heart and mind were consumed with grief for Aelwen; for the life together they had been denied; for the hopes that lay in ruin. Somehow he could not bring himself to deal with the practicalities of flight. Though he was forced to flee, every fibre of his being was calling him back to the one he loved.

Taine blinked, and returned to the present, half-surprised to see the walls of Cyran's apartments instead of the dark, reaching trees of that first, dreadful night when he had made his way into the forest, fleeing for his life. In order to reach the safety of Tyrineld he'd known cold and hunger, been forced to evade not only the Wild Hunt itself, but also the airborne patrols that Hellorin had sent in search of him. During that arduous journey he had taught himself perforce to find food and shelter in the wild, and the rudiments of stealth and concealment as he dodged the Forest Lord's hunters. Because of this the journey had taken far longer than usual, and when, filthy, exhausted and ravenous, he had finally crossed the border into the realms of the Magefolk, he had sworn never to set foot in the kingdom of the Forest Lord again – a vow he had broken over and over since that day for Cyran's sake and for another, even more pressing reason: Aelwen, the beloved he had lost on that terrible night of discovery and flight.

He had spent time in Eliorand ever since, disguising himself with glamourie, always just a step ahead of the Chahiri while collecting information for the Archmage. He had often watched Aelwen from hiding, his heart aching with the need to reveal himself, to speak to her, to hold her in his arms again. But she had always looked settled and content in her role as Horsemistress. Though she had never chosen a mate, would she thank him for disrupting her life once more? And if he should get her to come away with him, would she settle with the Wizards? How well would they accept one who carried none of their blood? One thing was certain: if he brought her back to Tyrineld, his days of taking such appalling risks for Cyran would have to be over. And if he could no longer spy for the Archwizard, would he still find a welcome here? Though Cyran had always assured him that this was the case, there was a constant shadow of doubt that had kept Taine braving the numerous perils of yet another return to Eliorand.

How would Aelwen manage without her beloved horses, to which she had devoted so much of her life? Would she harbour resentment, deep within her, if he took her away from them? Would it sour the love that they once shared? Always, his courage had failed him. As things stood, their love was a pure and perfect thing, preserved in his memory with absolute clarity. How could he risk finding out that Aelwen no longer felt as he did? No. Better, surely, to leave things as they stood. It was no good trying to demand the impossible. Not now, at any rate. This was not the time. But in the future? That might be a different story, and he was determined not to give up hope.

In the meantime, Taine told himself, he would grab a couple of hours' rest and then head off in pursuit of the ill-starred emissaries. He frowned. If the Archwizard was sending out his only son on such a hazardous venture, the situation must be a great deal more serious, not to mention perilous, than Cyran was prepared to admit. But though the unpleasant thought that he was being used had begun to cross his mind more and more often these days, Taine was prepared to continue for as long as he was needed. If he wanted to bring Aelwen back some day, it wouldn't do any harm to have the Archwizard deep in his debt.

14

THE ᴁRT OF COMDROMIꟙE

Now that Taine had departed, Cyran had other matters to deal with, and for the present, he put the spy out of his mind. 'My apologies,' he said to his fellow leaders. 'I will detain you but a moment longer.' He set wards of guard and silence, so that no one could approach undetected, or use magic to listen in on the meeting. Once all was secure, he sat down at the table, facing the others. Concentrating on their images, he reached out to them in thought: the gleaming golden form of Aizaiel, Matriarch of the Dragonfolk; the sleek, dark immensity of Kahuna, Speaker of the Leviathan, and the white-haired, brown-winged form of Pandion, Queen of the Skyfolk.

'Greetings to you all,' he began. 'Please forgive me for keeping you waiting. A messenger came with news of great importance.'

'Greetings, Archwizard.' As usual, Aizaiel of the Dragonfolk took the lead, using both her own language of light and music, and mindspeech, which was a language of thought common to all the races of magic-users.

'Greetings, Matriarch.' Cyran kept his physical voice low and even, and his mindspeech rigidly controlled, anxious not to betray to the others the puzzlement and concern he was feeling. Previously, it had always been he who called these meetings. What had changed? Had his fellow leaders finally decided that his fears were groundless, and these discussions a waste of time?

As usual, however, he could not deceive the Matriarch, who wasted no time in enlightening him. 'Cyran, we owe you an apology. It seems that you were right. Two days ago, Speaker Kahuna experienced visions similar to those you have described.'

'Save that most of them dealt with the destruction of the Leviathan race,' the Speaker added. He sounded very shaken.

'Yesterday I also perceived corresponding images,' Aizaiel said. 'The end of our beloved realm of Dhiammara, and the extinction of the Dragonfolk.'

'And I,' added Pandion, 'but mine came to me last night in a dream.' Her face was very pale. 'So much death, so much desperation. Nothing ever the same again.' She shook her head. 'Archwizard, I must confess that I have doubted you again and again these last two years. But no longer.'

Cyran's throat clogged with emotion. His mind whirled in a conflict between relief that he wasn't losing his sanity, thankfulness that he'd been vindicated at last, and horror at the thought of what the future might bring. There was also a good deal of puzzlement. Why now? And why had all the others received their visions at more or less the same time? A ball of ice began to form within his belly. Did this mean that the catastrophe – whatever form it would take – was about to begin? Or had the chain of events that would lead to disaster already begun to unfold?

Kahuna broke into his thoughts. 'Thanks to Cyran's timely warning, we are already aware of the situation. Now we must ask ourselves: what more can we do to prepare for the worst? Cyran, having experienced the foretellings first, you have been far more committed in your preparations. The fault lies with us, but now we must make up for lost time. Have we omitted anything that might make a difference? The nature of the visions tells me that we must have. Clearly, whatever we have achieved so far, it is not enough to avert disaster. Is there anything else we can do to save ourselves? Can anyone here think of something that we have previously overlooked?'

'One thing we should investigate,' Pandion said after a moment, 'is whether the problem is likely to come from within the ranks of the Magefolk themselves, or from without. Perhaps we should each investigate our own people a little more closely. Are there any malcontents? Troublemakers?' Her eyes lit with wry amusement. 'Folk who think they could fulfil our roles better than we can?'

'You are right,' said Aizaiel, 'though it comes hard to think that such devastation as we have witnessed might originate with one of our own.'

'On that score,' Cyran said, 'I have grave tidings for you all, which I have just received from my informant in Eliorand. That was why it was necessary to keep you waiting. The news gave me deep misgivings when I heard it, but now it has even greater import, coinciding as it does with you all witnessing the same horrors as I have these past two years.' Without delay, he related all that Taine had told him concerning the events that had taken place over the last few months within the realm of the Forest Lord.

After he had finally finished his tale, a long moment of silence stretched out while the Archwizard waited. He could hazard a fair guess at what his fellow Mages were thinking, for much the same thoughts had been racing through his own mind. Had the warning the others had received been connected in some way to this news of trouble in the Phaerie realm? Was this the beginning of the nightmare they had all foreseen?

Unusually, Kahuna was the first to speak. 'This is grave news indeed,' he said. 'Hellorin was wily, proud and difficult to deal with at the best of times, but at least we had all reached an accommodation with him over the long years. Now his people are ruled by a new and unpredictable faction. Tiolani by herself would have been difficult enough, but she is young, and we might have been able to help her through her grief, and lead her along the road of cooperation and common sense. As it is, however, she has apparently come under the influence of a dangerous exploiter—'

'And, if two and two still make four, an exploiter who is probably responsible for the death of her brother and the incapacitation of her father,' Queen Pandion put in. 'From what Cyran has told us, it seems obvious to me that this Ferimon used the rebel humans to rid himself of the Forest Lord. Once he weds Tiolani – which I'm sure is his plan – he will rule the Phaerie.'

'Unless Hellorin awakes, of course,' the Leviathan interrupted.

Pandion's great wings rose and fell as she shrugged. 'Hellorin won't awake,' she said. 'Ferimon will make sure of that. And once he can persuade Tiolani to wed him, Hellorin will become completely dispensable. Unless that stupid girl comes to her senses soon, she will lose everything: her power, her throne and her father.'

'If your conjecture is correct – and all the facts we have seem to point in that direction – my main concern is what Ferimon will do if and when he achieves his objective,' Cyran said. 'Having made the realm of the Phaerie his own, where will he look next? Already the accursed Wild Hunt is encroaching across our borders and killing our slaves.' He spread his hands. 'What shall I do? Fight? Wait to see what happens? Try to find a way to penetrate those closed borders and reason with Tiolani? Ultimately the decision must rest with me, but I would welcome your thoughts, for my actions now could affect all our futures.'

Aizaiel, who had remained silent during Cyran's revelations and the discussions that had followed, fixed the Archwizard with her glowing garnet eyes. 'I think we are all agreed that avoiding conflict must be our primary aim. But what if we cannot? What if the war we have foreseen is inevitable? The Phaerie wield the titanic powers of the Old Magic. As things stand now, could we counter that? Are we making the most of the magic we possess? I would say—'

'I already know what you would say,' Cyran interrupted. 'I am sick to death of hearing it. In how many more of our meetings do you and Pandion plan to keep repeating yourselves?'

'Until you finally listen. Cyran, the Dragonfolk are no more aggressive than the Wizards that you rule, but it is clear to us that currently we lack the means to defend ourselves. And the fact that all of us have now seen the dread visions you witnessed so long ago make the situation all the more urgent. In spite of Kahuna's doubts, in spite of your objections to the Magefolk using their powers for the purposes of war, we must make master weapons that will store and focus the combined powers of all our people.'

'Maybe your visions were different from mine, but it was plain to me that the wholesale, widespread destruction of our civilisation was due to the unleashing of vast amounts of power: in other words, magic produced by the use of exactly the sort of weapons you describe,' Cyran said. 'Can you not see that we are being warned? You would have us rushing headlong to our doom.'

'You say we have been warned, and you are right,' the Matriarch said, 'but could it be possible that the portents have a different purpose? The Phaerie now pose a threat to us. The creation of magical weapons has become inevitable. All our races have been researching the possibilities these last two years, since you first warned us—'

'*You've been doing what?*'

Cyran's voice was like ice. 'Did we not agree that the creation of master weapons would require the consent of all four races of Magefolk?'

'The creation, yes.' Pandion's eyes showed a steely glint. 'But no one forbade the investigation of ways and means to bring about such an implement, if the need should ever arise. If we do have urgent need to defend ourselves, we will have to move swiftly. There won't be any time to carry out lengthy research at that point. Even Kahuna finally agreed with us on that.'

'This is unconscionable,' Cyran protested. 'How could you be so duplicitous and irresponsible?'

'And how can you be so stubborn and blind?' Pandion shot back. 'Even your own people have been working on this project, and—'

'Enough, Pandion,' Aizaiel said, but it was too late. The Archwizard, his guts twisting in anger, realised that he had been deceived.

'Who has done this?' he demanded. 'As if I cannot guess. My ungrateful son and those devious Spellweavers – and I'm certain they were not alone in this. This time the Luen of Warriors has defied me once too often—'

'Do not be hasty, Cyran,' Aizaiel said. 'After all, what harm has been done? No weapon has actually been created. And it may come to pass that in the future you'll have reason to thank them for their foresight.'

'I'll thank them to respect my wishes. Am I right, Pandion? Is it my son? Is it Esmon and his Warriors? I want names.'

'I do not know their names,' the Queen replied. 'My own researchers have been in contact with them, and I knew of it, but I preferred not to ask their identities. What I do not know, you cannot ask me to reveal.'

'Come, Cyran.' The voice belonged to Kahuna. 'Maybe all is not lost. I also abhor the use of magic for war, but this may turn out for the best. If the Dragons and the Skyfolk want to make weapons, that is their prerogative. Wind and Fire are natural forces for violence and destruction. But our powers, those of Water and Earth, tend more towards nurturing and healing. If disaster should strike us, there will be great need for such magic, and my own people, far from researching a weapon, have been attempting to turn our powers towards more beneficial ends. Maybe you also should be bending your thoughts in that direction – as, indeed, should all of us, instead of fighting among ourselves. We need to concentrate not only on retaliation and aggression, but also on the preservation and protection of our people, our lore and our civilisation. Are those not good and worthwhile ends?'

Queen Pandion raised her eyes heavenwards. 'Kahuna the peace-maker,' she scoffed.

'Kahuna the wise,' Aizaiel corrected her. 'Cyran, please think on what our friend the Speaker of the Leviathan has said. What we – what *you* – could create need not necessarily be for destruction. Is that not a good end? And until you have considered, you have my word that none of us will forge any master weapons—'

'Artefacts,' Kahuna corrected. 'Not necessarily weapons.'

The Dragon nodded. 'Agreed. None of us will create any master artefacts until we have all reached agreement. And in the meantime, as Kahuna has suggested, can we turn our thoughts to preserving and protecting? Archwizard, you have accomplished far more than the rest of us to safeguard our accumulated lore. Have you any suggestions for us?'

Cyran took a sip of his neglected wine. 'I can think of one thing you can do immediately,' he said. 'Cooperate with me on sharing our magic. I know, I know,' he added, over the voices that Pandion and Aizaiel – but not Kahuna, he noted with interest – raised in immediate protest. 'I know that such an innovation is against all our oldest traditions, but at least my students have shown that it is possible, have they not?'

From the beginning, one of the Archwizard's main concerns had been the amount of magical knowledge and lore that might be lost forever when the disaster happened, plunging the entire Magefolk civilisation back into a primitive age of barbarism. His plan to explore the possibility of sharing magical powers between their races, however, had caused an uproar among the others. Nothing like it had ever been tried before, and the consensus of opinion seemed to be that it would be impossible for a Mage of one race to learn the magic of another. Even if Cyran was right, and such a thing could be accomplished after all, then they had been reluctant to give away the many secrets of their lore. Though they had accepted his three carefully selected delegates – who, incidentally, had been proving that they could learn, if not completely master the other forms of magic – their refusal to send representatives of their own had caused him great frustration. But could they now be persuaded to change their minds?

'Surely now,' he pressed, 'in the cause of protecting all we know and all we hold most dear – all the knowledge and lore we should be keeping in trust for generations to come—' He paused and looked from face to face. 'Surely now you will change your minds about an exchange of students, a pooling of our knowledge? The safest way to preserve our heritage,' he added, quoting his soulmate the Archivist, 'is by disseminating all the information as widely as possible, thereby increasing the chances that some, or most of it will survive.'

'I, for one, agree,' said the Speaker of the Leviathan. 'The hideous visions I experienced were enough to change my thinking on this matter. I feel that we have all been vouchsafed these warnings in the last few days because the danger is now drawing very near. It is already too late to be worrying about preserving our secrets. Our sole consideration now must be the survival – of our people and our civilisation.'

The Queen of the Winged Folk shook her head. 'When I was crowned, I swore to safeguard the secrets of my people, and never to reveal them to a living soul. What would you have me do? How long do you think my people would support a Queen who had turned oathbreaker?'

'But surely they would be able to see that these are exceptional circumstances,' Cyran protested.

'Would they? Until I saw those visions for myself, Archwizard, even I doubted your warnings. What right have I to expect more of my subjects?'

Aizaiel drummed her tail tip rapidly on the ground – a Dragon's equivalent, Cyran knew, of a frown. 'I agree with Pandion. Our powers have been kept secret for good reason. It's all very well for you Wizards, and even the Leviathan and the Skyfolk. But Fire magic could be appallingly destructive in the wrong hands.'

144

'And you think our powers could not?' Pandion snapped. 'Ever heard of whirlwinds? Hurricanes, perhaps?'

'Not to mention tidal waves, floods and whirlpools,' Kahuna added.

'Exactly.' The Dragon sounded pleased. 'Cyran, I should say that Earth magic is probably the most innocuous of all four elements. It tends to be more healing and nurturing than destructive. But can the rest of us afford to give our secrets away so easily? Pandion spoke of hurricanes. How much more destructive would such a tempest be when coupled with Water magic to produce torrential rain, tidal waves and floods? Then add Fire magic to produce lightning, and you have massive forces of destruction. Can we afford to let our knowledge become so widespread that any one of us could wield all four powers at once? If such a Mage turned to evil and destruction, they would be invincible – and for any one person to wield so much power would be a deadly temptation. We dare not take the risk.'

Aizaiel's words gave Cyran cause to ponder. For many years now, he had kept a secret of his own from his fellow Magefolk leaders. Should he finally tell them? After all this time? The fact that he had a Wizard who possessed the powers of all four elements might be just what was needed to persuade the waverers that magical knowledge could and should be shared. He had kept silent for all these years to protect Iriana. She had problems enough in her life without having to grow up under close study. But now things were different. He smiled to himself. The girl could handle the scrutiny of the others. He'd lay wagers on it.

Then, for an instant, Cyran thought of his son. He would have something – quite a few things, in fact – to say about this. But the two of them had grown up together, and Avithan had always been more protective of the girl than she had ever wanted or needed. Besides, right now, the Archwizard didn't feel that he owed his devious, recalcitrant son a thing. Iriana was a grown woman now, who knew her own mind, and Avithan would have to respect that. *And I should too*, Cyran realised. *I ought to speak with her before I make her abilities common knowledge; ask her if she minds, or at least warn her that the time is fast approaching when I must destroy her privacy. She may be just the person to persuade the other Mages that someone holding all four powers isn't necessarily a monster.*

Or do they know otherwise? For the first time, he wondered whether his young Wizard really was unique. Could it be that the others had Mages of their own who had mastery of all four elements of magic? Maybe everyone at this meeting was guarding a similar secret. Maybe the Magefolk were evolving, in some mysterious way, to meet the demands of this future catastrophe. Without exposing Iriana, however, there was no way of finding out. The way things were going, he knew he would soon be compelled to speak out, but ... *Next time*, he thought. *I'll tell them next time, for sure.*

In the meantime, however, nothing had really been accomplished. The Archwizard sighed, suddenly feeling very weary. 'We appear to have reached an impasse,' he said. 'If no one has anything more to add, we may as well adjourn for today.'

'Wait.' It was the calm voice of Kahuna. 'Perhaps there is a way out of this impasse in which we find ourselves.'

'Well I, for one, can't see it,' said Pandion bluntly. 'If you have any bright ideas, I suggest you get to the point. I have other demands on my time. I can't sit here all day.'

'And I will, if you could refrain from interrupting.' It was rare for the tranquil Leviathan to betray even a hint of irritation in his voice, Cyran thought, but the strains of this meeting were beginning to tell on them all.

'Please listen, all of you,' Kahuna said. 'Today we have failed to reach agreement in two vital areas: the exchange of knowledge and the creation of master artefacts. Might we not, then, compromise? If Cyran will consent to the artefacts being made, and Aizaiel to cooperating in the sharing of our magical lore, then I will agree to put aside my concerns and participate in both ventures. Despite the considerable risks, this seems to me to be the only way forward. Otherwise we may damn ourselves and all the Magefolk through our sheer inertia.'

Aizaiel was the first to reply. 'This sounds like a fair compromise to me, and I applaud the wisdom of our friend the Speaker of the Leviathan. Very well. I will agree if the others will.'

Though Cyran still had grave misgivings about the creation of such powerful magical artefacts, he realised that if he ever wanted to realise his dream of preserving knowledge, this was the only way forward. He took a deep breath, knowing that the very shape of the future would hang upon his next words. 'Kahuna is wise indeed,' he said. 'I too will put aside my doubts and agree.'

Pandion shrugged. 'I still think it's a mistake to give away our secrets, but if it means we gain a way to defend ourselves, then I suspect it will prove the lesser of two evils. I also will agree to the Speaker's suggestion.'

'Then for good or ill, we are decided,' Kahuna said, 'Now we are weary, and have talked enough for one day. I suggest we meet again tomorrow, to start working out all the particulars, for I fear we will find it is one thing to agree that the artefacts should be made, but it will be quite another matter to actually create them.'

15
~

A FAMILY AFFAIR

Iriana caught her first sight of the frontier town of Nexis through the eyes of a mighty mountain eagle. The magnificent bird of prey she had named Boreas long ago had started out as a gift from the Forest Lord to Cyran, in the days when relations between Eliorand and Tyrineld had been less strained. Little more than a fledgling, the young bird had officially been lodged in the menagerie at the Academy, only to be appropriated somewhat unofficially by Iriana, who had trained him, gradually and patiently, to be her watcher from above. In bringing him with her on a journey that would take him so close to the mountains of his birth, the young wizard knew she was taking a risk, but she hoped he was sufficiently imprinted on her that their bond would be enough to counteract the lure of his own kind. Now, through his keen eyes, her vision could pierce even the thin film of mist that clung low to the ground, and she could see four tiny horses cresting the ridge below him: three with riders – Avithan, Esmon and herself – and the fourth a packhorse carrying an assortment of baggage, including the basket that contained Iriana's owl Seyka, who helped provide night vision for her, and who slept as they travelled through the day.

Though the sun was obscured by grey clouds that were producing a fine drizzle, an hour of daylight remained as Iriana and her companions crested the last windswept ridge of the rolling green downs, and caught their first sight of the town. Iriana's view through the eyes of the eagle was better than that of the others. Seen from above, this northern outpost of the Wizardly civilisation was an unimpressive sprawl of primitive wooden buildings, centred on an island in the midst of a broad river that flowed through the valley, and spreading out along the banks and up the slopes on either side. According to Esmon, the buildings on the island now belonged to the northern branches of the Luens, providing housing as well as buildings set aside for teaching, study and experimentation. They seemed to have been erected with more thought and care than the remainder of the town, which was being constructed more with a view to speed, utility and expedience than any consideration of either beauty or permanence.

As the travellers rode down the last slope and into the outskirts of the town, Iriana shifted her vision from the lofty perspective of the eagle, changing to the eyes of the cat Melik, who was perched on the saddle in front of her. With a shrill whistle, reinforced by a mental summons, she called Boreas down from the skies. Esmon had warned her that one of the main sources of income round here was sheep, and she didn't want anyone shooting the great bird out of the skies because of the threat he undoubtedly posed to the half-grown lambs that dotted the hillsides. The eagle took his accustomed perch on top of the baggage on the patient packhorse – though as she dropped back to fasten the jesses, Iriana shuddered at the memory of the trouble she'd had teaching Boreas to ride there, and training the horse to accept the bird.

At close quarters, the differences between this raw, young northern settlement and stately Tyrineld were even more numerous and marked. In the ancient city of the Wizards, life proceeded on its orderly course, calmly and unhurriedly, with little changing from day to day. Here in Nexis, everything seemed to be in a constant state of flux as people worked hard to establish a new town in the wilderness.

Around the perimeter of the settlement, a thicket of tents had sprung up. 'Those are to house the folk who are still building, and the traders who are earning their stake to settle here,' Esmon pointed out. When Iriana looked more closely, she realised that the tents were a community of their own. Many folk were trading from the flimsy shelters, and in addition to merchants, she saw grog-shops, gambling dens and bawdy houses.

New buildings, in various stages of construction, were going up wherever there was a space, particularly around the edges of the settlement as it spread out into the countryside. Massive tree trunks, the branches of which must have been lopped off at the site where the trees had been felled, had each been chained down to two pairs of great wooden wheels, and were being drawn by teams of horses along the well-travelled track that led across the moors between Nexis and the edge of the forest. Their destination was a timber yard: a generously sized stockade that boasted a large, barnlike building and a collection of smaller sheds. Here the trees were stripped of their bark, planed smooth and sawn into the struts, planks, logs and shingles that would be used in the many structures that were currently in various stages of completion around the town by the teams of human slaves that swarmed all over the crude, skeletal frameworks of homes, stores and workshops.

As they rode along the rudimentary street that led down to the river, Iriana shivered in the cold wind that gusted down from moor and mountain, and felt the prickle of the moisture-laden air against her face as she pulled up her hood against the grey, misting drizzle. In this place, it was impossible to believe that it could be summer. 'If it's like this now, what is it like in winter?' she asked Esmon.

The Warrior Wizard made a wry face. 'Believe me,' he said, 'you don't want to know.'

Iriana was finding Nexis something of a disappointment. She missed the benign breezes of home; the cleanliness and order; the beautiful, ancient buildings and the mingled fragrances of ocean, blossom and herb with which she had grown up in her own temperate city. In Nexis, the predominant smell was woodsmoke, mingled with tar, new timber, the mixed aromas of supper cooking in the houses that she passed, animal dung and the damp, fresh odours of river, mist and rain. The inhabitants of the place appeared rude and uncouth to her: it hardly seemed possible that these rough-hewn people could be of the same race as the cultured inhabitants of Tyrineld.

As Iriana and her companions entered town, all sounds faltered for a moment as a wall of curious and sometimes hostile eyes stared at Iriana's animal companions, and the winged mask that Esmon still wore openly on his face. Over and over again, Iriana had to tell herself sternly that they weren't staring at her; that they couldn't know, just from looking at her, that she was blind. But no matter how much she tried to reassure herself, it was still unnerving, and sometimes even frightening, to be the focus of so many eyes. Once they had passed, the clamour broke out again behind them, made all the louder by the buzz of gossiping voices.

It seemed to Iriana that no one in this place could do *anything* quietly. She found herself actually flinching from the ear-bruising din: the rasp of saws; the rhythmic tapping of hammers; the scrape of planes smoothing wood; the loud clunks and thuds as the great baulks of timber were raised into position by levitation spells and the sturdy logs were dropped into place to form walls. Workmen bawled orders and curses; cartwheels rumbled; harness jingled and hooves clopped on the hard-packed surface of the road. People shouted greetings, instructions and imprecations at the tops of their voices, and shopkeepers stood calling out their wares in the doorways of their shops or from their roughly built stalls, which were little more than a wooden table with a canvas awning stretched above on a rickety frame.

Melik's ears flattened and he growled softly to himself as dogs ran about everywhere, barking loudly and adding their own contribution to the unearthly racket, with the pigs, chickens and other livestock doing their best to compete. Children yelled and shrieked as they raced around, getting under the feet of builders and risking the wheels of the carts with such reckless disregard for danger that they brought Iriana's heart into her mouth again and again. In a stone-built forge near the river, a sweating blacksmith was fabricating tools with the ear-splitting clangour of metal being hammered, followed by a long, searing hiss as its glowing heat was quenched in water.

As Iriana observed the Nexians, she suddenly felt very far from home. The people here were not just noisier than those in Tyrineld. She could sense something more: there was a rough-and-ready exuberance among the bustling inhabitants of the young settlement. Wizard and mortal alike went about with quick, purposeful strides, as if there were too many tasks to fit into their day. There was no sign of the brightly coloured, flowing robes worn by the Wizards of the great southern city. Here folk wore sturdy, utilitarian garb of leather and wool that allowed for quick and easy movement, as well as providing warmth and protection from the cold, damp northern climate. Even most of the women were clad in jerkins, shirts and trousers, just as Iriana and her companions, on Esmon's advice, had clothed themselves for their journey.

As far as the Wizard was concerned, there was one good thing about the place – the animals. Ducks and geese, magically marked with the colours and symbols of each owner, fished and swam in a rainbow flock at the river's edge, guarded by a barefoot little girl armed with a long stick, while three smudge-faced, ragamuffin boys, aided by a pair of rangy dogs, kept watch over a straggling flock of goats on the hillside above the town. In Tyrineld, no one would think of keeping farm animals in the city: butter, cheese, meat and eggs, as well as wool and hides, all came from farms beyond the city's bounds. Here, there seemed to be pigs and chickens in every back yard – and even, to her astonishment, the occasional cow. People kept their horses right beside their houses in rickety lean-to stables. Iriana approved of that. How often had she wished she could keep Dailika closer, instead of being forced to house her in the stables on the outskirts of Tyrineld?

Esmon led them down to the ford on the southern bank, but instead of wading their horses across the river to the island they turned left, and went a little way downstream. The only inn in Nexis was here, beside a simple bridge of planks balanced on piers of stone; just wide and robust enough to be crossed on foot.

Avithan viewed the flimsy-looking structure with a frown. 'Why don't they build a better bridge?' he asked Esmon. 'One wide enough to take carts and horses, instead of making people get wet sloshing through the river?'

The Warrior shrugged. 'I expect they will, eventually. Right now, though, their priorities are shelter, security and the means to make a living. Once the town has been established a little longer, I dare say they might get around to a proper bridge. There's one that you can't see from here, however. It goes from the northern bank to the other side of the island. The river there is too deep to ford, but here on the south side, the water is so shallow and silted that it's easy to get across – for most of the year, at least.'

By that time, Iriana had lost track of the conversation. She was scarcely listening to her two companions. Now that she had seen Nexis for herself, she was even more puzzled as to why Challan had abandoned his home and family in Tyrineld to come to this rough, isolated place. Why would anyone want to exchange the luxuries of Tyrineld, with its beautiful aspects and temperate climate, for this cold, wet backwater at the far end of nowhere? Why would Challan abandon a kind soulmate and a loving family for *this*?

It only supported her conviction that his leaving had been her fault. Her real parents hadn't wanted an abnormal child, so why had she expected more from her adopted father? She knew this notion was souring her relations with others, but she couldn't help it. For Iriana, to love someone held the very real risk of driving them away, and she would not chance that hurt again. As she grew up, she had learned to build barriers to hide her true feelings, and had always been careful to keep a slight but perceptible distance between herself and even her closest friends. It was safer to be close to her animals. At least she could be sure that their love was unconditional, and they didn't give a damn whether her eyes worked or not.

For years, she had tried not to think of the foster-father who had abandoned her, but now that she had come to Nexis, she could afford that luxury no longer. Challan was here, and though she was dreading the meeting, she could not avoid it. She didn't plan to seek him out because of love. All her regard and affection for him had perished a long time ago. But this might be the only chance to clear up some of the questions and doubts that had tormented her family for so many years, and she was determined not to miss the opportunity.

The inn was so new that Iriana could still smell the freshly cut timber with which it was built. A few extra coins from Esmon had ensured the innkeeper's cooperation in the matter of her bringing her animals into her room with her, though when he saw Boreas, his eyes grew so wide that Iriana was surprised they didn't fall out.

Iriana's chamber was fairly clean and very basic, containing only a bed made up with hairy and grey woollen blankets, a rickety wooden washstand with a pewter jug and bowl, a roughly built table and chair and wooden shutters to cover the windows. A row of nails was driven into the wall for hanging up clothing and equipment. She fed Melik and released Seyka from her carrying basket before feeding both birds of prey. As they travelled, it had already become her self-imposed task to tend to the horses, but for one night, it made a pleasant change to have someone else feed and groom them. Instead she washed and dug some clean clothes out of her pack, and when Esmon came to call her downstairs to eat, she was more than ready – she was ravenous.

The food was plain but solid, and there was plenty of it. Iriana had her first taste of moose meat – strong, rich and gamey – in a stew with onions and beans. It was good, she decided, once she got used to it. As she ate, she decided that this would be as good a time as any to tell her companions about her plans. With a hand on his arm, Esmon stopped Avithan from exploding into speech when she announced that she planned to visit her foster-father that evening, and looked at her with a flicker of concern darkening his eyes. 'Does Zybina know you're planning this?'

'Yes. We talked about it.' Iriana was glad, now, that they had. 'She's uneasy about the idea, but she understands that I have to try.'

Esmon nodded. 'Well, it's not my business. I barely knew Challan when he lived in Tyrineld.' She could sense his sympathy as he leant towards her. 'Iriana, sometimes people just change. It's like avalanches in the mountains. Sometimes any number of seemingly insignificant things, barely noticeable at the time, will build and build until—' He made an abrupt sweeping gesture. 'And like a real avalanche, the results can be very hard on the innocent bystanders in its path. Of course—' He took another mouthful of stew, chewed and swallowed. 'Of course, other avalanches are triggered by a single, major event: a falling rock, maybe, or a loud noise. However they start, it makes no difference to the people in their path. You still get the loss, the damage, the pain.' He looked at her very directly. 'After all this time, does it really matter how the avalanche got started?'

Iriana was impressed by his words and the understanding behind them. They invited serious thought, and she remained silent, keeping

Melik's eyes fixed on her plate, while she considered. This would be an easy way out for her, she realised. Was Zybina right when she said that no good would come from digging up the past? Yet ... All those years of wondering, of not knowing, of blaming herself. And what about Yinze, the brother who was as much a part of her as if they had come from the same womb? How could she not make the most of her chance to spare him the pain of this meeting?

And I'm fooling myself. I know that whether I do this or not, Yinze will come anyway. All these years he has just been waiting for the time to be right – and so have I.

Iriana turned back towards Esmon, and trained Melik's gaze on his face. 'I have to do this. Zybina warned me that whatever I hear from Challan will make me unhappy, and I suspect she's probably right. But I have to know. Only then can I put him in the past, where he belongs.'

Esmon nodded. 'I understand, and in your position I'd feel exactly the same.'

Throughout the conversation, Avithan had been fidgeting by her side, plainly bursting to have his say, but held to silence by Esmon's hand. At last, however, he exploded. 'Are you insane, Esmon? You can't seriously be allowing her to do this.'

'*Allowing?*'

Iriana turned on him furiously, but Esmon overrode her. 'Don't be an ass, Avithan,' he said firmly. 'It was never a question of allowing her or not. Iriana is an adult, capable of making her own decisions and dealing with the consequences. I only wanted to be sure that she had thought this all the way through – it's a serious matter – and I am convinced that she has. I know you're in the habit of protecting her, and I can understand why you want to, but there are times when it's simply not appropriate. This is Iriana's private family business, and it's none of your affair, or mine. Stay out. I mean it.'

Avithan scowled thunderously. 'My father trusted me to take care of her. If he knew—'

Esmon's words had given Iriana a chance to get her own temper under control. 'You think he doesn't?' she said coolly. 'I told you I discussed this with Zybina, and *she* tells Sharalind everything. But as Esmon said, this is private family business, and we shouldn't lose our sense of proportion. I am going to visit the foster-father who abandoned me. I want answers. I *need* them. Then I'll put it behind me, and get on with my life.'

'If you're lucky,' Avithan muttered, but he said no more.

'I'll talk to the innkeeper and do some asking around for you,' Esmon said. 'This is still a small town. Someone will know where Challan lives.'

'Thank you, Esmon,' Iriana said. 'For everything.'

By the time the Warrior had found out what they wanted to know, darkness had fallen outside, and Iriana knew that she could put off her meeting with Challan no longer, though now that the time had come to confront him, nervous tension was gripping her stomach like a clenched fist. Seyka glided above her like a silent white ghost, and Melik curled around her shoulders like a warm fur collar. Both of them were providing sight for her in the dimly lit streets, so that she had no problem making her way to Challan's house. Nexis was not a large place, and the innkeeper's directions had been very clear, so she found the right street with no trouble at all. It was on the island, where the buildings were more densely packed together, and the inhabitants thronged the boarded, lamplit walkways.

Iriana walked faster than she would normally have done on a dark night in a strange town. Firstly, because she was anxious to get the dreaded meeting over and done with, and secondly, she was walking off her annoyance at Avithan and Esmon, who had insisted on accompanying her. Fighting, as always, for her independence, she had wasted a good half-hour convincing Avithan that she would be perfectly all right on her own, only to be overruled by Esmon, who had insisted that all three of them should go.

At least the Warrior's bluntness had taken some of the sting out of the decision. 'Look,' he had said, 'this has nothing to do with your blindness, Iriana. I know that as long as you have your animals, you can manage very well on your own. But this isn't Tyrineld. It's a frontier town on the edge of civilisation, and it's inhabited by all sorts of rough, unsavoury types. These aren't the sort of Wizards we know at home. If they were, they probably wouldn't be here. In the main, these folk are misfits and adventurers, or worse, and most of them left our society and its rules behind with good reason. Even if you had your sight, a lovely young girl like you wouldn't be safe alone in the streets after dark. In fact,' the Warrior had added, 'I wouldn't be too happy about any of us going out alone tonight. Not even me, and I know how to handle myself in a fight.'

There was a tavern of sorts at the end of Challan's street, a rough structure that was little more than an open-fronted shed with lanterns hanging from the beams, a counter for serving ale and several tables and benches that had been hastily knocked together from scrap timber. 'We'll wait here until you're done,' Esmon said. 'This meeting with your foster-father is just between the two of you, and you certainly won't want Avithan and me tagging along.'

'Thanks,' Iriana said, feeling infinitely relieved that Esmon understood. 'I probably won't be too long.'

The Warrior grinned at her. 'You take as long as you need. Don't hurry yourself on our account. Avithan and I will amuse ourselves here with a drink or two, until you come back.'

Alone at last, Iriana made her way down the street towards Challan's house. When she'd found the right door, she held out her left hand, which was clad in the tough leather gauntlet that she always used for working with her raptors. At her whistle, Seyka floated down through the smoky night air and settled on her fist. For a moment, Iriana struggled with the temptation to turn around and return to her companions. When that door was opened, what would she find? 'Iriana, pull yourself together,' she muttered. 'You haven't come this far just to turn around and slink away again.' She took a deep breath and steadied herself. She wasn't a child any more. Challan owed her some answers, and by all Creation, she meant to get them. Trying to ignore the anxious churning in her stomach, she took a deep breath and knocked on Challan's door with her free hand, wondering what sort of reception would await her inside.

Iriana had been thinking about this meeting throughout the journey, and playing out all sorts of different scenarios in her imagination. From the moment the door opened, however, nothing was the way she had imagined it might be. Instead of Challan answering the door, Iriana came face to face with a tall, dark-eyed human woman whose abundant brown hair was streaked with grey and whose weathered face betrayed the remnants of what had once been a delicate prettiness. Standing there in the lamplight, she looked vaguely familiar, and the Wizard had an uneasy feeling that she knew her from somewhere – yet how could that be possible? She eyed Iriana with a chilly look. 'Yes?' she demanded. 'What do you want?'

Iriana was quite taken aback by her attitude. There was none of the usual respect or subservience that she had always seen in human slaves. What bare-faced effrontery! Why, this woman seemed to think that she was the equal of a Wizard. 'Is your master in?' she asked coldly.

'My *master*?' The woman laughed harshly. 'That'll be the day.' Looking back over her shoulder into the house, she shouted, 'Challan? There's some girl at the door wanting to know if my master's in.' She turned back to Iriana. 'Come in if you want, but you'll have to leave those filthy animals outside.'

'How dare you speak to me like that, human!' Never in her life had Iriana struck someone, but this was too much. Just as she raised her hand to slap this temeritous slave, however, Challan appeared in the narrow hallway. As he took in the tableau on his doorstep, he suddenly started, stared at her, and his jaw fell open. 'Iriana? Little Iriana? Is it really you? I scarcely recognised you.'

He looked different, and it surprised her. Wizards could look any age they wanted, and somehow, she had expected him to be as she remembered him: his angular face clean-shaven and his hair long and dark. Instead, he had allowed his face to age, and his hair, now silver, was clipped short to match his neatly trimmed beard. Only his hazel eyes were the same, and even in them, his wary, guarded expression as he failed to quite meet her gaze was something she had never known before.

Challan held out his arms as if to embrace her, but she ignored them. Melik, sensing her mood, hissed at him from her shoulder. Iriana took a deep, steadying breath. 'I would like to speak with you, if you don't mind,' she said. 'In private.' This last was directed very pointedly at the slave-woman, who was standing close to one side, listening to everything that was being said.

For a moment an expression of deep sadness crossed Challan's face. 'Ah. I see. Well, come in, Iriana, and be welcome.'

'Thank you.' Lifting her chin, Iriana swept past the human, whose scowl was thunderous. 'I told her she couldn't bring those dirty animals in here,' she snapped at Challan. 'Making a mess of my nice, clean house.'

'They won't make any mess, Lannala,' Challan said mildly, and at the mention of the name, Iriana remembered where she had seen the woman before. *Why*, she thought, *when our family was still together in Tyrineld, this Lannala used to be a servant in our house. What in the world is she doing here?*

What in the world was that wretched girl doing here? Lannala could only look helplessly at the two retreating backs as Challan and Iriana turned away from her and moved down the passageway into his study. When she tried to follow them, she found the door shut firmly against her. It was just like the old days in Tyrineld, she thought bitterly. The Wizards shutting out the lowly mortal slave.

A sensation like the cold, empty void of a winter's night passed through her, settling in her belly and her bones. She and Challan had been here for so many years: they had been one of the first pairs of settlers in this lovely, sheltered valley, and had watched the community grow from one or two lonely cabins to the busy, thriving town it was today. Stunned, resentful, she wandered back into the kitchen where the scrubbed vegetables lay on the table ready for a stew, and began to chop savagely at an onion. No matter what was at stake, she told herself, she had too much self-respect to listen at the door. Or maybe she was just afraid of what she might hear.

When her eyes began to sting and blur, she knew it wasn't just the onions. She'd thought they were safe here. She'd thought that time had erased the guilt that Challan felt at leaving Zybina and his children. The long, distant silences that Challan often fell into after they had left Tyrineld, which used to make her so unhappy and insecure because she knew he was missing his Wizardborn family, had tailed away long ago, until at last she had relaxed, felt less inferior, less dependent. She'd found her confidence, and truly believed she'd made a life for herself here as a partner and equal, not a slave. And if he had diminished a little since leaving Tyrineld, she had blossomed. So it all balanced out, and they'd had many happy years together.

She had never thought it would change. She'd been wrong. She hadn't counted on opening the door and finding Challan's past on the doorstep. Nor had she expected those old feelings of fear, inferiority and insecurity to come flooding back over her. The feelings of a slave. She knew that those uncomfortable emotions, not to mention jealousy and resentment, had made her shrewish and bad-tempered (and rude and ungracious to a visitor) but she couldn't help it. How else was she supposed to react to such a deadly threat to her happiness?

Though he'd tried to hide it, she'd seen the haunted look of guilt on Challan's face; heard the wistful emotion in his voice as he addressed his foster-daughter. Had Iriana come to ask him to return? Even though she didn't think he would leave his Nexian family, she knew that the girl's visit would stir up his emotions: feelings of regret, remorse, the ache of an uneasy conscience, the wondering what it would have been like if only he had stayed. If only she, Lannala, had not fallen pregnant ...

No matter what came of Iriana's sudden appearance, one thing was certain. Tonight would change everything.

Lannala's fingers tightened around the hilt of the knife. Damn it, she wouldn't give up without a fight – and not just for herself, or the love she bore Challan. She had her daughter to think about. Chiannala was loved by both of them, and indulged by her father – sometimes far too much for her own good, Lannala thought. It was as though Challan was some-how trying to compensate for abandoning Yinze and Iriana in Tyrineld. Challan had always given his new daughter anything she wanted, except for one thing. To Lannala's mind, the most important thing of all. Though she showed every sign of having inherited her father's powers, Challan refused to let Chiannala go to Tyrineld, and be properly trained in the arts of Wizardry.

New resentment against Iriana had her clenching her teeth. Why should Challan deprive his true – and plainly talented – daughter, when a blind nobody from who-knew-where had been accepted, taught, loved by the Wizards? Was he ashamed to face his peers in Tyrineld and recognise the girl he had fathered? Well, Lannala would see about that. No matter what it cost her, she would make sure that Challan did the right thing by Chiannala.

Just at that moment, the sound of voices raised in vicious anger, one of them belonging to her daughter, came down the passageway from Challan's study, making her jump. Her hand slipped and the sharp knife nicked her finger. Damn! Ignoring the welling blood, she hurried to the door.

Challan ushered Iriana into the narrow passageway, unadorned but for a shelf that held the lamp. There were doors to the right and left, and another open doorway at the end of the passage, through which she could see a kitchen with signs of a meal in preparation on the table. Opening the door on the left, Challan showed her into a cosy study, with books overflowing the shelves and piled on the floor and table, and a fire glowing in the grate. He led her to one of the comfortable chairs by the hearth, and Iriana settled herself, letting the owl perch on the back of the seat and lifting Melik down from her shoulder onto her lap. Challan did not sit, but paced nervously back and forth in front of the fire.

There was a long moment of silence, broken at last by Challan. 'My dear, you don't know how good it is to see you again.'

'Really. If you had wanted to see me that much, you knew where I was,' Iriana replied flatly.

Her words brought him to a standstill, as though she had dealt him a physical blow. 'Iriana, I cannot tell you how sorry I am about leaving; about everything. Please, try to understand—'

'Understand *what*?' Iriana's voice was like a whetted blade. 'You went off and left us without a word of warning. You didn't even have the decency to tell Zybina to her face that you were going, you just left her a cowardly note. What I understand, Challan, is lying awake all those long nights, listening to the woman I regard as my mother sobbing in the room next door. What I understand is that poor Yinze was forced to grow up without a father.' Suddenly she could bear to live in ignorance no longer. She *had* to know the truth, even if it destroyed her. 'Was it me?' she demanded. 'Was it my fault? I have to know. Did you leave them because of me?'

He stared at her. Through Melik's eyes, she could see the emotions crossing his face, one after the other: surprise, dismay and guilt. 'By all Creation, Iriana, is that what you believed?'

'Well, why else would you go?' Iriana demanded harshly. 'What other reason could there have been? I drove my own parents away as soon as I was born, because they didn't want a child who wasn't normal, and later I did the same with you. Only this time, it wasn't just me who suffered.' She was dimly aware, now, that tears were spilling down her cheeks. 'Zybina and Yinze's lives were ruined, too.'

Challan dropped to his knees beside her and gripped both of her hands. 'Listen to me,' he said. 'It wasn't your fault, I swear to you. It was mine; all mine. You see …' He hesitated, as if groping for the words, then plunged on. 'I fell in love with someone. Hopelessly, completely in love. I was besotted, spellbound. Forgive me, Iriana, but I had to choose her. She needed me far more than Zybina ever did. And things being as they were, with her expecting my child, we couldn't possibly stay in Tyrineld, so—'

But Iriana was no longer listening. All those years of pain and guilt – and for nothing. A colossal anger boiled up within her. 'Who?' she growled. 'Is she here now, this woman who was more important than your family?'

Prudently, Challan got to his feet again and stepped back from her. 'You've already met her,' he said. 'It's Lannala.'

The shock was like lightning jolting through her. '*What?*' she shouted, scooping Melik into her arms and leaping to her feet in turn. 'That housemaid? That *human*? You abandoned your family for a slave?'

'Hush! She'll hear you.'

'I don't give a damn if she hears me,' Iriana shouted. 'How could you? How could you do this to Zybina? To all of us? Rutting with a human – it's perverted and obscene!' She was aghast at such betrayal. All this time she had suffered. All this time she had lived in torture, blaming herself for destroying the family that had given her a home. And all this time the man she had looked up to as a father had been pleasuring himself with a mortal slave. Such things were done, of course, she was not such an innocent as to deny that, but never so openly as to actually set up home with one. And as for casting aside a loving family to be with the creature – why, such a thing was unheard of.

Challan sighed. 'I'm sorry you feel this way, Iriana, and I'm very sorry for all the hurt I've caused you. But your reaction only goes to prove that I was right to come here, where folk are more inclined to live and let live. My love for Lannala would never have been accepted in Tyrineld, and I would only have brought misery and shame on Zybina and you two children, not to mention Lannala and Chiannala.'

'Chiannala? Who in Perdition is *she*? Are you rutting with *two* of them now?'

Challan's eyes flashed angrily. 'Do not use that word again. For the love I bear you and the debt I owe you I've been patient, Iriana; but this is my family too, and I will *not* have you come marching in here and speaking of them in such offensive terms, as if they were mere animals—'

The door crashed open, cutting off his words. A thin-faced girl with flashing dark eyes and abundant brown hair stood there. Through Melik's feline vision, which was specifically designed to pick up small, abrupt movements, Iriana could see that she was actually shaking with anger. 'I can't stand to listen to this another moment,' she snapped. 'Just who in Perdition do you think you are? What right have you to come here, to our home, and speak of us like this? No wonder your parents didn't want you. No wonder my father couldn't stand to live with you! Why don't you go back to your stinking city, where you belong?'

Before Iriana could form a reply, Challan intervened. 'Iriana, I want you to meet Chiannala – my daughter.'

'His *real* daughter,' Chiannala said spitefully. 'His own flesh and blood, not some blind foundling freak with no claim on him at all.'

'That's enough, Chiannala,' Challan said sharply. 'It's not true – any more than the things Iriana was saying about you and your mother are true.'

But matters had already gone beyond his control. Iriana felt as though she had been stabbed through the heart. Somehow this ferret-faced bitch had managed to strike at the root of her deepest childhood insecurities. The only thing she could do was lash out in return. 'I may have been a foundling, but at least I'm not some half-blooded obscenity that should have been destroyed at birth,' she spat. Turning back to Challan, she added: 'The half-breed was right about one thing, though. You are no longer my father, and you never will be again.' With that, she made for the door. Chiannala, her face livid, stood there as if to bar her way, but Seyka flew at her face, talons extended, and she leapt aside with a curse, leaving Iriana free to go. Thrusting the door violently open, she almost ran into the accursed slave woman who had caused all the trouble. She had clearly been eavesdropping. Hardly surprising from one of *her* kind. Fortunately, Iriana only cared about getting out of that place, and away from the lot of them. It was just as well. She was so hurt and enraged that there was no telling what she might have done.

It was also just as well that she had the vision of the cat and the owl to depend on as she made her way back up the street, for even if she'd been able to see, her own eyes were too awash with tears to be of any use to her. When she reached the open-fronted booth that served as a tavern, Avithan and Esmon leapt up in alarm at the sight of her, and for once, when Avithan put his arms around her and held her tightly, she did not object, but leaned against his shoulder, grateful for the comfort and support of his arms around her. When they asked her what was wrong, however, she stiffened in his arms and shook her head. 'I don't want to talk about it,' she said in a cold, tight voice. 'Not now. Not ever.'

16

TRANSFORMATION

To his dismay, Challan realised that Lannala wanted very much to talk about what had happened – and at great length. He heard her slam the door that Iriana had left open, with a muttered, 'Good riddance.' Then she marched into his study and proceeded to give him her unvarnished opinion of his foster-daughter, with her daughter providing a harsh and bitter chorus. After a few minutes, Challan decided that he had allowed her to vent enough of her spleen. 'Lannala, is this going anywhere?'

It upset him to hear his previous family being impugned in such graphic terms. It was not that he hadn't loved them dearly. It was just that he had fallen so desperately in love with Lannala who, unlike the capable Zybina, had aroused such intense feelings of protectiveness within him that he couldn't help but choose her. It had been a long time before he had understood just how effective her clinging helplessness had been, as a means of attracting him – and it had been far longer than that before he'd realised, when their life in open-minded, who-gives-a-damn Nexis gave her so much more independence and freedom, that her vulnerability had only been an effect of her lowly status as a slave. She had changed, then; become his partner, equal, strong. It had taken some getting used to, but as the years had passed, he'd come to the decision that he liked this new Lannala better.

Until tonight. Now, seeing her face all twisted with rage, he knew a brief flash of longing for the old days, when she had been the malleable and timid slave girl.

'It is as far as I'm concerned,' she snapped. 'I heard what that little cow said about our daughter.'

Challan sighed. 'What Iriana said was reprehensible, it's true, but you obviously missed what Chiannala said about *her*. There was blame on both sides, and—'

'How *dare* you stand there and defend some foundling Wizard-whelp against your own flesh and blood! I'm not going to stand for it. Our Chiannala is every bit as good as some jumped-up little nobody whose parents didn't even want her.'

She took a deep breath. 'You really want to know where this is going? I'll tell you. I want you to stop putting me off. I want you to take Chiannala to Tyrineld, as I keep asking, and get her into the Academy to be trained as a Wizard. You know very well that she inherited your powers. Well, I want her to fulfil her heritage, then snotty bitches like the one who was here tonight won't be able to look down their noses at her.'

'Yes, take me, please.' Chiannala added her support. 'You know I have ability. Let me prove myself! If I was trained, I'd be every bit as good as *her*. And I'll probably be better, and that will knock the smugness out of the cow. Please, Father, please.'

Challan's heart sank. Not this again. It was unfortunate that Chiannala appeared to have inherited his powers in full. When she was a child he had taught and helped her, for power untutored and uncontrolled was a dangerous thing, but for some time now, he'd been wondering if he'd done the right thing. Now, of course, she was burning to go to Tyrineld for the intense, high-level training that only the Academy could give her, and her own ambition had only been exceeded by that of her mother. Time after time, he had fobbed them off with a variety of vague excuses, because he hadn't wanted to hurt Chiannala. But if she and her mother kept persisting like this, how much longer could he hide the truth from her? *I can't cope with this tonight – not after the shock of Iriana's visit*, Challan thought. *I brought Lannala here to Nexis to secure the freedom that she craved for herself and her daughter – why must they keep demanding more of me?*

He sighed. 'Chiannala, for the thousandth time, you can*not* be a student at the Academy. You—'

'Why not? Don't you think I'm good enough? Is that it?'

'I know very well that you're good enough to be a Wizard. More than good enough, but—'

'Then why won't you let her go?' It was Lannala again. 'It's not fair to keep her buried in this rough backwoods place.'

'It was good enough for *you* when you came here as a slave from Tyrineld,' Challan snapped, goaded and hurt by her ingratitude. 'You said you loved it here. That you'd never been happier.'

'It's good enough for me, but I want better for my daughter. There are greater things in store for her. She's not a human slave like I was. She has your blood, Wizard blood, in her veins.'

'She has your blood too.' There, at last he had said the words aloud. It had broken his heart to do so, but Challan knew that he had no alternative this time. Iriana's visit had brought matters to a head for all of them. 'Chiannala is a half-breed,' he went on, hating himself even as the words left his mouth. 'As such she will never be accepted by the Academy.'

Chiannala's face turned deathly white, but the glitter in her eyes was pure rage. 'Then make them accept me,' she snarled at Challan through gritted teeth. 'How do *they* know who my mother is? Tell them I'm truly one of the Magefolk, that my mother was a Wizard, but now she's dead.'

By the door, Lannala made a small, hurt sound that was halfway between a gasp and a sob, but Chiannala ignored her. 'Do it, Father. I know you can.'

Steeling himself against the pain, Challan shook his head. 'I could convince them, perhaps – but I won't.'

'*What?*'

'I'm sorry, Chiannala, but I've sacrificed everything for you and your mother. My home, my work, my friends. I abandoned my original family. Though I loved them dearly, I chose your mother over them when she became pregnant with you. I did it all for your future, so that you could grow up in a place where you wouldn't have to bear the stigma of a being treated as a slave. I love you both very much, and I would do almost anything to make you happy. But not this.'

'But—' Chiannala protested, but she had no chance to finish.

'Let me speak, Chiannala.' Challan overrode her words in a harsher voice than he had ever used towards her. 'All I have left of my former life is my self-respect. No matter what they think of my choice in Tyrineld, at least I acted with integrity, and I won't compromise that by going back now and lying to everyone. If I do, I'll lose the little that remains of the man I used to be. And I've hurt my other family enough – Zybina, and Yinze and Iriana – without shoving you under their noses by taking you to live in Tyrineld. I've already broken their hearts. I won't humiliate them besides. I'm sorry, but that is my final word. I promise I will teach you all I know right here, and I'll try to find other Wizards who would be prepared to train you too. But I cannot – I *will* not take you to Tyrineld.' Unknowing, he echoed Iriana's words to Avithan. 'I don't want to discuss this again. Not now. Not ever.'

A crushing weight of silence settled on the room. Then, without warning, Lannala blurted: 'I should have known it. No matter what you said, no matter what we did, we were never good enough for you, were we?

164

Well, if that's the way you want it, why don't you just go back to Tyrineld, and your precious family of stinking Wizards. *We* don't need you!'

'Lannala, I think you forget yourself.' Challan's eyes flashed with anger, but his voice remained quiet and controlled. 'You've lived here too long under my protection, enjoying privileges and liberties that, under normal circumstances, a mortal would never be granted. If I leave Nexis, they won't let you stay here as you are. You'll be sold to a new owner, and Chiannala with you, whether she has Wizard blood or not. Being the age she is, and with her looks, she'll probably be sold into one of the brothels. Is that what you want for her?'

Lannala turned as white as her daughter, but her pallor was pure fear. 'You wouldn't,' she whispered. 'You couldn't—'

'Don't you understand? It has nothing to do with what I want. If I leave here, your fate will be beyond my control. No matter how much I choose to elevate you, you're a mortal. As long as you dwell in the realm of the Wizards you're a slave and you always will be. And because of her human heritage, so will Chiannala.'

Chiannala stared at Challan in frozen disbelief. This couldn't really be her father saying these cruel, terrible things, could it? He had always loved her, spoiled her and, she now realised, shielded her from the reality of her situation. It was as though all the foundations of her life were crumbling beneath her. 'No!' she shrieked, unable to listen to any more, unable to take any further brutal truths. Clapping her hands over her ears, she turned to run from the room, but her mother tried to stop her in the doorway, catching at her arm as she passed. 'Leave me alone.' Chiannala struck out at Lannala with clenched fists, hitting out at her shoulders and face. 'This is all your fault. You and your accursed human blood, you've ruined my life. I hate you! I hate you both!'

'Chiannala, wait, wait!' She took no notice of her mother's anguished cries, but as she ran from the room, she heard her father's voice. 'Leave her alone. You've done enough damage for one night. See what you've brought us to, with your insane ambitions for the girl.'

'What *I've* brought us to?' Lannala shrieked. Fleeing the impending quarrel, Chiannala ran upstairs to her room, tears flooding her face. Locking the door, she flung herself down on her bed and struck the pillow with her fist. Downstairs, they were blaming each other as hard as they could, and judging from the raised voices, the argument was likely to continue for some considerable time. *She* blamed them both: her stupid, self-deluding mother for building up Chiannala's hopes all these years with her ridiculous expectations, and her cowardly, lying hypocrite of a father for letting her foster those hopes in vain. There was, however, someone she blamed even more than her parents: that arrogant bloody Wizard-bitch Iriana. She was responsible for the dreadful scenes that had taken place that night. For Chiannala's happy little family being torn apart by words that could never be unsaid. For the shattering of all her hopes and dreams.

'Curse you, Iriana,' Chiannala snarled. 'I'll hate you for this until the day I die. I swear I'll never rest until I've ruined you, and left your life in ashes and dust the way you've left mine tonight.'

To make matters worse, her anger was fuelled by guilt. She knew how much she had hurt her mother by trying to deny her. She hadn't meant it, not really. She loved Lannala. It was her mother's mortal blood that she detested, and tonight, the way she was feeling, it was impossible to separate the two. And as for her father's betrayal, it was much easier to be angry about that because anger kept away the unbearable hurt. After everything that had happened, all the terrible things that had been said, how could she ever face her parents? The way she felt right now, she never wanted to see them again.

Then don't.

The idea popped into her head as if it had been there all her life, just waiting for this crisis to occur. Angry, hurt and bitter as she was, it made complete sense to her. That was the answer. She would run away. Make a success of her life somewhere else. She would show her father that he had been wrong to dismiss her because of her blood, and make her mother proud of her.

It didn't take Chiannala long to pack. She was shedding her old life as a serpent sheds its outgrown skin, and she wanted to take no remnants of it with her. Enough clothes to get by, including her best gown – for like all girls her age, she was desperately concerned about her appearance. A comb and one or two other toilet articles. She parcelled her belongings into two blankets laid on top of one another, and tied the neck of the makeshift pack tightly with a long scarf, before putting on her boots and leather gloves, and her warmest cloak.

The cloak gave her an idea. Maybe she could buy herself a little extra time before her parents discovered that she was missing. Hurriedly, she pushed one of her pillows lengthways under her bedclothes, then bundled up the threadbare old winter cloak that she'd discarded last year and placed it above the pillow. There! With the covers pulled up high, it looked just as though she was snuggled under the bedclothes. Her parents would probably be too busy to take much notice tonight, and would only be too glad to have her out of the way.

Chiannala was about to leave, but as an afterthought, she took all of her jewellery: her little ring set with a garnet, which her father had bought her for her birthday, and a slender gold chain. When she got to Tyrineld, she should be able to sell them. She would need more money. She only had a small handful of copper coins to call her own, but it would be impossible to retrieve those meagre savings while her parents were fighting in her father's study, where his strongbox was kept. Then fate took a hand, or luck, perhaps. Suddenly, she heard the loud slam of the door into the street, followed by her father calling: 'Lannala, come back.' Then she heard the hollow sound of his footsteps running along the wooden floor of the passageway, and the slam of the street door again.

This was her chance! Without a backward glance, Chiannala darted from the pleasant little room that had been hers since her childhood. Across the landing was her parents' bedroom, and there in a drawer was her mother's scant hoard of jewellery. Chiannala hesitated, guilt churning in her stomach. Then she snatched up the lot and pocketed it without looking to see what she had. One day she would make it up to Lannala. When she had made a success of her life, she would replace these trinkets with far better stuff.

She hurtled headlong downstairs into the study, snatched the little iron strongbox from the cupboard, ran into the kitchen and swiped any food that could easily be carried, dropping everything, strongbox included, into the string-mesh bag that her mother used for carrying the shopping. She dropped flint and tinder into her pocket, stuck the sharpest knife into her belt – and was ready to go.

So far, so good. There were still no signs of anyone returning: her mother must be leading her father a merry dance through the town. Quickly Chiannala slipped out of the back door and found their sturdy brown horse in his little lean-to stable. She needed no lantern to see what she was doing. Along with her father's magical powers, she had inherited his Wizardly night vision, and she blessed it tonight. Though her heart was racing with panic lest her parents return and stop her, she still took the time to saddle him properly. It would be a long journey and she'd have to ride as fast as this fat and lazy creature would carry her, so there was no point setting off bareback. Tying bundle and net bag together with a bit of old rope that she found in the stable, she fastened them as tightly as she could behind the saddle, one hanging on either side. Then, pulling her hood up to hide her face, she mounted – awkwardly, because of the bulky bags – and rode the horse out of the stable, ducking low to miss the top of the doorway by inches. Out of the backyard and away: away from her childhood; away from her parents; away from her home.

And, best of all, away from that accursed taint of humanity for ever.

Chiannala galloped with reckless speed through the moonlit streets, praying that she wouldn't run into her parents, and dodging as best she could between the town's many nocturnal wanderers: gamblers, carousers and their predators – the street-hawkers, cutpurses, robbers and whores of both sexes. People leapt out of her way as she thundered past, and she heard a number of curses and cries of protest behind her; but to her relief no one came after her or tried to stop her. Nexians were great believers in minding their own business. She crossed the ford and pounded through the quieter streets on the outskirts of town. Soon she was passing through the new houses that were under construction on the very edge of the settlement, until at last the final half-completed buildings fell behind her, and she was away.

Once she had put Nexis behind her, things became far more difficult. A half-moon provided some light, but Chiannala was forced to slow down nonetheless. She might possess a Wizard's night vision, but her horse did not, and though the trail was well travelled, it was still rutted and rough in places. The last thing she needed right now was for her mount to fall, perhaps injuring one or both of them.

She had never been out alone at night before, and as her anger began to fade, her courage sank with it. The slopes and curves of the surrounding moorland, dark silhouettes against the moonlit sky, were vast and lonely. After the raucous, drunken din of nocturnal Nexis, it was almost shockingly still and quiet out here. The only sounds were the sigh of the night wind as it roamed the endless spaces of moor and dell; the inner rhythm of her heartbeat, slowing a little now that she had made her escape; the regular, soft thud of her horse's hooves and the huffing sound of its breath, loud against the whisper of her own quiet breathing. To a girl who had lived all her life in a bustling town like Nexis, the silence was unnerving and filled with threat. There should be no wild beasts on the moor tonight – they only came down from the mountains in the dead of winter – but what if there were robbers waiting to ambush unsuspecting travellers on the road? What if they leapt out, and attacked her?

At this point, Chiannala pulled herself together. 'Leapt out from where, you idiot?' she asked herself aloud. 'There isn't a tree or a bush within miles, and if they're hiding in a dell or behind a hill somewhere off the road, at least you'll see them coming if they decide to attack.' Firmly, she thrust the phantom robbers from her mind. If it happened, it happened, and there was no sense in worrying about it in the meantime. It was either this or go snivelling back home – which would never happen while she still had breath in her body.

Besides, there were far more real and immediate things for Chiannala to worry about. Pulling up her horse for a moment, she turned and looked back over her shoulder, peering into the darkness and listening as hard as she could for any sounds of pursuit. How long would it take for her parents to discover she had gone? They were so bound up in their own quarrel – would they even notice, until she didn't turn up for breakfast? Certainly, until they had discovered that the horse was missing, they would never for one moment imagine that she'd leave Nexis.

Yes, she should still have a little more time to get away.

It was just as well, at the speed she was going. After a while, however, the gentle pace began to lull her fears a little. Even though she still kept a vigilant watch all around her, and listened very carefully for any sounds of pursuit coming from behind, she finally found herself beginning to relax. Though she had been forced to run away from home, and though her former life was in ruins thanks to that miserable cow of a Wizard, Chiannala, much to her surprise, found herself almost enjoying this part of her adventure. Though it was summer, the nights were still cold this far north, but the sharp air on her face helped her to stay awake, and she could snuggle gratefully into her warm cloak and gloves. Everything smelled clean and fragrant after Nexis, with its permanent stink of garbage and worse, and the smoke from so many fires. The moonlit sky seemed to be sprinkled with far more stars than she could see when she looked at it from the lamplit town and, despite her earlier – and not *quite* vanquished – fears of robbers; despite the dreadful, hurtful scenes and revelations she had witnessed at home, she felt a quiet sense of peace settle over her.

She lost all track of time as she followed the moonlit trail across the endless stretches of moorland. After a while, monotony and weariness, together with the soothing rhythm of her horse's steps, lulled her into a half-doze, and she simply let herself be carried along, heading towards an unknown future, content to keep putting a growing distance between herself and all that she had known.

Chiannala awakened with a jerk, grabbing the pommel of the saddle to keep herself from falling. Somehow, without her knowing, the half-doze had deepened into sleep, and she had almost slipped right off the horse. She threw back her hood and took reviving gulps of pure, cold air. 'This won't do,' she scolded herself. 'What if robbers had come? What if the horse had shied at a shadow, or stumbled in a rut? You'd have been trying to walk all the way to Tyrineld, and they would have caught you for sure.'

She was just about to set off again when she noticed that the moon was on her left shoulder instead of her right. Chiannala blinked in confusion.

'What the—?' Then she realised what had happened. Making the most of her inattention, the tired horse had wheeled around and was heading back home to its stable, and it was the unexpected motion of the turn that had nearly spilled her from the saddle. 'Stupid creature,' she sighed. Or maybe not so stupid. Annoyed, she forced the reluctant beast to turn back the way it had been going, but its pace slowed, and it refused to go any faster, no matter how hard she urged it.

It was no good. The horse needed to rest and, if she were being truthful, she wasn't in much better condition herself after riding for about four hours. She would have to find a safe place to sleep for a while: preferably somewhere that would conceal her from any searchers who might come along the trail. She looked around, wondering how far she had come, and discovered to her surprise that while she had been oblivious to her surroundings, the horse had followed the road down a long hill into a deep, broad river valley. Down in this sheltered haven, away from the harsh conditions of the high moors, the landscape was very different. There were trees here: groves of ash and beech, with willow thickets along the banks of the river. More importantly, however, this was farmland: meadows dotted with cattle alongside carefully tilled fields of root crops, cabbages, beans and a few acres of ripening barley and oats. Wizards, with their powers rooted in Earth Magic, tended to make very good farmers if their inclination lay that way.

A track led off to Chiannala's right, and vanished behind a little copse. Hopefully, it would lead to the farm itself. Chiannala pulled up the horse and thought for a moment, her brows knotted in a frown, then turned the weary animal and swung off the main trail. The track, just wide enough for a cart, had sturdy, well-maintained fencing on either side, separating the fields from the road. Once past the copse, it curved down to her left, towards the river, and several hundred yards away Chiannala saw a cluster of buildings that was obviously the farm, with a big house for the farmer, byres and barns, henhouses and sheds, and quarters nearby for the human slaves. Now that the horse could smell a stable ahead, he perked up noticeably and picked up his pace, but Chiannala had no intention of going as far as the farm, where there would no doubt be dogs to sound the alarm and involve her in all sorts of complications. In the next field on her right there was an old stone barn that stood well back from the road, and Chiannala unlatched the gate and headed for this sanctuary.

The barn smelled pleasantly of hay and animals. The interior consisted of two separate areas: one a storage place for a clutter of farm implements, and the other divided by partitions into four stalls, two empty, and the other two housing a pretty, dappled, light-grey horse and a big brown mule. Above was a half-loft with a ladder, where hay and bags of fodder were stored.

Perfect. Chiannala put her animal into the vacant stall beside the other horse, and removed its gear and burdens. Scrambling up the ladder with the two heavy bags, she brought hay and corn from the farmer's plentiful supply down to her mount, who stuck his nose into the manger as though he had never seen food before. Having filled him a bucket of water from the stream, she climbed the ladder again, unwrapped her bundle and made a nest with her blankets in a pile of hay. Then, taking bread, cheese and an apple from the other bag, she fell to eating as hungrily as the animal had done.

As she ate, Chiannala thought about her parents. Would they have missed her yet? Would they be searching? She hoped not. If she could leave as soon as it was light, she could ride much faster, and put even more distance between herself and any searchers. Besides, they wouldn't be able to follow her immediately. Not only had she taken their horse, but all their money besides, so they wouldn't be able to afford to buy or hire another. For a moment she wondered how they would manage without their savings, and regretted the anguish and worry she'd be causing them once they found out that she was gone.

Feeling her resolve beginning to weaken, she hardened her heart. Who cared? Let them worry! The father she had loved so dearly had been lying to her all these years, letting her hope that she could attend the Academy like any normal Wizard, and her mother, with her miserable human blood, had ruined her life. If her absence was causing them pain, it served them right. But now that her mad flight from Nexis was over for a little while and she was forced to be still, anxiety began to gnaw at her. Running away was all very well, and for now she'd found a sanctuary, but she couldn't stay in this barn for ever. What would she do next? Where would she go? How could she show them that she was every bit as good as Iriana?

Then it came to her. The solution was so obvious! Never mind what her father said – she *would* go to Tyrineld. She would go on her own, as someone else – as a true Wizard, like the rest of them. The Wizard she was in her heart. Excited now, she forgot her weariness and sprang to her feet, pacing up and down while a plan began to take shape in her mind. Her father had been teaching her the spells of chimera and illusion, and although he had forbidden her to use them to alter her appearance until she was much more experienced, she didn't give a damn about that now. As far as she was concerned, he had lost any right to authority over her. When she got to the city, she would make herself look like someone else entirely. Someone beautiful. Someone that poisonous cow Iriana would never recognise. She would be trained properly, at the Academy, just as she had always wanted. She would work day and night, developing her abilities to their very peak. And when she was powerful enough, she would have her revenge on all of them: all those arrogant Wizards who wanted to enslave her mother and herself.

Chiannala smiled. First she would deceive them, then she'd outdo the lot of them – and first and foremost of them all would be that detestable Iriana.

Despite the whirl of hopes and plans that filled her thoughts, Chiannala found herself overwhelmed by weariness. Soon all her schemes and worries left her, as she leant back against the fragrant hay and relaxed into sleep.

A bed of hay could only feel comfortable to someone who was dead tired. It prickled, it tickled, it rustled with mysterious movements that could only be mice, or even rats... In short, Chiannala awakened after only a couple of hours' sleep. It was just as well, really, she consoled herself. The subdued, ghostly light that signalled the hour before sun-up was already glimmering through the open doorway below, and it was high time she was on the road again. The last thing she wanted was to run into someone from the farm now, and get caught up in endless explanations and lies.

At top speed, Chiannala began to pack up her belongings – then suddenly paused as she caught sight of the little hand mirror she had slipped in with her other bits and pieces. Picking it up, she looked at her face in the dim light and remembered that she had been planning, before she fell asleep last night, to use a chimera spell to disguise herself when she got to Tyrineld. But surely she could risk a few minutes now in such a good cause. If she looked different on her journey, she'd stand a far better chance of reaching the city undetected. Tucking the mirror into a pocket, she dropped her bag and bundle over the edge of the loft and scrambled down the ladder after them.

Chiannala took the mirror to the doorway where the light was better and looked at her reflection again. How she hated that narrow face, those mud-coloured eyes and that bushy, dull brown hair. Well, if she was going to disguise herself, she might as well do the job properly. Closing her eyes, she put together a detailed picture of the way she had always wanted to look, visualising every aspect of her new appearance in painstaking detail. Then, reaching deep inside herself as her father had taught her, she touched the wellspring of her powers and poured her magic into the vision, projecting the new image onto her own face as it was reflected in the mirror.

She had never done a spell this powerful, despite her earlier, confident words to her father. Nor had she attempted any magic so complex. But it was too late. Chiannala was committed. For an instant she felt a stab of terror, and a torrent of doubts flooded through her mind. What if she couldn't do this? What if it all went wrong? This was her *face* she was messing about with! Had she lost her mind? What if she turned herself into some kind of monster? As she watched with horror, a radiant nimbus washed down over her head, blurring her features – then suddenly, her entire face simply vanished, hidden behind a shield of pure light that looked as hard and shiny as the mirror she held. She gave a little scream, almost dropping it. What had she done?

Somehow, Chiannala pulled together the tattered shreds of her courage. She simply *had* to succeed. Everything depended on it. Taking a deep breath, she concentrated with all her might on the blank, shining oval in the mirror, willing the perfect new features to form. For a moment, nothing happened, then the reflection blurred and clouded as though a grey curtain had been drawn across in front of the mirror. When it cleared, the blank travesty of a face had gone, and a stranger looked out at her from the glass.

Chiannala gasped. For the first time in her life, she was beautiful. Her hair was a glorious mane of raven-black curls. Her eyes were large and green, with long, sweeping lashes, and though she had been careful to give her face the sculpted features that typified the Wizards, the bony angularity was softened slightly into a stunning beauty that outshone Iriana's stern, patrician looks as the sun outshone the moon. Chiannala laughed aloud. Nothing could stop her now.

As she gazed into the mirror, enraptured by what she saw, and delighted (not to mention a little relieved) that her first essay into such advanced magic had gone so well, she suddenly noticed that her surroundings looked brighter, and her skin had taken on a warmer hue. Damn it. Where had the time gone? The sun was rising already. The eastern sky had turned to apricot and gold, and a sliver of fiery light was beginning to show above the horizon. In the farmyard, a cockerel crowed. She had lingered too long here, and if she didn't hurry, the people from the farm would find her. Chiannala ran back into the barn, stuffed the mirror into her bundle with feverish hands and ran to fetch her horse.

The animal was far from pleased to have his rest interrupted so soon. He tossed his head and showed the whites of his eyes as she tried to put on the bridle. 'Stop that, damn you,' Chiannala muttered as the long brown nose was jerked out of her reach yet again. 'Come here. Why can't you be like that nice, well-behaved creature over there?"

She stopped dead, the bridle hanging limply from her hand. Could she? Dared she take the other beast? Why not? It seemed a fair exchange. And as she went on her way with her new disguise, she would be even less recognisable on a different horse. No sooner said than done. Within minutes the saddle, bridle and her baggage were all on the grey, who seemed a good-natured, docile creature. As she led it past the brown horse, she gave a little shrug. 'If you have to work harder now, you only have yourself to blame,' she said.

The new horse was of a lighter build than her father's stocky brown creature, which had mostly been used for pulling a cart. This was a proper riding horse; much more fitted to carrying a lady like herself, Chiannala thought smugly, than that thick-limbed, thick-headed creature which would be much more use on a farm anyway. She only hoped the farmer would see it that way. 'After all,' she told herself firmly, 'it's not really like stealing. I haven't left them any worse off.'

Chiannala turned onto the main road and saw the way to Tyrineld lying clear before her. At last! She couldn't wait to get there, with a new appearance and a new identity, and begin a new life. Leaning forward in the saddle, she urged her new horse into a gallop, and vanished down the road in a cloud of dust.

17
~

ABOUT FACE

The moment she heard her mother's voice calling her, Brynne was out of bed with a bound. Though she hadn't slept a wink, and the sky was still utterly dark beyond her curtains, she was much too excited to feel tired. Forming a ball of cool, bright magelight, the simplest of magic and the first spell her mother had ever taught her, she thought of all the wonderful, advanced and complex magic she would soon be learning at the great and far-famed Academy in the city of Tyrineld.

Brynne couldn't wait to get there, though her longing was tinged with a little trepidation. She certainly had ability, so there had never been any real doubt of her acceptance, or so her doting parents had kept on telling her, but she had spent all of her sixteen years living on a remote farm halfway between the city and the frontier, and had never had anyone but her mother and father to measure herself against. And her parents weren't especially talented.

Her father's name was Shelgan. His powers were nothing special, and he had left the Academy and the city to become a farmer to the southeast of the frontier town of Nexis, near the coast. He had sufficient magic to help him raise wonderful crops from the difficult environment of the windswept downs, and that was more than enough for him. Her mother, Larann, was a Healer, and though she was quite competent enough to tender good, practical service to the nearby fishing village and her own farm settlement, not to mention its animals (which were a speciality of hers), she would never be outstanding. They were completely lacking in ambition; content in their own little niche and wanting no more. A baby girl had set the crown on their happiness, and when her burgeoning talents had startled and amazed them, they had felt the warmth of tremendous pride, mingled with a little sadness and dismay that one day they must lose her to Tyrineld and the Academy – not that they would ever have let their own feelings hold her back. Brynne was glad that they trusted her enough to let her go, but she knew she would miss them.

She would miss her room, too, she thought, glancing round the snug little chamber with the walls panelled in dark wood, which had been hers for as long as she could remember. There were some spaces today on those walls and in the bookshelves, for she would be taking her favourite pictures and books with her, and they were already packed. She ran a hand over the brightly coloured patchwork quilt her mother had made, on the soft, warm bed in which she had dreamed so many dreams of magic and success, then turned away to brush her hair in front of the mirror.

This is the last time I'll do this, she thought, then snapped herself out of the nostalgic mood. *Of course it isn't. I'll come back for holidays, for visits. Maybe when I've finished my studies, it'll be my home again.*

She knew in her heart that it wouldn't.

How would she get on with the other students? Would she fit in? As an only child, she had never known the give and take of brothers and sisters. And there would be *boys* ...

'Pull yourself together, Brynne,' she said out loud. 'You've looked in the mirror often enough. Plump, plain, dull brown hair – you think you'll need to bother about boys?' She decided just to concentrate on her magic. Using her powers gave her such a thrill, and to think of developing them, working with them, seeing them grow day by day ... Who needed anything more?

Suddenly the serious face in the mirror broke into a smile, and the happy sparkle returned to those thoughtful dark grey eyes. She had wanted this, worked for this, dreamed of this for so long. These megrims at parting from her home and parents were only natural, for she would be leaving her childhood behind in every sense, but it was time to put them away and look to the brilliant future that she hoped would await her.

At that moment Mora, the family's human servant, entered the room carrying a cup of steaming taillin. 'What, up already?'

'I was too excited to sleep,' Brynne confessed.

'Well, my lovely,' she said, in the lilting local dialect of the north-western coast, ''tis hardly surprising. This is your big day at last. How time does gallop by. Why, it seems no time since ...' She shook her head. 'I'll miss my precious girl, I will. I'll miss you very much.'

Brynne opened her mouth to snap at the old woman, then shut it again with a sigh. Time seemed to have stopped for Mora when she, Brynne, was about three years old, she thought ruefully. But there was no point in causing strife and upsets on today of all days. It wouldn't change anything, anyway. Instead she hugged the servant, nearly sending the tea flying. 'I'll miss you too, Mora.'

When Mora had left, Brynne drank her taillin as quickly as she could manage without scalding her tongue, and turned to get dressed. She had chosen her clothes with care – she had a whole new wardrobe for the trip – and had laid them out ready the night before, so it didn't take long. Then, with one last look around the room, she ran downstairs.

The spattering sizzle and mouth-watering smell of frying bacon greeted her as she entered the kitchen. Her mother Larann, her brown hair escaping in straggles, as usual, from its knot and her normally pale complexion flushed pink from the heat of the stove, turned to her with a smile. 'There you are, punctual as always. I've done you two eggs this morning, Brynne – a good breakfast will set you up for your long journey.'

Brynne knew her mother was hiding a tumultuous mixture of emotions behind a mask of briskness. She glanced down at her waistline with a sigh. That was the thing about Larann: she firmly believed that good food was a panacea for everything from a broken leg to a broken heart. And because they were farmers, there was always plenty of good food around.

Well, maybe it would be different when she got to Tyrineld. Surely no one there would be telling her what she should and shouldn't be eating, and continually cajoling her to have more. In the meantime, she meant to enjoy her last delicious farm breakfast. While she was eating, her father Shelgan came in, chafing his hands against the early morning chill. 'Well, that's it, my Lady.' His florid bow to Brynne made her smile. 'We've harnessed the horses and the men have loaded all your gear into the cart. As soon as you've finished eating, we'll be ready to go.' His plump face (she definitely got her stocky figure from her father's side of the family) was glowing with exertion and beaming with pride at his daughter who was on her way to the Academy.

'Let the girl eat her breakfast in peace,' Larann protested. 'What about some more bacon, Brynne? Shall I toast you another slice of bread? Would you like another cup of taillin? What about you, Shel? Shall I pour you a cup?'

Father and daughter exchanged a wry and sympathetic glance. They both knew very well that Larann was putting off the moment of departure with every ruse at her disposal. Decisively, Brynne pushed her plate away and got to her feet. 'Thank you, but I couldn't eat another thing. You're right, Dad. It's time we were going.'

She didn't cry when she said goodbye to Mora or the farm workers.

She didn't cry when she said goodbye to her mother. But when it came to saying goodbye to the two dogs, Bracken and Bramble, and Moon the silver-grey cat, Brynne could not stem her tears. They would not understand why she had to go – they would only know that she was gone and miss her. And Bramble was so old now. Would he still be there the next time she returned?

Once she and her father were on their way, however, and the farm had vanished behind them over the brow of the hill, Brynne's excitement came to the fore once again. Tucking away her handkerchief, she turned to Shelgan with a grin. 'You've always said you would teach me to drive the cart when I was older. What better time than now?'

Shelgan grinned back at her and put the reins into her hands. 'What better time indeed?'

They travelled steadily southwards, not hurrying, camping as they went. Brynne enjoyed those last few precious days with her father: sleeping in the cart at night, well wrapped in cloak and blanket; cooking some truly horrible meals over a campfire; talking over all sorts of inconsequentialities. The morning of the fourth day, however, would be the last of their journey, and as soon as she awakened, Brynne's mind turned firmly towards the future.

What would it be like to live in the great city of the Wizardfolk, after coming from the tiny, self-contained world of a remote and isolated farm? Though she had been to Tyrineld once before, in the early part of the year, to complete the tests and assessments for her entry to the Academy, the nervousness and strain of that visit, one that would determine her entire future, had turned her recollections of the city into a bewildering blur of buildings, faces and magic. She was looking forward to seeing it again; now, when she would have the time and inclination to appreciate its beauty, and learn its ways and secrets.

Her one clear memory was reaching Tyrineld on a crisp, clear, brilliantly sunny winter's morning, and coming over the crest of the hill to see the magnificent city embracing the crystalline blue ocean, its intricate buildings gleaming white in the sunlight, and its glittering towers reaching, like her own dreams and ambitions, for the sky.

Always, in her imagination, Brynne had pictured herself returning to see that same vista. Looking down on the beautiful city where anything was possible, and knowing that it would be her home. That final morning, however, she awoke to disappointment. The clouds were down, looming low over the countryside, creeping across the high moors at ground level to form a mantle of dank, impenetrable mist, and filling the air with a light precipitation that prickled on her skin.

Brynne emerged, tousled and sleepy, from her nest of blankets in the cart, and muttered a word that made her father raise his eyebrows. 'Well, just look at this demons' brew,' she said crossly, in mitigation. 'I was so looking forward to climbing that last hilltop and seeing the city all spread out before me like a promise. Now we'll be lucky to find the blasted track. And instead of making a good impression, I'm going to arrive looking like a draggled refugee.'

'All right, all right now.' Shelgan put his arm around her shoulders. In the thickening of her voice he heard the sound of tears, suppressed but threatening to break loose, and he realised that Brynne, his bold, bright child who normally had the courage of ten Warriors, was far more nervous than she had admitted, even to herself. He lifted her chin with a finger. 'There now, my love, don't fret yourself. We'll stop before we reach the city. I'll use a drying spell on your hair, and you can change your clothes and spruce up a bit. And who knows, maybe this weather will have lifted by the time we get there, and you'll see your city after all.'

Brynne directed a scathing glance towards the soggy, dark-grey shroud that smothered their surroundings. 'And I'll sprout wings like one of the Skyfolk, and fly to Tyrineld,' she retorted pithily, but by making her realise just what a jittering mess her nerves were in, he had put the stiffening back into her spine. Suddenly she felt much better, and gave him a hug and a grin. 'Come on, Dad, it's your turn to make breakfast this morning.'

After a few days of practice, their campfire cooking was beginning to improve, and this time the bacon was only slightly burned. They were just rounding off their meal with a cup of taillin, smoke-flavoured from the fire but very welcome on this chill, damp day, when the sudden sound of hoofbeats came drumming out of the mist. A horse burst through the roiling curtain of grey and bolted right between them, reins and stirrups flapping. It swerved to avoid the campfire and found itself boxed in between the cart, the stream beside which they had camped and Shelgan's patient, tethered horses. Rolling its eyes, it skidded to a halt, ploughing up great clods of turf, but the presence of the other beasts seemed to calm it, and Brynne's father had little trouble catching hold of the broken, trailing rein.

'Well, well.' He stroked the sweat-damp neck and ran an expert hand down the heaving flanks and trembling legs. 'And where did you come from, my beauty? Grey as the weather itself, and a fine beast to boot with those pretty dapples. It doesn't seem to be hurt,' he added, speaking to his daughter now.

Brynne fed the animal a crust of bread left over from breakfast and it nuzzled into her hungrily, looking for more. 'Looks like it tossed its rider and bolted,' she said. 'I wonder how far it's come?'

Shelgan sighed. 'I suppose I'll have to go and look for the rider. We can't leave someone out there alone and maybe hurt, especially not in this weather.' He laid a hand on Brynne's shoulder and gave it a comforting squeeze. 'Don't worry, love, hopefully this shouldn't delay us too long. The way the beast was bolting, I doubt it's come very far. It wouldn't be able to sustain that sort of pace. You tether it to the cart and I'll take one of our horses and backtrack along its trail – it left a line of prints in this wet ground that you could see a mile off. I'll be back in no time, you'll see.'

And before Brynne could object or offer to go with him, he had leapt bareback on one of the carthorses and vanished into the mist, leaving only an echo of thudding hoofbeats behind.

How could an entire city lose itself? Driven by her purpose, Chiannala had never once doubted that she would attain her goals, but now that sense of certainty had been leached away by her desolate, empty surroundings. For the first time, she began to wonder if she would ever reach Tyrineld. The journey had been far more difficult than she'd anticipated. An inexperienced traveller, she had not brought enough warm clothing, or anything to keep off the rain. She must have lost her gloves in the barn, and now her hands were white and numb, making her grip on the reins uncertain.

Chiannala's stomach churned with hunger. She was chilled, wet through, weary, grubby, aching right down to her bones, and lost. On the first two nights of her journey she had been lucky: on the night she'd run away, there had been the comfortable barn where she'd changed horses, and on the second night, though the country was getting rougher and the area less populated, she had stumbled across a much smaller and less prosperous holding, where a root cellar had provided her with a temporary refuge, and some withered apples and carrots to eat.

Last night, however, she had not been so fortunate. Between Nexis and the outlying regions around Tyrineld was this wild, lonely stretch of hills where there was not even a tree to break the force of the unrelenting wind, and not a single building where she could seek refuge after sunset. She had tried to huddle at the edge of a thicket of whin that skirted the edge of the track, but when it had started to rain, she'd given up trying to rest. She might as well be cold, wet and moving, she decided, and mounted her reluctant horse once more. Getting the weary creature moving with an effort, she'd set off into the darkness.

Like an idiot, she must have been dozing when the horse wandered off the trail. When the sky reluctantly lightened to a sombre, clouded morning, Chiannala had found herself utterly lost, without any idea of the direction in which she should be headed. All day long she had been searching the lonely heights of the downs, but had never seen a trace of the road she was meant to be taking. To make matters worse, the terrain was growing increasingly rough and rocky, with spiny thickets of bramble and gorse that tore at her cloak to repeatedly thwart her progress, and more terrifyingly, stretches of glutinous bog covered with a green skin that made them look like innocent, solid ground – until an unwary horse took a step too far. The air was growing cooler against her face, and the thick, heavy cloud that darkened the sky seemed to be pressing ever lower upon her: a phenomenon that she initially ascribed to imagination, until she saw the far slopes of the hills fade and vanish into a misty haze.

Fog. The traveller's foe. The horizon seemed to be shrinking around her as the walls of grey rolled in towards her: an inexorable tide that left her stranded on a tiny patch of thin turf, in the midst of a cold, white void. At first she tried to keep going, but strange shapes loomed at her out of the haze, and nothing was what it seemed. A boulder suddenly bounded away with a startled bleat; a stream was running in the opposite direction from all those she had previously encountered. Had she somehow been turned all the way around? Or had she crossed some kind of watershed? She had absolutely no idea. A seemingly solid stretch of ground began to ooze water as her horse's hooves sank into it, and Chiannala backed hastily away from the bog, her heart beating fast with fright. This was no good. She would kill herself if she kept trying to move, and besides, what was the point when she had lost all sense of direction? It would be better to remain where she was.

She reined-in the horse and dismounted, looping the reins through her arm. The grey horse put his head down, hoping to find some grass long enough to graze. The minutes stretched interminably, with nothing to see but blank greyness and no sound to break the silence but her breathing and that of the horse, and the occasional bleat of a sheep. Though Chiannala had been very much alone on her journey, she had been too focused on reaching Tyrineld and the Academy of the Wizards to be lonely. In the fog, however, she felt desperately lost and isolated, longing for a kind word or a friendly face. She found herself thinking of the comfort of her mother's arms and the reassurance of her father's smile, and for the first time since leaving home, she did not think of them with anger and resentment.

As she waited in that eerie, silent world, all her worries, frustrations and discomforts gradually gave way to trepidation. As time crawled by, she began to wonder whether this cold, damp blankness that surrounded her would be gone by nightfall – and for the first time, she was beset by the gnawing fear that she might not survive.

It had all seemed so easy the night she had run away, any doubts overridden by anger, resentment and determination. All she had to do, she'd imagined, was follow the road. She had simply assumed that there would be inns, settlements and farms all the way to Tyrineld. Because her parents had been there to look after her all her life, she had taken it for granted that there would always be someone else to fill the gap. She had fled on the spur of the moment, instead of waiting long enough to formulate some kind of strategy, instead of taking the proper clothing and sufficient provisions – and, most important of all, finding out before she left about the route and the conditions she would meet.

What a stupid, naïve, reckless fool she had been, letting her anger overrule her common sense. *If I get out of this*, she vowed, *it'll never happen again. I'll be controlled and dispassionate ...*

If you survive.

The warning voice of fear cut across her thoughts. How could she even get through the next few hours, let alone make it to Tyrineld?

Even if by some miracle she did reach the city, she was beginning to harbour serious doubts that her plan would succeed. Why should they take her into the Academy merely on the strength of her own word? They would be sure to want to know about her family, and why, at her age, she was travelling all alone. She would be forced to lie to them, of course – and she had a feeling that the Archwizard, not to mention all the powerful Wizards who taught at the Academy, would be very difficult to dupe. Whatever tale she spun them, it would be easy enough for them to investigate her background, and once the truth came out, she was finished.

Chiannala buried her face in her hands. Why had she even bothered to try? It looked as though her desperate plan to better herself and be welcomed into the ranks of the Wizardfolk was doomed before it had truly begun. Thanks to her accursed parents, she would never have the life she craved, and by running away she had managed to make things a thousand times worse. After stealing from her parents, how could she possibly go back there? Yet what was the alternative? It would be easiest for everyone if she were simply to die right here in this ghastly wilderness. No one would miss her. No one would mourn. What was the point of fighting her background and her fate any longer?

Suddenly, her horse gave a startled neigh. Half-rearing, snatching the reins away with a sickening wrench to her arm, the animal bolted, knocking her aside onto the muddy ground. A pang of horror wrenched at her guts. Without the horse, she had nothing. She would wander lost out here until she dropped from hunger, weariness and cold. For the first time in her young life, Chiannala faced the certain prospect of her death. In that instant she forgot she'd just decided her life was no longer worth living. Stricken, helpless, terrified, everything in her life gone to wrack and ruin, she lay in the mud and sobbed.

'Ho there!' The voice echoed through the fog. 'Ho, is anybody out there?'

Chiannala was so stunned by thankfulness that, speechless, she lost those first few vital seconds.

'Ho,' the voice came again. This time it sounded further away.

Panic restored her voice. 'Help,' she yelled, as loud as she could. She scrambled to her feet. 'Here – I'm over here.'

It took them a good while to find each other, in spite of all the shouting back and forth, but finally, a dim shape materialised through the fog, and Chiannala stumbled, weeping, into the arms of a tall, portly man with a weathered face and a kindly smile. 'There now, there. No need for tears, little maid.' He patted her shoulder. 'You're safe now.'

Half an hour later, Chiannala was ensconced comfortably in the back of a wagon, wrapped in blankets, with a half-devoured chicken leg in one hand and a mug of warm taillin laced with honey in the other. As she felt warmth and strength creeping back into her body, her fighting spirit began to return, although she still had no idea what she was going to do, or how she would face the future.

Her rescuers were already starting to make her sick. She despised this smiling, pie-faced moron who had, by his own admission, thrown away all the opportunities that she yearned for to become a farmer, grubbing in the dirt like some common human. And as for his stupid, beaming lump of a daughter, who wouldn't stop chattering on and on like a bloody magpie about going to the Academy – Chiannala dearly longed to throttle her. She barely knew this girl, but she already loathed her for having everything *she* should have had – would have had – if her idiot father had possessed the common decency to wed one of his own kind instead of a common slave.

Then they started prying. Who are you? How did you come to be lost on the moor? Where are you going? How did a young girl come to be travelling all alone? There was no end to their questions.

Chiannala responded with the story she'd made up as she travelled from Nexis. Though she'd begun to doubt that it would pass muster with the Archwizard, she was sure it would fool these two innocent peasants. She told them that her name was Estella. Her mother had died when she was born, and grief had driven her father to become an anchorite – a solitary Wizard who dwelt alone, away out in the wilds, to study and perfect his art. Then, just when he was going to bring her to the Academy, he too had died of a fever. The poor orphan, with no other family to turn to, was heading to Nexis to beg desperately for admittance to the Academy.

They swallowed it whole. Of course they did. She knew she could be very convincing when she chose, and now, with her future at stake, there was everything to play for. The victory was almost too easy, and as she bathed in their kindness and sympathy, Chiannala began to believe that she might actually get away with her tale when she reached Tyrineld. Then the horrible daughter uttered the words that brought all her hopes crashing down in ruins.

'But at least you've been to Tyrineld before, right? It won't be completely strange to you. If you're coming to the Academy, you must have passed the tests and assessments.'

Tests? Assessments? Panic clawed at Chiannala's throat. Her father had never mentioned this! *Why would he need to?* she thought bitterly. *He never meant me to go to the Academy.*

What could she do now? She had told her lie to these people and now she was committed. With a gargantuan effort, she swallowed her shock and dismay, and pasted a smile onto her face. 'Why yes, of course,' she replied in bright, brittle tones. 'But I was so nervous, it's all just a blur to me now. I can't remember a single useful thing about the place.'

'Oh, me neither,' the girl – Brynne – said fervently. 'For all I can recall of my last visit, Tyrineld might as well be the moon.' She tucked her hand through Chiannala's arm in a companionable way. 'Still, at least now we'll each have someone we know when we get there. Maybe we can be friends.'

For a moment, some lonely part of Chiannala's soul that had been stunted and withered by the half-blood that had set her apart from everyone she knew bloomed and yearned towards this kindly, friendly girl. Then she remembered that Brynne had come so easily to everything for which she, Chiannala, so desperately yearned, and the bitterness and bile rose up to choke her once more.

Again she forced the smile back to her face. 'Why, that would be wonderful, Brynne. I'd love to have you for a friend.'

I hate you, you little bitch. You have everything that should have been mine. I wish you were dead, and that I could take it all.

Chiannala was shocked by the violence of her own thought, yet, as they drew ever closer to Tyrineld, her mood became increasingly desperate. What would she do when she got there? What *could* she do? She had passed no tests – the Academy would be closed to her now. Even if she were to apply immediately, it would be months before the next student intake. How could she possibly live in the meantime? And these assessments – would they reveal her mortal heritage? Surely they must.

By midday they had reached the road that ran along the coast. Shelgan steered the wagon across to the side of the track and halted. 'We may as well stop here for a bite to eat, girls,' he said. 'We still have plenty of time to reach the city before nightfall.' He beamed at Brynne and Chiannala. 'It will give you young ladies a chance to spruce yourselves up a little, before you make your big entrance.'

While Shelgan put a quick drying spell on a patch of turf so that they could sit down comfortably, and Brynne rummaged in the back of the wagon for bread and cheese, Chiannala's mind was working furiously, searching desperately for a way out of her dilemma.

Then Brynne gave her the answer, by handing her a mirror. 'Here you are, Estella. You might as well use this while I'm getting the food ready.'

Chiannala dug her comb from her pack and looked at the flawless reflection in the mirror. All that work to give herself this new and lovely face would be wasted now that she could no longer go to the Academy. She might as well not have bothered. Her reflection blurred as tears began to gather in her eyes.

Then, without warning, it slid into her mind. An idea so appalling that it dried her tears and drained all the blood from her face. But once it had surfaced, it would not leave her. A chance. Her only chance. Her entire future was at stake. She thought about the Chimera spell. Looked at Brynne. Shuddered. Doubted.

Can I do it? Could I? Am I capable of such an act?
You are. You must be.

It had to be now, or she would never find the nerve again. This one opportunity would slip by, and her life would be ruined for ever. She glanced around at Shelgan putting nosebags on the horses, at Brynne laying out bread and cheese, at the clusters of tall gorse bushes that dotted the edge of the cliff. 'Brynne, could you help me, please?' she asked, trying to keep her voice from shaking. 'I want to change my dress and it's much easier – not to mention neater – if someone else ties the laces.'

The plump girl beamed. 'Of course I will. I want to get changed myself. But why not wait until after we've eaten? Then we won't mess up our good clothes by sitting on the ground.'

A plague on the wretched girl! Chiannala ground her teeth in frustration. Yet how could she argue with such a sensible suggestion?

Luckily, they put her inability to eat down to nervousness about entering the Academy, though it certainly didn't seem to be affecting Brynne in that way, Chiannala thought irritably. Would they never stop eating, father and daughter? No wonder the girl was the size of a plough-horse. It never crossed her mind for a single instant that the two of them were trying to garner as many last precious moments together in each other's company as they possibly could.

At last, however, Shelgan got up with a sigh. 'We'd best be getting on,' he said. 'I'll clear this stuff away and get the horses ready, while you girls are putting on your finery.'

They retrieved their bags from the cart and Chiannala, her heart beating fast, pointed to the place she had chosen. 'Those bushes over there should hide us from anyone passing on the road.'

'All right,' Brynne said easily. 'Over there it is.'

There was only a narrow space between the bushes and the cliff edge. 'Goodness,' Brynne said. 'Do you think this is safe?'

'Don't be such a goose,' Chiannala retorted sharply. 'Of course it's safe, if we take care. Come on, help me out of my dress, then I'll help you out of yours.'

Brynne, clearly stung by the scathing tones, said nothing, her mouth set in a tight line as she helped her companion undress down to her chemise, then turned around so that Chiannala could do the same for her. As soon as her back was turned, Chiannala triggered the chimera spell that she had been preparing in her mind. In a way, it was easier this time, since she had done it before, but this time, she had her whole body to transform. It only took a moment, but before she was done she was trembling with exhaustion.

'Hurry up, Estella,' Brynne prompted. 'We don't have all day.'

'Sorry.' Hastily Chiannala pulled herself together and loosened the laces. Brynne stepped out of the dress, turned – and her mouth fell open in shock at the sight of herself standing there.

'I'm sorry, Brynne. Truly sorry,' Chiannala said – and pushed. It was all too easy. Yet she knew that Brynne's scream, cut off so horribly as she hit the churning water below, would stay with her to the end of her days.

'What happened? Brynne, are you all right?' As Shelgan burst through the bushes, she hurled herself into his arms. 'Dad, oh Dad,' she sobbed. 'Estella slipped. She was messing about, looking over the edge – and then she was gone. She fell off the cliff, Dad. Estella is gone.'

And my way to the Academy is open at last.

PART 3

~

THE FIALAN

18
~

THE MAD ONE

Pain perpetual. It was his whole life, his entire being. It devastated his mind, consumed all his attention, twisted his perceptions. It was his past, his present, his future. Ghabal's existence was nothing but pain.

Pain and one other thing.

The Stone of Fate.

The Fialan was the entire focus of the Moldan's world. It had to be. He both loved and hated it. The Stone had reduced him to the pitiful creature he had become, yet it was the only thing that let him recall who he was, and what he once had been.

He needed it. It allowed him to remember the face of his enemy.

Hellorin felt as if he was floating, high up among the vaulting of the chamber, where he could make out every detail of the intricate carving with its butterflies, flowers and twining vines. Down below, at floor level, the bed in the centre of the room was the focus of attention. He could see the healers fussing around it, going back and forth, and huddling together to confer in worried-looking knots.

He noted the occasional visitor. Now and again there was Tiolani, her manner changeful as spring weather, one minute pale and drawn with grief, the next, sparkling with love and happiness. When she looked at the bed and its occupant, her face, eyes shadowed and mouth tight-set, was haunted with a grim, guilty determination. At other times there was Ferimon, a cruel smirk distorting his features and triumph burning in his eyes. And, to his lasting horror, he saw the other healers, the three who came in the darkest watches of the night when the others were absent, and overturned all the progress their colleagues had made.

The worst thing of all was looking down at the bed, and seeing not a friend or a foe or a stranger, but himself. The body that had moved at his command with a combination of strength and grace. The familiar face that had looked back at him from the mirror every day of his incredibly long life. Though the details were veiled by the silvery shimmer of the spell that had taken him out of time, the sight of his seemingly lifeless form filled his mind with blinding anger and a sickening sense of dread.

Hellorin was trapped. Exiled from his body and from the mundane world by that accursed time spell, and by the fearful wounds that made its use a continuing necessity. Ensnared by Ferimon, with his dissembling words of concern, that sly and evil smile of triumph; his filthy hands on Tiolani's body and his vile, corrupting influence spreading poisonous tendrils throughout her mind.

The Forest Lord knew, now, how the ambush had come about. Knew who had supplied the fugitive slaves with weapons and orchestrated the attack. He was enraged by Ferimon's treachery, but beyond that, he was sickened to the core by such betrayal. When Ferimon and Varna had been orphaned, he had taken them into his own household, had seen that they were cared for, had given them every possible opportunity to make a good life for themselves as part of the Phaerie Court. And this was how they had betrayed him.

'You know why.' The rasping voice of Aerillia startled him out of his reverie. Clearly, the Moldan had been eavesdropping on his thoughts. 'You killed their father and destroyed their family.'

'Because their father destroyed mine,' Hellorin snarled.

'Blood for blood, life for life. Once you start heading down that endless path, you and all who follow you are doomed.'

'Spare me the homily, Moldan. I care only about getting back.'

'Then you must seek elsewhere,' the towering figure on the icy throne replied. 'I have provided you with a means of seeing into this world and your own,' – she indicated the patch of smooth, clear ice on the floor of her throne room, in which the Forest Lord had been viewing the images that tormented him so – 'but you know as well as I do that the only one who can assist, voluntarily or otherwise, in your return is Ghabal.'

'I don't need you to point that out to me.' Hellorin turned to give her a fulminating glare. 'You know as well as I do that search though I might, the Mad One has remained elusive so far.'

'Nevertheless,' Aerillia said, 'he knows you are here. I can sense it.'

Hellorin frowned. 'Ghabal may be mad, but he is not slow-witted. He sees me as too great a threat to confront directly. Our powers are too evenly matched, so he has opted for the safer course of evasion. This world is no longer mine but his, and he knows every trick, every ruse, every possible stratagem to exploit the powers of the Old Magic. He has concealed himself and the Fialan so well that he can stay hidden, if he wishes, for aeons, until my own people have forgotten me, and the mundane world has changed so much that there will be no point in my going back. Then the Stone will be safe, he imagines, for I will need it no longer.'

'If that is what he truly believes,' Aerillia said wryly, 'then he does not understand your capacity for vengeance. If he seeks to deprive you of your realm, he can conceal himself until the stars burn out, but you will still be waiting when he finally emerges. You will use any means at your disposal to destroy him and take the Stone, in redress for all that he has made you lose.'

'How very well you know me.' Hellorin smiled mirthlessly. 'You are clever, Aerillia.'

'Not clever enough to understand why you also seek the other stranger who came into this world when you did, and was befriended by those meddling Evanesar.'

'No, you would not. You never paid much heed to what was going on outside your isolated mountain form in the mundane world.'

The Moldan shrugged her titanic shoulders. 'I care little for the mundane world. Its magic and its beauties are crude and primitive in comparison to the wonders of the Elsewhere.'

'Is that so?' Hellorin raised a cynical eyebrow.

'Oh, I can understand why certain of my brethren prefer to dwell there,' Aerillia said carelessly. 'It has its advantages.' The look she gave him was softened, with memories kindling a happy light, and her voice, when she spoke again, had sunk to a murmur. 'The long, slow dream of eternal stone; the ever-changeful patterns of sun and wind and cloud; the deep vaults of crystal air where the eagles soar; the diamond crown of blazing stars; the dark, secret shadows of the forests; the inexorable power of the bear, the deadly beauty of the lynx and the grace and swiftness of the wolf. The pristine purity of snow and the sharp, icy tang of the air; the jewelled tapestry of summer flowers; the bounding, laughing young rivers where the silver salmon flash and leap—'

Hellorin cut short her reverie with a laugh. 'And these are crude and primitive beauties, Aerillia? We both know better. The Elsewhere will always be your birthplace, your first home, the mother of your heart, but with all its imperfections, you still love the mundane world as much as I do.'

'Very well, I admit it. You are right.' She sighed. 'I have lingered here so long that I often wonder if I shall ever again be part of those other mountains that are my beauty and joy, my refuge and my responsibility; my own lovely domain. Nevertheless, while Ghabal lurks somewhere in this world, hoarding the Stone of Fate, I have felt it to be my duty to remain. His body in the other world has been destroyed. He cannot return there in the normal way. But my greatest fear is that, with the Stone, he will discover another method of sending himself through, another form in which to exist within the bounds of the mundane world. The damage he could do there, the havoc he could wreak in his madness, is incalculable.'

Her eyes flashed. 'Is it any wonder that all my attentions are focused here, where the threat lies? Thanks to the trouble you left behind you, I have had little opportunity to take note of the happenings in the mundane world. So instead of sneering at me for paying little heed, you'd be better off answering my question, and telling me what I need to know.'

The Forest Lord bowed his head in acknowledgement, as much to hide the anger that he knew she would read in his eyes as in apology. He had done what he'd felt to be right for himself and his people, and had no regrets. What did he care if his actions had left the Moldai with some problems on their hands? Ghabal was one of their race. Let them deal with his madness. And as for those meddling Evanesar ...

'Hellorin, are you going to tell me about this other stranger?' There was a sharp edge of impatience to Aerillia's voice.

'Very well.' Hellorin reminded himself that he was there on her sufferance. 'What do you know about the Xandim?'

'Shapeshifters.' Aerillia's eyes stared off into the distance as she searched her memory. 'Unusual in that they take horses as an alternative form. Most polymorphs tend to use carnivores – the nature of the hunter corresponds better with the aggressive, predatory disposition of the bipedal form. Once, aeons ago, the tribe had a link into the Old Magic, but at some point in their history, the idiots repudiated their powers, which eventually were lost to them.' She looked at Hellorin. 'That's about all I recall.'

'But the Xandim loss of magic was not universal,' the Forest Lord said softly. 'Once in every generation the gift is passed on ...' As she listened, he told her about the new Windeye, Corisand.

The Moldan waited until he had finished, then shrugged. 'So? I thought you took care of the Xandim a long time ago. How can their Shaman be a danger to you now?'

'She was no danger to me – until the Evanesar brought her here at the same time that you brought me, and befriended her.'

'Interfering fools,' Aerillia snarled.

'Exactly. And no friends to your race or mine. While she is in this world, Corisand can access both her human form and her magic. With the Evanesar on hand to teach her to use her powers, she could become a significant threat.'

The Moldan drew in a swift, sharp breath. 'You think she can use the Fialan?'

Hellorin nodded. 'That is my belief. If the accursed Evanesar persuade her that the Stone can free her people – and they will – then she, too, will try to possess it.'

To his chagrin, Aerillia laughed. 'Hellorin, you astonish me. Why are you so concerned about her? Recently arrived in this world, untutored, newly come to her powers – how can she be a threat?'

'Because in this world, Corisand's powers are greater than she knows. And while I am holding her people captive, she will have everything to play for.'

The Moldan's expression hardened. 'In that case, Forest Lord, you had better stop watching and start acting. Difficult as it may be, put aside your concerns about what is happening in your own realm, and turn the scrying-glass that I have made for you onto this world instead. Find the Mad One. Do not rest until you have located him.'

She hesitated, fractionally, then continued: 'I will do the best I can to help you, though I will not be loved for it by my fellow Moldai. As for your Shaman, I would advise you to save your worries for later. Powerful or not, she still has much to learn. Concentrate on finding Ghabal and discovering a way to take back the Stone from him. When you hold the Fialan, the Windeye of the Xandim will be no more than an insect to be crushed beneath your feet.'

19

~

BRIGHT FACE, DARK HEART

Tiolani awakened early and slipped quietly out of bed. Drawing the drapes aside, she looked out of the window. 'Why, it's summer,' she said. Suddenly her heart grew lighter. Every year it happened like this. Summer came late to the northern realm of the Phaerie, but the long wait was always worthwhile. On one particular morning, all the imperceptible changes in the climate and landscape seemed to come together, and suddenly the world was a different place: golden, glowing and warm. Vibrant flowers, an emperor's cloak of purple, red and gold, massed beneath the trees, mingling their perfumes and crowded with bees. Colours were brighter. Birds flitted everywhere, filling the air with song, and streams and rivers, with a new, laughing note in their ever-running songs, flashed the sunlight back into the air. Green leaves fluttered at the end of each twig, and the grass in the meadows where the horses grazed grew rich and strong and thick. Suddenly, it was as though the cold, bleak darkness of winter and the pale and windy spring, which had seen her struggle to establish herself as ruler of the Phaerie realm, had never been.

For the first time since her brother had been slain, Tiolani felt she could look forward to the future. Since Hellorin was wounded, and she had suddenly found herself to be the Lady of the Forest by default, she had been finding life desperately difficult. But today she was filled with hope. At last she was beginning to feel in control of her father's realm. Until he recovered, she could function effectively as the ruler – and she was even beginning to enjoy it.

'What are you doing there, my love? It's early yet. Come back to bed.'

Tiolani turned away from the window with a laugh. 'Ferimon, you're wicked.'

The handsome courtier with the blond curls flashed that charming white smile that never failed to melt her heart. 'Only with you, my love. You know that my one joy is to be with you.'

Unable, as always, to resist him, Tiolani turned her back on the bright summer sunlight, and went happily into his embrace.

Later, as Ferimon slept again, Tiolani lay in his arms, relaxed, secure and sated. *My darling Ferimon*, she thought. *What would I have done without you?* It had been Ferimon who eventually broke through her grief, brought her comfort and, eventually, helped her take a grip on affairs within her father's court. When she looked back, she wondered how she would have managed to get through those first dark days following Arvain's death, save that she and Ferimon had been drawn together, helping each other through the difficult and lonely months. It had been Ferimon, for example, who had suggested that she ban all outsiders from entering the Phaerie realm at this time, and forbade all the Phaerie to journey to the world outside. That way, the news that Hellorin was incapacitated might be kept secret. It was well known that the Magefolk had a healthy respect for the Forest Lord and his powers, and it would be better at this difficult time if they believed he was still in command.

Ferimon was also encouraging her to take an increasingly firm stance with her father's old counsellors, and Tiolani's happy mood darkened a little at the thought of them. They would never take her seriously as a ruler, he had told her, if she allowed them to argue with her all the time; however, she suspected that most of them would never take her seriously no matter what she did. And, like Aelwen, some of the advisors were Hemifae, with their taint of treacherous human blood. How could her father have trusted them? Well, that was a mistake Tiolani didn't intend to repeat, even though she might be stuck with them for the present. Sometimes she would find herself falling into a daydream in which they were the quarry of her Hunt. The thought of them being ripped to pieces by the hounds, the notion of wading, for once, in *their* blood … sometimes these fantasies would frighten her with their savagery, yet they would make her feel better, at least for a while. And though she couldn't really hunt down her father's counsellors, she was beginning to manage them better. Since she had dismissed several of them from their posts, the quibbling and dissension had diminished markedly, but it had made her no friends within the court, and everywhere she went, she was sure that people were plotting and whispering behind her back, planning to wrest away the power that was rightfully hers.

Well, just let them try. Ferimon had arranged a personal bodyguard of loyal warriors to protect her at all times – just in case, he said, there was more trouble with renegade humans – but they could protect her from her enemies within the court just as well. She smiled at her lover as he lay dozing beside her. How wonderful he was. She had come to rely on his good advice, and his support had been invaluable as she gradually learned to make the great decisions that would affect an entire realm, and to wield the authority of a ruler with dignity and confidence. She would dearly love to make him her consort, but that was a decision of such magnitude that she could hardly take it without her father's consent.

When *would* Hellorin wake? He still remained in a suspended state while the healers worked on his injuries, and though they seemed to be taking an unusually long time about it, Tiolani didn't question their skills. With Ferimon by her side, she was beginning to like being ruler of the Phaerie ...

She was jerked from her romantic dream as Ferimon wormed his way out of her embrace and began to pull on his clothes. Tiolani sat up in bed. 'Where are you going?' she asked him, with a trace of peevishness in her voice. 'It's far too early to be getting up.'

He muffled her complaints with a kiss. 'It's a surprise,' he said. 'I won't be long. Anyway, you should be getting up soon yourself. You're holding public audience today, remember?'

Tiolani made a face. 'I *hate* holding those damned audiences. The entire court is looking at me all the time, waiting for me to make a mistake, and I never know what to say.'

'Well, it's time you learned.' Ferimon spoke sharply, and all of the pleasant good humour had vanished from his expression. 'You're the ruler of the Phaerie now, Tiolani. It's time you stopped acting like a pampered little girl.'

Tiolani dropped her gaze. 'I'm sorry. You're right.'

Ferimon took her in his arms and smiled down at her. 'Of course I am. And don't worry about the public audience. I'll be right there beside you. Trust me, Tiolani. I know what's best for you.'

When he had gone, Tiolani snuggled back down beneath the covers and stretched out luxuriously, looking round her room. How she loved this place, which had been hers ever since she'd been old enough to leave the nursery. The cold stone walls were panelled with golden wood, beautifully carved to resemble a forest scene, with trees, flowers, twining vines and a river that curled and flowed right around the room. Here and there, animals were cunningly concealed amid the vegetation, and she loved to pick them out one by one: rabbits, deer and slinking foxes on the ground, and squirrels, birds and even an owl perched in the branches of the trees. The carving extended to the stone surround of the fireplace, and in keeping with the general theme, the carpets and drapes were mingled shades of gold and green, as was the coverlet on her bed.

Thinking of Ferimon, Tiolani wondered how so much happiness could come out of such deep sorrow. True, her father was taking a worryingly long time to recover – but as Ferimon said, at least she knew that he was with the best possible healers. Her grief for her brother was more of a problem. Her feelings were still so acute, months later, that the pain could only be assuaged by the repeated spilling of human blood in the Hunt. Because she needed to hunt so frequently, she seemed to be locked in a constant battle of wills with Aelwen, who was forever fussing and complaining about the state of the overworked horses, until Tiolani had become sick of the sight of her. Only the thought of Hellorin's wrath, if he recovered and found that she had removed his precious Horsemistress, had prevented her from getting rid of Aelwen for good and all.

Yet, despite these problems and annoyances, things were getting better. While Tiolani had Ferimon at her side, everything would be all right, of that she was certain. She would have been far less sanguine, however, if she could have heard the conversation that was taking place at that moment across the corridor, in the rooms of her lady-in-waiting.

Ferimon could tell that Varna had been fretting. When he entered she was staring into the depths of the fire, her expression morose, her eyes clouded with troubled thoughts. She spun around quickly as he entered, unable to hide her unhappiness. Inwardly, Ferimon cursed his error. Whenever he left his sister alone for too long to be with Tiolani, she would start to miss both her brother and her friend, and uncertainty would begin to invade her mind.

'I thought you were never going to come,' Varna said. 'Did I not know better, I would think you were beginning to enjoy Tiolani's company more than mine.' Her bright voice tried to make her comment into a jest, but there was a slight tremor beneath the words that betrayed her uncertainty.

He put his arms around her and kissed her on the forehead, thinking, with wry amusement, that he'd done something similar not five minutes before to silence Tiolani's complaints. Women were so predictable. 'Surely you cannot think I would prefer the company of Hellorin's pampered daughter to that of my own dear sister.'

'I'm sorry.' To his dismay, the lines of tension had not moved from between her eyebrows and around her mouth. 'I sound jealous of poor Tiolani, and I have no right to be. After all, I still have you, but she has lost everyone: mother, father and brother.' Varna hesitated, then went on: 'Ferimon, are you sure we should be using her in this way? The death of our parents happened a long time ago, and Hellorin has always been kind to us.' She took his hand. 'My dear, could not our grief at losing Arvain and so many of our other friends have clouded our thinking? Tiolani might be spoilt, and not the easiest of people to live with, but I hate to think of hurting her.'

Ferimon shot his sister an anxious glance. These fits of conscience, to which she seemed increasingly prone, might ruin everything, and his plan was much too good to fail on such a ridiculous detail. Of course, Varna believed that his plot to encompass Hellorin's downfall had begun after Arvain's death. She had no idea just how long he had been hatching it in the secret recesses of his innermost thoughts, and how carefully he had plotted and intrigued to achieve the Forest Lord's downfall.

Even though she was his only remaining kin, though they had shared a close and loving bond since childhood, Ferimon felt not the slightest shred of remorse at duping her in this fashion. Best she stayed innocent, he told himself. She was convinced that the ambush had been an evil twist of fate, and had no idea that her brother had masterminded the entire trap – right down to providing those stinking ferals with the weapons that they so desperately needed. And, since she had been among the hunters on the night of the attack, it was certainly best she didn't know that he had risked her life to achieve his ends. Anyway, that was entirely her own fault. Though he had tried his utmost to persuade her to go with him in the net crew that night, she had insisted on accompanying Tiolani on her first Hunt.

Now it was more important than ever that he keep her on his side. 'Don't be angry with me, Varna,' he cajoled. 'How can we be hurting her when she so desperately needs our support at this time? And you agreed to help me avenge our family's name. It was your clever planning that won me Tiolani's trust in the first place, remember? That idea of wearing the same robes I wore for Arvain's funeral was inspired. And as for the ostensible gift from Arvain – that was pure genius, and well worth the expense. Do you know that she never takes it off?'

Varna sighed. 'At least it made her happy, poor creature. She doted on that brother of hers so much, she was blind to the fact that he was far too self-absorbed to think of buying the occasional gift for his sister. Now that he's dead, she has built him up into something he never was.'

'For certain, he was never interested in ruling.' Ferimon grimaced. 'In all those years I stayed close to him, he had no desire whatsoever for power, and I could never get him to influence Hellorin in any way. He was my friend, and I grieve for his death, but now that he is gone, Varna, I don't feel we owe Hellorin another thing. And don't worry about Tiolani. I've made her happy, have I not? And I promise I will do everything in my power to keep her that way – while you and I will be ruling the Phaerie through her, and no one will suspect a thing.'

His sister looked unconvinced. 'But what if Hellorin should awaken, and find out?'

He smiled. 'You needn't worry about that, dear one. Our associates among the physicians will make sure that Hellorin stays exactly the way he is.'

Varna shook her head. 'I still don't see why we have to keep him alive at all. That way, there's always a risk. Why don't we have our physicians rid us of him once and for all?'

'All in good time. Coming so soon after Arvain's death, the loss of her father might incapacitate Tiolani completely. No; let her gain some confidence first, and decide that she actually enjoys being ruler of the Phaerie. Then, when we make our move and Hellorin departs this life, she will not be so inclined to look into the matter too closely.'

'I only hope you know what you're doing,' Varna told him. 'Here.' She thrust a bunch of richly scented summer roses, with the dew still pearling on their petals, into his hand. 'I was up at some unearthly hour picking these. I knew you would never think of such a thing yourself – and besides, you're far too lazy to get out of bed at first light. I hope Tiolani appreciates them.'

'Oh, she will.' Ferimon smiled wolfishly. 'She loves surprise gifts.'

'I'd appreciate the occasional surprise gift myself,' Varna muttered, 'but you never think of that.'

Ferimon was too busy congratulating himself on his own cleverness to hear her. 'Your hard work will be worthwhile, I promise,' he told her. 'Every embrace, every gift, every little loving gesture brings Tiolani further into our power, and helps to deliver the realm of the Phaerie into our hands.'

The public audience was the aspect of ruling that Tiolani liked least. Every tenth day she was forced to follow Hellorin's custom of hearing the petitions of any who had a favour to ask or a dispute that needed settling. She dressed in all her finery. To make herself a little taller, she used a minor version of her father's glamourie spell, whereby he could make himself grow to a towering height. She even used magic to make her voice louder and more resonant, but nothing she did seemed to make up for her want of confidence. She was afraid she'd betray her lack of experience every time she opened her mouth. She hated having to make decisions on the spot in front of a crowd of courtiers, and she lived in constant dread of exposing herself to derision and scorn.

Today, in particular, she was beginning to wonder whether she had made a serious error. Ferimon's sources had told her that Ambaron, representing the interests of the small group of Hemifae traders who dwelt in the city, had been complaining about the restrictions she had placed on the movements of her subjects, but she'd expected him to request a private meeting to raise his grievances. Instead, however, he had apparently decided to corner her by raising his issues before the entire Phaerie Court, and there was no escaping a very public confrontation.

Tiolani sighed. 'Speak, Ambaron.' She tried in vain to keep from revealing her dislike of him in her voice. The trader had taken after the human side of his heritage in appearance. With his brown hair, stocky build and blunt, rounded features, he looked like a slave who had dressed up in his master's finery, and Tiolani was ill-disposed to look kindly on anything that resembled a human.

From the expression on Ambaron's face, the dislike was mutual, and his bow was a great deal more perfunctory than was required – especially from a Hemifae – to show respect for a ruler. When he spoke, he assumed a ponderous, didactic tone, as though he were speaking to a child. 'Lady Tiolani,' he began, 'as you doubtless know, it is the custom of the traders to travel each summer to the Wizard city of Tyrineld, where we trade moonmoth silk and gems from the mountains for the forged tools and weapons of metal that we cannot produce, and for the fruit and herbs requiring a warmer climate, that we cannot grow ourselves in this northern realm. This year, you have placed a ban on any Phaerie travelling outside their own lands – but surely you did not mean that restriction to apply to merchants? Would you truly deprive your subjects of the luxuries and necessities from the south in this way?'

Curse this miserable half-blood! In suggesting that she was deliberately depriving her subjects, he had placed her in an impossible position. Frantically she looked to Ferimon, who stood in his usual place, to one side of the throne. Usually his expression would tell her how she should proceed, but today, he simply looked thunderous, which wasn't much help. Nor did he reply to her frantic query in mindspeech.

Tiolani gazed around the throne room for inspiration. The imposing and beautiful hall was built of pale-coloured stone, its roof supported by a double row of great pillars carved to resemble trees, with the branches fanning out to provide the vaulting of the ceiling. Massive windows of stained glass pierced the walls at regular intervals, and behind the throne was a massive rose window in multicoloured hues that took up most of the wall, and filled the room with jewelled light. The richly clad courtiers who were in attendance, standing or sitting in scattered groups, were all looking up at Tiolani expectantly. She was the cynosure of every eye in the room.

She could think of no other way to respond, save with bluntness. 'The restrictions apply equally to all my subjects. Why should the traders be the exception?'

'But Lady,' the trader protested, 'what about the new weapons we need? How will our miners and farmers manage without tools? What about wine? Or herbs for seasonings and medicine? Or the good oil from the olive, which we use for so many purposes?'

Tiolani sat up straight on the throne. If she let herself be bullied over this matter, she would never manage to claw back the respect – albeit grudging – that she had managed to win herself so far. 'I thought I had made myself clear on this point,' she told the trader. 'I do not wish the Magefolk, particularly the Wizards, to know that the Forest Lord is wounded and currently unable to rule. They may decide to take the opportunity to encroach upon our borders, and following the ambush in the forest, the Phaerie are in no condition to fight a war over territory.' She looked him straight in the eye. 'The Wizards may decide that it will be easy to take advantage of a young, inexperienced girl. They would be wrong, but I would rather not risk the lives of my people to teach them that lesson.'

Ambaron glared at her. 'Are you suggesting that we traders would give away secrets to the Wizards?'

Hellorin's daughter met his glare with a stony look of her own. 'Frankly, I'm not prepared to take the risk.'

'But Lady, our livelihoods—'

'Enough!' Tiolani struck the armrest of the throne with her fist. 'You have heard my decision.'

The trader stood his ground, his own temper clearly beginning to rise. 'My Lady, this is ridiculous. You cannot make such a law—'

Utterly incensed, she leapt to her feet. '*I* am the ruler here. Do not presume to tell me what I can and cannot do.'

Ambaron's face went white. 'With respect, Lady, you are *not* the ruler here. You are merely acting in his stead. Wounded or not, Hellorin still rules the Phaerie – or do you know something that the rest of us do not?' Even as the words left his mouth, Tiolani saw his expression turn to one of dismay. In the heat of the moment, he had gone further than he had intended, and spoken words he had never meant to utter aloud.

There was a moment's deathly hush, then a buzz of horrified talk swept through the court as the implications of Ambaron's remark struck home. What was worse, the trader was closer to the truth than he knew.

So many times of late, Tiolani had found herself thinking how much more pleasant it was to rule than be ruled, and how convenient it would be if her father could remain out of the way for a little longer, and leave the field clear for her.

Tiolani's guilt focused her anger into a solitary diamond point. She found herself thinking very coldly and clearly, without a trace of emotion. There was only one punishment for such sedition. Time seemed to stretch as she remembered her father standing at bay in the forest clearing, pierced through and through by the arrows of the rebels, calling down the wrath of the heavens on those who had slain his son. Then, all at once, she knew exactly what he had done, and how he had accomplished it. True, it would be more difficult to accomplish within the hall, but nothing was beyond the new Lady of the Phaerie. Summoning the Old Magic to her bidding, she called upon the powers of the lightning.

As she lifted her hand, Ambaron must have seen his death in her eyes. He backed away from her, his face contorted with terror. 'Lady, please. Nooooo ...'

Tiolani opened her hand and unleashed a single, searing bolt that came out of nowhere and wrapped itself, sizzling and crackling, around the merchant's writhing form. He crumpled and fell – and suddenly the lightning was gone, leaving nothing but a vile odour of burning flesh, and on the floor, a blackened, smouldering lump that no longer resembled a Phaerie.

Tiolani swept the crowd with burning eyes, and felt them quail before her as her voice rang out through the hall. 'Let all take heed,' she said. 'So perish those who would speak treason.'

20

DHAGON

The death of the trader ended the morning's business. The fearful crowd, aghast at the smoking remains of Ambaron, cleared the room with amazing speed. Ferimon watched them go, and exulted. Tiolani sank down upon her throne and sat, expressionless as a statue, her face so white that it looked as though it had been carved from alabaster. Ferimon glanced across at Varna, and beckoned her with a tilt of his head. She hurried to join them as he insinuated his hand beneath Tiolani's elbow and led her from the room, with the warriors of the Lady's bodyguard grouped around them.

As they passed through the corridors of the palace, everyone melted out of their way. When they reached her suite, he stationed guards in front of her doorway. 'See that the Lady Tiolani is not disturbed,' he ordered, as he and Varna accompanied her inside and closed the door behind them.

Once she reached the sanctuary of her own rooms, Tiolani walked across to the window and stood in silence, staring out. Ferimon and Varna exchanged an anxious look, but Tiolani had a surprise for them. Before they had time to speak to her, she turned, staring through them with a cold, blank expression. 'Why are you two still here? I do *not* recall asking for company.' Her tone of voice was different from any she had used before: firmer, stronger, ringing with confidence. For once Ferimon found himself floundering, unsure of what to say. 'But ... but Lady,' he stammered, 'we were concerned – we wanted to make sure you were all right.'

'Of course I am all right,' Tiolani said icily. 'Why should I not be?'

'But my dearest Lady, I was afraid you were feeling bad about Ambaron's death.'

'As was I,' Varna added quickly.

Tiolani shrugged. 'You idiots. All I feel is rage, not remorse. How dare that half-blood trader accuse me of keeping Hellorin imprisoned out of time, so I could rule the Phaerie.' Her voice had turned to a snarl, and a cruel little smile curved her lips. 'But I soon corrected that. And you know, it finally made me realise that I have not been taking a strong enough hand with these insolent courtiers, or with my father's advisors. I won't make *that* mistake again.'

A shiver passed through Ferimon. He had done his work almost too well. He looked into her face and saw a familiar expression – the same one she had worn when she came back from the Wild Hunt, exulting in the bloodshed and slaughter. Had the horrors she'd experienced during the ambush that had killed her brother twisted her mind in some way? He was beginning to wonder. But no matter what had happened months ago in the forest, today had been a turning point for Tiolani. She had grown up, and proved she was her father's daughter. She had finally come to understand the extent of the power she possessed – and to revel in it.

Tiolani, in the meantime, had sat down before her mirror and was brushing her hair, as cool and unconcerned as if she had just returned from a morning stroll in the garden. 'Varna, you may go now. Send for some food, Ferimon, will you? I'm starving.'

'Yes, my Lady.' Her face tight with anger, Varna swung around in a swirl of skirts and marched out. Ferimon opened his mouth, closed it again, and quickly sent a message in mindspeech to the kitchens, requesting all the Lady Tiolani's favourite delicacies. Today it definitely seemed wise to stay on her good side.

After the events of the morning, Tiolani had been surprised to find herself hungry, but when the food arrived, she devoured hot soup, cold roast peacock and a big bowl of glossy, sweet cherries as though she had not seen food for a week. While she had permitted Ferimon to stay and eat with her, she was glad he had the good sense to remain silent unless she spoke to him first. Her actions that day had given her a great deal to think about, and the repercussions – both for herself and for those she ruled – were likely to be far-reaching indeed.

Hellorin's daughter was feeling very proud of herself. She had executed that perfidious trader using her own magical powers, just as her father might have done. Her subjects had been given a long-overdue demonstration that, just like the Forest Lord, she was not to be defied or thwarted – especially not by some filthy half-blood, first cousin to those animals who had killed her brother. How sweet and fitting it would be to remove their taint from the Phaerie race ...

'Whose taint?' Ferimon's voice broke into her thoughts.

Tiolani realised that she must have spoken the last part of her musings aloud. 'The Hemifae, naturally.' She reached into the cut-crystal bowl and selected another cherry, which looked like a drop of blood between her fingers. 'It was a mistake on my father's part to let them infiltrate our race. They twine like strangling briars into every aspect of Phaerie lives. Why should they own mines and farms, be in positions of power, wealth and privilege? They are no better than the human animals that spawned them.'

She saw Ferimon's eyes widen slightly in alarm, and exulted in her own sense of power. 'But my love,' he said carefully, 'the Hemifae were spawned, as you call it, by the Phaerie, too.'

'Their Phaerie blood is corrupted by human taint,' Tiolani snapped back, 'and that makes them just as bad as those filthy mortal scum. The hybrids are no better than slaves, yet they move among us in positions of authority, dressed in finery as though they believe themselves fit to be real Phaerie.' She clenched her fingers, stained blood-red with cherry juice, into a fist and smashed it down on the table. 'The Hemifae are an abomination, corrupting the purity of our race. Every trace of them should be cleansed from this world.'

'But Lady,' Ferimon said, still using that careful, coaxing voice, 'the Hemifae *are* our civilisation, or at least the greater part of it. They are our artisans, artists and architects, our agriculturists and traders. The humans might work our farms and our mines, but the Hemifae run them. It is they who decide what should be planted and when. They direct the mining operations by deep-sensing the whereabouts of gold and gem deposits, and they train and coordinate the cutters, setters and polishers. Hemifae design the jewellery, and the clothing that we make from moonmoth silk – which, incidentally, they produce. They are the ones who take these articles out into the world, and trade with the Wizards for the necessities, luxuries and delicacies that otherwise we could not obtain. The Hemifae train our horses. They—'

'Enough!' Again, Tiolani struck the table with her fist. How dare he speak to her as if she were still a child? 'Do not presume to lecture me, Ferimon. I know exactly what the Hemifae do. And I can see that it is only due to the laziness and indolence of the pure-blooded Phaerie that they have been allowed to gain such a stranglehold. Once, before the half-breeds grew so numerous, there were Phaerie who fulfilled all the functions that the Hemifae have now taken as their own, and we are perfectly capable of doing so again. My people may not possess many of these skills now, but they can learn – and they must. Then the Hemifae can be removed—'

'Lady, before you continue with your most interesting plans for the Hemifae, you should know that they are the least of your problems.'

The voice was strange to her. Even as Tiolani spun around, Ferimon vanished from sight, imprisoned within a silvery orb that enclosed him completely. Though she would have been willing to swear that there had been no one else in the room, a white-haired figure dressed in grey stepped out from the shadows in the corner. 'Now,' he said, in a voice that was iron and granite. 'That should take care of the minion. There is no reason why he should hear what I am about to say to you – in fact, when he is released, he will have no recollection that I was here at all.'

Tiolani was pleased to note that the intruder had the attenuated form of a true-blooded Phaerie. 'You're right, of course,' he said, as though she had spoken her thoughts aloud. 'Both my father and mother were pure-blood Phaerie, though it cost my mother her life to bear me. You will also notice,' he added with a chilling smile, 'that I have no compunction whatsoever about picking the most private thoughts from a poorly guarded mind, no matter what the person's rank. You would be well advised to work on your shielding, my Lady. I could never extract the faintest whisper of a thought from your father.' His eyes were what frightened her most. A strange, pale, silvery grey, they were stony and flat, reflecting rather than revealing, and utterly pitiless.

Not even during the ambush by the ferals had Tiolani been so afraid. Reacting from pure instinct, she lifted her hand in a blur of speed and hurled a sizzling bolt of lightning. But the stranger was faster. Even as she moved to attack, he had struck first. She saw the dazzle of the spell coming towards her – then it neutralised her own magic and enveloped her in a wave of icy cold that penetrated both her body and her mind, paralysing her limbs and slowing her thoughts.

With a sinking certainty, Tiolani realised that the interloper could only have one identity: he must be one of the Chahiri, the select, secret group of spies and assassins that Hellorin had formed long ago to be his eyes and ears – and when necessary his killers – in the world beyond the Phaerie realm. There were rumours that their services could be contracted by a private individual if the rewards were high enough, and by any standards, Ambaron had been very wealthy. Had his family hired this killer to avenge his death?

Again came the thin, mirthless smile that struck utter fear into Tiolani's heart. 'Not even close,' he said. 'Though you do have my profession correct. I am one of the Chahiri – in fact, I am their leader. You may call me Dhagon. Though I do occasionally permit my underlings to accept private contracts, I answer to your father alone. Until now, only he has known of my existence and, because he is still alive, I would have remained in secret, unknown to you – save that I am forced to reveal myself in order to bring you a warning. Danger is approaching. You must be on your guard.'

Tiolani, hypnotised by the gaze of those pale eyes, beckoned him to a seat by her side. 'Tell me,' she said.

He slid into place beside her as silently as a shadow. 'I am head of a spy network that Lord Hellorin seeded throughout the dominions of the Magefolk,' he told her. 'I managed to place an agent in Tyrineld who, for the last two years, has sent information about the Wizardfolk and their activities directly to me; and thence, to your father. Information from that agent has just come into my hands, and brought me here to disclose my identity and warn you in person. Lord Hellorin trusts no one but me to coordinate the activities of his spy network, and as I am now unable to make contact with him, I must come directly to you with my information, for the responsibility for the realm currently rests in your hands.'

He hesitated. 'Lady ... Do you think your father will ever recover?'

Was he questioning her ability to rule? Or was he testing her in another way? Unease crawled down Tiolani's spine. 'We do not know.' She looked away from this deadly stranger with the disconcerting eyes. 'My father's wounds were so grave, it was a miracle he survived at all. They say that they cannot bring him back into time for more than a moment or two because so many of his vital organs are malfunctioning, so they have given up that approach. Now they are trying to find some form of spell that will heal him all at once. If they cannot ...' She bowed her head, as if in grief, then suddenly her eyes snapped upwards and looked straight into the spymaster's own. 'Do *you* think I am responsible for his continuing decline?'

Her attempt to take him by surprise fell utterly flat. Dhagon simply gave her an unfathomable look. 'My Lady, I am the last person to believe you capable of evil. But if Hellorin does not survive, I must take steps to keep his intelligence network functioning for you, his successor.'

Tiolani let out a breath that she did not know she'd been holding. 'Thank you, Dhagon. I am glad of your loyalty, and grateful that you came.' Belatedly, she remembered her manners. 'Will you have wine? Or something to eat?'

He shook his head. 'Thank you, no.'

'Very well, then,' Tiolani said. 'So what are your urgent tidings?'

The spy leaned close to her and spoke softly. 'For some time, rumours have been flying in Tyrineld about what is happening in our realm. They knew nothing for certain; however, the Archwizard Cyran has discovered of late that the Wild Hunt has been crossing the border between our lands with increasing frequency, and killing a number of slaves belonging to the Wizardfolk of Nexis – genuine forest workers going about their legitimate business. In order to protest the depredations, and also to find out why we have cut off all communication, he is sending a delegation to you here in Eliorand.'

Those pale eyes became as sharp and cold as a sword blade. 'Lady, if you will permit me to say so, killing those slaves was most unwise. Did you not think there would be repercussions? Did you believe the Wizards would sit idly by and let their minions be slaughtered?'

Tiolani thrust out her jaw. 'The Wild Hunt is accountable to no one.'

'If that is your attitude, you'd better be prepared to deal with the consequences.' His tone was flat and uncompromising. 'Just as I have an agent in Tyrineld, it has now become evident that Cyran has also managed to place a spy in *our* midst. I have my suspicions as to his identity, and when I am certain ...'

For an instant his jaw tightened and those chill eyes flamed. Then the mask slipped back into place so swiftly that she was left wondering whether she had glimpsed the loathing and anger at all. 'I will find this spy,' Dhagon went on, and the chill tonelessness in his voice was far more terrifying than the earlier fireflash of emotion that he had let slip. 'I will use all the resources at my disposal to root him out, and when I apprehend him ... You have my promise, Lady, that the traitor will be screaming for death to take him, ere I am finished.'

He took a deep breath. 'In the meantime, however, we have more urgent business. Cyran's delegates have already left Tyrineld, Lady. What will you do?'

Tiolani's hands, which had been resting lightly on the table before her, clenched suddenly into fists. 'They may have left Tyrineld,' she growled, 'but I will see to it that they never arrive in Eliorand.'

The spy's pale eyes grew watchful; wary. 'You play a very perilous game, my Lady. Are you truly saying that you want me to ... dispose of them?'

'Yes, do so.' Her smile was as grim and mirthless as Dhagon's own. 'After all, the wildwood can be a dangerous place, filled with all manner of strange and deadly creatures. Travellers encounter them all the time. If Cyran's representatives were to meet with an accident, how could *we* be blamed?'

21

KEEPER OF THE TRUST

The Forest Lord's stables shimmered like a mirage in the sunshine. To the unmagical eye the scene might have consisted of trees and clearings, bluffs and boulders and banks of shrubs, for the glamourie that disguised the Phaerie city was very strong at this time of day, when the sun was highest in the sky. In order for them to be able to function, the mortal slaves who laboured in the city were bespelled to see through the enchantment. The companion animals, the horses, hounds and hawks beloved of Hellorin's folk, seemed immune to the deception.

By this time, Corisand had grown used to seeing both illusion and reality. It was one of the many changes that were taking place within her since the feral humans had slain the old Windeye, catapulting her into this strange new life. Luckily, the Phaerie had left her alone to work things out. Since Hellorin was not able to ride her, she was still turned out into the far pasture with its own stable. Now that the weather had improved, five of the brood mares who'd already delivered foals had been put into her field, ostensibly to keep her company, though in fact they all seemed to sense the sudden, inexplicable difference in her, and treated her accordingly. Sometimes she felt even lonelier among the other horses than she had been when she was on her own. Occasionally she found herself longing for the old days, when she had led a life of simple pleasures, comfortable surroundings and the good companionship of the herd. But those days were over, never to return.

If only Taku had called her back quickly to the Elsewhere, the problems of this world wouldn't weigh so heavily, but months had passed while the seasons turned from late winter to early summer, and there had been no summons. Her two friends among the Evanesar had explained to her that time flowed differently between the two realms. She understood that they would not bring her back until Hellorin was distracted, and no longer looking for her. Nevertheless, she couldn't help but be worried and impatient. And even worse, doubts had begun to creep in. Was it possible that she had dreamed the whole thing? Surely she could never have imagined the amazing, wonderful differences between her equine body and the human form that she had occupied in that other, magical world? In the face of all the doubts and difficulties, she somehow managed to cling on to hope and faith as the days slipped by.

If there seemed no solution at present for that particular problem, however, there were plenty of others with which Corisand *could* deal. As a priority, she continued to work on her mental shielding. A technique of retreating into a safe place in her mind had too many limitations, for it would not let her function efficiently among others, or cope with the practical demands of everyday existence. So how could she protect her mind from the intrusive mental emanations of others, yet still reach out with her thoughts and senses to the world beyond? After a number of ideas had been attempted and discarded, she'd finally hit upon a workable method quite by accident.

One fine day in spring, two of the Phaerie children had been brought down by their father to see the horses. The elder of the two, a little girl, had been enraptured, but her brother was much less impressed. While the elder child and the father were organising her first riding lesson, the boy wandered off, unobserved, and climbed on the fence of the enclosure that Corisand shared with the other mares. Corisand watched him closely, afraid that he might climb down into the paddock and be accidentally trampled, or kicked or bitten by mothers protecting their foals. She knew that she must be on her guard to protect the brat, for, if he should be hurt, the wrath of their Phaerie masters would fall on all her people.

Much to her relief, however, the child remained in place. As she continued to keep an eye on him, he began to amuse himself with a little magic. Putting his thumbs and forefingers together to form a ring, he held them in front of his face and blew. To the Windeye's astonishment, a gleaming, iridescent bubble appeared between his fingers and floated off across the paddock. Bubble after bubble he blew, which bounced and swirled among the startled mares, never bursting and continuing to hold their form, while the little boy sat on the fence and giggled with delight.

Corisand ceased to be aware of the child, as an amazing revelation struck her. Was this the answer? Maybe her problem would be solved if she could place a similar kind of barrier around her mind; one that would let her observe and interact with the world and her fellow creatures on the physical level, while keeping their thoughts and emotions at bay.

The idea was worth a try, but it turned out to be easier said than done. First, she had to work hard at her visualisation, in order to form her shield and make it function in the way she wanted, before learning how to maintain it in the face of all distractions. Time and again, her concentration would be broken at a crucial moment, the turmoil of outside thoughts and emotions came flooding back into her mind, and she would have to start all over again. Gradually, however, Corisand mastered the technique, and as spring blossomed into summer, she found that she could get her barrier to hold its form, and could finally call her mind her own once more. And with her protection in place, at last she could settle down in earnest to explore the ramifications of the new role that had been placed upon her.

She had always been different from the other horses, she could see that now. As a youngster she had perplexed her mother, the equable Maiglan, for she was more intelligent and curious than the rest, always the first to stick her nose into trouble. She had been more stubborn and rebellious than the others, too. It had taken Hellorin himself to get a bit into her mouth and a saddle on her back, for only in the Phaerie Lord had she discovered a will to match her own. And now, at last, she'd discovered the reason.

As the Windeye of the Xandim, a different world had opened up before her, ripe with possibilities and promise, yet with a set of challenges that were daunting in their immensity. She knew that, trapped as she was in her equine form, she could only scratch the surface of her new potential, and the same applied to the rest of the Xandim. Their enslavement had been far more cruel and complete than mere imprisonment. They had been confined as horses for so long that they had forgotten how to think and reason in the sophisticated way that humans could, and they had lost all memory of the history and heritage of their once-proud race. Deprived of their past, denied their future: what would become of them? As their Windeye, Corisand knew that no one could liberate them but herself. Yet, like her predecessors before her, she had already discovered the difficulty, ambiguity and frustration that lay at the heart of her role.

In the meantime, without even noticing, Corisand had risen to the position of lead mare among her people. When horses lived in their wild and natural state, it was a fallacy that the stallion led the herd. They were always led by a mare, more wise and clever than the rest: the one with the ability to find water and fodder, the safest grazing grounds and the best possible shelter from the elements. While it was the task of the lead mare to guide and provide for the other mares and foals, the stallion's role, apart from procreation, was to keep the herd together, and protect it from outside threats such as predators and other stallions.

Corisand had never aspired to the role of lead mare, and did not do so now. She had been so caught up in her own private world of challenges and discoveries that she had not noticed herself gradually changing positions within the strictly hierarchical system of the mares. In the spring, when the new grass came and all the horses were put out to pasture, the others, who had once preceded her, were now standing aside to let her go through the gate first. She drank first; she had first choice of fodder. If it had stopped at that, she would probably still have remained blissfully unaware of her altered status. But then, most inconveniently, they started to expect her to lead them and, though horses did not have a sophisticated language of words, they were able to communicate their needs with sounds, stance, body language and subtle movements of ear and eye.

They wanted her to let the grooms know that one of the older mares had taken ill and laid herself down in the long grass beneath the trees, out of sight and away from help. They looked to her to intervene in a squabble, when one mare took a fancy to another's foal. They expected her to keep the peace within the little herd, to quell any bullying and make sure that the weakest had their fair share of the food and water. When an unexpected spring blizzard hit the valley of the Phaerie, they immediately assumed that she would find them the best place to shelter.

It was very wearing. Time and again, she was tempted to chase them away, to ignore their needs, to make them leave her alone. But how could she? She was Windeye. No matter how unready she felt, they were her responsibility. If the tribe had been in its natural state, there would have been others to shoulder much of the burden: the Herdlord, and the Matriarch. But that was impossible now. It had been different for Valir, she realised. As a stallion, these problems would not have come his way. The group of mares would have found a natural leader amongst themselves. But now that she bore the Windeye's mantle, they sensed the change and turned to her, and would not be gainsaid. She had no alternative but to sigh, shoulder the load and lead them as best she could.

Corisand never considered that any of the Phaerie might notice that she had changed. Why should they, when the transformation had only taken place within her? In this, however, she had reckoned without the ever-vigilant Horsemistress.

It was a beautiful day, and with the horses all out at pasture, the workload for the stables should have been considerably lighter than in the winter. Normally, the horses would have been fit and well, the new crop of foals thriving, and Aelwen would have been enjoying the sunshine without a care in the world. This year, unfortunately, it wasn't that easy.

She was deeply concerned about Hellorin's condition. When a month had passed and brought no sign of a recovery, she had gone directly to his healers and demanded to know what was happening. They had explained their difficulties and counselled patience, and at first she had trusted their assurances that eventually the Forest Lord would recover. But as winter had run its course and spring had turned to early summer, she had found it increasingly difficult to believe them, and her suspicions that something was badly amiss had grown.

To make matters worse, Aelwen was unable to get close enough to Hellorin or his healers to investigate further. These days, she was no longer welcome in the palace, for her relationship with Tiolani had gone from bad to worse. Since the reins of power had been thrust into her hands, that foolish girl had gathered her own clique about her: sleek, self-serving courtiers who hadn't given two straws for her when her father had been whole, her brother still alive and she just an unimportant younger scion, and a daughter to boot. Once she had been given a taste of power, Tiolani, still in many ways a spoilt child, had no truck with those who tried to thwart her. Her relationship with Aelwen had foundered over the business of the Hunt, for Hellorin's daughter had not taken kindly to being upbraided for the ill-use of the horses, and had given short shrift to Aelwen's rebukes.

Hellorin's Horsemistress took her duties very seriously, and she was worried about the health of her charges. Also, she was losing sleep because she just couldn't work out what was amiss with the Forest Lord's favourite mare. Ever since she had returned from the massacre in the forest, Corisand's behaviour had been odd somehow: nothing too overt, nothing that could quite be pinned down, and yet ...

With her brows knotted in a frown, Aelwen leant against the paddock fence, put one foot up comfortably on the lower rail and watched Hellorin's mare with great concentration. What was *wrong* with the creature? None of the other horses involved in the ambush had returned like this. Some of them had been scared and skittish for a while, but that wasn't Corisand's problem. On the contrary, gone were the fidgets and the flashfire temper of old. Instead, the mare seemed almost oblivious to her surroundings for much of the time, walking round in a daze and standing for hours, simply staring into space.

At first Aelwen had thought that Corisand was ailing in some way, but Hellorin's expert equine healers could find nothing physically wrong with the animal. So what was the problem? If the Horsemistress had not known better, she would have said that the mare seemed preoccupied with something – but no, that was ridiculous. A horse deep in thought? The very idea was laughable, impossible. And though Corisand's fits of temper had gone, Aelwen couldn't say that her temperament had actually improved. When she wasn't ignoring her grooms, it seemed as though she actually hated them. To the experienced eye, her loathing could be read in her white-rimmed eyes and flattened ears, yet she made no effort to kick or bite her handlers, or threaten them in any way. Even stranger was the fact that, without apparently having made the slightest effort, this irritating animal had somehow become the leader of the mares. Experienced as she was in the ways of horses, Aelwen could see absolutely no reason for this change in the hierarchy of the herd. And there had been one other peculiar thing, one that she had never dared mention to Kelon or anyone else.

Not long after Arvain had been sent to his rest, she had walked down towards the lower fields one snowy night, unable to sleep, and wanting to distract herself from worry and sadness. When she'd reached the furthest pasture, she had seen a sight that had haunted her ever since. The moon, low on the horizon, had broken through the massed banks of cloud, and in the moonlight, the grey mare was dancing.

Hardly daring to breathe lest Corisand discover her presence, Aelwen had watched the horse dance amid the swirling snow; transformed, in those moments of magic, into some otherworldly creature. Then, as if someone had blown out a gigantic candle, the moon vanished abruptly behind the clouds, and the mare became flesh and blood once more, and paced quietly back into her stable. The sound of the bolt being slid back into place sounded loud in the still, frosty air, and a chill that had nothing to do with the wintry weather passed down Aelwen's spine, as silently she turned and crept away. When she had awakened next morning, falling snow had obliterated the intricate hoofprint patterns in the paddock, and the whole episode had taken on the tenor of a dream. But Aelwen knew, in her heart, that it was not.

At that moment Kelon came walking across from the stables, and the Horsemistress smiled to see him. She had known him for so long that he seemed almost to be an extension of herself. Her second in command, he had been her friend for years uncounted, and she knew that she could trust him with her life, as he could trust her. Though he was a Hemifae like herself, in looks he had taken after the human side of his ancestry, rather than the Phaerie. His hair was sandy rather than the burnished red-gold that was so common among Hellorin's folk, and his face was seamed and weathered, lacking the pointed delicacy of the Phaerie physiognomy. Though he was a kind man, it was a standing joke around the stable that he was rarely seen to smile.

'Are you still fretting about that animal?' Though Kelon would never openly criticise her, his voice held a hint of reproach. She knew he thought that she wasted too much time and energy worrying over Corisand's odd behaviour. The mare was healthy, wasn't she? And surely this new, quiet demeanour could only be an improvement? Well, then.

Aelwen sighed. 'I know you can't see it, but I am absolutely certain something is amiss with her.'

Kelon looked thoughtfully at the mare. 'You know, I'm beginning to agree with you. At first, I didn't think this new behaviour was of much significance – I put it down to shock after the attack, and thought she'd come out of it in the end. But this new business of becoming lead mare – now that's just plain unnatural. Totally out of the normal pattern of behaviour for the whole group.'

Aelwen frowned. 'It's not just her inattentiveness, or even this lead-mare business that's worrying me. It's only that – I don't know – there's just something about her. She was always a very difficult horse to handle, but now, though she's all right with the two of us, you would think she hates everyone else. There's something in her stance and the way she looks at the grooms that sends a chill through me ... Kelon, do you think she's going mad?'

For a thoughtful moment, Kelon gazed at Corisand again. 'What about breeding from her?' he said at last. 'She isn't doing anything useful right now – just lazing around, eating her head off, and she should come into season again about the end of the month. She's an outstanding mare – if we put her to that black stallion of yours, the foal could be spectacular. And if ...' he hesitated.

'And if this strangeness does turn out to be a problem, at least we'd still have her bloodline,' Aelwen finished for him with a sigh. 'Whatever ails her, we know it's not part of her heredity.'

Kelon put his hand over hers as her fingers tightened on the paddock rail. 'It's got to be faced,' he said softly. 'But don't despair. The worst hasn't happened yet, and probably never will. She's been acting strangely, but she hasn't shown any signs of aggression so far – at least, no more than usual. She's just odd, that's all.' His eyes went to Aelwen. 'Mind you, what can we expect? Everything here has been out of kilter since Hellorin was struck down.'

'I know.' With no one else would Aelwen have dared to be so open and honest, but Kelon was special. Abruptly she switched from open words to mindspeech. 'Don't you think, Kelon,' she went on slowly, testing each word with delicate and deliberate care, like a horse testing its footing as it crossed a bit of boggy ground. 'Don't you think that Hellorin is taking an unnaturally long time to recover?'

Their eyes, his grey, hers green, met in a look of understanding. Kelon switched to mindspeech too. 'It's wonderful, is it not, how well Tiolani has taken to ruling?' he said softly. 'She's her father's daughter. Having tasted such power, it must be hard for her to think of giving it up.'

In that moment he had never seemed so dear to her. Out of love, out of loyalty, he had taken it upon himself to voice the heresy she could not bring herself to name. She gave a barely perceptible shake of her head. '*Not here and now. It's not safe.*' Though mindspeech ought to be private, there were ways to overhear it, if the eavesdropper was determined enough. Suddenly she was filled with the overwhelming urge to get away completely from the whole mess: horses behaving mysteriously, Hellorin's illness, Tiolani's hostility and the atmosphere of sheer *wrongness* that poisoned the air of Eliorand these days. 'It's a beautiful morning,' she said out loud, 'and I would love to get out of here for a while. Shall we go for a ride?'

Kelon gave her one of his rare, fleeting smiles. 'What a good idea.'

With a mounting sense of panic, Corisand watched them depart. Damn those Phaerie! Why couldn't they leave well alone? She couldn't have a foal just now. It was the last thing she needed. As it was, finding a way to regain her human form and her Windeye's powers felt like a hopeless task. With a pregnancy and then a defenceless, dependent foal to care for, it would become downright impossible. But how could she prevent it? As the Phaerie reckoned things, they were about halfway through the month. By the time it ended, oestrus would be upon her and, though so far they had never let her breed, she already knew how powerful those drives could be. Would they prove so strong that the instincts of the animal would overcome the reasoning of the Windeye? Taryn was a very attractive stallion and she liked him. He also had an excellent record of success in getting foals. All things considered, she had a feeling that she would be a fool to risk an encounter with him.

Corisand raised her head to look over the fence at the forest beyond. 'There's only one thing for it,' she said to herself. 'I've got to escape.'

She was almost ready to try it then and there, so desperate did she feel – but her Windeye's intelligence made her hesitate. If she made her escape in such an obvious manner, the Phaerie would find out almost immediately. Without the flying magic that only Hellorin or Tiolani could give her, she had no power of flight, and would simply have to run away into the forest. She was Hellorin's own mare, and, as she had just discovered, Aelwen and Kelon considered her bloodline to be valuable. They would never rest until they had hunted her down and recaptured her.

No, she had to come up with a better plan than that. But what? How? The caring, conscientious vigilance of Aelwen and Kelon would thwart her at every turn, and it suddenly occurred to her that if she did manage to succeed she would bring a great deal of trouble to the two of them – the only Phaerie out of the whole tribe of them that she didn't detest.

Never had Corisand felt so helpless, despairing and very much alone. How could she escape this impossible situation? It would take a miracle.

22

NIGHT IN THE FOREST

The weather had improved at last. Since leaving Nexis the previous day, Iriana and her companions had been riding across rolling green downs beneath a blue sky streaked with high, racing clouds. Though it was summer, the air up here was cool and fresh, tingling against Iriana's skin. Now they were approaching the forest, and once again, Iriana was looking at the world from the perspective of Boreas the eagle. From such a height, the immensity of the wildwood was grimly apparent. 'I can't believe it,' she gasped. 'It goes on *for ever*.'

Esmon shrugged. 'Not quite. At a steady pace, it should take us about ten days or so to reach the other side.'

Iriana, far from being daunted by the endless miles of forbidding forest in front of them, was looking forward to the adventure. It might help her forget that dreadful night in Nexis. Now that she had put a goodly distance between herself and Challan's new family, she was finally beginning to shake off a little of the bitter rage that had clouded her spirits since that pointless and humiliating meeting with her foster father, but she didn't feel any better about it. Oh, how she wished she had ignored him as he deserved, and had never gone to see him! The thought of him sleeping with that human slave and fathering that nasty, poison-tongued half-breed made her physically sick.

Now, however, she could see a little more clearly, with her vision less clouded by anger. As she rode, Iriana thought back to the events of that night. Though she was forced reluctantly to admit that her own behaviour, fuelled by fury, had been less than exemplary, the conduct of Challan and his woman and daughter had driven her to such extremes. It was not so much the fact that he had abandoned his true family so heartlessly, or the fact that he had run off with a mortal slave and had bred a half-human offspring. It was both of those things together – added to the fact that he had seen fit to humiliate his original family by throwing his unnatural liaisons in everyone's face. Everyone knew that some Wizards – not all of them male – liked to pleasure themselves with humans, and the resulting hybrids did appear from time to time. But unlike the Phaerie, Wizard-human relationships were not acceptable within their society, and most Wizards had the decency to be discreet about their foibles, not move into a house with them and parade them as if they were a proper lifemate, for the whole world to see. And as for Chiannala, Challan's abomination of a daughter – apparently she had the temerity to think herself every bit as good as Yinze, the full-blooded child who had been deserted in her favour, and she could only have learned that attitude from her father.

How could Challan have put Zybina and Yinze in such an embarrassing position? Had he never loved them at all? As for herself, perhaps she had less right to such consideration – but all these years, she had lived with the misery and guilt of believing that he'd abandoned his family because of her. Now that she had discovered the truth, all the pain that had been festering within her for so long had come spewing out. It was too soon for her to feel relieved and grateful that she had not been the cause of such misery. She just felt sickened and stupid, and furious that she had wasted so many years in blaming herself. And how could she ever tell Zybina the truth? It would break her heart.

All these thoughts, however, had been churning in her mind for the last two nights and the day in between, and Iriana told herself firmly that it was finally time to stop. Challan had ruined enough of her life – she wouldn't let him spoil any more of her first real adventure. With the border of the trees coming closer, she switched back again to the bird's-eye perspective of the forest. It wasn't exactly easy. While she stood still, it was a simple matter to keep her mind focused on the eagle's viewpoint, but from the back of a moving horse, the experience was disconcerting in the extreme. She would only have dared try it on this particular horse. She had had Dailika since she was a youngster, and had trained her patiently for years to carry her rider smoothly and steadily at ground level while Iriana's mind was in the skies.

Seen from above, the vast tract of woodland spread like a dark cloak from horizon to horizon. The mountains that marked its northern boundary were so distant that they were nothing more than a smudge on the skyline. Directly below the bird, less than half a mile from the southernmost edge of the forest, the horses cantered steadily along a windswept ridge. They had left the logging road from Nexis the previous day in favour of a different, older trail, located further to the east, which wound its way through the wildwood to the Phaerie city. Iriana was glad about that. The constant stream of human slaves that passed to and fro along the Nexis road, and the mundane work that was being done, would have made this part of the journey much less of an adventure. Besides, the extensive felling operations had left ugly scars on the face of the land, and she didn't want to see any more of the churned ground and the pitiful stumps of the devastated woodland.

From her lofty perspective, Iriana watched with fascination as the little mounted figure that was herself drew ever closer to the border of the woods, and finally disappeared among the trees. As soon as she entered the forest, Iriana left the viewpoint of Boreas and began to alternate her vision between the cat and the horse instead. As the trees closed round the riders, she regretted losing the sense of freedom that she always experienced looking out through the eagle's eyes. He was still far above her, she knew; though she could no longer see him, he was linked to her by their unique bond. How she envied him the freedom of the skies ...

'You seem far away.' Avithan's voice interrupted her reverie.

'I was.' Iriana grinned at him. 'Literally. I've just been looking down from the skies with Boreas.'

'That must have been quite an experience,' Esmon said, 'but now that we've entered the trees, you'd better pay more attention to your immediate surroundings. There are any number of dangerous wild animals here in the forest: bear, puma, lynx and moose, to name but a few—'

'Moose?' Iriana interrupted. 'But surely they're herbivores?'

'That's as may be,' Esmon replied, 'but truly, they are one of the most dangerous creatures in the forest. They're big, evil-tempered and their hooves are sharp as razors. They would disembowel you before you could even blink. Also, there are wolves and wildcats, which are less dangerous to us but might kill your animal companions.' He shifted in his saddle and frowned. 'There are worrying rumours that the occasional monster penetrates Hellorin's wards and escapes over the border into our part of the forest. Unicorn, gryphon, basilisk and wyvern are all supposed to have been sighted at various times—'

'But I thought they were extinct,' Avithan protested. 'They were wiped out years ago, surely?'

'The wildwood here is big enough to hide anything,' Esmon told him. 'And it's rumoured that the Forest Lord deliberately let a few of them survive and breed here, to guard the approaches to his realm. So let's just behave as if it's true, all right? That way, there will be less opportunity for unpleasant surprises. Besides, we know that there are plenty of other animals here, and a bear that's ten feet high when standing on its hind legs is quite enough threat for us to handle. We must be on our guard. Now that we're among the trees and visibility is so limited in all directions, you'll need to rely on your other senses more – particularly hearing and smell. You should have the advantage over the rest of us there, Iriana.'

'But we don't know what these creatures smell like,' Avithan pointed out.

Esmon smiled at him. 'Good point. Well, a bear is probably easiest to describe. They smell something like wet dog …'

As they rode, Esmon taught them what he knew about forest survival – and he knew a great deal. Iriana reflected on how lucky they were to have him with them. He might be the high-ranking Head of a Luen, but he was refreshingly free of airs and graces, and was, in fact, the most down to earth of the three of them. He was a highly interesting, informative and useful companion who was more than happy to tell them everything they wanted to know – and more besides – about self-defence and survival in the wilderness. He was also excellent company, with a fund of amusing stories and bawdy songs. Best of all for Iriana, Esmon treated her blindness as nothing more than part of her life, never tiptoeing round the subject in embarrassment or pity, as so many of the Wizards in Tyrineld did.

The seldom-used forest road was little more than a primitive trail that wound between the trees, penetrating deeper and deeper into the dark, dim green of the wildwood. Since Esmon had warned her to pay attention to her surroundings, Iriana, switching between the eyes of Melik and her horse, had begun to notice that the forest was far more populated than it had first appeared. The liquid fall of birdsong was all around them, with small winged shapes flitting from bough to bough and darting between the trees. Squirrels whisked up tree trunks and sat on branches, chattering indignantly down at the travellers from their safe vantage. Rustles in the undergrowth betrayed the presence of rabbits and their nemesis, the fox, while deer fled on slender legs from clearings at the approach of the riders, their short tails lifted to show white flashes of startlement and warning. It was ironic, Iriana thought, that she was probably seeing more through the eyes of her animal companions than she would have through normal human eyes. With Dailika's vision giving her a panoramic view of her surroundings, and the keen eyes of the hunting cat, designed to catch the slightest flicker of movement in the undergrowth, she was able to detect the small, secretive creatures that she might otherwise have missed.

As afternoon wore on into evening and the shadows lengthened between the trees, Esmon decided that it was time to make camp for the night. Iriana felt a thrill of excitement. It would be the first time she had ever slept out in the open, in a tent. While they had crossed the realm of the Wizards there had always been somewhere for them to stay: inns, a farm, the sister of one of Esmon's Warriors. Now that they had entered the wildwood, however, such vestiges of civilisation no longer existed. The trail followed the course of a narrow, fast-flowing river, and they found a clearing set well back from the road but close to the water's edge. It felt good to dismount and stretch their legs after all the hours of riding, and as they began to set up camp, they found themselves falling naturally into a division of labour that would soon become routine.

Esmon cleared a space in the centre of the campsite, brushing away twigs, leaf litter and other debris from the area. Then he built a fireplace using stones from the riverbed. This first night, there would be no cooking, for they had plenty of supplies, including meat for Iriana's animals and grain for the horses, which they had bought from the farmer's wife with whom they had stayed the night before. The fire would be for light and safety rather than cooking, though they did want to boil some water to make taillin.

To Iriana's surprise, the warrior turned down her offer to use Fire magic to light the campfire. 'Thanks, but no,' he said. 'You're supposed to be keeping those abilities secret, remember?'

'But we're in the middle of the forest,' Iriana protested. 'There can't be anyone around for miles.'

Esmon looked at her with raised eyebrows. 'You know that for sure, do you?'

'As a matter of fact, I do. If anyone were around here trying to spy on us, the animals would have let me know by now.'

'Nevertheless, it's better safe than sorry,' Esmon told her. 'Much as I'd like to use your powers, Iriana, we should avoid it if possible.' He grinned. 'Though when it's pouring with rain, ask me again. But the Phaerie can go a long way on those flying horses of theirs, and we know the Hunt has been trespassing in our part of the woods. If we start developing slipshod habits we'll give ourselves away sooner or later, so let's save your magic for emergencies, shall we? Besides, it will only take me a couple of minutes to do this. I've been lighting campfires for years.'

Kneeling before the fireplace, he assembled the materials he needed: moss and dead leaves for tinder, twigs, then small branches and finally the bigger boughs close to hand. In no time he had a cheerful blaze going, and his two younger compatriots found it difficult to resist settling down close to the source of light and warmth to rest bones that were weary from a long day on the trail.

There were still plenty of chores to be completed, however. As well as foraging for more firewood, Avithan went to fill up the water bags. Iriana, who was alternating between the eyesight of Melik, whom she had lifted up onto Dailika's back, of Boreas, who had flown down and perched on a branch above her, and of the horses themselves, saw to the comfort of their mounts – brushing and feeding them, and unloading their packs, which Esmon carried to the fire.

Once these tasks had been completed, they pitched their small, light-weight tents made of the silken moonmoth fabric, while there was still light to see. Esmon got supper ready and set water to boil for taillin, while Avithan helped Iriana to feed her animals, including the owl, who was now out of her basket and perched on a low bough, fluffing her feathers as she prepared for the night. Then, their work finally done, the three Wizards sat down around the fire. The heat was very welcome, for the weather was growing colder by the day as they progressed towards the northern mountains.

'There'll likely be a frost tonight,' Esmon warned them. A shiver went through Iriana at the thought, but she stiffened her spine. She was finally having the adventure she had longed for all her life, and hardships were an important part of that experience.

They ate a meal of bread, cheese, hard-boiled duck eggs and some wonderful pasties that had been freshly baked early that morning by their former hostess the farmer's wife who, like her soulmate, had been born in Tyrineld. They had wanted a different life and, like the other farmers in the northern regions, had settled in the rough frontier country, using their Earth magic to nurture livestock and grow crops. She was truly adept at kitchen magic, Iriana decided. It wasn't only the appetite worked up on a long day's ride that made the supper so delicious.

As the travellers ate, they chatted inconsequentially about this and that, sipping their hot taillin and relaxing after a long day in the saddle. Iriana knew she would never forget that night: the sharp tang of woodsmoke; the rustle of the wind in the leaves and the crackle of the fire; the crowding of shadows beyond the light of the flames; the upward drifts of sparks as the burning wood collapsed in the fireplace; the flicker of flame and the play of firelight on faces; Melik's blue eyes as he purred in the warmth. Everything around her combined into a moment of pure enchantment.

After a time, their talk drifted down into a thoughtful silence, and Esmon said, 'Let's clear up, then we'll get some sleep and make an early start in the morning. Now, because of the dangers in the forest – not only from wild animals but also feral slaves, who've been known to creep into camps and murder people for their food and equipment – we'd better set watches tonight. Iriana, you take the first turn—'

'But surely—' It was out of Avithan's mouth before he could stop himself.

'Yes?' Though she spoke quietly, Iriana's voice was a whetted blade. 'Were you about to say I can't keep watch because I'm blind?'

'I didn't mean—'

'Then what, exactly, did you mean? Are you saying that just because I can't see in the normal way, I'm no use for *anything*? Because that's how it sounds to me. You're always hovering, always watching, waiting for me to make mistakes—'

'Iriana, I'm just trying to take care of you—'

Even though she could not use them in the normal way, Iriana's eyes were blazing. 'Who in all Creation appointed *you* my keeper?'

Esmon intervened, heading off the quarrel. 'As a matter of fact, Avithan, Iriana may be best equipped of all of us for keeping watch at night, because she can use the senses of her animals, which are far more acute than ours would be in the dark. Pay close attention to all your creatures, Iriana, not just the one currently helping you to see. The owl will spot anything moving around the encampment in the dark long before the rest of us, and the horses will soon warn you if there's anything dangerous around.'

He took a deep breath and looked at Avithan and Iriana. 'Now listen carefully, both of you. You're on watch tonight. That means you are responsible for the safety of the camp, yourself and your companions. You're not in the city any more – it's dangerous out here. It's time to grow up, the pair of you, and forget about squabbling. If you see or hear anything – *anything* – suspicious, wake the others at once. It doesn't matter if it turns out to be a mistake. Never, ever try to deal with trouble on your own. If you lose, the rest of us will have no warning. I would rather have an interrupted sleep than be attacked in my bed by a bear or a slave because some idiot has tried to play the hero. Always, if you're on guard, your first responsibility is to wake the others. Do you understand?'

'Yes, Esmon,' they chorused.

The Warrior got to his feet. 'Right. Avithan, go to bed – oh, and just before you go, there's one more thing. When you're on guard, don't sit facing the fire. Put your back to it and look out into the woods. If your eyes are used to the firelight, you won't see anything in the darkness. Remember to get up and move around from time to time. It'll give you a fresh perspective and help keep you awake.'

He turned to Iriana. 'Iriana, wake me in three hours. You know how to set up a charm to sense the passing of time ... And don't, on any account, let that cat go wandering off, even though you may be tempted to send him out to scout. Remember, here in the forest, he'll be prey for all sorts of wild creatures, and we certainly don't want him attracting any bears to our campsite.'

Startled, Iriana put a protective hand out to Melik. 'Don't worry, I'll keep him close.'

They all said their goodnights, then Avithan went to bed, though Iriana could plainly see that he was reluctant. She wished that she could somehow explain to him, and make things right between them, but how could someone who had enjoyed the privileges of sight all his life ever be made to understand just how important it was to her not to feel she was a burden on their group?

Esmon, who had lingered, squatted down beside her and spoke softly, so that only the two of them could hear. 'Iriana, I meant what I said about raising the alarm if you see or hear anything suspicious. I know you want to show Avithan that you can manage every bit as well as those of us with ordinary vision – I would feel the same myself, were I in your position – but he'll learn that as time goes on. Don't risk all our lives to prove a point. Only an idiot would do that.'

Iriana felt her face burning with embarrassment at having been so easily found out. How had Esmon known what was on her mind?

The warrior gave her a wry grin. 'I thought as much,' he said. 'It's just exactly what I would want to do.' Then the smile vanished abruptly. 'Just don't, that's all.'

With that, he scrambled to his feet and ducked into his tent, leaving Iriana in charge of the camp. Within each of their shelters, the Wizard could see a soft glow as her companions kindled a ball of magelight to light their way to bed. After a short while, the lights went out: Esmon's first, followed by Avithan's a little later. Iriana was alone on watch, thrilled that Esmon had believed her capable of handling such responsibility, and enjoying every moment of her solitary vigil. She looked around the campsite, switching between the eyes of Melik and the horses, then sent Seyka to glide into the surrounding forest on silent wings, circling the area around the clearing and scrutinising anything that moved.

Though she'd had a long day's ride, Iriana had no trouble staying awake. She was far too aware that the safety of the camp depended on her, too excited at the novelty of it all – and too determined to show Avithan that she could keep watch every bit as well as he could. With great firmness, she had expunged all encroaching thoughts of Challan from her mind. She had vowed that she wasn't going to think of him any more, and with so much else to distract her, she seemed to be succeeding. It wasn't so easy, however, to get Avithan out of her thoughts. She just couldn't shake off the irritation she had felt when he'd protested against her keeping watch. She knew he liked her – as, for that matter, she liked him. But somehow she just couldn't seem to make him believe that she could take care of herself, and until he understood that he didn't have to protect her all the time, she wouldn't let him come any closer to her. She wanted a partnership of equals when – and if – she finally chose a soulmate, and her pride wouldn't let her settle for anything less.

Iriana shrugged. Well, she would show him – and the best way to achieve that would be to give all her concentration to what she was supposed to be doing. Subsequently, she passed the time switching from the eyes of one of her animals to the next, utilising all the various differences in their vision to keep a careful watch, and she spent a good long while sharing the sights of the moonlit forest as Seyka flew her patrol. Using the senses of the owl and the cat, she soon found that she could put together a very accurate picture of all the living creatures in the surrounding area.

Sure enough, there was a family of bears in the vicinity, and Iriana's heart beat faster when Seyka spotted the mother and two young cubs. She was just about to wake Esmon when she realised that the owl had flown a wider loop this time, and the bears were almost a mile away. Furthermore, Melik's more advanced sense of smell could detect the wet-dog odour of the bear very clearly, and she perceived that the encampment was well downwind of the mother and cubs, so there was little risk that the Wizards would be discovered. Nevertheless, Iriana used the owl to keep a close eye on the bears until they had wandered far away in the opposite direction, leaving her very pleased with herself that she had discovered the potential threat. Avithan or Esmon would never even have known that any dangerous predators had been close by!

Sadly, she realised that she couldn't tell them. No one who saw in the normal way seemed to be able to understand her unique link with her birds and animals. Esmon would be angry that she hadn't awakened him, and probably wouldn't trust her to keep watch again, and Avithan would agree with him. Iriana ground her teeth in frustration. She would just have to find another way to prove herself to Avithan – and one way or another, she meant to do just that.

The object of her thoughts couldn't sleep. For one thing, this was the first night they had camped out on their journey, and Avithan wasn't used to a tent. His feet were frozen, and he was sure that the others must have saved all the lumps and bumps in the clearing, and put them under *his* blankets. What was worse, he felt very insecure with only the thinnest of fabrics between himself and the manifold dangers of the forest. The discomfort wasn't really the problem, however. It would not have mattered if he had been staying in the most expensive and luxurious inn in Tyrineld, with a feather bed to sleep on, while Iriana was on his mind. He was vexed and baffled by her behaviour. Why did she have to be so antagonistic? All he wanted to do was take care of her. Was that so bad? Did she really find him so unattractive that she just kept shutting him out, in the hope that one day he would take the hint and leave her alone?

After an hour or so of squirming around on his uncomfortable bed, it occurred to him that a different perspective might help. Esmon had plenty of experience with women – there always seemed to be a cluster of admiring females hanging around him when he was at home in Tyrineld. Maybe he would have an answer? Avithan hesitated for a while, reluctant to bring an outsider into his private business – as the son of the Archwizard, he had learned the hard way that there were very few people in whom he could safely confide. Also, if Iriana ever found out that he had been discussing her with Esmon behind her back, she would never forgive him. Eventually, however, his need for understanding overcame his scruples. He addressed the other man in mindspeech, shielding his thoughts very carefully so that Iriana should not overhear. 'Esmon? Are you awake?'

'I am now,' the warrior replied, with a touch of irritation. 'What's wrong?'

'I wanted to talk to you about Iriana.'

Esmon sighed. 'When you're trading night watches, the idea is to GO TO SLEEP when it's not your watch. Otherwise, when it is your turn on guard, you won't be able to stay awake. And, unless it's an emergency, you do *not* wake your comrades – who ought to be getting *their* sleep. Is that clear?'

'I'm sorry,' Avithan said. 'But—'

'Oh, all right. Tell me what the problem is, then with a bit of luck we can all get some rest.'

'Well, you've seen the way Iriana acts towards me? What makes her so angry with me, Esmon? I only want to take care of her. Why is she always pushing me away when I'm trying to help her?'

Esmon thought for a moment before he started to speak. He had a feeling that this matter, trivial as it first appeared, would have far-reaching consequences, and he had learned long ago to trust his instincts. 'Put yourself in Iriana's position,' he said at last. 'All her life she's had well-meaning people – especially Zybina and your parents – trying to protect her, when all the time she wanted to be independent and do things for herself. How would you have felt, growing up with such restrictions?'

Suddenly the Warrior began to mimic the overanxious tones which, when Avithan came to think about it, his parents and Zybina had always used around Iriana. 'Don't climb that tree, Iriana, you might fall. No, you can't learn to swim, you might drown. Don't run, dear – you might trip over something. Be sure and wrap up warm, we don't want you catching cold. Here, let me get it for you, let me take you there, hold my hand so you don't get lost. Let me cut your food up, let me help you with those buttons. You can't go travelling, it would be too much for you to manage, and far too dangerous besides ...' His voice went back to normal. 'Is any of this sounding familiar?'

'Oh.' Avithan's own thoughts from earlier that evening echoed in his mind: *She can't take a watch – it isn't safe.* How often had he been guilty of doing exactly what his parents and Iriana's foster-mother had done?

'Like any child growing up,' Esmon went on, 'Iriana wanted to make her own decisions, and learn how to do things for herself, and because of her amazing affinity with her animals, she's made a truly remarkable job of doing exactly that. But she just can't win. No matter how much she accomplishes, well-meaning people still want to do things for her, to protect her from taking any chances – and without a little risk now and again, it's impossible to achieve anything useful or exciting in life. With this overprotectiveness, they are denying Iriana her precious, hard-won independence and, at the same time, they are robbing her of her self-respect and undermining her confidence by implying that she's not good enough to manage on her own. And the tragedy is, they're only trying to help. Is it any wonder that she gets frustrated and annoyed?'

Avithan thought of all the times he'd acted just as Esmon had described. 'I've known her all her life, and it never once occurred to me—'

'That's the problem,' the Warrior told him. 'Most people have independence as a matter of course, so they don't think anything of it, and don't attach the same value to it, because they don't have to fight tooth and nail, every hour of every day, to preserve it. It would be much easier for the Irianas of this world – and when you look around, there are plenty of them – just to lie back and let other people do everything for them. Why do they fight so determinedly to do things the hard way? It's to preserve their self-respect. Without that, they might as well be dead.'

Avithan, dismayed and ashamed, rubbed a hand across his face. He couldn't say anything just yet. Esmon had given him too much to think about.

'Think about it in the morning,' the Warrior advised him, 'but right now, get some sleep. You still have a watch to stand tonight.'

Oblivious to what was going on in the tents, Iriana continued her watch, using Seyka to keep an eye on the retreating bears. When the female and her offspring had gone far upriver, there seemed to be nothing left to worry about – but something was puzzling her.

Melik was acting strangely. Usually, her bond with the cat was so close that he would look in whatever direction she wished, but tonight she found that wherever she pointed him, his gaze was soon dragged back to the same place: a tall chestnut tree directly across the clearing from the tents. Several times, Iriana sent Seyka to investigate the area, but the owl found nothing out of the ordinary.

Iriana fought a hard inner battle with herself. She writhed at the thought of waking Esmon over such a stupid thing. She kept sending her owl to check the tree and its surrounding area, and clearly, there was nothing there. Nevertheless, she could not shake off the uneasy sensation of being watched, and a growing feeling, like ice sheeting across her bones, that some dreadful evil lurked close at hand.

Much as she resented looking like a fool, Esmon's words came back to her: '*If you see or hear anything* – anything – *suspicious, wake the others at once.*'

Reluctantly, Iriana decided to rouse the Warrior. He had the experience to decide whether the unease of the cat and its owner was a sensible warning or a foolish fancy.

Using mindspeech to conceal from the intruder – if intruder there was – that she knew of its presence, she called the Warrior. Instantly he was wide awake and reaching for his staff. 'Wait,' she said, forestalling him just in time from hurtling out of the tent. 'Stay there, Esmon.'

'What's wrong?' Esmon was using the same mode of silent communication.

'I'm not sure,' Iriana admitted, embarrassment warming her face. Quickly she told the Warrior Wizard about Melik's suspicious reaction, and her own uneasy feelings.

'I'm coming.' Esmon crawled out of his tent, yawned and stretched in a casual manner – though Iriana noticed his eyes darting around as he did so – and sauntered over to the fire to sit beside her. 'Couldn't sleep,' he said aloud. 'Thought I'd keep you company for a while.' In mindspeech he added: 'I can't find the source, but you're right. There's danger near. We'll watch and wait for a while.'

*

Dhagon crept through the undergrowth on soft and silent feet, guided by a drifting tendril of sharp-scented woodsmoke. His prey could not be far away now. Where most hunters would be experiencing fast-beating hearts and the tension and excitement of anticipation, this killer maintained his icy calm. His lips tightened in a cold, cruel smile as he thought of the oblivious Wizards up ahead. They were about to learn the hard way not to interfere in Phaerie concerns.

As usual, Dhagon was travelling alone. Though he had trained an efficient pack of spies and assassins in Hellorin's service, he had not brought any of them with him. For one thing, he preferred to work alone; for another, this matter was far too delicate to trust to anyone else. Only he and Tiolani knew where he was and what he planned to do, and it was vitally important that he gain her trust by succeeding in this mission. Though he was acting on her instructions, however, he had his own objectives to fulfil.

He felt no particular loyalty towards his new ruler, and he certainly did not trust her. Long ago he had sworn an oath of allegiance to Hellorin, and though he was incapacitated at present, Dhagon had never given up hope of seeing him restored to health and power. He knew perfectly well that the healers should have effected a cure, or at least some considerable improvement in the Forest Lord's condition by now, and he recognised the stench of treachery when he smelled it. He had tried many times to reach his Lord, but the sickroom was so well guarded that it defied even his skills. Day or night, Hellorin was never left alone for a single moment, and the chamber had been warded against any use of spells from the outside. Furthermore, the old, loyal guard had all been replaced, and several – those who had been asking too many questions – had either met with accidents or, in certain cases, had simply vanished under mysterious circumstances. Clearly, Ferimon was at the heart of the plot, but how deeply was Tiolani involved? Only by gaining her trust could Dhagon discover the truth, hence the need to make a success of this mission. And there was no doubt in his mind that he *would* succeed. The Wizards would not live to see another dawn.

He climbed into a twisted old tree and lay among the branches cloaked under a camouflage spell, watching the scene below. From his high perch, he had an unimpeded view of the enemy encampment. Three small, light-weight tents made of moonmoth silk, bespelled to take on the colour of their surroundings, were barely visible in a semicircle around the edge of the clearing. Loose gear such as the travellers' packs, the horses' tack and utensils for cooking and eating, were stored nearby beneath a tarpaulin, for the shelters were so cramped that there was no room for anything more than a single person inside. On the other side of the clearing from the tents, taking advantage of the fire's protection from wild animals, the four horses were picketed.

He had been watching for some time, and listening to their careless chatter as they made camp. Only three of them – one a blind girl who fawned over a bunch of filthy animals, and would be absolutely useless if it came to a fight. He could pick them off at any time – but he had decided to wait a little longer. Already, he had discovered one or two startling facts, such as the presence of the Archwizard's son, and the ability of the girl to use the magic of all four elements, instead of just the one.

Dhagon's plan had already changed. He wanted to shadow them, to see what other vital information they might inadvertently reveal. There was no hurry, after all. Then, when he was ready, he would strike.

23
~

THE SHINING MOUNTAIN

The Windeye was becoming desperate. Everything was going wrong. Why couldn't Aelwen and Kelon just leave her alone? She had no intention of letting any of the Xandim stallions near her at this time; yet judging by what the Horsemistress and her assistant had been saying, who knew what her fate might be if she did not cooperate? Time was running out, and she was still unable to get back to the Elsewhere and regain her powers. Why didn't Taku and Aurora summon her? Surely it must be safe to let her return by now?

Flicking her tail irritably at a cloud of flies, Corisand moved out of the blinding noon sunshine into the shade of the trees. She thought wistfully of the lake in the Elsewhere with its shimmering glacial waters the misty colour of blue chalcedony, surrounded by deep, dark-green coniferous forests with the snowy mountains towering beyond. How her heart yearned towards the place. If only she could be there now, learning from Taku and Aurora, the awe-inspiring Evanesar. She could be developing her powers and practising her skills instead of wasting her time as a captive in this miserable, magicless place.

Even as she longed for that lovely lakeside, with the magnificent glacier towering like a great white cliff on the other side, Corisand felt her world give that odd little sideways jerk, followed by the uncanny twisting sensation deep within her. Almost before her spirits had time to give a joyous leap, she found herself stepping hurriedly through the mist and out into the grassy clearing that stretched back from the lake into the trees.

This time, the bipedal body was familiar; she felt easy and at home in it. She marvelled at the smile that had spread across her face when she'd found herself back, at last, in this marvellous and longed-for place. How amazing it was, this new body. All those tiny facial muscles that could make a million infinitesimal changes in her expression, just to reflect the emotions that were playing in her mind. She stretched tall; felt the tingle of her magic running through her body. She couldn't wait to use it again.

Alight with anticipation, the Windeye reached down into her centre to the radiant essence of her magic and felt the power flare up within her, flooding her body and mind. Once again the arcane vision of her Othersight turned her eyes to silver. She saw the mountains become dazzling prisms blazing with a host of rainbow colours; the crystalline shimmer of the lake; the jewelled trees and grass. Across the lake, the breathtaking blue of the glacier's heart now coloured its entire winding length.

Corisand looked up at the glowing streams of wind that swirled over the lake, and with a delighted laugh, reached up to snatch a handful of the fluid strands into which she poured her Othersight. In response, they blazed incandescent silver, and once again she spun them out across the lake to form her bridge.

Before she had reached the other side, the great serpent, its coils the dazzling white reared up to meet her. 'Greetings, my friend Windeye,' Taku said, his blue eyes glittering. 'It is good to see you once again.'

Pure, scintillating colour flashed across the sky, with drifting curtains of emerald and ruby, sapphire, amethyst and iridescent diamond. Vast wings stretched from horizon to horizon as the immense form of a golden-eyed eagle materialised from the veils of rippling light. 'Hail, little sister.' Aurora called out her greeting. 'Welcome back to the Elsewhere.'

Their friendship wrapped around Corisand like a warm cloak, filling her with the joy of belonging. 'I feel as if I've come home,' she said softly.

'You have, in a way,' Taku told her. 'To your heart's home, at least.'

'But your chief place is still in the mundane world,' Aurora warned. 'There lies your future, and the great task of liberating your people.'

Corisand had not yet become accustomed to controlling those strange and wayward facial expressions to conceal her feelings, and her disappointment must have shown in her expression, for the eagle added: 'But always remember, little sister, that in freeing your people you also free yourself. Once you can occupy this body in your own world, you will have your powers at your fingertips there as well as here, so that you can use them to come to the Elsewhere whenever you like.'

'And there will always be a welcome here for you,' Taku added. 'Until then, however, we must make the most of your brief visits. If you truly intend to take the Fialan from Ghabal, you will have to develop your powers, Windeye. You have much to learn, and we must teach you all we can.'

Corisand felt her heart give a bound of excitement. Sternly she tried to tell herself that this was serious business, that what she would learn here could save her life and dictate the future of her entire race, but still she could not control the thrill of excitement that passed through her. As a horse, she'd had no concept of gifts, but she realised now that what Taku and Aurora proposed to give her would be an offering of infinite value. 'Thank you,' she said. 'Thank you both. I can't tell you how much this means to me.'

'Then let us begin,' Taku said.

Aurora looked down at the Windeye with her piercing, golden gaze. 'I will teach you your first skill, little sister. Though you will need to learn to fight, it is sometimes far better if you can pass by your enemies unseen. I will show you how your magic can be used to hide you whenever there is need.' She flexed her great wings, and ripples of colour chased across the sky. 'Let us begin with your feet on the ground. Then you can avoid the distraction and drain of maintaining your bridge, for at first, the task in hand will take all your concentration.'

Everything blurred, and Corisand found herself standing back on the grassy swathe by the lakeshore, with the image of the serpent still towering up from the glacier, and the form of the eagle stretching across the sky.

'Now, take back your bridge,' Aurora commanded.

For a moment, Corisand was nonplussed. She had managed to create the structure without too much difficulty, but how did she go about taking it back?

'Be at ease,' Taku said softly. 'In your heart you know what to do.'

The Windeye knew she must relax and let her instincts take over. Countless generations of Windeyes had lived before her. Surely their knowledge must be imprinted in her mind, her heart, her soul – even her very bones. So ... Logically, taking back the structure must mean doing the opposite of what she'd done when she created it. She steadied herself with a deep breath and lifted her hands towards the bridge, her fingers spread wide. This time, instead of reaching deep within to the core of her power, she opened herself out, embracing the magic of her bridge. Letting it flood into her, she gathered it and folded it back within herself. Gradually, the elegant, gleaming arch vanished, leaving a ghostly image of itself etched upon the air in a shimmer of silver sparks that were caught up by the rivers of wind and blown away.

'Excellent.' Taku's voice echoed approvingly across the lake.

'Well done, little sister,' Aurora said, 'but that was the easy part.'

Corisand schooled her features into a motionless mask, so as not to reveal her irritation. 'I'm ready when you are.'

'Are you, indeed?' There was a ripple across Aurora's veils of colour that might have been laughter. 'Well, we shall see. Now,' she continued, 'I want you to take some air and spin it, as you did when you were making your bridge.'

Obediently, Corisand gathered handfuls of streaming air, feeling their cool smoothness twine like silk around her fingers. Pouring her Othersight into them, she spun them into a whirling silver disc that hovered in the air in front of her.

'Now, you see those shadows, down to your right beneath the trees?'

The Windeye spared a glance from her spell, and nodded.

'Good,' said the eagle. 'Now, go over there, snatch up the shadows and weave them into your disc.'

'What?' Corisand was so startled that she lost concentration on her disc. The glimmering form shredded and was borne away on the currents of air. 'Curse it. Now I'll have to begin again. But before I start, what in the world am I supposed to do with a bunch of shadows?'

'It's perfectly simple,' Aurora said. 'All you have to do is snatch the shadows in the same way you pick up the wind. Then you weave them into your disc.'

'Can I do that?' the Windeye asked in astonishment.

'Why don't you try it and see?'

'Very well,' said Corisand, a little doubtfully. With all her concentration, she spun her silver disc once more. When she had it well established, spinning slowly in the air in front of her like a great silver wheel, she skewed a glance out of the corner of her eye towards the shadows that gathered beneath the trees. She reached out for them, tried to incorporate them – only to have the entire construct collapse on her again. '*Pox on it!*' The curses she had learned from her grooms while wearing her equine shape came easily to her when she was in this form.

Corisand gritted her teeth – another thing this human body seemed to do instinctively – and started again. And again, and again. No matter how hard she tried, she was unable to gather the two components of her spell together without losing one or both. It was galling, it was frustrating, and she was beginning to tire, but she refused to give in. This was her first spell of any complexity – what would happen if she failed? She was not only responsible for herself, but for all the Xandim. Whatever the cost, she could not let herself be beaten.

After several more attempts, Corisand's temper was at boiling point, with this world and its insane challenges, with Aurora and her ridiculous, impossible demands – and most of all with her maladroit self. What was worse, with every botched attempt, she could feel her confidence slip a little. She knew in her heart that she had to accomplish this soon, or she would never manage at all. And once she failed at one piece of magic …

'Perhaps this was not such a good spell with which to begin, Aurora,' Taku said gently from the sidelines. 'I would suggest that we work on something else, and return to this later.'

'That's all very well,' the eagle argued, 'but the way things stand at present, the ability to conceal herself may well save her life.'

Corisand closed her eyes and tried to shut out the sound of their bickering. Humiliated beyond bearing, determined that she wouldn't let herself be beaten by a simple spell, she steeled herself to try again, despite the insidious suspicion that Taku might have been right, despite the weariness of body, mind and spirit that was slowly seeping through her. Why did this have to be so bloody hard? Her mind went back to her first serious spell, the construction of her bridge across the lake to Taku's glacier. She remembered the ease of it, the sheer exuberant joy of being able to let her magic loose at last …

And all at once, she had the answer. With Hellorin after her, with the Fialan at stake, with Taku and Aurora, kindly and well-meaning though they were, being so desperately and understandably *serious* all the time, she had put herself under pressure and tried too hard, and in doing so had lost all the ease and joy of her magic.

The Windeye laughed aloud, took a deep, cleansing breath and shook herself to remove all the tension and frustration from her body. This time, things would be different. Above her, in some detached corner of her mind, she heard the voices of the Evanesar cease as she whirled the strands of air together, pouring her Othersight into the disc until it blazed with coruscating silver light. This time, instead of trying to snatch at the shadows, she called them to her as if they were hounds lying at rest beneath the trees, just awaiting her command. At the snap of her fingers they streamed across the grass towards her, and leapt obediently into the whirling circle of light.

Even in her moment of triumph, Corisand was astonished at the transformation. The wheel changed, becoming a flickering, insubstantial, almost translucent ghost of its former glory, so that even its creator could scarcely see where its boundaries lay.

'My compliments, little sister.'

'Fine work, Corisand. Your persistence was admirable – and most effective.'

The praise of the Evanesar filled her with relief. A grin compounded of pure happiness, pleasure and satisfaction stole across her face. What wonder, what joy was to be found in pushing out the boundaries of her magic. She gave the shimmering, phantom disc a quick flick with her mind and sent it spinning faster through the air. 'All right, Aurora. Now that I have it, what shall I do with it?'

'Spin it around your body,' the eagle said. 'Make it into a cloak to conceal yourself.'

Corisand's eyes opened wide in sudden understanding. 'Oh ... Now I see ...'

Now that she knew what she was creating, this stage was much easier. A clear visualisation, a slight tug from her will, and she moulded her creation into the form she wanted – more or less a cone shape – and pulled it around her.

Taku chuckled. 'Remember your head.'

The Windeye imagined her disembodied face floating above the ground and spluttered with laughter. When she had calmed herself, she extended the apex of her spinning cone over the top of her head. 'Is that better?'

'Much better,' Aurora said with warm approval. 'Now, go and look at yourself in the lake.'

Holding her cloak in place around her, Corisand walked to the lakeshore and knelt to look down into the water. She saw the wavering, rippled reflections of mountains, trees and sky, with Aurora's intense bands of colour flowing across it. There was absolutely nothing else. 'Great stars! That's incredible.'

'You can be proud of yourself, Windeye,' Taku told her. 'That was not an easy spell to master.'

'Indeed it was not,' Aurora agreed. 'You have done well, little sister. Now all you need is practice, both to create your shadow-cloak and to keep it around you wherever you go. It must become like a second skin to you. Then, when you venture into this world, you will be able to conceal yourself at need.'

'Shadow-cloak.' Corisand smiled. 'I like the sound of that.'

'May it serve you well,' Taku said. 'For this is only the beginning. Dispense with your cloak for the present, and spin the air again.'

'Is this spinning of the air the foundation of all the Windeye's magic?' Corisand asked curiously.

'Most of it,' Aurora replied. 'Your powers centre on the manipulation of the air and the wind, little sister, and nothing is more intangible and elusive. But spinning the air into a disc, as you do, turns it into a more manageable substance, and gives you all the control you need.'

'I see,' said Corisand. 'Very well, Taku, I'm ready.' With a shrugging gesture, she shed the tatters of her shadow-cloak and snatched a handful of clear, streaming air, infusing it with the incandescence of her Othersight, then stretching and moulding it to spin a new disc, smooth and gleaming as a mirror.

'Good,' Taku said. 'Look now, Windeye. See with the eyes of your power and mind. Look into the mirror, and tell me what you see.'

Her heart beating fast with excitement, Corisand gazed into the silver depths of the disc she had created. Despite the difficulties she had experienced in the construction of her shadow-cloak, she felt calm and confident as she faced this new challenge. Having mastered one spell, what had she to fear from another? Not rushing, she watched patiently, relaxing and opening her mind; trying to send forth her thoughts through the shining barrier to the realms of potentiality that lay beyond.

The silvery radiance shimmered and cleared, like drifting clouds banished by a gentle breeze. And the Windeye saw.

There was the lake, exactly as it appeared from her position on the shore. Then suddenly there was an odd shift in her attention, and she realised that she was inside the image. It was as though she had fallen into the mirror. Suddenly she found herself flying, circling above the lake beneath the sheltering arch of colour from Aurora's wings and seeing Taku's icy, sinuous white body overlying the ribbon of the glacier that wound away into the mountains. She turned to follow and . . .

'Not that way.' Both voices, the serpent and the eagle, spoke in her mind together.

'Explore away from us,' said Taku. 'Forge your own path.'

'Go your own way,' Aurora added.

Torn between reluctance and excitement, the Windeye turned away from the familiar, protective comfort of her friends, letting her heart and her magic and her instincts choose her path. Delighting in the thrilling sensations of flight, she swooped down the length of the lake to where it finally narrowed into a river which raced down a series of rapids and little waterfalls to the lands below. These lower regions, with skeins of grey cloud drifting across them, were a patchwork of muskeg: an intaglio of black and silver with its areas of bright water and dark trees.

She made for the broad expanse of ocean that lay beyond, following a coastline toothed with a series of coves and inlets. Inland, to her right, the land was rising, and the muskeg was changing to forested mountains, with dark peaks of rock above their treeline. Small, tree-covered islands were dotted along the coast, looking so tempting to explore that she had to keep reminding herself that this flight was only a vision, and in reality, she was still standing on the shore of Taku's lake, gazing into the mirror she had made.

Then, in the distance, she saw a tall pinnacle of rock that appeared to be rising directly out of the ocean, a few hundred yards offshore. It drew her as though it had reached out long fingers and yanked her towards it. When she drew closer, she discovered a massive chimney of rugged rock more than a hundred feet tall. Though made of stone, it resembled the stump of an ancient tree that had been ravaged by lightning in the distant past, and was still holding its remains up straight and proud and tall. It stood in an ocean inlet with a background of tree-covered mountains, on a tiny island that was no more than a spit of gravel, so small and flat that it looked as though the rock was rising directly from the waters. Real, living fir trees, straight and tall like dark-green spears, clung to its sides, and bushes clustered on its pinnacle, while the mouth of a cave at its base promised a safe haven for those it chose to protect.

A shiver, part awe, part delight, passed through Corisand as she sensed the vast intelligence and living power, primordial and immense, that it contained. Was it a Moldan? Another of the Evanesar? A different entity entirely?

'Who are you?' Even as she sent the thought out, the Windeye cursed herself for a fool. She had just worked incredibly hard to learn the shadow-cloak spell from Aurora, with the precise aim of keeping herself hidden. Now she had revealed her presence to a total stranger, without a thought for her own safety. Was this entity friend or foe? She had no idea.

Then suddenly a voice sounded in her mind: deep, with growling, grinding undertones that held the weight of aeons. It reminded her, a little, of Taku's voice, but older, darker, more sorrowful. 'I will not commune with a mirror-borne phantasm. Have the courage to seek me out in your corporeal form. Then we will talk.'

Corisand was desperate to investigate, to learn the identity of this newfound being, but this time, journeying through the images in her mirror, she could only observe – and clearly, that was the wisest course. Even so, she sent out a cautious thought towards the newfound entity. 'I'll come back,' she promised. 'One day I'll come here in person and find out who, or what, you are.'

'Come back soon, then. Time is growing short.'

Did these ancient beings get some sort of perverse pleasure out of being so cryptic? Irritated, reluctant, the Windeye left the astonishing stone formation behind and flew on, watching the mountains to her right becoming higher and changing from dark, bare rock to great white peaks, dazzling with snow and ice. Ahead of her the horizon was lost in mist, and a low-hanging bank of ominous cloud bruised the sky. The darkness was spiked with jagged flashes of madness and rumbling concussions of sullen anger, and Corisand could sense the resentment, the resistance barring her way. She was not wanted here. She felt a tight clutch in her belly: part fear, part excitement, for she knew what must lie beyond that barrier of cloud. She had found Ghabal.

The Windeye battled onward, pushing against the ever-strengthening barrier of insanity and fulminating rage. The Moldan hated the world, and was determined to keep it out at any cost. Soon Corisand was finding it increasingly painful to continue, as her mind was buffeted by wave upon wave of scalding fury and an overwhelming torment that jarred every flinching nerve in her body. She was finding it difficult to remember that she was observing this scene through her mirror. Every sensation was as vivid and real as if she had been physically present. And if it could make her feel such pain, could it actually harm the form that awaited her on the shores of the lake? She was absolutely certain it could.

She plunged into the cloud bank, unsure of how far it stretched or what dangers it concealed, but determined to penetrate the Mad One's disguise. Blackness engulfed her, and she could do nothing but force her way forward blindly, with that savage will trying to beat her back and the howls and curses of the demented Moldan ripping through her mind. It was impossible to tell how much progress she was making, or in what direction she was headed. She could only keep pushing forward painfully, fighting the torrent of resentment, pain and rage. Corisand realised that she was sharing Ghabal's agony, and was overcome with pity for him. How could he bear such torture? How unthinkable, to be forced to carry this burden of suffering down all the long ages. The Windeye felt as if her mind and body were being torn to pieces. The temptation to turn and flee was overwhelming, but she thought of her people enslaved, herself trapped for ever without magic in the form of a dumb beast, and from somewhere found the courage to keep going.

As she penetrated further into the smothering darkness, the Windeye discovered something beyond the turbulence of Ghabal's emotions, which lifted her hopes and stiffened her determination. Power, vast and eternal. Profound and ancient magic that beat like a living heart.

The Fialan.

Emerald light began to pulse through the thick cloud and the barriers of dark, churning vapour finally began to thin. Without warning Corisand broke through, and found herself in the open. She floundered and halted in mid-air, suddenly very glad that she was not physically present in that place. At least now she would have the perfect opportunity to observe and study her enemy: hopefully the tormented entity was still unaware of her presence.

The Windeye looked down at the Moldan's stronghold, a vast eminence that towered thousands of feet above the surrounding pinnacles of the northern range. Closer study, however, revealed that it was not what it first appeared to be. Unlike the other mountains, which were veiled in ice and snow but with solid rock beneath, this peak had a pale, translucent glow like an uncut gemstone. With a shock, the Windeye realised that it was formed from solid ice, with no foundation of stone whatsoever. What was more, its heart was hollow. The green radiance of the Fialan, hidden deep within, shone out through the ice, and there was something more – the vague shadow of a dark, twisted shape, the very sight of which filled Corisand with profound and chilling fear.

The Windeye switched to her Othersight to penetrate the clouded depths of the ice mountain – and gasped at what she saw. The Moldan was so badly twisted and deformed that it was difficult to guess at its original shape. It seemed to be writhing in and out of a number of forms, as if trying to find one in which its pain could be allayed. The only constants in that black, amorphous monstrosity were a pair of glaring crimson eyes that smouldered with the intensity of its suffering. In writhing limbs it grasped the Fialan – though, by the way it was constantly shifting its burden, the Stone was hurting the Mad One just as much as its injuries.

Corisand looked on, her horror vying with compassion. 'Is there no one, in this world or the other, with the power to heal such suffering?' she murmured to herself. 'Surely there must be some way to help this tormented creature.' Shocked and saddened, she turned to leave, but ...

Suddenly those mad, red eyes glared upwards, transfixing the Windeye like burning spears. He saw her. *He saw her.*

In her mind, his voice sounded like the tortured grate of rock upon massive rock. 'There is no help or healing for me. Flee, puny creature, unless you wish to meet the same fate.'

Corisand fought down the instant panicked urge to turn tail. 'I don't want to leave,' she said stoutly. 'I want to aid you.'

'I am beyond all help.' With his words, Corisand found herself trapped; held in a grip that surrounded her as though she had been entombed in solid stone. The pain that she shared with the Mad One increased tenfold, a hundredfold, a thousandfold, until she could barely think, could barely remember her identity. The inside of her brain was one solid, eternal scream

With every ounce of her strength, every fibre of her being, she reached within herself, seeking the power to pull free. It wasn't working. Again she strained; in fear she tried to strike out, but nothing was happening.

Slowly but surely, she felt herself being drawn in, to become a prisoner, part of Ghabal's rage and agony for ever.

Then it happened. *Something* came out of nowhere – a force, a presence, a personality … It all happened so quickly that she could not tell exactly what transpired, but the image in her mind was that of the strange towerlike rock formation in the midst of the ocean. It struck out at Ghabal, at the same time yanking her free. Then it was gone, leaving one word:

Basileus.

Corisand fled. Only when she felt she was truly at a safe distance did she turn back to address Ghabal.

'I will leave if that is your wish,' she said, 'but your pain will stay in my thoughts, and if I ever find a way to assuage your suffering, I promise that I will return.' Backing away, she made her retreat – not slowly, exactly, but at least in good order.

'If you ever return here, then the more fool you.' With that final threat, the Moldan was lost from sight.

Then Corisand felt the peculiar sideslip of reality that meant she was being returned to her own world – presumably the Evanesar were reacting, somewhat belatedly, to the peril in which she had found herself.

Not now, she thought. *I have so many questions.* Even as the protest formed in her mind, she found herself back in her paddock beneath the shady trees, helpless in her equine form once more. Corisand stamped her foot in frustration. If only she could have stayed longer in the Elsewhere. How could she find the answers she sought if she was yanked back every time she started to get somewhere? The Evanesar looked at things differently. They had the perspective of aeons to govern their thinking, but she did not have forever at her disposal. *Next time*, she vowed, *I'm going to find the Stone of Fate, if it's the last thing I do.*

The memory of the Moldan, of his strength and his insanity, loomed in her mind, and a shiver passed through her. She only hoped that her vow would not end as prophecy.

24
~

THE GRIM FACE OF TRUTH

Another day, another camp. Taine examined the remnants – not that there were many, for Esmon excelled at woodcraft – of the dismantled campsite, scrabbling with his knife blade at the patch of new-turned earth that covered the fireplace. The ashes were fresh, and still held the faintest trace of heat. Over by the river, a little area of grass had been grazed down by the hobbled horses, and he could discern both hoofprints and human footprints on the bent and flattened turf.

Rising, Taine straightened his back and returned to his own mount. Even though he had taken an extra day's rest in Tyrineld at Cyran's insistence, he would catch up with Avithan and his companions today – probably within the next hour or two. While they had been travelling at a careful pace through the forest, he had been hard upon their trail, but had been delayed because one of his horses had gone lame, and had needed to be left with a group of loggers. With only one horse, his pace through the forest had necessarily been slower, and he didn't like travelling with but a single animal. Too much could go wrong. It was a relief to think that he was finally in reach of the others. He would make it on time after all. At the rate they were going, it looked as though they wouldn't reach the border of the Phaerie realm until tomorrow.

He watered his horse and tethered it so that it could graze for a little while as he sat with his back to the trunk of a willow, and took an apple and some cheese from his pack. As he ate, his mind drifted, as always, to Aelwen. He didn't like the course events were taking in the Phaerie city. When he'd left, Tiolani's hatred of humans had been growing at an alarming pace. If her thirst for revenge had not abated, then the Hemifae were the next logical targets.

Including Aelwen.

Taine cursed himself for not bringing her with him when he'd made his last escape from the city. Plagued by doubts that she would no longer want him and afraid that she might come to harm in the escape through a closed border, he had hesitated, and left her behind. Now he regretted it with all his heart. But wait! The apple dropped from his hand and lay on the ground unheeded. Maybe it wasn't too late to rectify his mistake. He would catch Esmon and tell him to return to Tyrineld. Then he would press on to Eliorand with all speed, as he had promised Cyran, but he would not stay there to risk his life again. He would quickly garner what information he could, then – whatever it took – he would persuade Aelwen to come away with him.

Suddenly these pleasant thoughts were interrupted. The quiet peace of the clearing was broken by a sound like a massive boulder rolling rapidly downhill towards him. Taine leapt to his feet with a curse. Bear!

It burst out through the trees with incredible speed, a mountain of muscle and black fur. Its ears were laid back, its eyes wild, and its jaws dripped bloody foam. Taine jumped up and down and waved his arms, making himself as large as possible, and yelled and screamed, making as much noise as he could.

The bear was supposed to turn away now. They always had before – but this one just kept coming. Taine dropped to the ground, curling in a defensive position, and let himself go limp.

Play dead when they're coming at you, that's the only option.

He stifled a scream of pain as the maddened creature ran right over the top of him, its powerful claws tearing at his back. It turned quickly and was on him again, its great paws battering him left and right, hitting him on his chest and side. It had the terrifying power of some huge unstoppable force of nature: a tornado, a hurricane, an avalanche. Taine's heavy leather jerkin gave him some protection; nevertheless he felt the claws rip into his skin and the flesh beneath, while its teeth just missed tearing his face off and sank into his shoulder instead, grating on bone. Then suddenly the attentions of the maddened creature fastened on his horse, which was screaming and fighting its tether to escape. With contemptuous strength, it tossed Taine away. He flew through the air and hit a tree in an explosion of pain and darkness.

Aelwen was lungeing Corisand, making the horse move in a circle on a long line and walk, trot or canter on command. The Horsemistress had decided that some schooling would remind the animal just who was in charge, lest she become too difficult to handle altogether.

After a sticky start, Corisand was working smoothly now: stopping, starting and changing gait on command, much to Aelwen's relief. It was nice to see something going right. Three days previously, the mare had come bounding into season – and had steadfastly, and violently, refused every stallion in the place. Worried about injuries to the precious studs – not to mention the three grooms who would be laid up for days – Aelwen had given in and left Corisand alone, but she was becoming increasingly concerned about the future of the animal. If they couldn't ride her and couldn't breed from her, then her fate was tied to that of Hellorin. They couldn't keep a useless, unpredictable horse in the stable indefinitely. If the Forest Lord failed to recover, Corisand would have to be destroyed, even though it would break Aelwen's heart to see the end of such exceptional beauty and spirit.

The Horsemistress was so preoccupied that she didn't hear anyone approaching, until a harsh voice from behind made her jump. 'I have just been told by some upstart of a groom that on your orders, I may not ride Asharal tonight.'

She turned to see Tiolani, who, judging by her sumptuous gown of emerald velvet, had just come from a hard morning of audiences and meetings. Her eyes, as she addressed Aelwen, had an unpleasant glint. 'Who do you think you are, to deny me the use of my own horse? How dare you?'

Aelwen signalled a groom to take Corisand away, then turned to face the angry gaze. 'As your father's Horsemistress, the welfare of the horses is *my* responsibility, and—'

Tiolani flushed darkly. 'My father's Horsemistress you may be, but *I* rule here!'

'I am resting Asharal because he is lame,' Aelwen continued, ignoring the outburst. 'You rode him to exhaustion yesterday, despite my warnings—'

'How I handle my horse is my own affair,' Tiolani blazed.

'When your horse is being damaged unnecessarily, it becomes *my* affair,' Aelwen told her. 'And Asharal is not the only one in trouble.' She knew that she was being dangerously rash in confronting the girl this way, but the horses were her responsibility, and she could only stand so much of seeing them ridden into the ground. 'You know how hard the flying magic is on our mounts, Tiolani. Once cast, it feeds upon their energy to sustain itself. Hellorin was experienced in minimising the effects, but you—'

'Are you trying to say I don't know what I'm doing?' The girl's voice had a dangerous edge.

'I am telling you, as I have told you so many times before, that this is the wrong time of year for the horses to be working so hard. You know the Hunt never rides out in the summer. That was Hellorin's edict, and he was right. These are the months when the horses rest, bear their foals, feed on the new grass, roll in the meadows and enjoy the sunshine. You cannot expect them to keep going indefinitely.'

The Horsemistress might as well have been talking to herself, for all the good it did. 'The Hunt will ride out when I say so,' Tiolani snapped. The hardness in her voice and in her eyes, which had been growing more and more marked of late, made her look like a stranger to Aelwen. 'Never before have we faced such a threat from these accursed wild humans, and I will not rest until that threat has been eliminated once and for all. That is *my* responsibility, Horsemistress. Yours is simply to do as you are told, and enable these horses to fulfil their function. You have until sundown to get Asharal fit to ride, or there will be serious repercussions. Be warned.'

'No matter how much you threaten me, Asharal is still lame, my Lady,' Aelwen said coldly. 'If you wish to ride out tonight, you must choose another mount.'

Tiolani's eyes flicked across the retreating figure of Corisand who, as usual, was fidgeting and playing up the groom. 'Very well. I will take my father's horse. She, at least, will be fresh, since no one has ridden her for months.'

'But you can't ride Corisand!' Aelwen was aghast. 'Only Hellorin can ride her, and if he were here, he certainly would not permit this.'

'But my father is *not* here.' Tiolani's eyes were hard: the eyes of a stranger. Not a trace remained of the unworldly, affectionate young girl that Aelwen had held in her arms as a newborn, had taught to ride, had watched growing up. She was overwhelmed by a crushing weight of sorrow. Whether or not Hellorin recovered, that demanding but delightful child would never return.

'You will either learn to obey my orders, or suffer the consequences,' Tiolani snapped. 'For my father's sake I will give you one more chance, but if you defy me once more, you will regret the outcome. Have the mare ready for me at nightfall.' She turned on her heel and stalked away, almost knocking over the approaching Kelon as she went and leaving Aelwen fuming – and not a little afraid.

When Kelon strode over to her with a scowl on *his* face, she didn't have to ask him what was amiss.

'What's going on, Aelwen?' he demanded. 'I just came back from seeing to the brood mares and found the grooms getting everything ready for the Hunt as usual – and they said that you told them to do it. I thought we agreed that the horses must rest. Is that blasted Tiolani still making impossible demands?'

'Hush, Kelon,' Aelwen said quickly, with a swift glance around to make sure that no one was within earshot. 'I can't help it. Tiolani won't stop the Hunt. I told her it was vital that she cancel it – at least for a few days – but she refused.'

'And I take it she was far from happy that you'd been insisting?'

'You might say that. She threatened to get rid of me if I gainsay her again.'

'I would like to see her try!' There was real anger in Kelon's voice. 'If she thinks to replace you with me, she'll have a surprise coming to her. Because if you go, I go too.'

A shiver went through Aelwen at his words. 'I don't think you'd want to go where she plans to send me,' she said softly. 'I saw the look in her eye when we argued. It wasn't so far from her expression in the Great Hall when she killed Ambaron.'

Kelon went very white. 'Then we have to do something,' he said.

Aelwen nodded. 'You're right. I suspect that Ambaron isn't the only one who has been getting in my Lady's way lately. If the rumours are true, others have disappeared in the last few days: Ambaron's brother Jarmil; Tanoram, head weaver of moonmoth silk; Gestil the master miner; Essenda, who owns – *owned* – the biggest of the valley's farms.'

'All of them Hemifae,' Kelon said softly, 'and all of them in prominent positions. I had heard rumours that Lady Tiolani wanted to get rid of us all because of our human blood, but such an idea was so outrageous that I didn't believe it. Until now.'

Their eyes met. 'We need to exercise our own mounts,' Aelwen said. 'The grooms can finish getting the other horses ready for tonight.'

'I think that's a good idea.'

It took no time to saddle their own horses. The two of them had developed the habit of riding out lately, whenever they wanted to discuss the state of affairs in Tiolani's court without being overheard. As usual, they rode away from Hellorin's stables, down and around the foot of the hill to the forest beyond. Aelwen was mounted on Taryn, her black stallion, while Kelon rode Alil, another stallion, a stocky light bay with a white star on his forehead. Though Alil was a decent horse, he wasn't particularly good-looking compared with his brethren in Hellorin's stables and, since no one else seemed to want him, Kelon had somehow managed to turn the animal into his own mount without ever having asked for, or been granted, the privilege.

It was cold beneath the trees, with a raw, whistling wind that tossed the restless branches and tugged spitefully at Aelwen's long braid, and the manes and tails of the horses. After they had put some distance between themselves and Eliorand, they turned away from the well-used track, taking a narrow side path that threaded its way into the woodland. The two of them rode knee to knee along the winding pathway, with the scents of greenery and earth in their nostrils, and the soft, muffled thudding of their horses' hooves on the springy surface of decaying leaves that carpeted the ground. They chatted inconsequentially about the small doings of the stables, each of them reluctant to return to the perilous subject of their talk beside the paddock fence. It still preoccupied their thoughts, however, to the extent that when Kelon blurted out: 'Surely it can't be possible,' Aelwen knew exactly what he meant.

'How should I know? I certainly don't find myself very welcome up at the palace nowadays.' Her voice came out sharper than she had intended. 'Tiolani has gathered her own clique around her.'

'Yet for most of her life, she has been almost like your own daughter.' Only Kelon would have had the nerve to say it.

Aelwen shrugged, trying not to let her expression betray the bitterness that she felt. 'Well, that's all over and done with now. My Lady doesn't like the way I'm constantly upbraiding her for wearing out our horses with this endless Hunt nonsense. If she carries on this way, she's going to run out of humans on which to take her vengeance – but that's no affair of mine. It's our poor charges I'm concerned about. At this rate, she cannot help but do them permanent damage.'

'I agree,' Kelon said. 'Hunting in the summer! Such a thing has never been known, and for good reason. The flying magic is hard on the poor beasts, and they need the summer to rest. Tiolani never had the feel for horses that her father and brother had,' he went on. 'If Hellorin would only recover, he would never permit such abuse.'

'Still,' Aelwen said, 'Tiolani may be young, inexperienced, stubborn, wrong-headed and unwise, but she has always loved her father, and Hellorin is all the family she has left. I find it hard to imagine that she'd keep him incapacitated so that she can hold on to the throne.'

'Power can do strange things to people.' Kelon locked eyes with her. At last they were approaching the subject that they had come out here to discuss, and for an instant Aelwen found herself shrinking from having to mention the unthinkable: that the attack by the feral humans that had slaughtered Tiolani's brother and almost killed her father had twisted her mind in some way, and turned her against the Hemifae because of their human blood. But the time had come for Aelwen and Kelon to face the realisation to which all the Hemifae had to come: as long as they remained in Eliorand, within the reach of Tiolani's arm, their lives were in constant danger.

Aelwen sighed, recalling that morning's confrontation with Hellorin's daughter; remembering the flat, hard, uncompromising look in the girl's eyes. *Human*, it said. *Tainted*. Her heart breaking, she thought of the girl who had once been like her own daughter; of all her beloved horses that she had nurtured for so long; of her comfortable, pleasant little house close to the stables; of her grooms, who might have started out as mere human slaves, no better than animals, but were now skilled, cheerful, important and valued members of her stable, with self-respect and a role in life. She had trained every single one of them, listened to their problems, shared their sorrows and triumphs. Even they were part of her family.

Kelon, as usual, seemed to know what she was thinking. 'Aelwen, there's no way out,' he said. 'She has her eye on you now. You'll have to get ready to run, and you should leave this place as soon as you possibly can. It just can't be helped.'

Looking at his dear, seamed face, Aelwen thought back down all the years they had been together. How many thousands of days had they worked side by side, rearing and training Hellorin's stable of splendid beauties? How many long nights had they sat up together, talking quietly throughout the peaceful hours of darkness, waiting for foals to be born? It seemed as though he had always been there beside her, steadfast and sensible, as necessary to her as her own right hand.

Maybe it was time she faced up to the unthinkable. Taine must be dead. Were he not, then surely he would have come back for her before now? He was so clever – surely he would have found some way to send her a message, at least. The alternative … Well, she couldn't bear to consider that, either. Had he forgotten her, found someone else to love?

It didn't matter. She would never stop loving him. That, however, did not preclude her from including her dearest friend in her escape – especially when his safety was also very much at stake.

Aelwen took a deep breath. '*We* will have to get ready to run.'

For an instant she saw a bright flash of hope cross Kelon's face, before his expression returned to its normal, serious mien. 'But Aelwen,' he protested, 'what about the horses? If we're both gone, who will take care of them?'

'Kelon, if I could, I would take every single damn one of those horses with me. The thought of anyone else trying to care for them twists me up inside. But what can we do? We won't be able to look after them if we're dead – and with Tiolani in her current state of mind, that's exactly how we'll end up if we stay. You have to come with me. You're Hemifae too, and however we try to conceal it, you'll be implicated in my escape. How much longer will she keep *you* alive?'

This time, the hope brightened and stayed. 'Of course I'll come,' he said.

Aelwen looked away, trying not to see. *Am I being cruel?* she thought. She knew that by including him she was raising false expectations. But such complications were trifling in the face of the danger. Right now, all they should be worrying about was survival. There would be time later, when their lives were not at stake, to deal with all the rest.

'If we're going to escape, then it had better be tonight,' she said. 'If we leave just after the Hunt has set out, we won't be missed for several hours.' She sighed. 'I wish they didn't have such an advantage over us with the flying magic. No matter how far we travel on the ground in that time, Tiolani should soon be able to track us down.'

Kelon nodded glumly, his brows knotted in a frown. 'The sooner we can leave the better, but we'll be taking a dreadful risk. They'll hunt us down from the air, so unless we can find a really good place to hide within a few hours' riding distance from Eliorand, we'll be caught for sure.'

They rode back in silence, deep in thought. As they left the woodland behind and headed up towards the stables, they were no nearer a solution. Then, just as they were passing Corisand's paddock, Kelon's expression suddenly cleared and he pulled his mount to a halt. 'I've got it! The perfect solution – at least I hope it is.'

'Tell me,' Aelwen demanded, catching his excitement.

A grin slowly spread across Kelon's face. 'I know a way for us to steal some of Tiolani's flying spell. Once all the horses have gone up to the palace courtyard for the Hunt, we'll follow them with our own beasts and hide them just inside the tunnel mouth.' He was talking fast with excitement. 'You've seen Tiolani's flying magic in action. She lacks the control over the spell that her father had. The enchantment extends much further, and it's very diffuse round the edges. Instead of having proper boundaries, it continues to spread until it eventually fades away due to a lack of targets. So if we hide our horses inside the tunnel mouth, when she casts the spell we should be in range.'

'Kelon, you're brilliant – absolutely brilliant!' Aelwen felt excitement bubbling up inside her. 'As soon as the Hunt leaves, we'll fly away ourselves in a different direction, keeping low above the treetops. Before the spell wears off, we'll be far away – and since they will be expecting us to have escaped on foot, they'll never imagine we could travel that distance, and they'll be looking for us much closer to the city. This could work, Kelon, it could really work. We might have a fighting chance to get away after all. Presuming that your wonderful plan works and we *do* escape, shall we head for Tyrineld and throw ourselves on the mercies of the Wizards?'

'I think that's our best option,' Kelon agreed. 'In fact, it's our *only* option.'

'Come on, then,' Aelwen said. 'Let's not waste any more time. We've lots to do to get the horses ready for the Hunt tonight, not to mention putting together all the stuff we'll need for our escape. Sunset will be on us before we know it.'

They went out of the stable, leaving a stunned and horrified Corisand behind them. Aelwen and Kelon were leaving? Tonight? But now that Hellorin was gone, they were the only ones she could tolerate and trust. There was no alternative. Somehow, she would have to find a way to escape, as soon as possible. It they were heading for Tyrineld and the Wizards, she wanted to go with them, but as the hours wore on she found no inspiration. Hellorin valued his horses highly. He had made every possible effort to safeguard against their theft or escape. All too soon, the sun was dipping towards the horizon, and she was no closer to a solution.

When Kelon came for her, she couldn't have been more surprised. Driven by curiosity, and the hope that he might reveal more of his and Aelwen's plans in her hearing, she let him put a halter on her with unaccustomed meekness, and suffered herself to be led from the far paddock that she had occupied for so long, leaving the mares and their foals looking curiously after her over the fence. She was taken up to the main stable block, which was bustling with the frantic activity that always accompanied the preparations for the Wild Hunt. But surely they couldn't mean for *her* to join the Hunt?

Apparently that was exactly what they were intending. She was so aghast that she actually let Kelon lead her into a stall and tether her, and he had started to groom her before it occurred to her to take any action. Corisand was furious. Why, without any warning, had she been brought in from the paddock? Why was Kelon grooming her so carefully? And why the saddle and bridle? Hellorin had not recovered – she had been listening very carefully to the talk around the stables, and if there had been any change, she certainly would have heard. That could only mean another rider – but these stupid Phaerie should know perfectly well that the Forest Lord was the only one who could ride her! Who else would dare to attempt such a thing? Corisand came to the conclusion that it could only be Tiolani, and this ... this ... travesty was the upshot of the girl's visit to the stable that morning. It did not take her long to discover that she was right. Out of earshot of Aelwen and Kelon, she overheard the lowly human grooms making wagers about Tiolani's continued good health, using what scanty items they possessed. From their talk, it was clear that the Hemifae were not the only ones who feared Hellorin's daughter.

'I hate that bitch. She gives me the shivers, the way she looks at us all. For two pins, I reckon, she'd have us all dead, like those poor buggers in the forest.'

'Bet you my gloves that she doesn't last more than a dozen heartbeats tonight.'

'What? That long? I bet you my belt with the brass buckle that our Corisand'll have her on the ground in five.'

'Whose heartbeats? Yours or mine?' Corisand heard laughter.

Five heartbeats, eh? she thought grimly. *She'll be lucky if she lasts that long.*

When she was almost ready, Aelwen joined Kelon in her stall. Though they spoke in very low voices, Corisand strained her ears to listen above the stable's raucous din.

'What about the horses?' he asked her.

'They're in the smaller stable,' she replied. 'They're ready to go. Let's get this lot moving out, then we'll follow at a distance, so they won't hear us coming behind. You take Corisand out for Tiolani, and I'll wait in the tunnel mouth with the horses. I only hope this works, Kelon.'

'It'll work. It has to.'

In that moment, a flash of inspiration came to Corisand. This was her own chance to escape – and even better, it was on the same night as Aelwen and Kelon intended to flee Eliorand. Her mind raced, as a whole treasure chest of possibilities opened before her. Why, if she thought this through, she might even be able to find a way to cause a distraction to help them get clean away! Somehow, it made her feel a great deal less alone to know that the two Hemifae would also be making a run for it. Maybe she could even find them, and play the dumb horse for a while longer while she let them take her with them to Tyrineld. If anyone could free her from this imprisonment in her equine form, surely it must be the Wizards.

In the fading daylight, the Windeye's excitement was like a blazing beacon – but its fire could not burn brightly enough to wipe out the shadows of her fear.

25

OUT OF THE DARK

Iriana and her companions were late making camp that night. Over the last few days they had moved steadily onward into the heart of the forest, climbing all the time as the land rose steadily towards the flanks of the mountains. After following the course of the river for so long, the road had finally veered away and the look and feel of the terrain was changing as oak, birch and chestnut began to be mixed with aspen, maple, pine and spruce. Even the sound of the forest was different, Iriana mused, as her tired horse trudged up the trail. The flutter and rustle of the breeze through the broad-leaved trees was now mingled with a rushing whisper that rose and fell like the sound of the sea, as the cool, resin-spiced wind soughed through the soaring branches of the conifers.

Though every one of Iriana's senses combined with the vision of her animals in showing her surroundings of heart-lifting beauty, she'd had enough for one day, and wished with all her heart that Esmon would find a campsite and let her rest. Now that they were nearing the borders of the Phaerie realm – for tomorrow they would be entering that hostile territory – the Warrior was determined to find a spot in which the travellers and their horses would be invisible from the air. There would be no more comforting campfires from now on, either. Not while there was a risk of the Wild Hunt riding overhead.

The sun was sinking into a leaden mass of dense grey cloud that was stacking around the southern and western horizon, and Iriana felt a shiver of foreboding.

'We'd better hurry up and find somewhere to camp, Esmon,' she said. 'It looks as if there's a storm on the way.'

'We can't stop until I find a safe place,' the implacable voice floated back over Esmon's shoulder. 'We're too near the border and I want us hidden from the Hunt. Better tired now than dead before morning.'

Avithan sighed. 'We can't argue with that.'

Boreas, the great eagle, would be ready to land and rest for the night, and Iriana called him down to her arm, planning to transfer him to his perch on the back of the packhorse, which Avithan was currently leading. But to her astonishment, there was no response from the bird.

This had never happened before. Iriana, concerned, abandoned the vision of her horse and flung her mind into the skies, searching for the errant one. He made the link with reluctance, barely acknowledging her presence, almost brushing her away. Grimly, she held on, looking out through his eyes, trying to see where he was and why he had strayed.

Iriana gasped at the soaring white peaks that surrounded them in stunning grandeur. Boreas had sped north, to the mountains beyond the Phaerie realm. Iriana's heart sank. Deep inside she knew why he had flown so far afield. She would do anything not to face the truth, but unfortunately, there was no choice. He had followed an imperative even more urgent than his loving bond with her. Whirling and tumbling around him was another eagle – and she sensed from his mind that it was a female. Boreas, the lonely, solitary creature who'd been taken so far from his natural home had returned at last. And he'd found a mate.

He was going to leave her. Her heart breaking, Iriana remained a part of their dizzy courtship dance as the pair swirled and spun, looped and circled and soared, going higher and higher until even the mighty peaks looked like insignificant hillocks beneath them. Then suddenly they locked claws and fell together in a flutter of wings and racing heartbeats. Iriana tore herself away then, leaving them to find a suitable ledge and mate at last; to build their nest and rear their chicks.

Eagles mated for life.

He wouldn't be coming back.

'Iriana, what's wrong?' She felt Avithan's arms around her, and the hot flood of tears that were soaking her face. 'Esmon, stop. Something's happened to Iriana.'

When she choked out her news they were kind and sympathetic, but how could they possibly know how much this meant to her; how deeply she felt the separation? She had been closely linked with the bird since Boreas was hatched. Yet even as she grieved for her loss, Iriana felt a sense of immense pride. Boreas had found his own mate, his own life. In bringing him on this journey she had brought him home, to his own world. He had found a mate, and one day his offspring would wheel among the peaks, fishing in the sparkling mountain lakes.

After a time, Melik helped her pull herself together by sticking his claws into her arm with high-pitched wails of irritation.

'What's the matter with him?' Avithan demanded.

'Shut him up, for goodness sake,' Esmon added.

'He wants his supper, and a nice, cosy tent instead of a moving horse,' Iriana replied.

'He has my sympathy.' Avithan fidgeted and stretched in the saddle. 'I want exactly the same things.'

'Don't we all?' Iriana said ruefully. 'Esmon, surely we can't go much further?'

'What do you want me to do? I can't find a place.' For the first time since they had set out on their journey, Esmon sounded worried.

The clouds were moving inexorably towards them, and shadowy dusk lurked beneath the thick boughs on either side of the path. The horses were stumbling with weariness.

When darkness fell, the Wild Hunt would ride, and they were out, unprotected, on the open trail.

Iriana hesitated, then spoke. 'Esmon, perhaps I can find somewhere for us. Seyka can look further off the trail.'

'At this point, I'd be willing to consider anything.'

Iriana let an impatient Seyka out of her basket. She stroked the bird, running her hands over the soft white feathers. At least Seyka had stayed with her. The white owl gripped the wicker rim with her claws, stretched her wings a time or two, and floated, silent as a ghost, away into the woods.

Iriana pushed her horse alongside Avithan's mount. 'Keep an eye on Dailika, will you, please? I'm going to link with Seyka and take a look around, or we'll never find anywhere to stop tonight. Maybe there's a camping place further from the road.'

Avithan nodded. 'Do you want me to lead her?'

'No, I can trust her to follow her companions – she's trained to do that. Just be there to grab her bridle if anything spooks her.'

Iriana let herself share the owl's vision for a few moments as she hunted. The world lost its colour as she made the link, turning monochrome as she flew with Seyka, swooping and banking low beneath the trees. Every detail: each flake of bark, each vein of a leaf, every single blade of grass had become absolutely clear and distinct; the keen eyes of the bird searching for any unusual movement that might betray the presence of prey.

With a little more difficulty, she concentrated hard and tuned into Seyka's hearing, which was far more acute than her own. Each tiny rustle, each buzz of gnat and fly, the breathing and heartbeats of the horses, their riders and the tiny creatures in the undergrowth: all were magnified, and it was even possible to discern their distance and direction.

Iriana was so immersed in the sensations of the flight and the hunt that she almost overlooked the sound of the river. It was different now, its tranquil murmur changed to bubbling laughter as the young stream skipped and raced along. 'Esmon, stop,' she called. 'I can hear the river again, away to the right of the trail.'

Up ahead, the sound of hoofbeats stopped, then started again as Esmon rode back. 'You've found the river? Good girl. But are you sure, Iriana? I can't hear anything.'

'Neither can I, with my own ears. But Seyka heard it.'

'How far away do you think it is?'

'Not too far, but I'm not exactly sure of the location. It's sometimes difficult to keep track of where she's going when she's swooping and banking through the trees.'

Esmon thought for a moment. 'Avithan, hang on to Iriana's horse. Iriana, link with Seyka again. Can you get her to find the river?'

'I've never tried with the owl,' Iriana told him, 'but sometimes I can get Melik and Bear to go to a place if I put an image in their minds.'

'Well, let's find out. I'll head off the trail in that general direction, and when you've found the river, send Seyka to me and I'll follow her back. If she can't do it, give me a call in mindspeech. We shouldn't be shouting this close to the border if we can possibly help it.'

Iriana nodded and settled herself in the saddle. Casting her mind forth, she found the owl, who had just spotted a fat mouse scurrying between the tree roots, completely oblivious to her silent presence. She was just tensing herself to swoop when Iriana called her back. 'I'm sorry,' she told Seyka in mindspeech, 'but you've got all night to hunt. I just need to borrow your eyes for a little while longer.'

Reluctantly, the owl abandoned its prey and flew on into the trees. Iriana tried to send images of water into its mind, and after a few moments of weaving flight between tree trunks, she heard the sound of the splashing stream again. Seyka burst out of the trees into the open, and to Iriana's delight, she had found the perfect camping place. It was not so much a clearing as a wide margin around a large pond that had been created by a beaver dam. The young river poured in from the north over a step of rock – about waist-high, it was too small to be called a waterfall – and flowed out across the tangled barrier of sticks at the opposite end of the broad, shining pool. On the side closest to the trail a massive chestnut tree grew, its broad, sheltering boughs overhanging the area between the water and the forest's brink.

Water, shelter, cover from the air. The place was perfect, and Iriana could not have been more gratified by Esmon's nod of approval as he rode out of the trees, picking leaves and twigs from down the neck of his tunic, and looked around. She left the owl to continue her interrupted hunting, and returned to the very different vision of her horse. 'Esmon liked it,' she said to Avithan, with a big smile. 'I could tell by his face. Oh, thank goodness we can stop and rest at last.'

'Listen – he's coming back now,' Avithan said.

The Warrior emerged from the trees onto the trail once more, mopping at the blood from a scratch on his bald head. 'It's something of a scramble to get there if you haven't got wings,' he said, 'but the place is too perfect to quibble about that. Besides, there's no harm in being fairly inaccessible from the road. Let's get going, you two. We're already losing daylight. Once we're down, I'll come back up here on foot and do my best to hide the place where we left the track.'

Avithan and Iriana exchanged an uneasy thought. Now they were so close to the border, what had seemed like a light-hearted adventure to begin with had become deadly serious. As they turned their horses to follow Esmon, the Warrior's posture and demeanour communicated a new sense of caution and the need for stealth.

Esmon was right – it *was* something of a scramble, down a steep bank thickly overgrown with trees. Iriana, using her horse's eyes to navigate the slope, had to crouch low in the saddle: not the ideal position under the circumstances. Every moment it felt as though she would slide over Dailika's head, and the horse was finding it difficult to keep its balance with her weight thrown so far forward. The wild, hair-raising slither was soon over, however, and they were out in the open again on the banks of the pond. She straightened up gratefully, pushing her hair, which had been caught on twigs and pulled out of her braid, back from her face.

Esmon, however, scarcely gave his companions time to catch their breath. 'Get this camp pitched. We won't be lighting a fire tonight. We'll manage all right with our night vision, but I want everything sorted out and under cover before nightfall. Beneath that big chestnut tree is best for the tents – that should hide them from the air – and keep those horses well out of sight, Iriana.' Though she was tired, Iriana went to work with a will. The sooner they dealt with the camp and the animals, the sooner they could eat something and get to sleep.

As usual, they fell efficiently into their routine, and Iriana picketed their horses beneath a huge old hawthorn that stood near the bank of the stream where it flowed out of the pool. After their quarrel on the first night in the forest, Avithan had been careful to see to his own tasks and allow her to get on with hers, and the only time Iriana felt a twinge of regret about the new arrangements was when she had to remove the weighty, unwieldy saddles. Her own Dailika was easy enough to deal with, but Avithan and Esmon rode bigger horses. As Iriana reached up and pulled off Esmon's saddle, the additional weight made her stagger slightly, and a loose stone turned and rolled under her foot. She stumbled two steps backward, teetered, toppled, and, with an enormous splash, fell flat on her backside in the stream, with the saddle resting on top of her. 'Bugger! Shit, arse, pox, plague and sod it.' All this time with Esmon had been improving the scope of Iriana's vocabulary no end.

'Are you all right?' Esmon and Avithan came running up. Though their faces were a picture of concern, their eyes sparkled with mirth and their lips were twitching in a desperate attempt not to laugh.

Even though Iriana was using Seyka's eyes, she still managed to turn a fulminating scowl in their direction. 'What the bloody blazes are you clowns waiting for? Get this blasted thing off me.'

The two men made the mistake of catching each other's eyes, gave up the unequal struggle and roared with laughter. Avithan, helpless, mopped at streaming eyes while Esmon simply sat down on the ground, clutching his ribs.

Iriana, her face hot with mortification, abandoned any hope of help from the pair of grinning morons and managed to roll out from beneath the saddle herself. As she climbed out of the water, she was suddenly filled with a wonderful warm glow of camaraderie and belonging. If this had happened when their journey started, the two men would have been falling over themselves to pick her up, dust her down, make sure that she hadn't hurt herself. Now, at last, she had truly become one of them: a member of the team who could pull her own weight, take care of herself – and be laughed at. Dripping and delighted, Iriana joined in the mirth.

'Time to wake up. It's your turn to watch.'

'What … ? Oh. All right, Avithan. Give me a minute, I'm coming.' Iriana rolled over carefully in the cramped confines of her tent and wormed her way out of her blankets. She groped for her warm coat and shrugged into it, then found the edge of the doorway by touch and crawled out of the shelter, sending a mental call to Melik as she did so. Seeking the cat's mind with her own, she found him nearby, and settled happily into their habitual bonding. As she looked out of his eyes, she saw the forest floor through the monochromatic light and dark of feline night vision. He was slinking through the bushes, heading towards the dim shapes of the tents that he could see between the leaves and branches.

Suddenly, Iriana saw herself and Avithan as Melik burst through the bushes into the clearing. 'That's better,' she said with a smile for her fellow Wizard, knowing that he had been waiting, as was his tactful wont, until she could see him before starting a conversation.

'Here.' He held out a cup of water. 'That should wake you up a bit. I wish it could have been a cup of hot taillin, but it was the best I could manage with no fire.'

'Thanks – it's just what I need.' Iriana lied. She would have killed for taillin, but she took the cup and sipped.

'Esmon picked his time to start doing without fires,' Avithan said. 'It's getting colder the further north we go.'

'And this is the coldest night so far.' Putting her cup down, Iriana pulled her coat more closely around her. 'Oh, drat. I left my gloves in the tent. Could you fish them out for me, please?'

The fact that she had asked him demonstrated the change in their relationship. Formerly, she would have been too determinedly independent to ask for help. Formerly, he would have been offering to get her the gloves before she'd even had time to think of it herself. Recently, however, she had been surprised and pleased to notice that Avithan was giving her more credit for being able to manage her share of all their little tasks of survival, and as a result, she'd begun to be a little more relaxed about letting him help her occasionally. Also, now that they had ceased their constant bickering, Iriana was beginning to find his company very congenial – though she was scarcely ready to admit it as yet, even to herself.

Now, it occurred to her how handsome Avithan looked in the firelight. While they were travelling, he had started to grow a beard, and it suited him. Why had she never really *noticed* him before? Because she'd been too busy fending him off, she realised; trying to guard her independence from his stifling attempts to take care of her. Well, maybe it was time to stop evading him. Maybe she should try taking care of him for a change, and see how he coped with *that*.

Right now, for instance, he looked tired out, and it was high time he left her and got some rest. 'Go on, Avithan,' she told him with a smile. 'Get into your tent and go to sleep. It's my turn to watch now.'

'All right. Goodnight, Iriana. Have a peaceful watch.' To her utter astonishment, he leant over and kissed her lightly on the lips – then disappeared swiftly into his tent before she could either reply or respond.

For a moment, the Wizard sat open-mouthed, staring at Avithan's tent through Melik's eyes. The thin moonmoth silk walls glowed faintly with magelight, and she could see his shadow moving about as he wriggled into his blankets. What in Perdition did he think he was playing at? she thought indignantly. Kissing her out of the blue like that, and then, just when she was starting to like it, vanishing off to bed without a word? For a moment she had an overwhelming urge to call him out again to demand an explanation and – she suddenly found herself grinning – maybe give him a taste of his own medicine by kissing him back.

Then the inward voice of her sensible self took control, reminding her that she was supposed to be on watch now, and was responsible for the safety of the camp. Besides, she ought to think about this interesting new development a little before taking any action. It might only be an affectionate little kiss after all, in which case it wouldn't do to make a fool of herself by reading too much meaning into it. Nevertheless, the grin refused to leave Iriana's face as she settled down to watch, and she felt a pleasant warmth inside that more than compensated for the lack of a campfire.

Dhagon, hidden above Avithan and Iriana in the broad limbs of the chestnut tree, watched this tender little scene with contempt. These two pathetic idiots deserved to die. And they were still letting the blind girl take watches! It was utter lunacy on Esmon's part. He looked down at the creature with distaste. Imagine the Archwizard having the nerve to send such a flawed freak of nature as his representative to the Phaerie Court. *Had she been one of our race*, he thought, *she would have been strangled as soon as the deformity had been discovered.*

As the one called Iriana settled down to guard the camp, Dhagon wondered if he should begin with her. She would be easy prey. No trouble at all. But there was always the chance that she, or one of those filthy creatures that she used as eyes, might let out a sound and awaken the Warrior Esmon – who would immediately call Avithan, and then Dhagon would have two men to fight. No, that wasn't the way. Even though the danger was small to a trained killer like Dhagon, the best option was always to take no risk at all. He would wait until Esmon came on watch and kill him first. With the only Warrior among them dead, the other two would be easy pickings.

The assassin licked his lips, his body tingling with anticipation. For days now he had shadowed these fools, using the Phaerie spells of glamourie to hide himself from the Wizards and from the girl's accursed animals – he'd learned from his mistake the first night when that foul cat had almost seen through his spell. Every night since, he had spied upon their camp, listening to them talk, tucking away all sorts of information about the Wizards of Tyrineld and their defences and, thanks to Cyran's peaceful policies, their paucity of trained Warriors.

Tiolani was going to be very interested in that.

Dhagon hoped he'd not left it too late and let his quarry get too close to the border. It was important that they should be killed while they were still within the realm of the Wizards – he planned to make it look as though they had been attacked by an animal, by dragging the corpses to the vicinity of a bear den and letting nature take its course.

Time went by while he hid in his tree with the deadly patience of a spider, making his plans and waiting for the right moment to put them into action. He could have killed them with magic, of course, but Cyran and his Wizards would be able to detect the traces of the spells, and know that Phaerie had been involved. Besides, he preferred his butchery to be more intimate: the deadly glitter of cold steel, and the gush of warm blood across his hands. And apart from the sweet joy of killing, there was also the girl. Dhagon began to entertain himself with ideas of taking her. Without her sight, she would be utterly helpless and in his power – exactly the way he liked his women. The killer ran his tongue over his lips in anticipation. They were best when they were afraid; re-sisting. Their terror and struggles gave a delicious edge to his pleasure. And when you added pain: that was the best of all. Once he had killed the two men, he would have all the time in the world to torture her, and take every pleasure he wished. He knew the tricks of keeping his victims alive while he toyed with them.

Finally Iriana roused Esmon, and Dhagon's killer instincts snapped alert. Irritably he waited, wishing that the blind girl would make haste and go to bed. Then he tensed as he heard what she was saying. The wretched creature was still blathering to Esmon about feeling uneasy, as though she were being watched. The Warrior replied patiently, but sounded a little weary of the whole business. Dhagon observed and listened, his lip curled with scorn. *That impaired slip of a girl has better instincts than you*, he thought. *Soon you'll be sorry you ignored her – and so will she.*

Once the girl had gone into her tent, the assassin bided his time for a good while longer, to make sure she was well and truly settled and asleep. Then, soundlessly, he slid down from his perch and crept up behind his victim. At the last instant, Esmon seemed to realise that something was wrong. But before he could raise the alarm or reach for his weapon, Dhagon's knife sliced across his throat, then plunged into his heart.

26

STORMFLIGHT

At nightfall Corisand waited in the stable yard with Aelwen and Kelon until the other grooms had taken the rest of the horses into the tunnel entrance. Once they were safely out of sight, Aelwen crossed the yard and ducked into the smaller stable, emerging with Taryn and Alil, each laden with bulging saddlebags and with blanket rolls strapped behind their saddles. To Corisand's surprise, she also saw another mare, the very flashy (in Corisand's opinion) strawberry roan named Rosina, who was laden with packs and tied to Taryn's saddle with a long tether.

Kelon raised his eyebrows. 'You want to take a *packhorse*? Aelwen, are you sure about this? An extra animal to control could be a dreadful liability while we're trying to escape.'

'I wasn't thinking so much about a packhorse as a brood mare,' Aelwen replied. 'She's just been to the stallion, Kelon. I thought if we could manage to take her with us, we could continue the line of Hellorin's horses in Tyrineld, or wherever we end up. We would never leave Taryn or Alil behind, but from a breeding point of view, where's the advantage of having two stallions and no mares?'

Kelon considered briefly, then nodded. 'It's worth a try. Come on, then. We'd better hurry.'

They set off, Kelon leading Corisand in front, while Aelwen came behind with the other horses. Behind the stables was a low cliff where the hillside fell away steeply, and set into the face of the escarpment was the entrance of the tunnel. Steadily they began to climb up the wide, curving way, and as he led Corisand on, Kelon looked over his shoulder and grinned. 'I notice you just happened to choose that precious pink mare of yours.' With her coat a mixture of deep fiery chestnut and white hairs, Rosina did seem to have a rosy blush. Aelwen scowled at him.

'She's a very good mare, and I think her colour is beautiful. Do you have a problem with that?'

'Me? Not a bit,' Kelon chuckled. 'I think Corisand does, though.'

Corisand did. When she saw Aelwen with Rosina, she felt an unanticipated pang of jealousy and, even while castigating herself for being stupid, she couldn't resist turning her head to put her ears back at the other mare.

Aelwen chuckled. 'Would you look at that? Still, it won't be a problem to us, as Corisand isn't coming. I would love to take her, but even if Tiolani had not been riding her tonight, we'd never be allowed to get away with Hellorin's own mare. They would hunt us to the ends of the earth.'

Kelon shrugged. 'Besides, what would be the point of taking her? She's just rejected every stallion in the place. Ouch!' He jumped. Corisand had nipped his arm.

All the time they had been talking, they had been climbing within the underground passageway, moving up through the hillside beneath the city. The walls and floor of the tunnel had the smooth, perfect look of any structure that had been carved out by magic, though the floor was covered with a thick layer of sand, to prevent the horses from slipping. The ceiling arched high above, leaving lots of headroom. The lamps, filled with captive lightning, crackled and buzzed as they cast their brilliant bluish light across the passage, and the ozone smell tickled the nostrils of horses and riders alike.

Eventually, Aelwen halted the other horses in the shadowy mouth of the tunnel, and let Kelon and Corisand go on ahead. They emerged into the courtyard before the palace, with Kelon keeping a firm grasp on the mare's bridle. Corisand discovered a very different scene from the last Wild Hunt she had attended. Everything felt wrong tonight, and out of place: the mildness of the evening, with its scents of sun-warmed vegetation, the luminosity of the summer sky, with a golden crescent moon overhead, and some ominous-looking banks of dark cloud forming on the western horizon. It was all so different from the crisp, frosty air and velvet blackness of a winter's night. Beyond the city, the soft, rounded outlines of leafy treetops marked the forest, instead of the intricate lacework of winter-bare boughs.

Even the hunters themselves had changed. Gone was the atmosphere of anticipation; gone was the savage joy. On previous Hunts the courtyard had been brimming with excited, chattering Phaerie, but now only a grim handful remained, the weaker of them held to their purpose by fear of Tiolani, and the stronger – mainly those who had lost friends or kin in the ambush – filled with a merciless, driven sense of purpose, desperate to find more wild humans on whom to wreak their revenge. There was no sense of pleasure here any longer – only the vicious desire to hunt, and maim, and kill.

A sudden silence fell across the courtyard, and Corisand looked up to see Tiolani standing alone at the top of the steps. She too had changed out of all recognition from the excited young girl with nothing in her life to worry her save acquitting herself well on her first Wild Hunt. Now she had aged and hardened.

Corisand, with her Windeye's senses, could perceive the aura of darkness that surrounded her; could smell the miasma of bitterness and bloodlust and hate. The mare shuddered and, for a fleeting instant, felt unprecedented doubt. Would it really be wise to cross this dangerous, unpredictable creature whose very sanity was in question?

Then her head came up, and her pride took command.

I am Corisand. I know things, O daughter of Hellorin, that you could barely imagine. Your father might have bested me when I was a dumb beast and knew no better, but you *will never master me!*

Kelon led Corisand forward as Tiolani descended the steps, and all eyes were upon them as they met. A silence had fallen in the courtyard. With a curt nod to the stony-faced head groom, Tiolani went to put her foot in the stirrup. Corisand laid back her ears and sidestepped.

'Hold her, you fool!' Tiolani, in temper, lashed out at Kelon with her whip, and a red line opened on the side of his face. Corisand smelled the blood, and felt the slow boil of building anger within her. *You'll pay for that*, she thought, but for the present, so as not to get Kelon into more trouble, she decided to stand quietly and let Tiolani mount. Kelon let go of the bridle and stepped well back out of range, and Corisand felt Tiolani's legs clamp her in a vicelike grip and her hands tighten on the reins, ready to deal with any trouble. Smirking to herself, the Windeye stood, meek and obedient as the gentlest old nag, and listened to the murmurs of surprise, coupled with respect for Hellorin's daughter, that were running round the courtyard. How had Tiolani mastered her father's untameable horse with such ease?

With a great show of obedience, Corisand let Tiolani turn her to face the assembled Phaerie. 'Let us ride,' Tiolani cried out in a ringing voice, and activated the flying magic that was the heritage of the Forest Lord's line. Instead of the glittering splendour of Hellorin's spell, however, his daughter's magic emerged as a faint greenish, luminous mist that clung to the horses, hounds and riders, giving them an eerie, eldritch pallor that resembled corpse-light. Corisand sensed the difference immediately.

This flying spell, lacking the practice and polish of Hellorin's long life-time, was raw and brutal, gnawing painfully at the life-energies of the recipients to fuel itself. *No wonder my people have been coming back so exhausted from Tiolani's Hunts*, the Windeye thought furiously. *Does she not realise what she's doing? Does she not care?*

As the hounds took off, Tiolani spurred her into the air in their wake. Still Corisand chose to bide her time. She was far too close to the city to make her move yet – and in the meantime, she had to admit that it felt wonderful to fly again. Moving easily through the warm summer night, the Wild Hunt was heading southward once more, veering towards the south-eastern boundaries of their kingdom and, with every league they flew, coming closer to the lands of the Wizards. Tension and excitement made her heart beat faster. Soon now, soon. With her equine vision she could see almost all the way around her, and as she gained height, she kept an eye out behind her for Aelwen and Kelon. Only when they were well on their way could she act.

Aelwen, standing with the three laden horses in the shadowy tunnel mouth, watched Kelon walking back to her, and felt a searing rage at the sight of his bleeding face. Damn that Tiolani! How *dare* she? As he approached, she pulled him into the shadows with her, and dabbed gently at the whip cut with a corner of her cloak, feeling her anger flare even higher as he winced. 'That little bitch,' she muttered. 'Are you all right?'

'I'll live,' he muttered. He wouldn't meet her eyes. 'Look – she's starting.'

Aelwen peered out of the tunnel to see Tiolani sitting on a curiously placid Corisand, her hands upraised as she summoned the flying spell. She shuddered as the sickly green glow began to spread out across the riders of the Hunt. 'Ugh! I don't much fancy *that* crawling all over me. Do you remember Hellorin's flying magic, Kelon? All the sparkle and the shimmer, and the glorious colours against the winter sky. It was so beautiful.'

Kelon nodded. 'All the same, just at this moment I prefer Tiolani's enchantment. If we had picked up Hellorin's flying magic, we'd have been visible for miles, but this spell is so dim that we'll just fade into the background once we've put a little bit of distance between the Hunt and ourselves.'

'Here it comes!' Aelwen gripped Kelon's arm tightly as the magic spread across the courtyard, entering the tunnel mouth and flooding across the two Hemifae and their mounts. Neither of them had been subjected to the flying spell before. It took them completely by surprise.

Aelwen felt a cool tingling as the magic passed over her, covering her from head to foot in the spectral green glow – then suddenly she staggered, clinging to Kelon's arm as a wave of weakness overwhelmed her. There was a loud buzzing in her ears, a blizzard of brightly coloured spots before her eyes, and the world swirled dizzily around her. She could feel Taryn tugging on the reins and neighing shrilly in distress, and was dimly aware that the magic must be affecting the horses in a similar way.

Aelwen gasped, pressing her hands to her throbbing temples. She wasn't sure at that moment whether she could even stand upright, let alone pull off a daring escape. She was not to know that Hellorin's flying spell, refined by long years of practice and reinforced by the colossal strength of the Phaerie Lord himself, would not have affected her this way. Tiolani's magic, however, was not strong enough to power itself throughout the long hours of the Hunt, and must therefore feed instead upon the energies of its subjects, as Corisand had discovered already. And because Aelwen and Kelon had never been part of the Wild Hunt, they'd had no chance to build up an immunity to the magic.

The worst of her torment was short-lived, however. After a few moments, the spell stabilised, the world stopped whirling and those dreadful feelings of nausea and weakness receded into the background. Aelwen looked at Kelon. Beneath the translucent green haze that covered him, he was white as a ghost. 'How are you feeling?' she whispered.

He took a deep, shuddering breath and pushed himself away from the wall against which he had been leaning. 'Well,' he said softly, 'at least now we know why our horses are coming back exhausted every time.'

'They're leaving.' Aelwen gestured towards the courtyard. The Huntsman and his hounds were already aloft, and the horses and riders were climbing steeply into the air as they followed, with Tiolani at their head. Her face was set and grim, and her eyes were bright and savage with bloodlust. Aelwen and Kelon watched them soar and dwindle until they were nothing more than a glowing speck in the distance, then turned and looked at one another.

'This is it,' Kelon said. Warily he crept out into the courtyard once more, scanning the windows of the palace for people looking out. After a moment he beckoned to Aelwen, who led the horses out, trying to stay in the shadows beside the high wall. In a trice they were mounted, and Aelwen quickly fastened Rosina's tether to her own saddle.

'Come on – quick,' Aelwen whispered.

'Er ... How do we start?'

They looked at one another in consternation. How, exactly, *did* one get airborne? Aelwen frowned, trying to remember what the hunters had done. 'It was as if they were putting their horses at a jump, then they just ... went.'

It was Rosina who solved it for them. The mare had taken part in the Wild Hunt several times before and, having been held back while her herdmates set off without her, she was desperate to follow. Tugging at her tether, she suddenly bounded forward and Taryn followed, taking with him an unready Aelwen who, preoccupied with trying to work out how to get aloft, had let her attention wander. Before she had time to gather herself, she felt a tremendous lurch and heave that made her lose a stirrup. When she looked down, she was no longer on the ground.

Aelwen groped frantically with her foot until she recovered the missing stirrup. Then, to her everlasting shame, she did something that she had not done since she was a little girl learning to jump high fences. She twisted both her hands in the stallion's long, black mane, shut her eyes tightly and hung on with all her might.

With her eyes closed, things felt better. Taryn might have been galloping uphill on the ground, on any normal day. After a moment or two she gained enough confidence to open her eyes, and looked around anxiously for Kelon. Fortunately, Alil had followed the other horses, and was running easily along on Aelwen's right, while Rosina matched Taryn stride for stride on her left, at the extreme limit of her tether. Aelwen gave Kelon a watery grin. 'At least we're up here,' she said in mindspeech, to save having to shout against the whistling wind. 'But by all Creation, that was scary! I very nearly wet my pants.'

Kelon's mental voice sounded shaky. 'You're not the only one. But now we're up here, it's not so bad. It's just like riding normally on the ground – as long as we don't fall off.'

Aelwen looked down at the treetops, horribly far below, and felt her stomach tighten at the thought of falling. 'Let's definitely not do that,' she agreed. But to tell the truth, he was right. Riding up here was perfectly easy – if you didn't think about what lay below. She glanced back at Eliorand as it receded into the distance. It looked beautiful, and she felt a pang at the thought of leaving it. Her home was back there, and her beloved horses. Her friends, her grooms, her memories ... All her life before this night was far away now, and being left further behind with every passing moment. She gritted her teeth and looked ahead. 'It's not your home any more,' she told herself. 'It's a nest of vipers, and you would have died, had you stayed.'

Kelon broke into her thoughts. 'I'll lead the mare for a while, if you like. Then you can relax and enjoy the view.'

Aelwen rolled her eyes to the heavens. 'Wonderful,' she said, but was happy to hand over the lead rope. 'As long as you're sure that being seen with a pink horse won't damage your masculine dignity.'

'Well … I can make a concession this once, since there's no one to see me up here.' Kelon grinned as he attached the rope to the pommel of his saddle. After the dangers of their escape, it felt good to break the tension a little. 'Better change direction,' he said, growing serious once more. 'The horses are trying to follow the Hunt. That's the last thing we want.'

'You're right,' Aelwen said. 'We need to lose some height, too. We're a bit conspicuous all the way up here.'

The Hunt had set off in a south-easterly direction, so the fleeing Hemifae turned their horses towards the south-west.

'Perfect,' Kelon said.

Aelwen nodded. 'If we're going to Tyrineld, this is a much better direction.'

Getting their mounts to lose height was a little more tricky, but after some trial and error they discovered the knack. Descending was a lot more terrifying than the ascent, and Aelwen, looking down into the forest through the dizzying void of empty air, was hanging on to her horse's mane once more, and gripping Taryn so tightly with her knees that her legs were aching by the time they levelled off just above treetop height. It felt much better down here, the trees giving the illusion that it wasn't far to fall. Aelwen loosed her stranglehold on the mane as she finally began to relax and enjoy the ride.

'We'd better go as far and as fast as we can while the magic lasts,' Kelon said. 'Hopefully, we can put enough distance between us and the Hunt to give us time to find a hiding place when we're finally forced down.'

Suddenly Aelwen went icy cold all over. 'How will we know when the spell is wearing off? We never thought of that.'

Kelon looked at her in horror. 'It lasts about ten hours, doesn't it? So we shouldn't have to worry till after sunrise?'

'When Hellorin cast the enchantment, it lasted ten hours,' Aelwen said. 'But we've already seen that Tiolani's magic is different, and it's definitely weaker. We can feel it sapping our energy all the time to feed itself. We'd better be careful, Kelon. I don't *think* we'll suddenly lose the magic and go plummeting to the ground, but I wouldn't want to stake my life on that.'

'Maybe the horses will know instinctively when the spell is wearing off, and they'll head back down,' Kelon suggested.

'For all our sakes, we'd better hope so.'

They rode on for a moment in an unpleasantly thoughtful silence, before Aelwen spoke again. 'Thank providence there's still no sign of pursuit. It looks as though we got clean away, though I'm amazed that no one saw us leave the courtyard.'

'It was supper time at the palace,' Kelon replied. 'Probably no one was looking out of the window. Apart from Tiolani and her bunch of die-hards, nobody is much interested in the Hunt any more.'

Aelwen frowned. 'As soon as she comes back we'll be missed, though. Do we go down to the ground and look for somewhere to hide? Or do we simply try to get as far as we can, and hope we'll be able to outrun them?'

'She may notice we've run long before she returns to Eliorand. It will only take one of the Hunt to look back, and we'll be in trouble.'

'You have a masterly talent for understatement, Kelon. That cloud bank could hide us. Possibly.' She shuddered. 'I don't like the look of it at all, though.'

But no matter that she didn't like it, Aelwen suddenly found herself out of options. Across the skies, she heard a cry go up. The Hunt had seen them.

For an instant, Aelwen's blood froze in horror, her heart dropping like a stone. Then, she yelled 'Go!'.

Aelwen and Kelon plunged towards the cloud. Because they had no experience of flying, they did not understand the dangers of heading into such a storm. Nevertheless, as their approach took them closer and closer to the black and turbid agglomeration, Aelwen felt the tightening of fear in her belly. The wind was rising to a howl and the temperature dropped rapidly. They could clearly see the blue-white flicker of lightning as it darted about inside the cloud. The Horsemistress frowned. How would the horses fare in such a maelstrom?

But the Hunt was now in full cry behind them, the great hounds closing the distance fast.

Suddenly the cloudbank was upon them, and they were swallowed up by darkness. Aelwen was flying blind in a maelstrom of titanic forces that hurled Taryn about as though he was an autumn leaf, not solid horse-flesh. It took all of her skill to stay on his back, while the thunder made a deafening assault on her ears, and the lightning flickered and sizzled around her while she tried not to think of metal stirrups, and buckles, and Taryn's bit. She was soaked right through her clothes, and so cold that already she was losing the feeling in her hands and feet. Desperately she called Kelon's name, but the howling gale whipped her words away. She switched to mindspeech. 'Kelon, Kelon, are you there?'

'I'm on the ground.' Kelon sounded dazed. 'I got into a downdraught, and it just *pushed* the horses out of the sky. Where are you?'

'Up here in the storm,' Aelwen replied tersely. She needed all her concentration just to stay on Taryn's back.

'Get down, quickly,' Kelon urged her.

'What in the name of Perdition do you think I'm trying to do?'

Desperately she wrestled Taryn downwards, using every trick she knew to force the exhausted stallion to fight his way through the violence around them. Sometimes the wind seemed to be trying to help them, but more often, it picked them up and hurled them back the way they had come, so that they had a constant fight to regain lost ground. It seemed to take forever, but somehow they made it to the treetops at last, which deflected the wind enough to let them get down.

She only just managed to spring clear as Taryn went crashing into the undergrowth, stumbled and fell. Aelwen, frantic in case he had hurt himself, scarcely felt her own bruises and scrapes as she tore herself free from the spiny bushes and rushed to examine her mount. He could easily have broken a leg ...

Taryn was shocked and shivering, and Aelwen was forced to settle her own nerves before she could begin to calm him. Groping in the gloom, she felt her way down each of his legs in turn, trying to discern whether he was putting his hooves firmly on the ground, or lifting them in pain. This time he might have been lucky. As far as she could tell in the darkness, he didn't seem lame, though she would have to wait until daylight to lead him and see his gait, to be absolutely sure.

Aelwen's thoughts turned to Kelon, but there was no reply to her frantic queries in mindspeech, though she tried for a long time to reach him. 'He'll be too far away, that's all,' she told herself stoutly, but she worried nonetheless. Had the Phaerie found him? Had he been attacked by some wild beast?

There was nothing she could do about it. Aelwen knew that she must concentrate on her own survival at this time. In the morning, when it was light, maybe she would be able to find Kelon somehow. For the present, all her energy had to be directed towards getting herself through the night. She was cold, exhausted, soaked and hungry – and the food was with Kelon, on the packhorse. The forest was a wild and frightening place that night, with lightning sizzling down through the trees, the gale screaming in the treetops and the thunder ripping the air apart overhead. The trees tossed and creaked, bent right over by the force of the storm, and occasionally there was a loud crack as a branch broke off and went crashing to the ground. Aelwen was aware of her perilous position beneath the trees, but there was nowhere else to go. She would just have to shelter here, and hope that her luck held out.

Everything seemed hopeless to Aelwen. It was dark, wet and freezing; she had lost her companion, and she had no food. She was still in danger of being hunted down by the Phaerie, the forest was full of dangerous wild animals and she was far from the edge of it. She hated not having a plan of any kind. 'But that's only temporary,' she tried to comfort herself. 'I have the rest of the night to work something out.'

I hope.

27

IRIANA ALONE

Iriana was curled with Melik in a nest of cosy blankets. Though the warmth felt wonderful after her long, cold vigil over the camp, she was finding sleep elusive. She had experienced a whirl of emotion that day, swinging between joy and sorrow, laughter and tears, belonging and loss.

The link between her and Boreas was severed utterly now. He had gone to make his own life, no longer an appendage to her. In her head she was proud and glad for him – but that didn't assuage the ache in her heart.

Then there was the feeling of discomfort and unease she had felt, yet again, while she was on watch. It was happening every night now, to the point where she no longer dared awaken Esmon. At first he had taken her seriously, but as night after night had passed without incident, his concerns had diminished, and she knew he had begun to put the whole thing down to the nervous imagination of a novice traveller.

Well, if Esmon wasn't unduly concerned, maybe she should stop worrying about it. Shifting an indignant Melik, Iriana wriggled over onto her other side and tried to concentrate on the good things that had happened that day. She and Seyka had found this wonderful campsite for everyone. How satisfying it had been finally to feel herself to be an equal, functioning member of the group, instead of the blind girl who had to be guarded, helped and cared for. Iriana smiled in the darkness. Men were so pig-headed. It had taken her a long time to convince them, but today she'd succeeded at last. Then the strangest thought crossed her mind.

Maybe, before I could convince them, I had to truly convince myself, deep down inside.

However it had come about, she was glad that it had happened and proud of her achievement.

And of course, Avithan's kiss had changed things. She wanted it to happen again, and maybe *again*. If Avithan was willing, of course. *Don't take it too seriously*, she warned herself. *Not until you know whether he does.* But her first real kiss ... She felt as if she was beginning a new journey that night, and wondered where it would lead.

By this time, Iriana was beginning to grow drowsy and, as was her nightly habit just before she fell asleep, she linked with Seyka for one last look around the camp and its environs. She found the bird hunting in the forest, but it accepted her presence and let her distract it easily enough, and she suspected that it had eaten already. Sure enough, a quick scan of its recent memory revealed two fat mice that had lately gone the right way – at least as far as the owl was concerned.

Flying a sweeping arc through the trees, Seyka circled back over the campsite for her, and swooped low towards the tents. All at once, Iriana smothered a gasp as she saw a clot of blackness detach itself from the surrounding darkness and transform into a figure. It glided up behind Esmon and sliced a knife across his throat, then plunged the glittering blade deep into his chest. Iriana saw blood spray across the ground; saw his body slump and fall. There was no time to catch her breath, no time to absorb the horror and peril, for that sinister shadow was gliding rapidly towards the tents.

'Wake up,' she shrieked to Avithan in mindspeech. 'We're being attacked!' Desperately she hurled the images that she'd seen and was seeing into his mind.

The dark killer bent down to reach for Avithan's tent flap. Like lightning, a blade thrust out straight through the flimsy fabric of the shelter, piercing the assassin's shoulder above his sword arm. With a curse he danced swiftly backward and, with a deadly economy of motion, transferred the weapon to his other hand. As he did so, Iriana caught her first good look at his face through Seyka's eyes. A Phaerie, as she had suspected.

On silent feet, he stole around the side of the tent and slashed downward – but just as the tip of his blade tore the moonmoth silk, Avithan's sword jabbed out again and caught him in the side. Iriana heard him hiss with pain and frustration as he jumped back once more. Though he must have been in pain from his wounds, he gave no outward sign: only stood very still for a moment, thinking, then looked long and slowly around the camp. To her horror, he abandoned Avithan and turned towards her tent.

Then his gaze lit on Seyka, perched on a nearby branch, and to Iriana, it seemed as though he was looking directly at her, not at the owl. Without warning, a bolt of dark power flashed across the clearing from his eyes to those of the bird, and Iriana's vision went black in an explosion of intense pain. Horror, grief, disbelief: all these emotions struck through her in the space of a heartbeat as she searched frantically with her mind for the bird. But her mind could only confirm what her heart already knew. Seyka, beautiful Seyka, was dead.

Stunned by rage and sorrow, Iriana had almost forgotten her own plight, and left herself with little time to escape. Switching to Melik's eyes, she grabbed her knife and sliced open the rear of the tent. The cat, catching her panic, shot out ahead of her. She began to crawl through – but it was too late. The killer grabbed her ankle, his fingers grinding cruelly into flesh and bone, and jerked her backwards, out of the tent.

The terrified cat had fled, and Dailika was in the bushes, out of sight of the clearing. Iriana was left utterly blind. She twisted herself around and flailed wildly with the knife, but it found no target and her assailant took it out of her hand with a cruel twist of her wrist. He dragged her roughly to her feet and struck her hard across the face. Had he not been holding her arm, the blow would have knocked her off her feet. As it was she staggered, her head reeling. No one had ever hit her before, and the fact that she had never seen the blow coming only exacerbated the shock and pain.

Yanking her towards him, he pinioned her arms from behind. Iriana struggled until she felt the cold bite of a blade across her throat, then suddenly became very still. How had it all happened so fast? Never had she been so helpless; never so terrified. Now that her life hung in the balance, her blindness mattered more than it ever had before. From childhood, she had always found ways to circumvent, to compensate, to cope. Now, weaponless, all her animals dead or fled and a knife at her throat – now, for the first time she truly found her blindness to be a grave disadvantage.

Behind her back, the shadowy killer laughed, a sound as cold as the steel that threatened to take her life. 'That's better,' he said. 'I knew your little blind friend would bring you out of your lurking-hole. The best way to catch a cowardly dog is with a bitch in heat.'

Iriana stiffened. He wasn't talking to her but to Avithan. She didn't need eyes to know that her companion had emerged from his tent, sword in hand. She was one of the few people who knew he'd trained to fight in secret with the Warriors' Luen – but she was sure he'd be no match for one who could creep up so silently on Esmon and slit his throat.

'Leave her alone,' Avithan snarled.

'Make me.' That same cold, grating laugh came from the killer.

Iriana's heart was breaking over Esmon, over Seyka; she was terrified to the depths of her being, for she knew how it would end – Avithan would attack and die, they would both die at the Phaerie's hands. Yet this final threat to her companion froze the fear that had turned her knees to water into an icy, deadly fury. This murderous bastard thought she was helpless – well, he would soon learn otherwise.

Though her wrath was cold, she struck with fire. With a roar, flame enveloped her assailant's body. For an instant, just an instant, his grip loosened and the knife fell away, then to her horror the fire was gone; extinguished. How had he done that? Even as the thought flashed into her head, she kicked him hard in the ankle and slipped from his grasp.

'Run, Iriana,' Avithan yelled. 'Hide. Warn Father.'

Iriana ran. Not through cowardice, but sense. Blind like this, she would be no good to Avithan, and a downright hindrance if the Phaerie got his hands on her again. If she could only get to Dailika, find another pair of eyes, then maybe she could help her companion – her love.

She fled in what she hoped was the right direction, but she was hopelessly disorientated. Suddenly there was no ground beneath her feet, and for the second time that day, she found herself floundering in the frigid stream. Gasping, she struggled up again and clawed her way out, and continued to fight through the bushes.

The forest was a dangerous place for one who could not see. She ran into a tree with bruising force, and kept stumbling on the uneven ground, barely catching herself before she fell. Branches whipped across her face and snatched at her hair, and her heart was almost beating its way out of her chest with terror. All she could think of was Avithan at the killer's mercy. She had to help him, she *had* to. Where were those bloody horses? Where was she, anyway? Without the vision of her animals, everything was so bewildering. She could be running right back into the arms of the killer.

Yet she couldn't stop. Some primeval instinct kept her moving, searching. 'Warn Father,' Avithan had said.

It won't save us, she thought, *we're too far away from anyone who could help. But it might save others from walking into this trap.*

Yet how could she manage it? Mindspeech would never reach as far as Tyrineld. Not even to Nexis, unless the link between the participants was exceptionally close. She had but one solitary, unlikely spark of hope. Maybe ... With all her heart, all her power, all her strength, she tried to fling a desperate message back to the frontier town. To the only one she knew there. To the one who'd been her foster-father. Even as she did so, something – a fallen tree trunk, she realised – swept her legs out from underneath her. She fell hard, fast, and oblivion claimed her.

Now that Iriana was out of danger, Avithan was free to concentrate on staying alive. Clearly, this cold-eyed Phaerie had some way of circumventing Wizard spells, for the bastard had smothered Iriana's flames in an instant. All Avithan had to rely on was Esmon's legacy of sword-training to avenge his murdered friend.

Unfortunately, his opponent was a much better fighter. Avithan circled defensively, trying, as far as possible, to avoid that lethal blade. 'Who are you?' he said.

'Your Death.' The voice was granite hard and utterly without emotion. 'Why?'

'Because I can.' With a deadly swiftness, the assailant moved, weaving a dance of death around Avithan, who could only try to defend himself as far as possible, hanging on to his life one moment – one breath – at a time.

Had his night vision not been superior, and if he hadn't already wounded the Phaerie twice, leaving the killer bleeding from shoulder and side, he would have been dead in no time. As it was, he could barely hold his own. He ducked and wove around the clearing, forced ever backwards by the cold-blooded ferocity of the Phaerie's attack. The flash and flicker of the lethal blades filled his blurring vision, and the clang and clash of steel jarred his ears. His legs felt heavy as iron bars; his arms were soon numb from the repeated impacts as he tried to defend himself. Sweat dripped into his eyes; strands of his long hair plastered themselves across his face. His footing was uncertain, his boots slipping and sliding on the soft earth.

Avithan's only hope was that the Phaerie's wounds would eventually slow him down, but that didn't seem to be happening. Though that cold, mocking smile had become a grimace, though his breathing was harsh and laboured, his movements were still fluid, swift and lethal. Suddenly his sword flicked across the Wizard's face, leaving a long slice down his jawline and a flash of shock and pain. Distantly, Avithan registered the pain of other wounds, to left arm, belly and thigh, but could not say when his foe had nicked him. He could hear the pounding of his blood and a distant buzzing in his ears that marked the onset of exhaustion, yet somehow he found the strength to keep on fighting. Not only was his life at stake, but Iriana's, too. The more time he could buy her …

Who am I deceiving? he thought desperately. *He'll wear me out; sooner or later one of these brutal blows will land, and that will be the end. Then he'll hunt her down – she'll be easy enough to track – and she'll never see him coming.*

Her death would be cruel.

And that thought was enough to distract him. Only for an eyeblink, but it was enough. The killer's sword snaked past his guard: a hot, vicious pain exploded through his chest. No, no! Desperately Avithan tried to stop his weak knees from buckling, to keep to his feet, to raise his sword arm to defend himself, but there was no control any more. His throat filled with choking blood. He couldn't breathe. His vision greyed and clouded, and the last thing he saw was the cruel triumph on the face of his foe, as he pitched forward and down, down into the bottomless black void.

Iriana swam blearily back to consciousness with blood trickling down her face and a throbbing head. All was confusion. How had she come to be here? Where *was* here? She sought for Seyka, so that she could get a good look at her surroundings – and sat up abruptly with a stifled cry that could have been grief, pain, fear – or all three together. Seyka was dead. Esmon murdered. And Avithan ...

I've got to get back!

How long had she been unconscious? Was she too late? Was Avithan dead, and the killer stalking her even now?

She took a firm hold on her panicking thoughts, and cautiously felt the gash on her forehead. Good. The blood wasn't crusting yet, so she hadn't been out for long. Now, where was Melik? But the cat had run off in terror and search as she would, she could not reach him. She didn't know how far away she was from the campsite, but she *had* to see what was happening, and she had to help Avithan. Frantically, she located Dailika, the only one of her animal companions she had left.

When the Wizard linked, she heard the clangour of blades, and fear for Avithan warred with incredible relief that he was still alive. But she had tied the animals in the bushes, away from the clearing. Though it sickened her, she had only one option. For the first time in her life she overrode the gentle partnership they had always shared, put forth her mind in an iron grasp and took control of Dailika, forcing her to pull and jerk at her rope again and again, attacking it with hooves, teeth and all her considerable strength. The knowledge that she was hurting the poor creature and betraying a trust tore at Iriana's heart, but she had no choice. She drove the mare without mercy, until finally the tether snapped.

The mare stumbled backward and Iriana turned her and goaded her towards the clearing; towards the clash of weapons and the fearsome stink of spilt blood. The terrified mare fought back, striving with every sinew to run away from the horror. The Wizard was bleeding inside, knowing her actions for the betrayal of trust that they were, but she gave Dailika no choice, even as she herself had none.

Dailika burst into the clearing, just in time for Iriana to see Avithan fall, and the Phaerie raise his blade for the killing blow. Ruthlessly she forced the horse forward – fast, faster, too quickly for the killer to turn. He never saw what hit him. Dailika ran him down, trampling him into the dirt beneath her hooves. Even as he tried to rise, Iriana turned the mare back and attacked again. Even as she reared over him to knock the sword from his hand, Dailika felt its bite as he tore her flank with the tip of her blade. Caught in the remorseless grasp of the Wizard's will, goaded against her instincts to a kind of madness now, the horse pounded the killer into a bloody pulp.

Iriana, weeping, loosed her grip on Dailika's mind, and the mare fled screaming into the darkness. A trust and a bond, which had been there since the Wizard was a youngster and the mare a stilt-legged foal, had been irredeemably shattered tonight. Her grief a crushing force, she put her face in her hands and knelt – but only for an instant. There was no time for such indulgence. Avithan could still be alive – *oh, let him be alive* – but he could be bleeding to death in the clearing. She had to get to him. But how could she find her way back without her animals to see the path?

Panic gripped her. Blind, lost and alone in hundreds of miles of wilderness. What if she fell over a precipice? Encountered a bear? Wandered aimlessly in circles until both she and Avithan died?

'But I won't.'

Iriana fought down the terror and told herself to *think*. She used the fallen tree to haul herself to her feet. Her legs were bruised and abraded, a vicious pain lanced through her right ankle and her right arm throbbed from shoulder to wrist. Her face was scratched, the wet clothes from her earlier tumble into the stream clung to her soaked and shivering body, and kindly nature had clearly arranged a sharp stone in just the right place to cut her head open. Ignoring the aches and pains, she orientated herself by the tree trunk that had been her undoing. Now she had a rough – very rough – idea of the direction in which she needed to go.

Though her heart urged her to hurry, Iriana stood very still and listened, trying to catch the distant sounds of the stream. How far had she run? Not that far, surely. Though her instincts were screaming out at her to run again – towards Avithan this time, instead of away – she knew she would never find him that way. Blundering around the forest all night would help no one. She listened again for the stream, trying to separate its bubbling murmur from the sounds of the forest all around, and turning her head from side to side to try and fix on its direction. As soon as she was sure she had it firmly in her mind, she followed the sound, concentrating with every fibre of her being and changing direction if it seemed to move or diminish.

It wasn't easy. Between the Wizard and the water lay an obstacle course of rough ground, briars and trees. Iriana stumbled, tripped and was hit by low branches. She realised for the first time that she'd been fortunate to have run so far without seriously injuring herself. Then, of course, she had been fuelled by terror, not registering the obstacles, the collisions, the falls. Now, as she tried to retrace her steps, the forest was making her pay. Far worse than any physical pain, however, was the unrelenting fear that Avithan might already be dead.

'Please, Avithan. Please be alive. Just keep holding on – I'm coming as fast as I can.' Desperately Iriana called to him in mindspeech, but there was not the slightest whisper of a response. All the time she tried to keep the sound of the tumbling water ahead of her, and finally she found the stream exactly as she had found it last time – by falling into it. It was deeper here than the previous place, and icy. Iriana surfaced, spluttering and spewing curses, and sloshed doggedly to the far bank, turning to the right to follow the watercourse up to the pool and nearby clearing. After a few moments she could hear the churning of the little waterfall, and the remaining horses nickering and stamping restlessly among the bushes. She was just opening her mouth to call out when it occurred to her, belatedly, that there might have been more than one Phaerie present. Who was to say that the killer didn't have friends nearby?

It was no good. She *had* to see what was happening in the clearing. Once more she tried casting her mind forth for Boreas, or little Melik, lost in the forest, but received no response. She couldn't find them anywhere. All her animals were gone.

But there was an alternative.

Maybe.

She crept up to the remaining horses, quieting them with her familiar touch. They had excellent night vision. She knew they could see all she needed. Though one part of her was screaming with impatience, she suppressed it somehow, knowing that the animals would pick up on her state of mind. Lightly, she touched the mind of each horse, testing which, if any, would be amenable to her presence and this unusual form of control, which was, in reality, more partnership than domination.

To her astonishment, it was Esmon's black warhorse who acknowledged her presence, and let himself be guided. As a stallion, trained to fight, he was the last one she'd have expected to respond. There was no time to wonder, however. Gently she seated her awareness within the warhorse's mind and sent him to poke his nose out of the bushes and look into the clearing.

'The bastard! I *knew* it.' In her dismay, Iriana almost uttered the words aloud. Anger and terror curdled in her blood as she saw another assailant kneeling over Avithan's still form. Though his back was turned to her, he had an indefinable look of Phaerie about him. The Wizard's main feeling was one of outrage. She had driven her beloved Dailika mad in dealing with these murdering scum. Now she'd have to do it again, this time using Esmon's mount as a weapon. At least it was a warhorse; hopefully it wouldn't be driven past all endurance this time. But if Avithan was already dead, if this second killer had finished him while she was still unconcious, for she had felt no death pang, then what would be the point? In that case, it would be more sensible to take the horse and sneak away. How could she find out? If there was the slightest chance of saving Avithan's life, she was damned if she was going to leave him.·

No, she couldn't take that risk. Steeling herself to perpetrate the unthinkable for a second time, Iriana clenched her fists and sent the warhorse charging into the clearing.

This time there was no conflict. Esmon had trained this animal to attack on command. Like dark lightning, the horse leapt forward, but at the last split second the shadowy figure rolled aside, out of the way of the lethal hooves. At a slow, half-staggering run, he headed straight towards the horrified Wizard. 'Iriana, please stop him! I'm a friend. From Cyran.' On the other side of the clearing the warhorse stopped and spun, turned and charged again.

Trust him?

Let him die?

The stranger stumbled and fell. With only the space of a heartbeat in which to make her decision, Iriana went with her gut. With an effort she pulled up the horse, letting it stand close to the man, stamping and snorting. The threat of power and danger were still very evident, but judging from his struggles, he seemed unable to rise in any case.

'Who are you?' she called.

With an effort, he pulled himself up to his elbows. 'Taine. Cyran sent me to warn you—'

'Then you came too late.' Iriana snapped. 'Is Avithan still alive?'

'Yes, but he's badly hurt. I've tried to stop the bleeding, but … He needs a proper Healer. And I—' He collapsed face down on the muddy ground.

'Oh, merciful Creation!' Iriana ran out of the bushes, and brought the fractious warhorse close enough for her to get a good look at the stranger. He stank of bear. His thick hide jerkin had protected him from being disembowelled, but the leather and the shirt below it were in tatters across the front, and soaked with blood from the deep scratches across his stomach. A torn piece of cloth tied roughly over his right shoulder and under his arm was soaked with blood. Iriana swallowed hard, and swore. She could sense no other horses nearby. How far had he come, alone and on foot, and so horribly mauled?

You came too late. Well, now she knew why, and how she wished she could take back those angry words.

She wondered who he was, for she had never seen him in Tyrineld, or heard his name. Her friendship with Avithan had given her a fairly close association with the Archwizard and his family, and she tended to recognise members of Cyran's trusted inner circle. With a shrug, she put the puzzle aside for the present. She had far more pressing matters to deal with.

At first glance his wounds didn't look life-threatening, so she left him where he was and ran across to Avithan, Esmon's stallion trotting obediently behind her. She sank down beside her companion, almost afraid to look. He was still breathing, though there was a dreadful gurgling sound when he did so, and his lips were covered with a bloody foam. That bastard had got him in the chest, then. Quickly she assessed his other hurts. A long gash in his thigh was bleeding badly, but the slice into the muscle of his left arm and the cut across his belly didn't look too deep, and the wound on his face was, compared to everything else, only a scratch.

How thankful she was that one of her best friends was such a talented Healer. Melisanda had taught her a lot over the years. The first thing was to stop the bleeding. Now, of course, she understood why the stranger had failed in his attempt. With such serious injuries of his own, he would never have the strength to heal another. Also, he probably didn't have the knowledge she had picked up from her friend. Iriana put her hand over the thigh wound and summoned what healing magic she knew. She had no need of normal eyesight for this. Where her palm rested, she could 'see' inside the leg, the images coming directly into her mind. She knew spells to seal off the bleeding, to repair damaged tissue and muscle, to close the wound and imbue it with the magic to kill infection. She worked quickly, keeping the horse's eyes on the injuries, rather than Avithan's face. That way she could somehow hold herself together; keep at bay the urge to curse and weep; hold back her own weariness for long enough to complete her work.

The chest wound was more difficult. When Iriana saw how close the killer's sword had come to Avithan's heart, she felt sick. Still, there was a great deal she could do. Close off the wounds in the lung and chest, stop bleeding, prevent infection. Lastly, though she was shaking with exhaustion now, she performed the spells that eased the shock to the body and stilled the pain. The rest would be down to time, and Avithan himself.

Blessing her talent for Fire Magic, she lit a fire to keep both men warm. If the Hunt passed that night – well, she would just have to take the risk. It was a question of survival now, she thought, as she wrapped Avithan in a blanket. Iriana was weary beyond measure. Magic did not come without a price. The more complex, or expansive, or powerful the spell, the greater the toll on the Wizard. Iriana knew – it had been driven home by her tutors again and again during her training – that if she expended too much of her own energy in the use of her power, she would fall into a state of oblivion from which she might never awaken. After healing Avithan, she needed desperately to eat and rest, and recoup her energy – but there was the stranger to care for yet. Sighing, she moved across to the other recumbent form and sat down by his side to check the damage. As she did so, there was an ear-splitting crash of thunder and the first splutters of rain hit the fire.

One thing after another.

Iriana, too weary even to curse, dropped her head onto her knees and tried to think. The rain was falling harder now, and the wind tore at the branches of the trees. Then a whiplash of lightning seared across the skies, followed by thunder loud enough to make her ears ring. She would have to do something, fast. Though she weighed nothing like as much as these two tall men, somehow she must get them into the tents – supposing that the tents would stay up in this storm. With their wounds, they couldn't lie out in the rain, and she couldn't shield them magically or apport them into shelter: she had already exhausted too much of her power in healing Avithan. In addition, supposing she did manage to get them inside, how could she even see them without Melik or Seyka?

The thought of her animals – one dead, one insane, one lost in the perilous night-time forest – was almost enough to break her. But even as she felt a sob rising in her throat, Iriana gritted her teeth and swallowed it back down. *You wanted adventure,* she told herself. *Well, now you've got one, so stop feeling sorry for yourself and get moving. There are things that must be done, and no one to do them but you.*

The lightning flashed again. 'Well said, Lady.' The voice was so unexpected that Iriana, who had just started to get to her feet, sat down abruptly. The eyes of the wounded stranger – in the midst of all these crises she had forgotten his name – were open. Iriana felt her face heating with an embarrassed blush. Had she spoken her thoughts aloud?

'Just about. You are very close to me, and you've forgotten to shield.' As she frowned, he added, 'I'm truly sorry, but you were thinking *very* loudly.'

'Just don't do it again.' She hadn't the energy to snap at him for such a transgression. 'Since you're awake, let me help you inside—'

'Let me help *you*. I only have one working arm at present, so I can't lift your friend into the tent, but if you pull him, I can help with an apport spell to support his weight.'

'If you can apport, why not transport Avithan inside the tent yourself?'

Iriana demanded, aware of sounding ungrateful even as she said it. 'He's too badly wounded for me to be hauling him about,' she added apologetically.

The newcomer shrugged, the gesture sending a grimace of pain across his face. 'If only I could. But like yours, my power is down to the dregs now. I've been drawing on it to keep myself going, ever since the bear attacked.'

Stranger or no, Iriana's heart went out to him. If what he'd said was true, then the Archwizard had sent him to warn them of danger, and though he had come too late, it was not his fault. Though he had been injured, alone and on foot, he had not given up, but had found them in the end. 'Then let's get Avithan under cover between us,' she said. 'Afterwards I'll take a look at your wounds.'

The rain and wind were by this time tearing savagely at the tents. Her companion looked at them doubtfully. 'Maybe we should try to seek some other shelter. I doubt these will stay up much longer.'

'Yes they will,' Iriana said decisively. 'Avithan bespelled them to stand firm whatever the weather. He's very good at practical magic like that.'

'Come on, then. By the Light, Cyran would never forgive me if I failed to save his son.' Again, the grimace passed over his face.

As they moved Avithan, he stirred and moaned. Once she had him inside the tent, however, Iriana spent a little more of her power putting him into a deep, healing sleep. Working by touch, since she had no way of seeing once she was inside the shelter, she made sure he was comfortable, tucked his blankets warmly around him and dropped a gentle kiss on his brow. With a sigh, for she hated to leave him, she crawled out again into the cold rain, relieved to be back where she could use the eyes of Esmon's patient horse, to see what she could do to help ... 'Your pardon, sir, but with everything that's happened, your name has flown right out of my head.' She felt a bit of a fool, but she couldn't go on without knowing.

He was bending over the now dead fire, which was clearly beyond all saving in this downpour. When she spoke he turned to face her, and his quick smile was like the sun coming out from the clouds. 'With all that has happened, Lady, I've almost forgotten it myself. I am called Taine, by your grace.'

His accent was strange to her, Iriana realised, but pleasant, and she was charmed by his courteous manner. 'Come on,' she said. 'Leave the fire. It's hopeless. We'll get out of this infernal rain and—'

At that moment another lurid flare of light came streaking across the sky – but this time it was no lightning. Taine's face blanched to the colour of bone. 'The Hunt! The Phaerie are upon us!

28

NOTHING BY CHANCE

When she left Eliorand with the Hunt, Corisand kept a lookout behind her for Aelwen and Kelon. From the corner of her eye, she finally saw them rise above the rooftops of the palace, and breathed a sigh of relief. By Creation, they seemed to be making heavy weather of such a simple business! Soon they were safely aloft, however, and she noted the direction in which they were heading. Sorely as she was tempted, there would be no point in trying to follow them right now. She would lead their enemies directly to them. No, she would have to wait patiently for a little while longer, and let them put some distance between themselves and the Hunt. Besides, the further she was from Eliorand, the more chance she had of bringing off her own escape.

Tiolani urged her to stay a few paces in front of the other riders, and Corisand galloped along, meek and gentle, the absolute picture of a well-trained, obedient horse. After a time, she felt her rider beginning to relax on her back, lulled by the rhythm of that smooth, swinging stride. And the more the girl's vigilance slackened, the more delighted the mare became. Tiolani's golden-haired lover, whom Corisand detested, closed the gap between them. As he rode up close, the mare's skin twitched as though she could feel the prickling feet of a swarm of filthy flies. Why were these Phaerie so dense? Had they no deeper instincts? Why couldn't Tiolani *see* the evil aura of treachery, greed and deceit that clung around Ferimon?

He was riding Vikal, an ill-tempered white stallion with pale-blue eyes, who had recently crossed Corisand's path when she'd refused to mate with him. As a matter of fact, Aelwen had tried every stallion in the place except Vikal, as she didn't particularly want to pass on the blue-eyed trait, but he had broken out of his paddock one night and tried his luck anyway. Kelon had found him in the stable yard the following morning, a sadder but wiser beast. The horse was well known as an attacker of other males, and had inflicted some terrible injuries in the past, so Kelon thought that he must have been fighting with another stallion, and was still wondering which of them it had been, for he had never found any evidence of injuries on the others. One thing was certain – this time it had been Vikal's turn to come off worst in the encounter. Corisand looked at the torn ear and the partly healed scars on his white hide and flicked her tail in derision, before turning her attention to the conversation between their two riders.

'How are you finding your new horse?' Ferimon called out.

Tiolani made a little sound of disgust. 'I cannot think what Aelwen has been doing to her,' she said. 'I would have more fun riding a nursery rocking horse than this dull, spiritless beast.'

You wait, Corisand thought darkly. *Just you wait*. With her panoramic vision, she saw Aelwen and Kelon peeling off in a south-westerly direction, and sinking furtively down towards the treetops. Now would be the time to act, before she lost them completely, but before she could tense herself, or take another breath, she heard the Huntsman Darillan cry out.

'Look – over there!'

Corisand cursed to herself. Then without warning she exploded into violent motion: rearing, plunging, bucking, twisting in the air and lashing out with her feet; trying every trick she knew to unseat her rider.

Tiolani was completely unprepared. On the first buck, Corisand felt her lose a stirrup; the mare plunged and bucked again, and the other stirrup went. The third buck was so violent that it hurled Tiolani out of the saddle, and with a fading scream, the girl plummeted towards the treetops far below.

Corisand didn't stop to watch. As she had hoped, every rider in the Hunt went hurtling down towards Tiolani, hoping that one of them might catch her before she crashed to her death. They had forgotten about the fugitives now. In the meantime, the riderless mare doubled back sharply and sped as fast as she could in Aelwen's direction. She planned to put some distance between herself and the Hunt during the panic over Tiolani, then plunge down and lose herself among the trees before they noticed where she had gone.

It was the best plan she could come up with – but Darillan had turned his horse, leaving his hounds to scatter, and was coming after her. She spun in the air and charged on a collision course with the astonished Huntsman. Ramming into the shoulder of his horse as hard as she could, she grabbed Darillan's arm in her teeth and wrenched him bodily from the saddle. She didn't wait to see him hit the ground, but wheeled around once again and raced away at top speed. She couldn't let them catch her now. Even if Tiolani lived through the fall, as she probably would – someone was sure to catch Hellorin's precious heir – Darillan was unlikely to survive. Corisand was marked for death. She had killed, and she doubted very much that being the Forest Lord's horse would save her if they caught her again.

Which was not unlikely. Corisand was just thinking about turning down into the shelter of the trees when she saw movement behind her. A group of riders, led by Ferimon, his face contorted with rage, was streaking unbelievably fast across the sky. His wicked-looking horse Vikal quickly outdistanced the others, his white coat shining in the gloom, the red glow of murder in his eyes mirroring the twisted expression of rage on Ferimon's face. There would be no fighting this pair; no taking them by surprise. If Corisand could not find a way to escape them, she could measure her life in minutes.

She ran faster than she had ever run before, galloping for her very life across the night sky. As she went, she noticed that the clouds were blowing up very fast from the west, and now covered half the sky in a menacing mass that was growing larger by the second, reaching from treetop level right up into the heavens. And she was heading towards it. In the midst of the clouds she could see flickers of lightning, and the wind was blowing up into a gale as the weather front advanced. Corisand dared to hope. Livid with rage though he was, would Ferimon dare risk the peril of such violent tumult? Even if he did, she stood a good chance of losing him in the thick cloud and, if she was really lucky, the lightning or the tearing winds might finish him for her.

If they don't kill me first.

But there was no other choice. Hopefully the storm would give the rest of the Phaerie quite enough to think about, without any more of them chasing after her. It was exceptionally dangerous to fly in the midst of a thunderstorm. She had enough at stake to risk it, but she doubted that her pursuers did.

She turned her attention away from Ferimon and his followers and plunged towards the cloud – then suddenly realised, to her dismay, that she was not alone. Darillan's mare, prettily marked in patches of white and coppery red, was galloping along at her side, showing an impressive turn of speed. Corisand's heart sank. It was the herd instinct, of course. Naturally the mare – Corisand couldn't think of her name – wanted to stay with the only other horse nearby, and of course all the other horses *would* insist on treating the Windeye as lead mare. This idiot animal trusted her to keep it safe, and instead she had led it straight into the worst possible danger. Quickly she grabbed the mare's loose reins in her teeth and set herself to hang on tightly. At least she might be able to keep the two of them together – but that was all she could do.

If Corisand had known what it would be like inside that malevolent mass of cloud, she would never have entered. She shot straight into the heart of an inferno: a dark, chaotic maelstrom of searing lightning, deafening concussions of thunder, and tearing winds that buffeted and blasted her beyond all hope of control, sending her tumbling and reeling helplessly across the skies. Dimly, beyond the roar and thunder of the storm, she could hear the Huntsman's mare screaming with terror, but all she could do was keep her teeth clamped around the other horse's reins, and hope they would hold. She could see nothing but the lightning, which lanced through the clouds on every side, sizzling past them, horribly close. The ozone stink was overwhelming.

Then out of the murk came Ferimon, oblivious to the danger in his fury, bursting through the clouds on his screaming white stallion. Vikal arrowed in on her, and since she was hampered by the other mare, Corisand was forced to let go of her, before attacking in a fury of flashing hooves. One blow struck Vikal on the head, and with a grunt of pain the stallion lurched aside, leaving Ferimon open to her attack. Snaking her head out, Corisand plunged her teeth into his shoulder, trying to jerk him from the saddle as she had done with Darillan. Ferimon, however, was prepared for such a move. Clinging to Vikal's saddle bow, he locked his legs tightly around the stallion's ribs. Though he screamed in pain as her teeth grazed his collarbone, he kept his hold, immovable as a rock, even managing to briefly free a hand and strike out at her face with his fist – a hard, painful blow that left her sickened and dizzy with pain.

Corisand, in disengaging, tore a great bleeding chunk of flesh out of his shoulder. She had the satisfaction of hearing another scream, and seeing his face go grey with agony and shock. In disgust she spat out the mouthful of torn muscle, drooling and champing in an attempt to rid herself of the foul taste of blood.

Recovering himself, Vikal charged her from the side, goaded on by his rider, a demon with the fire of madness in his eyes and blood streaming down his shoulder, dripping from his hand. Corisand jerked herself violently aside, using a savage gust of wind to hurl herself away, and felt his teeth meet with a snap barely a breath from her throat. As she spun away she kicked out violently, and felt the satisfying impact of her hind hooves meeting his shoulder before she leapt back to a wary distance.

On the ground, had he been able to close with her, Vikal would have had the advantage, using his greater mass and strength to assert his dominance. Up here, however, they were almost equal, with Corisand's speed and manoeuvrability giving her the edge. In addition, she had one other advantage: intelligence. She could think and plan, use her brains to outwit her foe.

Which was all very well, until she saw the sword appear in Ferimon's hand.

Luckily I tore his shoulder – at least he can't pull a bow.

But he could keep her from coming too close to Vikal, until the other Phaerie finally got over their fear of the storm and came to his aid. The two horses circled, fighting for position in the screaming wind, the stallion wary of Corisand's snake-fast hooves and teeth, the mare heedful of the long bright blade in the rider's hand.

A spear of lightning lanced between the combatants, blinding them with its actinic glare. And Corisand, blinking the dazzle from her eyes, spotted the opening she'd been waiting for. Ferimon lurched in the saddle, his sword arm trembling with the strain of holding up the heavy blade.

One hand for the sword, one trying to hold on to the saddle with a wounded shoulder – and he's weakening from blood loss all the time.

Seizing the moment, Corisand feinted one way, then dodged in the opposite direction, using the force of the gusting wind to drive in, hard and fast, on the side that had no blade. Ferimon was lifted clean out of the saddle and vanished with a howl into the depths below. Vikal, caught off balance, was snatched by the gale and, spinning helplessly away, smashed heavily into a tree and plunged down out of sight below the forest canopy.

Corisand, through her own momentum, was beyond all control and seemed to be about to share his fate. In a flash of terror she saw the tree hurtling towards her.

No time to—

Even as the thought flared in her mind, a weight crashed into her from the side, knocking her out of danger's path. The tree flashed past in a blur of green, its branches almost close enough to rake out her eyes. Straining every muscle in her body, she managed to right herself and get back under control. And who would have guessed it? Galloping at her side was Darillan's red and white mare, whose quick action had saved her life. Infinitely grateful and relieved, Corisand took hold of the trailing reins once more, determined to stay with the one who had aided her. The fight was over. Vikal must surely be dead, and she doubted very much that Ferimon could still be alive. Now her only battle was with the storm.

Utterly weary, bruised and spent from the conflict, the Windeye had to find a way to get herself and her companion safely to the ground.

Fighting the strength of the storm, she plunged downwards, dragging her companion with her, moving as fast as she could, heedless of the risk of crashing into the trees below. Somehow, despite being hurled about by the violent wind, she managed to keep a generally downward direction, until finally she almost reached treetop level. The storm had blown her so hard from her original course that she had given up all hope of finding Aelwen and Kelon again. Her only concern now was survival.

Just then, to her utter horror, she felt a peculiar ebbing sensation in her body. The flying spell was fading – and fading fast. Cold shock swept over her as she realised what she had done. Tiolani was unconscious or dead. The girl's powers lacked the force and finesse of Hellorin's magic and she had never created a safeguard, as her father had put in place, to give the Hunt that extra time to get safely home. Corisand, carelessly, had assumed that the spell would work as it always had. She had been wrong. Dead wrong.

Down. It was the only thought in the Windeye's mind. *I have to get down!*

Tiolani was falling, tumbling through emptiness, her heart stuttering in terror, the sky and trees changing places in a spinning blur as she turned, raindrops pelting her skin with stinging force and the cold wind whistling past her face so fast that she could scarcely breathe. In her tear-filled vision, the dark-green blur of the forest was looming closer and closer ...

Suddenly horses were flashing down on either side of her, and her headlong plunge was stopped short as she landed on her back with a jerk that jarred every bone in her body. Gasping great gulps of air, she blinked the tears from her eyes to see the stars above her, and a cautious turn of her head showed her the four riders of a net team, who had swooped down and, with speed, skill and tremendous presence of mind, had caught her in their net before she hit the ground. Drenched, aching all over, sick and dizzy, her head still spinning, Tiolani turned over and vomited copiously through the meshes, into the forest below. Only then did she see just how close to death she had come. Had she wished, she could have reached an arm through the net and touched the topmost branches of the nearest tree. Tiolani felt a clutch of coldness in her belly. Her quick-witted rescuers could have anything that was in her power to bestow.

As her head began to clear, Tiolani heard shouting from above her. At first she thought it was simple concern for her – but no. They were not calling out to her, but to each other, and she could hear a definite note of panic in the voices.

'Darillan! Catch him, someone.'

'He's too far away—'

'What a dreadful way to die.'

'The hounds! We'll lose them. Doesn't anyone know how to call them?'

'Curse that demon horse.'

'It must have gone mad.'

'Put an arrow through it.'

'No need. It's heading straight for the storm.'

'Ferimon, no, don't follow.' This last was Varna's voice. 'You'll be killed!'

'Ferimon?' Tiolani struggled around in the net with difficulty, for the riders were no longer concentrating on holding it straight, and she was being tipped and tossed in the billowing folds. To her horror, she saw her lover, the hide of his white stallion gleaming luminous against the blackness beyond, being swallowed by the monstrous mass of cloud. The slower riders who had been following managed to peel away in time and turn back, but the foremost, like their leader, were pulled into the storm and lost.

'No …' Tiolani's wail rang out across the skies. Her brother, her father … Not her beloved Ferimon, too. He must survive the storm. He must still be alive. He couldn't die. Someone must go after him. He must be found at once.

Her rescuers, however, had other concerns. With the extra weight pulling on them, they had neither the speed nor manoeuvrability to escape the tearing winds, and were losing height fast. Suddenly the net smashed into the top of a tall tree, and though the folds cushioned some of the impact, Tiolani cried out in pain as she was scraped and battered by the clutching branches.

From above her came curses and flying instructions, then somehow they were all down in a scramble: horses, riders and a frantic Tiolani in her net. Even as she sank to the ground, weighed down and trapped beneath a tangle of meshes, she heard the slithering hiss of an arrow storm. Suddenly, it was as though she was back in the ambush that had robbed her of both father and brother. Her rescuers fell around her, Phaerie and horses crashing into the mud, bleeding and kicking up great gouts of earth in their death throes, mown down by the deadly hail. Karinon, the brave and handsome, with dark hair and flashing smile; Damascena, who had shared the tedium of childhood lessons with Tiolani; Roseire, with her love of jokes and mischief; and Sheran the dependable and strong. She had known them all her life. They had saved her life. They had been her friends.

Tiolani, pressed flat into the ground, was the only one to survive. Screams, bubbling groans, the sickening smack of arrows striking into flesh, the stench of blood and voided bowels: it was all so hideously familiar, except this time there was no Hellorin to save her, no Ferimon to comfort her. None of the other hunters had come down, as she had expected, to see how she fared. This time she was all alone.

It was unthinkable.

Fury, outrage and grief consumed her.

Harsh voices rang out above the roaring wind, with one that sounded both young and female raised above the rest. 'Plague take the cursed weather! It's going to be a bugger of a job butchering those animals in this rain. Evnas, Nira, Traig and Nurt, you make a start on that. Laika, Margeli, Thu, you help them. Be careful of the hides – we want them as near in one piece as we can get. Renol, Shaima, collect all the unspoilt arrows. Make sure you don't miss any. Teluk, Sparay, Sirit, keep watch. You others, loot the bodies then help to pack up the meat for carrying. And don't forget to grab the net – it'll come in handy for all sorts of uses.'

Tiolani's rage and sorrow froze into terror. *Play dead, play dead.* The words screamed in her mind. She closed her eyes, willing herself to be elsewhere – anywhere but this dreadful place. All around her, she heard sounds of activity as the ferals began their gruesome tasks. Nausea rose up into her throat at the stench of blood and ordure as the horses, so free and beautiful only an hour ago, were butchered, and she fought back tears when she was forced to listen as the bodies of her friends were casually despoiled.

'See their cloaks. Surely this lightweight stuff cannot be warm?'

'Well, they would need warm cloaks, flying up in the air like they do.'

'Maybe they use their filthy magic.'

'I used to belong to Phaerie who weren't too proud to hand out their cast-offs to the lowly humans. The cloaks are warm, all right, and water-proof, too.'

'And such beautiful clothes.' The voice held a touch of pure feminine delight.

'Are you going soft in the head, Arina?' It was the voice of the girl who led the band. 'What use will beautiful clothes be to us out here? So long as they're warm and hard-wearing, it doesn't matter if they look like potato sacks. It's the food and the weapons that will do us far more good – and the fact that these bloody bastards won't be killing any more of us.'

'They're carrying good swords and knives – not to mention bows just like the ones that back-stabbing turd Ferimon got for us so we could ambush the Forest Lord for him ...'

In the coils of her net, Tiolani went rigid, her own dreadful situation forgotten in her horror. How could this be? It couldn't be true – no, surely it couldn't. Yet how did these monsters know Ferimon's name? And they had no idea that anyone was listening, so why would they make up such a story?

'We bought Ferimon's bows with our blood. I told my father not to trust a Phaerie, but he wouldn't listen, and it cost him his life.' For a moment, the leader's voice was swallowed in grief, then it hardened again. 'I'll never make that mistake. In future we buy our weapons with *their* blood, as we did today.'

There was a moment of silence, then someone, a man clearly seeking to lighten the moment, spoke up. 'Hey, Danel, who'll get this loot? Is it to be finders-keepers?'

'In your dreams, Benon,' the leader scoffed. 'The weapons and other stuff will have to go where they'll do most good, and that will have to be decided in council. And you may be sure that no one will be trusting a sword to the man who nearly cut his foot off when we stole that axe.'

A gale of laughter followed, and Tiolani ground her teeth with rage. How dared they? How *dared* they stand over the bodies of her friends, the butchered remains of her horses, and laugh? She wanted to kill them – but dared not try. She didn't know how many there were, and she did not have her father's power to kill a number of enemies with one spell. How she wished she had not been so lazy while growing up, dodging lessons whenever she could and counting on Hellorin's indulgence to save her from her tutors' wrath. Nothing could save her now.

Tiolani shrank within herself as she heard the voices drawing closer.

'Get a move on, you lot,' Danel urged. 'Hurry up and finish stripping those corpses and don't forget the one in the net. You lookouts – keep an eye on the skies. I'm guessing that the storm will stop the others coming back this way for now, but we won't have long.'

Someone touched her. Tiolani felt her flesh trying to cringe away from those intrusive hands, and it took every ounce of control that she possessed to remain as limp and silent as the corpse she was pretending to be. They had her surrounded now – close, so close – she was desperate to vomit from the human stink of them. Their filthy hands lifted her, prodded her, turned her this way and that as they tried to disentangle her from the net. Somehow, she kept herself still while they released her from the net's folds. She didn't move, she barely breathed, she didn't make a sound. She let them paw and handle her, fighting down her fury and disgust in a desperate effort to survive.

All to no avail.

When they began to remove her clothing, Tiolani finally betrayed herself. A gasp, a flinch – she had no idea what she'd done, but suddenly the dreaded cry rang out.

'Hey! This one's alive.'

Tiolani's eyes flew open, as another voice cried, 'I know her – it's Hellorin's daughter.'

'Good,' someone else said. 'Then we can put an end to the bastard's line right now.'

Above her, Tiolani saw the flash of a knife, but suddenly the leader shouted, 'Stop. Wait. Don't kill her yet. This wants thinking about. Just put her out of action for now.'

Tiolani never saw what hit her – a crashing blow to her head. There was a flash of light, and blinding pain, then only black oblivion.

Survival was the imperative for Cordain, once the Forest Lord's Chief Counsellor. Demoted to a wary outcast in the Phaerie Court, he followed the Hunt nonetheless, for he deemed it wise to keep a close eye on Hellorin's daughter. To his utter horror he saw her fall, saw the fate of Ferimon and Darillan and, with fast-beating heart, saw the net crew streaking down in pursuit of the plummeting Tiolani. Automatically, he turned to follow – then the calm pragmatism that had always proved so invaluable to Hellorin took over.

If the net-bearers could not reach Tiolani in time, then no one could. Meanwhile, with Ferimon, Darillan and their ruler having fallen, the remaining Phaerie were leaderless and milling in confusion, right in the path of the storm. Someone had to take command. Calling loudly with both voice and mind, Cordain rallied the hunters to him and by a miracle they obeyed, speeding away from the advancing bank of sinister cloud. His relief was short-lived, however. Even as they fell into place behind him, he felt the flying magic beginning to drain away. His horse dipped a little, then recovered, but he knew that the animal was working harder now to stay aloft and keep going. A wrenching feeling of grief and dismay joined the ebbing sensation of the spell. What had happened to his old friend's daughter? Clearly the rescuers had not reached her in time. But was she merely injured and unconscious? Or lying dead and broken on the forest floor?

Cordain's mind raced, his thoughts flying this way and that in panic: *With the flying spell weakening we can't stay aloft in the storm.*

If we aren't dashed to pieces we'll be stranded.
Ferals now have weapons to attack even a large group.
No protection from lost and scattered hounds.
On the ground, we change from hunters to prey.

The way became clear. He must save what lives he could. Leaving Tiolani and the net bearers to their fate, he gathered the remaining Phaerie and fled homeward at breakneck speed, in a desperate attempt to reach Eliorand before the spell ran out completely.

No matter how unstable she had become, no matter how badly she had treated him over the last months, he hated leaving her, and every stride through the sky was dogged by strangling feelings of guilt that pursued him as relentlessly as the advancing storm. Hellorin was his dearest friend and he had known Tiolani since she was born. Even in the privacy of his own thoughts he shied away from the stark truth – that the death of the Forest Lord's daughter would solve a great many problems.

To Corisand, the battle with the storm seemed an unending nightmare as she fought against the swirling gusts, desperately trying to find a safe way down. Suddenly something hit her, hard enough to knock the breath out of her. The wind had hurled her into the upper boughs of a tree, pulling the other horse after her. Luckily this part of the forest was mainly evergreen. If she had tangled up in an oak, Corisand hated to think what might have happened. She might easily have been impaled, broken a leg or, worse still, her neck. As it was, the brittle upper branches snapped and splintered, and she managed to struggle free of the fir with only bruises and scratches to her name.

Her heart in her mouth, the Windeye set course upwards once more, dragging her companion after her. She began to wonder how much longer she could keep the two of them together like this. Her neck ached, and her jaws were nearly breaking from hanging on to the slippery, rain-soaked leather of the other mare's reins. Yet what else could she do?

Keep going. The keening of the gale and the loud concussions of thunder hurt her ears, and made it difficult to think. The Windeye struggled on, soaked and frozen; fighting to maintain a height that kept her beneath the worst of the turbulence, but above the level of the treetops. Though her only concern had been to reach the ground, she must now strive to avoid hitting another of the forest giants. In lightning flashes, she could see that she was currently above a dense belt of woodland. She had no other choice but to persevere, and hope to hit a thinner patch soon, so that she could get herself and her companion down. Because of the thickly mounded storm clouds, the night was utterly black, so apart from the brief glimpses she gained during the flashes, she had no idea how close she was to the tops of the trees.

Corisand was peering anxiously downwards, ready to snatch all the information she could from the next split-second flare of lightning, when she sensed, with the extra intuition that seemed to come with being a Windeye, the presence of horses somewhere far below. As another flash split the sky with a streak of blue-white light, the veils of rain below her blew aside and she saw a pool that shimmered brightly in the lightning-glare. She glimpsed a clearing – a wonderful, blessed *clearing* – far beneath her and, without hesitation, she plunged downwards, hauling her companion (Halira – what a time to remember that) behind. Down here, the trees broke the force of the violent gale, and she managed to fight for enough control to glide safely down, though the ground itself was now obscured once more by the violent downpour.

She almost landed right on top of them. Just in time, Corisand wrenched herself aside as she saw the dim forms below, and came down hard in a fountain of mud. The ground was cut up in the centre of the clearing, and two dark corpses slumped nearby. There was the rank smell of a terrified horse, and the stench of blood and death. Something very bad had happened here, and she had put them right in the middle of it. She spun, ears flat, ready to fight or flee, and caught the glint of a sword in the murk. On the wind came the ringing challenge of a stallion, and then two voices, raised in surprise:

'It's not the Hunt.'

'It's only horses.'

Cautiously, two people emerged from the trees at the edge of the clearing, accompanied by a magnificent warhorse – an ordinary animal, not a Xandim, Corisand was disappointed to note – who clung as close to the woman's shoulder as a shadow.

'But where are the riders?' the female of the couple said.

'They *would* decide to land here.' The male frowned. 'These animals have been lost from the Hunt – they still glow with the flying magic. The bloody Phaerie will be right on top of us, searching for them, with these two in our clearing lit up like beacons to lead the enemy right down on top of us.'

Corisand was sure she'd seen his face before. He looked so familiar, but she couldn't think ...

The woman, however, was a complete stranger and, like the man, looked as though she had already been in a dreadful battle that night. Her clothes were torn and soaked through with blood and rain. Her hair hung in snarls, and her face was chalk-white with exhaustion. Corisand was impressed to note that she made a visible effort to rally herself, and deal with the problem. 'I'll put them with the others,' she said. 'If I tuck them right under the hawthorn and put blankets on them, hopefully we can hide that glow.'

She put out a gentle hand towards Corisand. 'You poor thing, you're cold, wet and scared.' Her voice was the same low, reassuring croon that Aelwen used. 'You're safe now – no one here will harm you. Come along with me, and I'll soon make you more comfortable.'

Corisand's instincts, both horse and Windeye, said *trust*. These people were right – while she and her companion still glowed with the remnants of the flying spell, they were a conspicuous target from the air. She allowed the strange woman to put a gentle hand on her bridle, and permitted herself and Halira to be led away.

Recognising Iriana's superior touch with animals, Taine offered to stay with Avithan while she concealed the new arrivals. Fighting the rain and the wind that blew her hair across her face and made every step forward an effort, the Wizard led the horses across the clearing, trying not to alarm them with any sudden movements. They were splendid creatures, the most beautiful she'd ever encountered. One, slightly smaller than the other, was prettily marked in copper and white, while the taller was a beautiful grey with black legs, mane and tail, and dark dappling on her shining coat. Esmon's warhorse, still acting as her eyes, was craning towards the newcomers and nickering a welcome, and as Iriana drew closer she realised that they were both mares, which accounted for his enthusiasm.

'How in the world did you come to be here?' she murmured to the two beauties. She loosed the stallion's halter rope, counting on his interest in the females to keep him with the group and, using his eyes and moving carefully, she took the strangers beneath the sheltering hawthorn to tether them with the other horses.

'Come along, my pretty ones,' she crooned. 'We'll soon have you warm and comfortable.' They were both trembling with shock and cold, and seemed to appreciate her attentions as she covered them with warm, dry blankets and fed them from the camp's dwindling grain supply.

She knew she should hurry back to the tents. Avithan would need constant watching through the remainder of the night. But she felt an overpowering reluctance to return to the clearing, past poor Esmon's body lying beside the corpse of his killer. Physically and mentally drained, Iriana paused – just for a moment, she assured herself – and stroked the velvety muzzle of the grey. Leaning into the powerful arching neck, she could feel the warmth and strength of the horse seeping into her; helping her to keep going for just a little while longer. 'Just look at you, you beautiful creature,' she murmured. 'Now I finally understand why Hellorin sets such value on you – *and* why Archwizard Cyran is so interested in you.' She ached with longing as she remembered poor, lost Dailika. 'I wonder if you would let me ride you?'

It occurred to her that there might be a way to discover what had happened to the horses: she would look into their minds as she looked into those of her own creatures, and see if she could discover anything from their memories about the proximity and direction of the Hunt. Laying a gentle hand on the grey mare's neck, she let her thoughts drift into the animal's consciousness – but suddenly, shields slammed down and she found herself shut out.

'Get out of my mind!' The words, spoken quite clearly in mindspeech, echoed through Iriana's head, startling her so much that she stepped back hastily. This was impossible! However, when she tried again to probe the mind of the grey horse, all she encountered were very firm, impassable shields. The animal made no attempt to speak to her again, but seemed to be scrutinising her with a look which was so intelligent and acute, she was sure that something more than a mere animal lurked behind that penetrating stare.

'Did you just speak to me?' she asked the mare out loud this time, as mindspeech would not penetrate the shields. 'Did you just tell me to get out of your mind?'

The horse took a step backwards, looking as startled as Iriana felt. Then the Wizard was engulfed by a wave of joy and relief so strong that it almost knocked her off her feet, as the mare dropped her shields abruptly. 'You heard me? You actually *heard* me? Oh, but this is a miracle.'

The astounded Corisand could barely contain her excitement. That she could actually communicate with this Wizard was good fortune beyond all her expectations. The surface of the other's thoughts was dark with an agony of grief, but beneath it, the Windeye could feel a similar delight and astonishment welling up, together with acute curiosity. Suddenly her heart was filled with hope. Would everyone in Tyrineld be able to hear her like this? If so, she saw a new future stretching before her, filled with a multitude of exciting possibilities.

She came back to herself at the touch of the Wizard's hand on her neck. 'You *did* use mindspeech, didn't you?' the girl was saying. 'I didn't imagine it?'

Corisand moved firmly away from the caressing hand. If she was to identify herself as more than a simple animal, it was important to establish respect and dignity between herself and the Wizard from the very start. She looked her in the eye. 'No, you did not imagine hearing me. My name is Corisand, and I am one of an ancient race, the Xandim—'

'The *Xandim*?' The girl interrupted with a gasp. 'The lost race of shapeshifters? I learned about you in history lectures when I was a student at the Academy. But they said you were extinct, or possibly even a myth.'

'Do I look like a myth to you?' Corisand snapped.

'I'm sorry, but that's what I was told,' the Wizard said. She smiled. 'I'm glad it isn't true. My name is Iriana, and I'm a Wizard from Tyrineld—'

'Yes, I guessed as much,' the Windeye told her, 'when you mentioned Archwizard Cyran. This meeting is good fortune beyond my wildest hopes.'

'But where have you been all this time?' Iriana asked her. 'The Xandim, I mean.'

'A very good question,' Corisand replied grimly. 'Down all the ages that the Xandim were deemed to have been lost, we have dwelt in captive slavery in Eliorand, imprisoned in our equine forms by Hellorin, the Forest Lord.'

'Merciful Creation! So all this time the Phaerie steeds have really been the Xandim?'

'Exactly. And I am their Windeye, or Wise One, which means that of all of us, I am the only one capable of human thought and communication from mind to mind. I escaped from Eliorand, desperately hoping that the Wizards would hear me, as the Phaerie could not, and would help my people escape the bonds that Hellorin has laid on us.'

The eyes of Corisand's companion had been growing wider and wider during this explanation. 'Of *course* we'll help you,' she said. 'I'm not very senior as Wizards go, but I'm sure that when you meet Archwizard Cyran, he'll think of a way ...'

The Windeye felt a flash of guilt and worry leap across Iriana's mind. 'I'm sorry, but I must get back to my companions who are both wounded, one very badly. Can we talk in mindspeech—'

'There you are. I was getting worried.'

Iriana jumped and spun round. Corisand was astonished to see a fireball in her hand, raised ready to strike.

'Whoa! It's only me.' The intruder stepped back hastily, hands raised in surrender, also staring at the fireball with undisguised curiosity. Behind his eyes, the Windeye could almost see his brain speeding through possibilities. With a stifled curse, Iriana snuffed the fireball. 'Taine! What a shock you gave me. You almost stopped my heart.'

'I should say that I was in the worse danger. Where did you learn to do that? Wizards aren't masters of Fire Magic.'

Corisand had ceased to listen to them – her thoughts were otherwise occupied. Iriana had called him *Taine*? But that was the name of Aelwen's lost lover. She had heard the Horsemistress and Kelon speak of him on occasion, and she had come to know him when Aelwen was working with her, or grooming her, and the two of them were alone. Taine was on Aelwen's mind so often, and so intensely, that Corisand had been unable to avoid picking up the thoughts, once she had become Windeye. In fact, she had become almost sick of the subject – though a lot of the memories had been a fascinating insight into the courtship and mating rituals of the Phaerie. When she looked at him closely, she certainly recognised him from Aelwyn's thought-pictures, though he looked older and more careworn now, and his face was pale and drawn, with black-shadowed eyes. From his torn and bloodstained clothing, it was clear that he'd been hurt in some way, and from the rank scent that still hung round him, the Windeye suspected an encounter with a bear. She shuddered. He was lucky to be alive. How tragic, if he and Aelwen had finally come so close to being reunited, and he'd been killed by a wild animal.

'Corisand?' Iriana's voice in mindspeech pulled her back from her own thoughts. 'Can you speak to Taine as well, or am I the only one? I don't think he believes me when I say you are a rational being.'

Corisand tried, but as she had half-expected, her thoughts only reached into Iriana's mind. 'Only you. I have tried to reach the Phaerie many times, with no success.'

'Taine and I are going back to our tents now. We'll talk to you from there. It seems that we have a lot to tell each other.'

'Iriana, you don't know the half of it,' Corisand replied. But even before Iriana got as far as her tent, the Windeye succumbed to her exhaustion. Her legs folded beneath her, and almost before she could lie down on the soft, cushioning moss, she had fallen asleep.

29

~

DAYS OF JOY AND SORROW

Dael had no plans that night except to stay as close to the fire as he possibly could, which was why he was staggering up the steps from the cellar with a huge wicker basket filled with dry logs. 'I've brought some more wood, Athina,' he called, as he tottered into the main living chamber, his knees threatening to give way any moment beneath the weight of his burden.

Athina turned from the window to watch his unsteady progress. 'Thank you, Dael,' she said in her beautiful low voice. 'But why must you always be carrying such heavy loads? One of these days, you'll hurt yourself.'

'I just want to make sure we're going to be comfortable for the night,' he protested. 'We'll need a good fire, with that storm raging outside.'

She let him dump his basket with a thud beside the hearth, looking at him shrewdly. 'You don't have to prove anything to me, Dael. You're not a slave any more, and you don't have to work like one. This is your home, here with me, and no one can take that away. You've been here half a year now, and we've become a family, you and I.'

Dael shook his head. 'You know, I still can't believe how lucky I am. I lived my whole life as a slave, I never had a mother – she was sold not long after I was born – and I never knew what it was to have a proper home. To *belong*.'

Athina smiled. 'I think we're both lucky,' she said. 'Before you came, I never realised that I was so lonely. Come along: we'll sit by the fire and mull some wine. On such a dreadful night as this, we may as well be cosy.'

They sat beside the glowing fire, sipping mulled wine, toasting bread on the end of a long, metal toasting fork and passing a crock of honey back and forth between them. When the loaf ran out, they settled back in comfortable silence, looking into the heart of the fire. *What a difference*

Dael has made to my life, the Cailleach thought. *Before his coming, I never realised how lonely my existence was.*

Dael seemed to share her pleasure in this extraordinary partnership. They would spend hours in conversation about all sorts of inconsequential things. He was delighted to find someone at last who was happy to listen, and she found great pleasure in sharing the outlook of a new, young mind. He delighted in doing things such as fetching wood and water, performing small repairs around the tower, or simply making her a cup of tea. When he told her about his upbringing in a fishing settlement by the sea, she used magic to create a little rowing boat for him, and he loved going out on the lake and fishing with a line. Though she could have done these little tasks much more easily using her powers, she soon came to realise that he enjoyed helping her, and that it was important to his newly burgeoning sense of pride to feel that he was doing his part.

The Cailleach enjoyed Dael's company more and more. At first she had looked on him as merely an amusing pet, but as the months went by, he grew increasingly close to her heart, until finally she began to understand why the natives of the mundane world set so much store by their offspring. She, who had given birth to worlds, was now discovering the joys of having a son of her own.

To her relief, he had never questioned the magic that brought them so many necessities and comforts in the tower. Since she was clearly not one of the Phaerie, he simply made the assumption that Athina – she had no idea why she had told him her true name, but somehow it had happened – must be a solitary Wizard. And though he was very much puzzled by her disinclination to treat him as a slave, he was too thankful for his own good fortune to place it at risk by questioning the (to him) eccentric behaviour that was making his life so happy.

Though she remained a mystery to him, the Cailleach soon discovered the details of Dael's miserable short life. He had grown up in Bourne, one of the settlements on the western coast, where the human slaves supported the Wizard community by going out on the ocean to fish. His mother had been sold inland somewhere to pay off her master's debts while he was still a babe in arms. Dael's Wizard owner had worked his slaves hard, and Dael had hated him for selling his mother. The greatest tormentor in the young man's life, however, had been his bullying father, who had finally led the escape of a number of slaves and forced Dael to go with him.

It was clear that the Cailleach's new companion had never been used to kindness, for it had taken a long time for his suspicion and wariness to recede. Finally, she had managed to half-convince him that this new, happier life would not be taken away from him, but even then he had been pathetically anxious to please her; terrified that he would accidentally say or do something to make her change her mind. As time went on, however, and she neither hurt him nor sent him away, Dael's confidence began to grow, and these two oddly matched companions became increasingly close.

'Athina?' Dael's sleepy voice broke into the Cailleach's thoughts. 'Will you show me some pictures in the fire?'

'Why not?' Athina agreed. This was a pastime she had started some months before, when Dael had not been with her for long. The entire point of her coming to this world had been to find the young women of her vision, and warn them, somehow, of the momentous events that were about to be set in motion. That way, there was a fragile hope that some of the damage, at least, might be averted. Unfortunately, Athina had not taken into account that, because she had brought herself into the mundane world, she had become subject to certain of its constraints. She had found it impossible to identify the women she sought, no matter whether she scried by fire, water, mirror or crystal, because the events that would reveal their true identities and destinies had not yet taken place. Her only option had been to keep searching through a multitude of images of the world outside her secret vale, until the people she sought should reveal themselves – and her task was made much more difficult by the growing suspicion and hostility between the cities of Eliorand and Tyrineld, both of which were now protected by magical shields of concealment and illusion against prying, spying eyes.

When Dael had first arrived, his presence had interfered with these activities. Though he was well aware that she had magical powers, how could she explain her constant scrying in search of a small group of strangers? Rather than becoming enmeshed in a web of explanations and lies, Athina had invented the 'pictures in the fire' game, a form of scrying that let her search through a multitude of images for those three special women. It had been a simple matter to let him share her visions. He thought he was viewing them with his own eyes, and did not realise that she was slipping them into his mind.

She had also not told him that she had been watching the Wild Hunt. After hearing about the massacre of his brethren, and discovering what Dael himself had been through at the hands of the Phaerie hunters, she had not wanted to distress him further by letting him see them in action again. So she had watched alone, in the depths of the night when he was fast asleep, and when she saw for herself the savage bloodlust and the merciless slaughter of the Hunt, she wondered what had happened to the shining, perfect world that she and her brethren had created so long ago.

Then she had seen Tiolani, and had immediately known that this was one of the Three she sought. Following that recognition had come the dreadful knowledge that this was not the saviour of the world for whom she had hoped. Horror had sheeted like ice across her skin as she became aware of the aura of darkness, cruelty and hatred that shrouded the girl. The death of her beloved brother had twisted the girl's mind. The incapacity of her father had removed the only member of her family who remained to comfort her, while leaving her with plenty of freedom to seek vengeance and the power with which to accomplish it. To make matters worse, she was being misled by those who pretended to be her friends.

But the worst thing of all about the situation – the one that kept the Cailleach from her sleep each night – was that Tiolani's intense and abiding hatred of humans knew no bounds. Having embarked on the comprehensive slaughter of the ferals, and executing the human slaves in her realm on the slightest pretext, she was now turning her attention towards the Hemifae. How long would it be before the whole of the Phaerie civilisation collapsed completely? Tiolani was hurtling headlong towards evil, and the Cailleach knew, with a sinking feeling of certainty, that it was already too late to stop her.

One hope lost, then. But what of the others?

For a little while following her dreadful discovery, Athina had no more heart for searching. Instead, she had immersed herself in the pleasure of Dael's company, and had occupied her days in pottering around the tower and its environs with this human she had so serendipitously found. Tonight, though she didn't think much would happen in such foul weather, the Cailleach realised with a pang of guilt that she had been neglecting her search through cowardice, and that this was hardly meet behaviour for one of the Guardians of the world. To salve her conscience, she was more than happy to go along with Dael's suggestion. Once he had built up the fire, she held her hands out to the smoke and flames that streamed up the chimney and put forth all her powers, casting out from the tower in ever-widening circles to find the ones she sought.

The flames blurred in the fireplace, and were hidden by a glowing golden haze that darkened rapidly into an impenetrable pool of blackness. No vision could pierce that rain and wind, and the cloud-shrouded darkness beneath the trees. Only in the brief lightning flashes could a disjointed series of images be seen. The slanting silver curtain of the downpour. Branches writhing wildly in the gale. A flooded river; a savage, surging mass of foam that swept great chunks of its banks away and tore up trees and bushes that lay in its path. A mighty sycamore split apart by a searing bolt from the churning cloud above.

The Cailleach shuddered at such violence. In her sojourn here she had come to love the forest, and it pained her deeply to see the fallen giants, the broken branches, the leaves torn from the boughs and the rivers and streams overflowing and wreaking such havoc in their path.

For a time, Athina scanned the area around the tower. She didn't mind keeping up this vigil for hours: roaming around the shadowy glades of the wildwood, widening her circle to take in the busy frontier town of Nexis, trying to penetrate the walls of chimera and enchantment that protected the cities of Eliorand and Tyrineld. Tonight, however, with nothing to see but darkness, downpour and desolation, she rapidly grew weary. 'Dael, I don't think there's any point in going on with this—'

The words died on her lips. In the captured instant of a lightning flash, she saw a skein of brightly clad figures among the clouds: the Phaerie Hunt rode, as she had seen them ride before – but this time, the elements were the hunters, and the Phaerie were the prey. Though they were beyond the leading edge of the storm, Athina knew just how fast those clouds could move. 'Fools,' she muttered under her breath. From what she had seen of the Wild Hunt in her months of watching, she viewed its members with anger and contempt. However, she had also seen, with great astonishment and unutterable joy, that their mounts were Xandim – the lost race that she herself had created in the far-distant past, when she and her brethren had spun the world from their imaginations, for nothing more than the sheer joy and fulfilment of practising their art.

Though she had believed, at first, that the Xandim must have some kind of alliance with the Forest Lord, Dael had soon made her think otherwise. On hearing his version of the situation between the Phaerie and their mounts, she realised that the race could only have been enslaved by Hellorin. Enraged as she was, however, the Cailleach knew that she had not come here to right every injustice of this world: that would have been unpardonable interference, and the more she meddled, the more likely her brethren were to find out what she was doing, and move to prevent her. Her only mission was to locate the three from her vision, and do what she could do set them on the right path. So Athina was forced to leave the Xandim to their fate. But it was hard to watch them tonight, being heedlessly ridden into peril by their Phaerie conquerors, for they were innocent, and beautiful and brave, and did not deserve to die.

Suddenly there was a commotion in the ranks of the Phaerie. One of the horses seemed to go mad ...

Wide-eyed, Athina saw Tiolani's fall, the ambush of her rescuers and her capture. She saw the horse attack the Huntsman, watched him plummet into the forest below. The hounds, uncontrolled now, scattered to the winds, their instincts telling them to flee the lethal wind and lightning. She saw Ferimon vanish into the clouds in pursuit of the girl's runaway mount – and there was something about the horse itself, something that drew her attention and set warning bells ringing in her mind … But too much was happening all at once; there was no time to look closely before the creature was gone, deliberately hurling itself into the maw of the storm.

Athina cursed loudly, causing Dael to stare at her in mute astonishment. Concentrating, she redirected all her focus towards the missing horse, hoping against hope that it would survive the storm and the wrathful Phaerie; scanning the shadowy depths beneath the trees in the certainty that it would not be able to remain airborne for very long in the face of the violent elements.

After a time of fruitless searching, she was positive she saw something: a glimpse of colour that was surely not a natural part of the forest. Dael had seen it too. He leant forward to peer into the vision in the fireplace as they waited for the next flash and what it would reveal. 'Was that an animal?' he said.

In the next dazzle of lightning, Athina saw clearly. Two miserable-looking horses, one a light bay, the other a prettily marked roan that had caught her eye in the first flash. She bit her lip, disappointed. They were Xandim, for a certainty, but they were not the one she sought. They were standing dripping under the outspread boughs of a large pine, and with them, scarcely visible in the shadows near the trunk, was a huddled figure.

They had only time for the briefest of glances before the lightning died away, plunging the image into darkness once more. Athina frowned. 'Was that one of the Phaerie?'

'Maybe.' Dael kept his eyes fixed on the darkness in the fireplace.

'And were those two beautiful horses the legendary Phaerie steeds I've heard about?'

'Looked like it.'

Athina shot him a searching look. 'You don't need to worry, you know. You're safe with me. They might have had you once, but I'll never let them take you back.'

Dael managed a smile, but she could see that the sight of the Phaerie had unnerved him. 'I don't want to look any more,' he said. 'I'm going to bed.'

When he had gone, the Cailleach sighed. *Poor Dael*, she thought. *I hope that in time he'll come to trust me to keep him safe from his former masters. In the meantime, let me see if I can find out what a lone Phaerie and two Xandim horses are doing in the forest on a night like this. I didn't notice him leaving the Hunt. I wonder if he has any friends nearby?*

It didn't take her long to find the second stranger. Another Phaerie – a woman this time – with a superb black stallion. The Cailleach frowned. What were they doing out in the forest on such a foul night? They certainly weren't acting as though they belonged to the Wild Hunt. She scanned further. There – what was that? Amid the trees?

When she looked closer, she saw the faint radiance that had caught her attention: a phantom glimmer of magelight, shining through the walls of one of three tents clustered together in a clearing. A jolt of excitement shot through her. She had finally found one of the three! She used her scrying powers to penetrate the walls of the tent, and saw the young Wizard with the long, dark-red hair talking with a strange young man, in whose features both Wizard and Phaerie were mingled.

Relief flooded through Athina. She had found another of those she sought. And she was absolutely certain that the third woman, the mysterious, unidentified member of the trio, would not be far away.

As she moved her vision away from the tents to scan the surrounding area, the Cailleach finally blundered into the one she was seeking, who was sheltering beneath the overhanging branches of an enormous hawthorn on the edge of the clearing. But wait – surely she must be mistaken? Those weren't people beneath the tree, but horses. Yet the tingle of recognition was so strong, how could she have made a mistake? She looked again, sending her vision beneath the branches of the tree. Several patient animals stood there, but one of them, the dappled grey ...

Athina gasped. 'That's the one!'

Suddenly everything became clear. 'That's why I could never identify her before,' she muttered. 'The last thing I looked for was a horse.' A radiant smile spread across her face. It seemed that the Fates had been hard at work and had managed quite well, for once, without her assistance. But her task was not done yet. The Xandim had been imprisoned in their equine forms for time out of mind, so how could this one possibly influence the future of the world? And what about the other two Phaerie she had seen sheltering, in their separate misery, beneath the trees? She could sense that, in some way, they would be important to the grey mare.

Before she could see what happened, however, the images in the fire became dim and hazy. Athina blinked. 'It can't be getting misty out there,' she muttered. Then, with a jolt, she realised that the haze was not within the Seeing, but was coming from the fireplace itself. Before her eyes, it began to pour out into the room, rising and spinning in the air to form a tall, columnar shape that began to glow with a coruscating radiance, sparkling with a multitude of iridescent hues.

The Cailleach gasped. 'Uriel!'

'My sister.' The voice echoed, deep and resonant, in the vaults of her mind. It was not filled with censure, but with a deep regret.

'You've come to tell me that you and the others want me to go back.' Athina sighed.

'Beloved one, you must. When we gave birth to these worlds of ours, we gifted them with self-determination and free will. They are our children, but they must learn and evolve of their own accord. It is not fitting for us to return here, tampering with fate. You know in your heart that this is true.'

'But this child is heading for self-destruction,' Athina protested. 'I foresaw it in the Timeless Lake! Why was I vouchsafed such a vision if not to render our creation all the help I could?'

'I do not dispute that, my dear sister,' Uriel said, 'but any assistance you give must come from within your own realm in the Elsewhere. The Guardians dare not venture into this mundane reality; not because of the risk to its inhabitants, but due to the danger to ourselves. Already this place has changed you, infecting you with emotions and attachments that are unnatural to our kind. And ultimately your interference here will avail you nothing, Athina. This world must grow and develop as it will, and its inhabitants must pursue their own fate. However much you try to interfere at this time, their destiny will ultimately be shaped by them alone.'

Though Athina knew he spoke the truth, she still could not bring herself to let go. Though Uriel, of all her siblings, was the closest to her heart, in that moment she almost hated him for making her face the truth. 'But Uriel,' she protested, 'what if they destroy this beautiful world that we created with such labour and love?'

'Even if they do, it is their world to destroy,' Uriel reminded her gently. 'I am more concerned for you, Beloved. If you try to stay here, you will change and diminish, losing your powers one by one until you are trapped in this place for all eternity. Already the changes are beginning – I have arrived here just in time. Your first mistake lay in loving this world so much that you took the physical form of one of its inhabitants, instead of the pure energy that is our natural state. You must not compound your error any further or you will coarsen and dwindle to the same level as your mundane creations. You know as well as I do that there is no climbing back from such a fall. You will cease to be a Guardian, and be lost to us for ever.'

Uriel was right. In her heart she knew it – just as she knew that he had not come to condemn her or punish her, but because he knew she was in deadly peril, and was desperate to save her. 'Do the others know what I have done?' she asked him softly.

'Not yet. I came as soon as I found out, in the hopes of persuading you to return before the others discover your error.'

Athina sighed. 'Uriel, I am grateful for your discretion in this matter, and for your timely reminder that I do not belong here. I know I must leave now – but what of this poor world?' She turned her face away from him, too overwhelmed by grief to say any more.

As if he sensed the depth of her sorrow and distress, Uriel relented a little. 'Leave such instructions and clues as you may for the human you have adopted,' he told her kindly. 'Then he will have a purpose, and you can at least leave with the knowledge that you have done all you can. The fate of the world will be back in the hands of its own children, but you will have armed them for the battle ahead.'

'And how can I explain where I'm going to my poor Dael? He loves and depends on me, and knows nothing of my true identity, but I am the only person who has ever cared for him. It would break his heart to think I was deserting him.'

But Uriel had an answer even for this. 'Athina, you have no choice. Let him believe that you are dead,' he advised. 'It will be much kinder than letting him live with the knowledge that you have deserted him, and the vain hope that one day he will find you again.'

'And you'll also be removing any temptation on my part to come back and visit him from time to time,' Athina pointed out drily.

'That is also important,' her fellow Guardian confessed. 'We can use our powers to leave the facsimile of a body behind, and you can leave him a message of some sort to warn him of the dangers faced by the world, and advising him to help the ones from your vision.'

Though her heart was breaking, Athina spread her hands in surrender. 'Very well,' she said, fighting to keep her voice strong and steady. 'It shall be as you say. Help me make my preparations swiftly, Uriel, for this world has such a hold on me that I dare not linger here.'

The colours of the energy-shell that was Uriel flickered and grew brighter. 'Come, then. Let us leave as soon as we may.'

Yet Athina hung back, hating to think of causing Dael such unhappiness; unable to contemplate the idea of leaving him. 'I wish I could say goodbye,' she whispered. But she had no choice. Tomorrow, when he awoke, he must, of necessity, grieve for her death, and she must return to her lonely eternity by the Timeless Lake. Could she do that to him? Could she leave now, just when she'd finally discovered those she sought?

Athina had her doubts.

'No, wait. I must have a little more time, Uriel. Only a few days longer, to leave the instructions and clues of which we have spoken, so that these children may be armed for the battle that lies ahead.'

Uriel's energy darkened. 'Beware, my sister, lest you go too far. Already your peril is growing.'

'Just a little while,' Athina argued. 'It will not take long for me to set my plans into motion, then you have my word that I will leave immediately.'

'You must,' Uriel said. He sighed. 'Very well. Soon the sun will be rising. I will give you this dawn and the next to make your arrangements. But be warned. If you have not returned by the third sunrise, I will come back – and this time I will bring the others. You know what that means. The penalties for you will be severe. Farewell, Beloved. Think carefully, and act wisely. Your time here is running out.'

Then he was gone, and the room seemed very dark without him. Athina shuddered. Full well she understood what a narrow escape she'd had. She would have to act swiftly indeed if she wanted to save this world, of all her creations the dearest to her heart.

The Cailleach turned back to the fireplace and once again began to summon her visions in the flames. Now that she had found the others, it was important that she relocate the captive Tiolani. Already the game was afoot. All the important pieces had been brought together in the storm-torn forest, but currently everyone was lost and scattered, beset by dangers on every side. So her first task must be to gather them all together, for only then could she position them to her satisfaction. And there was no time to waste.

With the ghost of a smile overshadowing her sadness, Athina summoned her powers, and sent her magic forth into the woods.

30
~

TRUST AND TREACHERY

Athina already had the early stages of a plan worked out. Once she had brought together all the major protagonists of her vision, plus the handful of others that her instincts told her were important – and had told them all the salient facts – they would have a chance to formulate a common vision and work towards it. She might have to leave this place, but at least she would put its future into the best hands possible. It was all she could do. It was vital she accomplish as much as she could in the hours she had left – no matter what the cost to herself.

Resolutely she searched, scanning the shadowy spaces beneath the crowding trees, sending forth her mind while her body stayed safely in the tower. To her relief, she discovered that fate had lent a helping hand. The Xandim of her vision had already found Iriana, so that was one less thing to worry about. The others she sought, however, those strange half-Phaerie who had been grounded in the storm with their Xandim mounts and must be somewhere in the forest – they would need to be gathered too.

It did not take her long to find them, sad, soaked and separated, try-ing to shelter from the wild elements as best they could. With relief, Athina sent her magic to each of them in the form of a glowing red globe: a guide to bring them together and unite them with Iriana and her companions. After she sent the spells forth, she noticed for the first time a drag of weariness in her mind and in her bones, and felt fear twist its icy coils inside her guts. Uriel's prediction was already coming true. Her powers were beginning to weaken in this place. If she persisted in using them here, where they could not be renewed, she stood a good chance of losing them altogether.

Athina gritted her teeth. 'I'd better hurry, then,' she muttered.

All at once the fatigue fell away, dispelled by a jolt of excitement. She had found Tiolani at last, and the fate of Hellorin's daughter was hanging by a thread.

A pounding headache.

Cramped and aching limbs.

The clammy, dank chill of wet clothing.

The sickening, sinking sensations of horror and fear.

All these feelings avalanched down on Tiolani with returning consciousness. Making things worse was the disorientating knowledge that, although she couldn't seem to move a muscle, somehow her body was in motion. Between pain and confusion, it took a little while to pick through her memories and establish what, exactly, was happening to her. From the pattern of meshes digging into her skin, she realised that she was thoroughly cocooned in the net that had saved her life, and was being carried along between two or more of the accursed ferals who had captured her. She was wrapped so tightly that she couldn't move, and there were too many layers around her to let her see out properly.

Her original hope – that this was all some horrible nightmare – was soon quashed. Not even the worst dream could produce such an abominable smell. Ever since the first ambush, all those months ago, human odour had been unbearable to her, but this stench of feral, unwashed humans – only the fact that her stomach was empty from her earlier vomiting saved her from throwing up again.

She remembered falling from that thrice-cursed Corisand; being rescued, then the grim rain of arrows, the death-screams of her friends and their mounts. She remembered the terror and the helplessness, waiting for the ferals to get to her. And, seared like a brand into her mind, the recollection of hearing them say that Ferimon, her beloved, had betrayed her father and herself, and been responsible for her brother's death.

No! It's not true. It's NOT!

Desperately she pulled her thoughts away to other matters, telling herself that the ferals lied, that their stupid wild tales were of no importance now, when her life was at stake. Pretending that the knowledge was not now lodged, like a poisoned dart, in the bitter depths of her soul.

What else did she remember? Only discovery, and seeing her own death in the flash of a knife in the darkness. Well, she had been spared for the present, though she knew her reprieve would not last long – and that her death, when finally it came, would be a drawn-out agony that would make her wish for the clean, swift, merciful ending of the blade.

In order to distract herself from thoughts of the hideous, and probably brief, future that lay before her, Tiolani began to listen to the soft conversations of her captors, hoping against hope to hear something – anything – that might help her escape.

'Damn it, Danel, she weighs a ton.'

'Aye, and carrying her like this, it's a bugger to get through the bushes,' another voice complained. 'Why we had to bring her along, I don't know. She's a cursed nuisance, and a danger to us all.'

'Evnas is right,' a third voice added. 'Let's just stick a knife in her right now. A few inches of dirt over her, and the bloody Phaerie will never know what happened to her.'

'I think they'd guess, don't you?' Danel asked, with a deceptive mildness. Tiolani, with her own will of iron, was quick to recognise the same trait in another.

'So what?' It was Evnas again. 'I'd rather the labour of digging than have to carry the bitch any further. In fact, if they'll guess anyway, why dig at all? Just kill her and be done, and leave her for carrion. The wolverines and bears and worms will take care of the rest.'

'No.' The leader's voice was like steel. 'If you're tired, Evnas, change places with Thu. He hasn't had a turn at carrying her yet.'

As Tiolani was lowered to the ground then lifted again, Danel carried on speaking. 'We need to take some time to think about this. There might be some way we can use her as a hostage, or a bargaining counter. They're bound to want her back.'

'They'll want her all right,' Evnas said. 'Enough to return with their hounds and bows and stinking magic, and slaughter the lot of us. The bloodshed we've already suffered will be as nothing compared to the massacre that will happen if they think we're holding her. They'll wipe us out, down to the last man, woman and babe in arms.'

'No they won't,' Danel said decisively. 'Don't you see, we have a chance to make them stop hunting us now? We'll tell them that if any more of us are harmed, we'll kill their ruler.'

'And then what? We can't keep the bitch for ever, clothing her and feeding her and tying up men who can ill be spared from hunting to guard her every hour of every day. And what about her accursed magic? Sooner or later she'll escape, or be rescued, or we'll be forced to kill her. Then the Wild Hunt will be back for us with a vengeance.'

Danel swore imaginatively. 'You have a point,' she said at last. 'But maybe there's another way. She might buy us a little time, at least, to get our people out of the Phaerie realm. We could go south, away from the Hunt—'

'And right into the hands of the bloody Wizards. Have you lost your mind, Danel? Do you *want* to be a slave again?'

There was the sudden, meaty sound of a fist striking flesh, and a grunt of pain. '*I* lead here, Evnas.' Danel's voice was as cold and inexorable as stone. 'Before my father died he nominated me to stand in his place. I may be young, but our losses have diminished since I took over and so far, I've led you well. If you think otherwise, you can call for a vote in council – and much good may it do you. Now, I'm telling you for the last time, we don't want to be hasty in killing Hellorin's daughter. Because you're right about one thing – if they find out we've murdered another of their leaders, the bloody Phaerie won't rest until they've hunted every one of us down.'

She sighed. 'I almost wish she hadn't landed in our territory tonight. Those stupid Phaerie *would* have to come crashing down practically into our laps – we didn't have much choice but to defend ourselves. But since we have her, let's wait and see if there's any good we can wrest from the situation. Remember, as long as she's alive we still have options, but once we've stuck a knife in her – much as I'd like to do it myself – well, we can't bring her back again.'

For a moment, there were mutterings among the band, until another voice, female this time, spoke up. 'Well, maybe you're right, Danel. I truly hope you are. Though I think—'

But what she thought was never to be revealed.

Suddenly the ferals froze, startled as wild hares, then dropped down into the undergrowth, dragging Tiolani with them. What had alarmed them? She had heard nothing. The storm was finally blowing itself out now; the rain had ceased, the thunder and lightning had rolled on towards the mountains, and even the ravaging wind had dropped significantly.

The ferals, signalling to one another in some code of their own devising, left her in the bushes and crept forward, silent as drifting smoke. Then from somewhere up ahead, Tiolani heard what had panicked them, and her heart leapt with hope. Horses, she heard horses, and two raised voices. She caught her breath at the sound of familiar, beloved tones. Ferimon! He had survived. He was here. He would save her.

Before she could act, a hand gripped her shoulder through the meshes of the net, and she felt the sting of a knife point in the hollow of her throat. 'Make a sound, you die,' a voice hissed. 'Use your mindspeech or your filthy magic, warn them in any way, and I'll dismember you piece by piece.'

Tiolani froze; helpless, terrified, scarcely breathing. Even as she cursed herself for her cowardice, even as she steeled herself to risk all in a mind-cry to her love, she heard Ferimon speaking.

His words turned her heart to gall and ashes.

Kelon had spent a cold, wet, wretched night beneath the minimal shelter of the wind-blown trees. But while his body was wracked by the storm, his thoughts were tortured with concern over Aelwen. When last he had heard from her, she had still been airborne, battling the tempest. Had she landed safely? The fact that he could no longer contact her by mindspeech did not bode well. And even if she had reached the ground in safety, she might have been captured. Tiolani would execute her out of hand for trying to make away with Phaerie steeds.

If, by some miracle, she was safe, but too far away to communicate with him, he was still far better off than the Horsemistress. Because he had kept his hold on the packhorse, Aelwen's precious Rosina, he could huddle between the two animals and share their body heat. The roan mare also carried food, but at first Kelon tried to ignore the gnawing in his stomach. It didn't seem right, somehow, to touch the food in the saddlebags of the packhorse while Aelwen was somewhere out in the woods alone, with nothing to eat. Occasionally he would call out to her in mindspeech, hoping for the comfort of hearing her voice and knowing that she was all right, but there was never any answer. It took a great deal of energy and effort to project mindspeech over any distance, and she was obviously far away from him. The other alternative – that she might not have survived the storm – he simply refused to countenance.

That didn't stop him from thinking about her, however: how deeply he cared for Aelwen, how long he had lived with the mingled joy and pain of a love that was not returned. He knew that he was very dear to her, that they were the closest of friends, but always she seemed to carry an invisible barrier around herself. Her heart was shrouded in secrets; he knew that she had long carried the shadows of sorrow and loss. Maybe now that they had left the perils and intrigues of Hellorin's court, and were away from their many responsibilities; now when they only had each other to depend on – maybe now, if they survived, things would be different. He could only keep on hoping, and wait to see what the future would reveal.

After what seemed an eternity, the violence of the storm abated, and the darkness began to give way to an eerie grey world of mist and shadow. As yet, however, the light was too faint to be any of practical use for travelling, but Kelon could see that the forest floor was a quagmire covered with broken foliage and fallen boughs: the debris of the savage gale's destruction. Water dripped from the trees overhead, and he shivered in the dismal damp. Though the wind and rain had faded away, there was not the slightest hope of lighting a fire, so he finally succumbed to his hunger and wolfed some bread, meat and cheese from the saddlebags, in the hope that the food might give him more energy to stay warm.

When he looked up again from his meal, Kelon was sure he must have dozed, and dreamed. A globe of crimson radiance hung before his face, dazzling him after the dismal gloom of dawn. He shook his head and rubbed his eyes, but the strange vision remained. He stretched out a hand to it and felt a gentle heat, but it glided away from his touch, remaining tantalisingly just out of reach. Drawn by the cheerful glow and the hope of some much-needed warmth, he took a step or two after it, but it slipped away from him again, retreating whenever he moved towards it, yet remaining motionless, just as if it were waiting, whenever he stood still.

This was not Phaerie magic – but it was some sort of enchantment, of that he was certain. It did not feel evil. Glowing there so bright and warm and cheerful, it felt beneficent to Kelon. Half-dazed from cold and lack of sleep, craving the comfort that it brought, he followed it along a narrow track that was no more than a game trail, as though he were in a trance.

So when he stumbled across the body of the horse, the shock hit him like a lightning bolt. Kelon recoiled with a cry as his own mount shied into the bushes, dragging the packhorse behind. Calming the snorting, trembling Alil, he dismounted and tethered his own animals, then went forward reluctantly to examine the dead creature.

It was the most appalling thing he had ever seen, its limbs broken and twisted in unnatural places, its hide split and leaking and its skull smashed open. Only the bloodied scraps of white hide and a glazed blue eye that the ravens had not yet found betrayed the poor creature's identity. Vikal. Ferimon's horse.

The poor creature must have fallen from a tremendous height. All around the body lay splintered branches, some even impaling the flesh, obviously broken off when the animal came crashing down through the trees. Kelon turned away and vomited into the undergrowth, but even as his stomach wrenched and heaved he could feel a chill of fear crawling between his shoulder blades.

What had happened to Ferimon? Where was he? Had he survived?

No, surely not. Who could live through such a fall? But Tiolani was bound to be searching for her lover, and the more distance Kelon could put between himself and this place, the safer he would be. Besides, it was more urgent than ever that he find Aelwen. Anxious to put his gruesome discovery behind him, he skirted as far around Vikal's body as the undergrowth would allow and hurried on his way. The burning globe had hung in the air all the time he had been preoccupied, and there could be no doubt that it was waiting for him. Now, as if sensing his urgency, it moved ahead of him faster than before, leading him through the shadowy ranks of the trees.

With all his attention focused on the light, Kelon was careless of other dangers. He never even realised that he was being watched until a tremendous weight crashed down on his head and shoulders, knocking him out of the saddle.

He hit the wet ground with a stunning impact. Dazed and shocked, the breath knocked out of him, his vision smeary with mud and his nose and mouth filled with cloying filth, he was in no condition to fight for his life, but there was no choice. The assailant was also on his feet.

Ferimon.

Kelon barely recognised the Phaerie as the handsome, charismatic young man who had won Tiolani's heart. He had come off badly in the fall. His blond hair was matted with dirt and leaves and clotted blood. His face was scratched, bruised and swollen, and his tattered clothes were stained crimson where he had been hurt. A gory socket was all that remained of his right eye, and the left held a searing glare of hatred and red wrath. There was madness in that look, and Kelon was pierced by a fire-ice bolt of fear. Though he had been taught the basics of combat with bow and blade, by nature he was no fighter.

Vile epithets spewed from Ferimon's twisted mouth, then a snarl. 'Would have ruled. *Should* have ruled.' His voice rose to a scream, then that one eye fixed on Kelon with a terrible intensity, and the slurred tones fell to a whisper. 'Stupid Tiolani. Had her fooled, everyone fooled. All my plan. Give bows to filthy ferals, bring down Hellorin.' He spat blood. 'Should have killed him, like her brother. Wed Tiolani. Rule. *Rule!*' His face was contorted with rage. 'Accursed horse demon,' he spat. 'You made it kill Tiolani. Aelwen bitch did. How? Why?' The voice rose again to a howling crescendo. 'Kill you now. You. *I should have ruled.*'

Pulling his knife from its sheath, he took a lurching step forward, and Kelon knew a split second's disbelief. *Surely he can't really mean to fight me? Wounded as he is?* His head cleared rapidly of extraneous thoughts, his instincts working at lightning speed as he backed away to give himself a little more room to react. Almost without his knowing it, his own knife was already in his hand, memories of a hundred stable brawls filling his head. Apprenticeships in the stables were a test of toughness, and the youngsters perforce learned to fight if they wanted to survive.

Then Ferimon, as if he had realised that in his condition he could never hope to win a physical combat, had a change of heart – either that, or the knife had been a ruse all along. Without warning, he launched a spell: a magical call that shot like a bolt of silver into the shroud of blackness that lay beneath the trees.

From the secret heart of the forest, something answered.

Fast, fast, fast: shreds of shadow streamed from beneath the bushes to pool at Ferimon's feet. They gathered, entwined, clotted together to form a shape like the terrible heart of the night: a creature like a wolverine, black as nightmare with eyes like searing embers burning in a narrow face. Eyes of hatred. Eyes of savagery.

Eyes of death.

They fastened on Kelon, affixing him as though he was held in a vice, while within him, his soul cried out in despair. Legends of this hypnotic stare were manifold – but he had never heard of anyone escaping it. The creature was a Culat: rare and lethal, and possessed of its own magic. Despite its size, it was numbered among the most deadly magical beasts and was one of the most feared.

Ferimon laughed: a sound like a knife blade scraping an exposed nerve. 'Like my pet, Kelon? Took a long time to find one, longer to tame. Now it comes to my summons. Kills for me.'

The creature opened its mouth to reveal needle-tipped teeth that glittered white as bone. It gave a low hiss, and scores of shadows sprang up around it, ghostly images of itself replicated over and over again. Concealed by the undergrowth, they spread out and clustered around the periphery of the clearing, the claws on their thronging feet making not a single sound, even among the rustling dry leaves.

Ferimon raised a hand, holding the monstrosities in place with his will, enjoying the sight of his enemy's horror and fear. The Culat's power lay in the shadowy army of facsimiles that surrounded it. They housed the souls of every living being it had slaughtered, subsumed and enslaved; all given animation by its will. Each one of them was as capable of dealing death as the entity itself. And as each victim they slaughtered was absorbed into the Culat's sinister power, its army of doomed and captive souls increased. The only way to destroy this threat was to find and finish the original, the leader, the progenitor. It was the only one that truly lived; the only one that could die. And if it could be killed, the rest of the soul army would be freed at last from their ghastly imprisonment. But how to kill it? It would be too fast for blade or bow.

As if reading his thoughts, Ferimon laughed again. 'Needs magic, pure

Phaerie magic. Not your pathetic powers; your blood tainted by human slave filth. *You* can't kill it, Hemifae.'

'I think you're lying.' Rage swept through Kelon, an anger so powerful that it broke the Culat's hypnotic spell. He took a deep breath and looked his foe in the eye. 'Or maybe not – but at least I can take you with me.' And on the last word he lunged through the shadow army, his knife piercing upward between Ferimon's ribs, finding his heart with deadly accuracy. The Phaerie sank to the ground, his last breath rattling in his throat, pulling Kelon, whose hand was still locked around the hilt of the jammed blade, down with him.

And in eerie silence, the Culat's minions attacked.

They were in no hurry now. They closed in on him slowly, stalking, feeding on his fear. Kelon abandoned the futile struggle with the knife and dived behind Ferimon, putting his back against a tree and trying to use his enemy's body as a shield, but he knew it would be useless. Against so many foes, there could be no defence. He fixed the image of Aelwen in his mind and waited for the end.

And an end came – but not the one he had expected. Kelon cried out in shock as a hissing hail of arrows swept the clearing in a lethal storm. The Culat horde ignored them, the missiles passing through their wraith-like forms, but the onslaught was so heavy that one was bound to find the leader. One of the creatures fell with a piercing scream, spraying gore – and in the blink of an eye, the rest had vanished.

'You can come out now.' The laconic voice was female, and sounded quite young. A feral human, she had to be, Kelon thought with dismay. How would they react to someone of Phaerie blood – even half?

'It'd stupid to hide – you can't get away.' This time the voice betrayed impatience – and just a hint of puzzlement.

Though Kelon's position, tucked down among the roots of a tree behind Ferimon's cooling corpse, had kept him out of the way of stray arrows, it certainly would not conceal him. Furthermore, he knew that these unknown assailants must have seen him when they made their attack. So what unpleasant game were they playing? They had him helpless. Why toy with him now?

Then he happened to look down, and for an instant, until his sight adjusted, he saw what they must have been seeing.

Nothing.

Kelon was absolutely stunned. He had made himself invisible. But he had no talent for glamourie! He could only imagine that need had ignited some unknown, deeply buried spark of ability within him, a legacy from his Phaerie father. With his survival at stake, instinct had taken over.

'I said come out, damn you!' But behind the anger in her voice, he could hear the uncertainty. 'We just saved your life, stupid,' she went on.

He had no idea who she was, how many were with her, or what she wanted. He wasn't *that* stupid. So he waited, staying very still lest he betray his position.

From somewhere out of sight, there was a murmur of voices. 'Look here, you idiot.' The female spoke again. 'We have this place surrounded and you can't get by us. You might as well come out. You killed that slimy, cold-blooded, treacherous turd, and that puts us on the same side – at least for now. I'm only disappointed I didn't get to do it myself. So show yourself, stranger. Come out and parley.'

Not in this lifetime, Kelon thought – but once again, his deepest instincts seemed to be one step ahead of him. This time he actually felt the magic coursing like cool wine through his veins as the glamourie fell away.

'There he is!' From all sides, the cry went up. The only way for him to salvage any shred of dignity was to pretend he'd revealed himself deliberately, so Kelon stood up, his skin prickling all over in expectation of an arrow.

They materialised like ghosts, out of nowhere, curious, wary-eyed, hostile; armed with slingshots and bows, and dressed in badly tanned hides and tatters of cloth. Then from the midst of the throng stepped a young woman with short, brown hair that stuck up in tousled spikes and looked as though it had been hacked off with a blunt dagger. She was skinny but wiry, her face smudged with dirt, but she wore her ragged clothing with the dignity of a queen, and her hazel eyes, the colour of forest shadows, snapped fire. 'Throw the knife away,' she ordered.

With a bristling thicket of arrows pointed at him, Kelon had no other choice

31

THE GATHERING

The feral leader scrutinised Kelon with those serious, cool eyes. 'Hemifae, he called you.'

Kelon nodded, though from her tone she had stated a fact, not asked a question. 'I have human blood in my veins, the same as you.'

She spat. 'You also have cursed Phaerie blood in your veins, so you'll never be the same as us. But you killed that snake, so you get to live – at least till we've talked.' Never taking those appraising eyes off him, she jerked her head in an 'over there' gesture. 'Move away from that scheming bastard.'

'I like your way with words,' Kelon said. He kept his voice light, but he was not sorry to put some distance between himself and Ferimon. Before today, he had never killed anyone. Inwardly, he was quaking and his heart was thundering, but he held himself together by sheer force of will so as not to betray any weakness to the ferals. Nonetheless, he could not help but flinch as the girl marched over to the Phaerie's corpse and gave it a number of vicious kicks, the last of which was full in the face. He wondered at the venom in her expression; the hatred and anger betrayed by her violence and her tense, jerky movements.

That was personal, he thought. It was more than a gut reaction to a dead oppressor. So how did this grim-faced crew know Ferimon?

Given the feral leader's current mood, he decided this was not the time to ask her. With a final kick, she turned away from Ferimon's body. 'Loot that carrion, Sim,' she said. 'Make sure you get everything – we've a use for it all, that's for sure. We'll leave now and go somewhere safer, so we can talk with this stranger.'

'How do we know we can trust him?' someone asked.

She gave a wry, one shouldered shrug. 'Who says I trust him?' Her eyes went to the glowing sphere that still hovered just beyond him. 'And what the bloody blazes is *that* thing?'

'I wish I knew,' Kelon admitted. 'Some sort of magic, I think. It attached itself to me in the forest, and it was leading me somewhere when I stumbled across Ferimon.'

'Maybe it was his spell. He seemed to hate you enough. Maybe he used that thing to lure you.'

Kelon shook his head. 'Spells don't normally last long after the caster's death – apart from the magic that makes the horses fly. If that failed immediately, then—' He noticed her foot tapping impatiently. 'Never mind,' he went on quickly. 'That spell is no Phaerie magic. It's like nothing I've ever seen.'

She cast her eyes to the heavens. 'Then why in the name of thunder were you stupid enough to follow it, instead of heading off as quick as you could in the opposite direction? I may not have any fancy Phaerie blood in my veins, but I've got enough sense to know you shouldn't mess with strange magic.'

'You should be grateful you've a choice.' Kelon glared at her. 'It seems to have attached itself to me in some way. It sticks with me wherever I go, but really it appears to want me to follow it. I decided that the only way to shake it off was to find the caster.'

The feral girl's eyes grew round as moons. 'My friend, I salute you. You must have balls of iron.'

'Balls of fire, more like,' jested some wit from among the bowmen, gesturing to the glowing sphere. 'Still,' the wisecracker added, 'this wants some thinking about, Danel. Seems to me we don't want nought to do with no strange magic. And if we take him with us, the thing's latched on to us, too. Seems to me that we have but two choices. Either leave him to go on his way, and take that bloody unnatural thing out of our territory – or kill him, and get rid of it that way.'

Kelon thought fast. 'If you kill me, what's to stop the spell attaching itself to one of you instead?'

Danel – as her name had turned out to be – hesitated a moment, gnawing on a grubby, bitten fingernail. 'Let him go,' she decided. 'It's not worth the risk, and I'm certainly not taking him to any of our hideouts with that thing following him.'

'We could take his horses, at least,' a woman said hopefully. 'There's enough meat there to feed everyone twice over.'

Kelon's hand tightened possessively on Alil's bridle as he surveyed the ring of ferals. Though they looked like a murderous crew, with their bows trained on him and their grim, uncompromising eyes, a closer look betrayed gaunt, shivering flesh beneath the threadbare tatters of clothing that hung from their bony frames. Their hollow, pinched faces spoke of hunger and privation far beyond his own understanding. For the first time, he realised that the Phaerie view with which he had been raised – that humans were little more than useful animals – was wrong.

Danel interrupted his thoughts. 'No,' she said. 'Not that it isn't tempting, but I don't want to risk causing any trouble with that cursed spell thing. If whoever cast it is leading him towards them, then they want him for something, and I'm not going to get in their way.'

She nodded brusquely to Kelon. 'On your way, stranger, and our thanks for killing that whoreson filth, though we could have done it ourselves anyway,' she ended on a note of pride. 'Go on – what are you waiting for? Get you gone, and your strange spells with you.'

'Wait.' Kelon did not want to push his luck – every instinct was screaming at him to get out of there as fast as possible – but he had to know. 'Why do you hate Ferimon so much, Danel? How do you know him?'

'Don't tell him,' someone cried, but the feral leader ignored the interruption.

'I don't see the harm in telling him. Not at this point. And someone ought to tell the Phaerie the truth, before any more of us get slaughtered by her bloody Hunt.'

She turned back to Kelon. 'It's like this. A few months ago, when the winter was at its coldest and we were having a real struggle to survive, *that* one turned up.' She gave Ferimon's body another vicious kick. 'Brought us food and blankets, didn't he? Warm clothing and healing herbs and stuff. Said he sympathized with our plight. My father was leader ...' She paused, closed her eyes and swallowed hard. 'He trusted the lying weasel. Ferimon had a plan, he said. If Hellorin was out of the picture, the human slaves in Eliorand could be freed. He gave us weapons, these good bows, and set up an ambush—'

'That was *Ferimon*?' Kelon gasped.

'None other. I never liked his scheme, but my father thought the risk worthwhile, and so we walked into the trap like a lot of innocent babes. Since Hellorin fell, his accursed daughter has hunted us down like rabid dogs, along with all the other ferals in the forest. Who naturally blame us for their troubles, and now we're beset by enemies on all sides.'

'While Ferimon seduced Tiolani and gained power in Eliorand,' Kelon said.

'And my father was killed by the Hunt.' Though her voice was steady enough, she could not keep the telltale tremor of emotion from her voice.

'I'm sorry,' Kelon said softly. 'I wish I could help you. My deepest thanks for saving my life from Ferimon's creature and its minions. Go well, all of you: especially you, Danel.'

'Go well – what's your name, stranger, anyway?'

'Kelon.'

'Go well then, Kelon. Good luck to you.' And with that, she and her companions melted back into the forest, leaving him alone with the cooling body of his foe – and the mysterious glowing sphere that waited to lead him on his way.

Hidden, helpless in the undergrowth, a deadly blade at her throat in the hands of a desperate human, Tiolani was forced to listen as her life was smashed into jagged shards. The only way she could ever have believed that Ferimon would betray her was if she heard it from his own lips – and now she had. Much as her mind twisted and turned to try to evade and deny, there was no escape. Thoughts and memories cascaded through her mind with lightning speed, as all her actions of the past months came crashing down on her. Her unquestioning trust in Ferimon, the way he had persuaded her to dismiss her father's old counsellors and surrounded her with his private guards. The way he had been always at her side, enfolding her, as she had thought, with love and security, even though he had never shown the slightest interest in her through all the years she had worshipped him as a young girl, before she had lost her father and brother. Why had she not suspected? How could she not have *seen*? Through advising her, helping her, influencing her decisions and her thoughts, he ruled the Phaerie just as effectively as if he had been Forest Lord himself. And she had let him. Her face was hot with shame.

She had loved him with all her heart, and he had made a fool of her. It had all been a lie – an evil, calculated lie. For cutting him down like a dog, Kelon deserved any reward she had in her power to give.

A chill ran through Tiolani as she thought of her father. Was it not strange that he was taking so long to recover? Ferimon had always been so very quick to lull her fears and concerns, encouraging her to enjoy this chance to rule. Had he bribed the physicians somehow? If she had thought to investigate more closely, would she have had Hellorin back with her by now, as healthy and powerful as ever?

Oh, how she wished he was back!

She thought of Aelwen, whom Ferimon had represented as a meddlesome hag who deemed Tiolani unfit to rule. She realised how wrong she had been to distrust and resent the Horsemistress. Aelwen, whose help she had lately scorned, had taught her to ride and had been there, steadfast and stalwart, all through her life, and Tiolani had repaid her with anger and vicious threats.

Oh, how she wanted her now!

If that were not enough, there was worse, far worse, to come. She could blame Ferimon for so many things, but she, and she alone, had been responsible for all the slaughter. The image of Ambaron came back from the dead, his face contorted with fear, his eyes fierce with accusation, filling her with horror, guilt and remorse, and behind him the other Hemifae she had executed on the slightest pretext: partly because they had dared to question her actions, but chiefly because of their part-human heritage. She had carved a bloody swathe through the slaves in Eliorand, and in the Hunt she had bathed in gore, and revelled in her thoughts of retribution and revenge.

They deserved it. They killed my brother.

True. But Ferimon had arranged that deadly ambush; he had provided the weapons and used the ferals as his tools. And how many of their fathers, mothers and children had she slain? While she'd been forced to listen to the ferals talking among themselves, it had no longer been possible merely to view them as savage forest animals. The leader, in particular, had struck a chord with her – a young girl just like herself who had been thrust into the responsibilities of leadership after her father had fallen.

Tiolani's mind was in turmoil. It was impossible to let go of so much hatred all at once, and yet ... She was beginning to understand that she'd been wrong about so many things: she had been granted the privilege and responsibility of ruling, and she'd made an appalling mess of everything. If Hellorin ever did wake up, he would be so angry with her ...

Don't be ridiculous. You aren't going to live that long.

If only there was some way to put everything right. She would do anything, *anything* ...

Anything? A desperate plan began to form in her mind. But it would depend on reaching some kind of accommodation with the ferals: prohibiting the Hunt and even helping those she had previously hunted to survive and thrive in the forest. To save her life, could she bring herself to forgive the stinking humans for what they had done, or even enforce such a bargain? And even then, the discontinuation of the Wild Hunt was going to be an extremely unpopular decision, and Tiolani did not deceive herself about her current lack of popularity in Eliorand. And what of Hellorin, supposing he should ever recover? He would not only be furious with her, but would probably refuse to honour any bargains she might make.

Well, that wouldn't be her fault.

Very slowly and carefully, she turned her head a fraction and whispered to the man with the knife. 'I want to see Danel. I can help you. I swear, no tricks.' If only she could get the leader's attention while Kelon was still there ...

But it was no good. 'Shut up, you,' the guard hissed, and followed the words with a vicious kick in the side. Indulged and pampered all her life, Tiolani had never been struck before. Silenced and cowed by pain and shock, she huddled into herself, despising her own cowardice as the vital moments slipped away from her until, despairing, she heard Kelon depart, and knew that she had failed.

Now she was alone indeed. There would not be a second chance. She had only her wits and her will to survive to depend on. She hoped they would be enough.

This was the moment Athina had been waiting for. It was a simple matter for a being of her power to look into the minds of these lesser creations, and while the situation between Kelon and Ferimon had been unfolding, she had been monitoring Tiolani's thoughts and reactions very carefully. Now, while the Forest Lord's daughter was distressed, terrified and above all contrite, Athina knew the time was ripe to act.

She cloaked her thoughts in light and watched, amused, as the jaws of the feral humans dropped open in shock when her image shimmered into existence, right in their very midst.

There was a sudden tumult of curses, yells and running feet. Athina shrugged as a fusillade of arrows passed harmlessly through her illusion. These primitive creatures were always so predictable. Danel, who had been in the clearing looting Ferimon's body, came at a dead run and pulled up short at the sight of the ghostly figure. 'Hold your fire,' she shouted. 'You're only wasting arrows.' Then, swallowing hard, she straightened her shoulders and stepped forward. 'Who are you, Lady? What do you want with us?'

'I want her.' The Cailleach pointed a finger at the trussed-up form of Hellorin's daughter. An explosion of light flared forth, causing the humans to scatter in terror, shielding their eyes. When they emerged, drawn back by a power they could not understand and blinking the dazzle from their vision, Tiolani was gone.

The image of Athina still stood unmoving and unperturbed, ignoring the cries of dismay and the scattering of arrows that came her way despite Danel's orders. 'Where is she?' Danel demanded. 'She was our prisoner, damn it. What have you done with her?'

The Cailleach smiled. 'You were on the right track all along, Danel. There is a great deal that you and Tiolani can do to help one another – though it is as well for you that I came to you when I did. She is her father's daughter, and would not have honoured any bargain she made with you, were I not here to hold her to her word. Go as quickly as you can to the tower by the lake. You will find Tiolani there, as well as myself and certain others who will influence your fate.'

She beckoned to the feral leader, and her voice now held a compelling note that seemed to resonate within the very depths of Danel's mind. 'Come now. Bring your followers. You will be fed and sheltered there, and I can protect you from any of the Phaerie Hunt who might be searching for Tiolani. Do not delay, Danel. Do not be afraid. Believe me when I say that I have your interests at heart, and represent the best chance of a safe future for your people that you are ever likely to find. Will you trust me, O leader of the free humans? Will you hasten to the tower?'

'But – but there isn't a tower by the lake,' Danel protested.

'There is now.' Athina gave her a beatific smile, and vanished.

The dismissal of her phantasm released the rigid control under which the Cailleach had been holding herself during her encounter with the ferals. As her consciousness returned to her physical form she staggered, overcome by a wave of dizziness and weakness, and collapsed to the floor.

Dael came running. 'Lady, what happened? Are you ill? How can I help you?' Putting an arm around her, he helped her back to her feet, and supported her while she sank into a chair. Athina sent him off for some water that she did not need, just to give herself a moment to collect her reeling thoughts. Uriel's warning echoed in her mind. She was shocked to discover the rate at which her powers were diminishing. She wondered if she would be able to accomplish everything she needed to achieve before the loss of her powers left her stranded. For the first time it became crystal clear to her that, much as she loved this world, the idea of being trapped here for the brief span of a limited life filled her with the utmost horror and fear. She couldn't let it happen. The cost was simply too great. She must hurry, and make the best possible use of the little time she had left, and then must leave before it was too late, whether or not her work to secure this world had been completed.

Athina sighed, and dragged herself heavily to her feet. She had better go upstairs and deal with Tiolani, before Dael discovered her – but first, there was one more person to set on the proper path.

Aelwen was too uncomfortable to sleep. The dripping trees offered little shelter from the cold wind and driving rain, and she was forced to huddle miserably beside her wet and unhappy horse, trying to share a little of Taryn's body heat to keep her going. She couldn't sit or lie on the wet ground. All she could do was stare into the disquieting shadows of the forest and worry about Kelon, how long the Phaerie would search for the two of them and what they would do next if they did, against the odds, escape their pursuers and get together once more.

There was no point in trying to go on in the darkness. It would be foolhardy to risk herself and Taryn on such a wild and turbulent night. The wind was strong enough to tear off whole branches, and once, too close for comfort, she had heard a rending creak, like the last cry of a tortured spirit, followed by an earth-shaking crash as an entire tree came down.

Beneath the forest canopy, it was impossible to see the sky. After a time, however, Aelwen noticed that light had begun to filter through the surrounding woodland – but not the pale, ephemeral luminescence that preceded dawn. This was a smouldering red glow, as if the forest was burning somewhere nearby. Her heart gave a couple of uneasy thumps before her common sense told her that there was no crackle of burning wood or roar of flames, and no smoke or smell of burning. Besides, a blaze would never survive on this wet night. So if not fire, then what?

Aelwen blinked, and knuckled her sleepy eyes. A small globe of light, about the size of her head, was coming towards her – bobbing through the trees at chest height. It came to rest in mid-air about a yard away. Aelwen stretched out a hand, stopping a few inches away from the mysterious, radiant orb. She could feel no heat or cold coming from it, and a faint tingle in her fingertips hinted at some form of magical energy emanating from the thing. Very, very cautiously, she reached out with her mind, forming a telekinetic spell – and gave the sphere a push. It was like trying to move a mountain. Aelwen staggered back a step or two as her magic rebounded off the impervious orb and recoiled hard against her.

The glowing light suddenly began to move again, floating slowly away from her through the trees, then hovering steadily a dozen feet away as though waiting. When she had shown no sign of moving after a moment, it looped back to her, bobbing up and down impatiently in front of her nose before floating off again into the forest and stopping in the same place. There was something familiar about the pattern of its movement: it reminded Aelwen of a hound she'd once owned, which used to race off in the same way and then wait for her, crouched low, tail wagging, inviting her to follow.

It wanted her to follow? Oh, surely not. But once again, as she hesitated, it started to move, repeating exactly the same sequence: return, retreat and wait. It was magic, for sure, but not of a kind that she had ever come across. She had met Wizards of Tyrineld, come to Eliorand to trade in less suspicious times, and this did not have the feel of Wizards' magic. Besides, the magelight they produced was not red but a silvery blue.

The light bounced up and down in the air before her, as if growing impatient, and the sight of it made Aelwen smile. She stopped dithering, deciding to trust her instincts and follow.

'Very well,' she told it. 'I'm coming.' Leading her horse, she set off through the trees. As soon as she began to move, the shining orb moved too, keeping a short distance ahead of her, and leading her on through the dark forest. At least the movement helped keep her warmer, though her legs were aching and her head buzzed with weariness. After a time, she noticed that the first dim glimmers of daylight were stealing between the crowding trees.

Maybe now she could ride again, and give her aching legs a rest. The Horsemistress swung into the saddle – and found a pair of blue eyes staring into her own. Clinging to a branch, right at her new eye level as she sat on the tall stallion's back, lay the most extraordinary feline that Aelwen had ever seen. She had heard of the blue-eyed cats that the Wizards bred in Tyrineld, but the strange reality, with long, luxuriant fur that seemed to be created out of light and shadow and the stunning eyes in the sable mask, went far beyond the tales.

At its best, it would be magnificent. For the moment, however, the poor creature was clearly suffering. Its fur was soaked into spikes and it looked small, bedraggled and pathetic as it crouched flat to the branch, its eyes dull and glazed. Aelwen knew perfectly well that she was in no position to be taking care of sick animals, and should simply ride away and not look back – yet the sad little figure tugged at her heart. How could she leave it? She doubted very much that it would survive for very long all alone in the forest.

After a brief inner struggle, and smiling wryly at her own folly, she disengaged its claws from their stranglehold on the branch and carefully lifted it down. At least it would be company. Though she had been ready for it to erupt into a fury of clawing and biting, it lay limp and unresponsive in her arms. Aelwen ran expert hands over its body, and it did not seem to be physically hurt in any way. She suspected that it was simply in shock. Something had terrified it, probably the storm itself, and it had fled until terror and exhaustion had overcome it completely.

But this was no wild creature, and there was no way it could have come right into the darkest heart of the forest by itself. So who had brought it here? Where were its owners, and what had happened to them?

She had almost forgotten the mysterious light. When she had stopped it had paused with her, hovering in place about three feet away. Now it came closer, zooming and swerving wildly through the air, right in front of her nose. With a muttered curse, she drew her cloak over the cat so that it wouldn't be frightened, and set off after the impatiently bobbing globe. She began to wonder if, perhaps, this strange light belonged to the owners of the feline. She knew little of Wizards' magic – could they produce something like this?

As she rode, she couldn't help speculating about what was happening in Eliorand following her escape. Tiolani already knew they had fled, taking three of Hellorin's precious bloodstock with them ... The Horsemistress shivered. The furious ruler would stop at nothing in her attempts to hunt them down. So where was the Hunt? And where was Kelon? Again she called in mindspeech, hoping against hope that he would answer this time, but there was no reply.

'What's that?' Aelwen pulled up her horse. The breeze had picked up a little, blowing into her face. It carried a wonderful smell of woodsmoke and fried bacon. As if on cue, the red sphere in front of her vanished. Through the trees she heard the sound of voices.

32
~

THE CLEAR LIGHT OF DAY

Since Corisand had succumbed so quickly and completely to exhaustion, they had left her to rest until morning. When the first of the birds started singing to usher in the new day, and Taine emerged from Esmon's tent and went to seek Iriana, who was crowded very tightly into the same tent with Avithan. She was sleeping, curled up in a way that could not be comfortable, lying across the feet of her wounded companion. Taine took one look at her pale, strained face, and decided to let her get what little repose she could.

The morning was cool, damp and grey, and he very much wanted some taillin, and something hot to eat, but all the wood was soaked through from the rains of the night before, and he found it impossible to get the fire started. Eventually he was forced to awaken Iriana after all because he needed her rather specialised powers.

Grumbling under her breath, obviously not awake enough yet to hold a conversation, she emerged bleary-eyed from the tent and stumbled across to the fireplace. With a careless gesture, she launched a sizzling little ball of yellow fire into the midst of the pile of kindling, which immediately burst into spluttering, rather smoky flames. He would never have believed it, had he not seen it with his own eyes. A Wizard with the powers of all the elements – as far as he knew, such a thing had never happened before. He wondered uneasily if this was some kind of omen – a sign that the catastrophe foreseen by Cyran was not far away …

In the meantime, however, life went on. Iriana, still using Esmon's black horse as her eyes, tended the animals while Taine fried bacon, then Corisand joined them, with the warhorse standing nearby.

While they ate, Taine watched with bemusement as Iriana and Corisand – the grey horse that apparently was not a horse – exchanged histories and information. The Wizard had had a hard time convincing him that this creature – for no matter how magnificent it was, it still looked like a simple horse to him – was one of the legendary Xandim, and that all of Hellorin's precious steeds were descendants of the same long-lost race, enslaved aeons ago by the Forest Lord's magic. He wondered whether Aelwen had ever guessed.

However, there was no denying Corisand's tidings from Eliorand. Her tale, as relayed by Iriana, filled him with increasing alarm; he heard with dismay of Tiolani's deteriorating mental state. For a moment his thoughts drifted away from Iriana's words as he imagined bringing this bad news to Cyran, who would already be devastated by Avithan's fate. The Archwizard had trusted Taine to guard and help his son. What would he say in the face of such abject, terrible failure?

Through the night, Avithan had slipped further and further away, until Taine and Iriana had to face the fact that they were losing him. Out of sheer desperation they had cobbled together a time spell – a risk in itself, for Taine had never attempted time magic, and Iriana, though she had read the theory, was similarly lacking in experience. Nevertheless, it had been Avithan's only chance. Now he lay in the tent, unmoving beneath the magic's eye-defying shimmer, and until they got him back – somehow – to Tyrineld, and the spell could be removed, they would not know whether they had saved or killed him.

Looking at Iriana now, Taine marvelled anew at her courage. For a little while the previous night, before they had performed the spell, she had sobbed broken-heartedly and he had tried in vain to comfort her. Having given vent to her grief and anxiety, she had pulled herself together and set about doing what needed to be done. He had nothing but admiration for the young Wizard. When she spoke of Esmon's death, Taine had realised how deeply she was grieving for the murdered Warrior. The loss of her animals had affected her profoundly, both emotionally and practically, and he sympathised with her frustration that she could no longer see unless the stallion was near, or be of much practical assistance to her companion. Yet she had remained capable and steadfast throughout her ordeal. He felt humbled by her courage. How would he have managed, sightless, bereft and in peril from both assailant and storm?

All at once, his wandering attention snapped back to her words, as she translated Corisand's thoughts: 'And then Tiolani threatened Aelwen, Hellorin's Horsemistress. So Aelwen decided to flee, and I decided we should escape together, along with—'

'What? *What?*' Taine all but pounced on Corisand. 'Say that again. What about Aelwen? She escaped? Where is she? Is she all right?'

He leapt to his feet, pacing the clearing, scarcely able to contain himself as Corisand's narrative continued. When he heard that his beloved had been lost in the storm, his heart turned over. So close. He had come so close, and now she might be dead.

Iriana had stopped speaking and was watching him open-mouthed. Even Corisand looked astonished, and he realised that he must have been babbling out loud. 'We have to find her.' His voice grew urgent as he rounded on Corisand. 'Tell me again – I mean, tell Iriana. Tell us exactly what happened. How far away from her were you? What direction was she moving in, when you went down?'

'I'm sorry, Taine, but I have no notion.' Corisand's words came back through Iriana. 'Too much was happening – we were a goodly distance apart, and as well as the storm, I had Ferimon and that accursed Huntsman to deal with. You have no idea what it was like up there. The wind hurled us around so much, I had no idea of anyone's direction. Aelwen could be anywhere – close by, or fifty miles away. We can't possibly hope to find her.'

'And what about Avithan?' Iriana laid a hand on his arm. 'We must get him home now. We must take him back to the healers.'

In his heart Taine knew she was right, and that only made it worse. But how could he leave Aelwen?

'Taine, we can't stay here,' Iriana said urgently. 'The Phaerie—'

'But Corisand said she threw her rider,' Taine protested. 'If Tiolani has fallen, there will be no flying magic. It will take them two or three days to come out this far – and even then, this is a big forest to search. If they cannot see us from the air, they can't find us. We have a little time left, surely?'

'But there is something I didn't tell you. Cyran may know very soon that we're in trouble. Last night, when I was running from the assassin who killed Esmon, I sent out a cry for help in mindspeech. I think the distance was too great, but I was desperate. I called to Challan, my foster-father in Nexis. We had such a close bond once, I thought there might be a chance. If he heard, he could have sent a message through by carrier bird—'

Taine sighed. 'Iriana, I'm sorry to have to tell you this, but your foster-father can't have heard you, because he wasn't in Nexis. I met a Wizard called Challan on the road a few days ago. He was going to Tyrineld, to search for his daughter. She had run away, apparently, after some sort of family quarrel.'

He wondered at the bitter look that crossed her face. 'Chiannala,' she muttered, then he saw her square her shoulders, shrugging away whatever had upset her. 'All right. So Cyran can't know of our danger. But Corisand also said the others tried to catch Tiolani, and she didn't see whether they succeeded or not. She may not be dead, or even badly hurt. What if she's planning, right now, to bring the Hunt out after Corisand and Aelwen and her friend? We must get away, as far and fast as we can—'

'There is no need to run away. I will protect you.'

She had come out of nowhere, the woman with the face of ageless beauty and the fine-spun silver hair that glowed around her head like an aureole.

Taine and Iriana leapt to their feet, she with a cry of astonishment, and he with a curse. Corisand's head snaked out aggressively, her ears going back flat to her head. Swiftly though Taine snatched at his weapon, the stranger was faster. His hand closed on emptiness as the blade sailed through the air and thudded to earth on the far side of the clearing.

'See? I can protect myself, too,' the woman smiled wryly. 'But you have nothing to fear from me, Iriana, Corisand, Taine.'

'Then what do you want?' Taine demanded.

'How do you know our names?' Iriana asked at the same time.

'I am not from this world, and I am here to help.' She smiled as their jaws dropped at this bald statement. 'You may call me Athina, or the Cailleach. Trust me. The fate of your world is truly hanging in the balance, and I know that your Archwizard has also foreseen this, Iriana. I have, shall we say, a very great interest in your world, and I am trying to save it from utter destruction. I too believe that the crisis is nearly upon us. I have had my own visions. I know that the future lies in the hands of a very small group of people: one is Hellorin's daughter—'

'*Her?*' said Corisand. 'Are you insane? That must be wrong.'

Even as Iriana began to translate, the woman held up her hand. 'There's no need for that, Iriana. I understand the Windeye of the Xandim perfectly. Which is just as well, because you, Corisand, and you, Iriana, were the others in my vision.'

A storm of protest broke out, with everyone speaking at once. All but the strange woman, who stood quietly and let their words break around her like waves. 'Then let me prove it.' Her quiet words were suffused with such powerful compulsion that the others were silenced as effectively as if she had shouted at the top of her lungs. 'Both you, Iriana, and you, Taine, are yearning for missing companions.' She turned to the trees behind her, and cast her arm out in a sweeping gesture. 'Behold, I restore them to you.'

There was a snapping of twigs in the underbrush, then out of the trees stepped Aelwen, riding her midnight stallion.

Her face was drawn with weariness and her hair hung down in tangles, snarled with leaves and twigs. She was shivering, Taine noticed, and her clothing had been darkened by the soaking rain. The linen shirt under her leather jerkin clung to her body in sodden wrinkles, and was ripped down one sleeve. There were bruised shadows under her eyes, a scratch on her forehead and a long smudge of green bark down one cheek.

He had never seen anyone so beautiful.

She froze, staring at him with wide, stunned, vulnerable eyes. He could see the emotions chasing across her face: disbelief, amazement, joy. A mirror of his own feelings. For Taine, time stopped. For a moment they simply stared, utterly transfixed, drinking in the sight of one another like desert travellers who, parched with thirst, reach an oasis at long, long last.

Their absorption was broken abruptly by a cry from Iriana. 'Melik! Oh, my Melik.' As she ran forward, the cat struggled out of Aelwen's unresisting arms and was scooped up into the Wizard's familiar, safe embrace. Though tears ran in profusion down Iriana's cheeks, her face was radiant with happiness. 'I thought you were dead,' she sobbed as she stroked the soft fur. 'I thought I had lost you too.'

Iriana's reunion with her cherished companion broke the enthralment that had held the other two. Even as Aelwen slid down from her horse, her beloved ran forward with a choking cry. Then they were in each other's arms, and to Taine, it was as if all those years of loneliness, of yearning, of not belonging, had never been.

'Oh, my love—'

'I thought I would never see you again—'

'I can't believe it's true—' They were both talking at once, their words tangling with kisses.

The Cailleach stood to one side and smiled. The joys of bringing such happiness far transcended Uriel's threats and warnings – whatever the cost to herself.

Kelon walked along in a daze of weariness and unreality that had come in the wake of his fight with Ferimon. In one way he regretted parting from Danel and her outlaws. Now that he was on his own once more, he was very lonely without them. But he could not desert Aelwen, though how he could ever hope to find her in this vast tract of wilderness, he did not know. The glowing sphere floated on ahead of him, tantalisingly out of reach, luring him towards some unimaginable fate.

Hunger gnawed at him and fatigue dragged at his bones. He was finding it increasingly difficult to keep his eyes open, so when he heard the sound of voices, he wondered if he was dreaming. He followed the globe forward to where the undergrowth thinned – and walked into a nightmare. A clearing, a lake, light and horses. A young woman embracing a cat, an old woman looking on with a benign expression: all of these details were noted and forgotten in an eyeblink. He only had eyes for the couple embracing in the centre of the clearing.

Aelwen had found her lost love – and all Kelon's dreams and hopes crashed down in ruin.

The sight of them together seared into his mind like poison. Oh, she had never been his; had never given him any encouragement but good, honest friendship. He had always known where he stood. And yet … How could he be blamed for yearning, for wanting, for hungering? So he had persuaded himself that given time, he must succeed with her. Taine had been gone for years – how much longer would she continue to wait for a lover who clearly would never return? Chances were that the wretch was dead. He was almost certainly dead. So Kelon had told himself over and over until, eventually, he had come to believe it.

The truth almost brought him to his knees.

There had never been anyone else for him – and for Aelwen, there had never been anyone but Taine. He was a fool. He should have known better. A crimson mist of anger boiled up from some dark place inside him – though he knew not whether he was more angry with Aelwen for not loving him, or with himself for his folly in loving a woman who would never return his love. Alil, sensing his mood as horses were wont to do, squealed out a strident challenge to the unknown black warhorse in the clearing. Aelwen tore her eyes from Taine's face, and saw Kelon.

He had been watching her for so many years now that he recognised every emotion that chased across those expressive lips and wide, green eyes. Surprise; delight at seeing him safe; dismay that he should have the joy of their reunion tarnished. But the pity was by far the worst – and in that instant, Kelon knew he could not stay, could not bear to watch them happy together, hour after hour, day after day. Every time he looked at Aelwen, worked with her, spoke with her, it would be plain that she felt sorry for him. Even their friendship could no longer exist now, for with the sudden appearance of Taine, everything had changed.

Better to go, and keep his pride. It was all he had left.

Aelwen, who had recovered her equilibrium, hastened towards him, her hand outstretched. 'Kelon, thank providence you're safe. It's good to see you, my friend.'

'I can no longer be just your friend.' Coldly, Kelon knocked the proffered hand away.

Hurt and anger flashed in her eyes, tightened her mouth. 'I never led you to believe you could be otherwise.'

Despite all his rancour, how could he deny it? And seeing her standing there, her eyes stormy with distress, how could he hate her? 'I know.' He sighed. 'I know. You can't help who you love, any more than I can.' Then he glanced across at Taine, who was watching the exchange, wary and alert as some forest animal whose mate is threatened. Kelon had no trouble hating *him*.

His mouth thinned to a bitter line as the future seemed to unroll before him: sooner or later there would be words exchanged between himself and Taine, then blows – there was a chance that one of them would die. And he still would not have Aelwen's heart.

'I can't stay.' The words were out of his mouth almost before he realised what he was saying.

'Here.' He thrust the leading rein of the packhorse into her hands, then, not without a dreadful pang, he gave her Alil's reins. 'I can't take them with me. The ferals eat horses. You're better able to protect them. You seem to have found yourself among friends.' He could not keep the sneer out of his voice. 'I'll take the provisions, if that's all right. I'm sure these folk have more.'

A frown darkened Aelwen's face, and her eyes grew hard as flint. 'Curse it, Kelon, don't be stupid. I don't care if you're angry, or upset, or disappointed, you can't go marching off alone into the wildwood. You'll die.' She gripped his shoulders. 'There'll be someone else in time. Someone who's meant for you. But that can't happen if you get yourself killed.'

He twisted out of her grasp. 'There was never anyone else for you.'

'Kelon, stay, please,' Aelwen begged. 'It's too risky out there. What about the Phaerie?'

'I don't have to worry about Ferimon at least.' He shrugged. 'I killed him.'

'What? Kelon, wait.'

But he turned and walked away, grateful when the trees swallowed him in their shadows and hid her from sight.

Sorrowing, Kelon walked, neither knowing nor caring where he went. Climbing the steep bank, he came to the trail and crossed it, heading north-west. With his eyes fixed on the ground, he walked in a black haze of loneliness, misery and self-pity, his thoughts whirling with images of Aelwen in Taine's arms; the incandescent joy on their faces; the aura of absolute unity that surrounded them. And himself, standing on the sidelines, alone and ignored.

'Watch where you're going!' Kelon jumped, his heart hammering, and heard the sound of a soft female laugh. There in front of him was Danel, the leader of the ferals.

Kelon swore, his temper snapping. Her laughter was one humiliation too many, and he rounded on her savagely. 'What the bloody blazes do you think you're doing?'

She shrugged. 'When you left, I thought I would stalk you in case that spell you were following got you killed.'

'Then you could loot my gear and take the horses after all.'

She shrugged. 'Well, *you* wouldn't have been using them.'

He looked at her coldly. 'I'm sorry my survival has proved such a disappointment.'

'*We* gamble on our survival every day.' Danel threw up her hands in exasperation. 'Will we find food? Will the shelters hold up to the weather? Can we stay warm enough and keep our bellies full enough to live to see another sunrise? Or will the Hunt come in the night and lay waste to everything we've become?' Her voice sharpened with a harsh edge of bitterness. 'We do what we must – and sometimes that's not enough.'

For a moment the jaunty courage left her stance, and she looked weary and beaten and sad. For the first time, Kelon looked at her closely and realised how thin she was: how pale, hollow-cheeked and pinched with the cold. The ragged clothes she was wearing must offer little protection from the elements. In that instant, his heart went out to her. She seemed so young for her responsibilities. She put his own troubles in perspective, he realised. Shame flooded over him as he contrasted her courage in the face of such appalling difficulties with his own self-pity over nothing more than a broken heart. The Phaerie viewed ferals as nothing but vermin, a dangerous nuisance to be exterminated wherever possible. He had never truly understood that they were people too, with the same feelings and physical needs as their masters.

'Let me join you.' The words sprang unbidden from his lips.

Danel cocked her head, put her hands on her hips. 'And why would I be wanting another hungry mouth to feed?'

'Because I can be a help to you, not a burden. My human grandfather, my mother's father, was a forester. He taught me how to set snares, how to track and to hunt with a bow, how to butcher my kill and prepare the hides. Thanks to him, I also know how to catch fish and find dry firewood, and how to build a shelter in the open.'

Though less than an hour before, Kelon had been convinced that he would never smile again, he somehow found a smile for Danel. 'So you see how useful I could be, if you'll have me?'

The feral girl's tired eyes brightened. 'Everyone in our band was an escapee from the city. When we fled out here, none of us knew a damn thing about surviving in the wilds. All these years, we've been scraping by as best we could.'

Kelon remembered from several years ago the mass escape of slaves that had so angered Hellorin. Though a search had been made for them, using the Hunt, they had scattered far and wide into the depths of the forest. A goodly number had fallen prey to the Phaerie hunters – Hellorin had decreed that none of the troublemakers were to be brought back alive, no matter how great the inconvenience and expense to their former owners in Eliorand – but apparently, some had managed to keep both their freedom and their lives.

'I think that what you've done is admirable,' he told Danel. 'Truly, I would be honoured to be part of your group, and glad to help you in any way I can. Eliorand holds nothing for me any more. Even if you won't accept me, I won't be going back. I'm finished with the Phaerie for good.'

'Well, why didn't you say so in the first place? Join us and welcome, Kelon.' She offered him her rough, nicked, dirty little hand, and he clasped it in his own.

'Follow me. I'll take you back to the others. We're following the instructions of someone who wasn't there, and heading for a place that doesn't exist.'

'What?'

'I'll explain on the way – though in all honesty, I don't expect you'll believe me.' With that, Danel slipped away through the trees, a shadow among shadows, forcing Kelon to hurry after her in order to keep her in sight. From over her shoulder, her voice came floating back to him. 'I wish you'd hung on to the horses, though.'

Back in the clearing, Aelwen, swearing bitterly, began to hurry after Kelon, but was restrained by a hand on her arm. She swung round. 'Taine, I can't just let—' But to her surprise, she looked into Athina's face.

'Take comfort, Aelwen.' The Cailleach's silver eyes turned as huge, sharp and gold as those of a bird of prey, gazed far into the distance, as though her vision could pierce the intervening trees – and not only the trees, but the veils that hid the future. 'Kelon must walk his own path now, but do not fear. He will be as safe as any of you in these troubled times, and he will not be alone, or friendless, for I brought him hither to encounter some new companions, and to these he will go now.'

She took Aelwen's hands. 'Do not fret for him. It is better so. It would not be good for either of you to remain together now. You both need to be heart-whole: you to walk the ways of the future alongside the one you lost long years ago, and Kelon to live for himself and forge his own fate, instead of ever walking in your shadow. All will be well, child. All will be well.'

'How can you possibly claim to know these things?' the Horsemistress demanded.

Athina reached into thin air and brought out another red globe, tossing it carelessly to hover beside the others that had led Aelwen and Kelon to her. 'I know them. And I brought you here, as I was explaining to the others before you arrived, because this group, all of you, will greatly influence the fate and survival of the world that we know.'

'But—'

'Enough. I want you all to come with me to my tower now. It is safe there, and we can deal with all the explanations, and plan our next move in comfort and safety.'

'But—' said Iriana.

'Yes, I can use my power to move your injured friend without risk. Hopefully, I will be able to help him.'

'But—' said Corisand.

'Yes, of course there will be food and shelter for the horses.'

'But—' said Taine.

'Yes, you can trust me. Yes, it's not that far. Yes, it is concealed from the Phaerie Hunt.' By this time, the Cailleach's voice was beginning to hold an edge of irritation.

Iriana swallowed hard. 'Athina?'

'*Now what?* Oh, I see.' Her voice dropped from irritation to gentleness. 'Yes, my dear, of course we can tend to your fallen friends before we go.'

For Iriana this was a necessary task, but one fraught with deepest sorrow. Save for Avithan, the newly united companions clustered around Esmon's body. The Warrior had been moved from the trampled, blood-soaked mud of the clearing to a gently sloping bank, soft and green with cushioning moss and overhung with fern, that reached down to the edge of the pool. Iriana had cleansed his body as best she could, and the others had helped her array him in the spare clothing from his pack, which hid the wound in his chest. But his clothes could not conceal the gaping gash in his throat, and Aelwen, seeing Iriana's distress, went to her pack and took out the one treasure she had allowed herself to bring from Eliorand: a scarf of moonmoth silk, coloured by Phaerie magic in the shimmering hues of the rainbow. It had been a gift from Taine many years ago, before they were parted, and had absorbed many of her tears during the lonely years of their separation. When he saw what she carried, their eyes met in a lingering, secret look, and he nodded almost imperceptibly. Aelwen gave the scarf to Iriana.

'But I can't take this,' the Wizard protested. 'It's a treasure of yours, I can see that.'

'Don't worry about it,' Aelwen told her gently. 'During all the time that Taine and I were parted, this was always a token of hope to me, that one day he would come back and our life together would be renewed. Now that he has returned,' – she glanced at Taine, her heart in her eyes – 'I have no need of such keepsakes. Let it stand instead for Esmon, as a symbol that one day he too will return, to another, happier life.'

'Thank you, Aelwen.' Iriana arranged the scarf around Esmon's neck, hiding all evidence of the dreadful wound. Then, with a glimmer of tears in her eyes, she turned and took the limp body of Seyka, and laid it on Esmon's breast. At least the owl would not be alone. Melik, still a little weak and nervy, but determined to fulfil his usual task as Iriana's eyes, touched his nose once to the owl's wing as if making his own farewell. Iriana stroked the cloud-soft feathers one last time and clasped Esmon's cold hand in parting.

'Stand back,' she told the others softly. Lifting her staff to help her concentrate her power, she reached inside and found the hottest fire she could conjure. With a soft word she loosed the fierce energy. The bodies of the fallen vanished in a single flash of incandescent flame, and when the dazzle faded from the eyes of the watchers there was only a drift of soft ash, already blowing across the surface of the pool like a grey, translucent veil. Thus passed Esmon, consummate Wizard and dauntless Warrior; leader, mentor and friend. Thus passed Seyka, windchild, spirit of dusk and dawn; with courage and heart too great for one so small. Long would her winged ghost whisper on the winds of Iriana's memory.

When the last of the ashes had blown away, Athina raised her hands and a shimmering silver mist rose up from the ground, enveloping the reunited companions, the horses, the entire campsite. When it dissipated, the clearing which had been the home of both tragedy and joy was empty once more.

33
~

TO SAVE A WORLD, TO SAVE A LIFE

Avithan lay on Dael's bed, looking like the corpse he had so nearly become, the gashes of his horrific wounds standing out livid on his body, and his skin appearing bloodless and translucent under the silvery sheen of the time spell. The Cailleach looked down on him, with Iriana standing at her side. Melik was in his favourite place, slung like a heavy fur collar around the Wizard's shoulders, lending her his sight.

The girl remained composed, her face betraying none of the anxiety she must be feeling. Athina could see, however, that the cat, so deeply attuned to his lifelong companion, could sense the feelings that she concealed so well. His eyes were wild, his ears were flattened, and the tip of his tail beat a restless tattoo against her shoulder. *He's on guard*, Athina thought. *He's ready to protect her against whatever is causing her so much distress.*

I wish I could do the same.

Having received a glimpse of Athina's abilities when the Cailleach had brought them here, Iriana had been confident that this uncanny and powerful being would be able simply to wave a hand, and Avithan would spring to his feet, healed and restored. But she was doomed to disappointment.

Athina regretted bitterly that she was unable to help the girl. For the first time in an unimaginably long existence, she knew failure, and it filled her heart with fear. Her time in this world was running out fast, she knew. The strain of bringing the companions and their horses to her tower, following so closely on her similar transportation of Tiolani, had drained her power almost to the dregs. On their return, she had been forced to ask Dael to tend to the comforts of the new arrivals, instead of producing an instant hot meal out of thin air, as she had planned. It had cost her every shred of strength and control that she possessed to hold herself upright long enough to instruct him and welcome her guests, and she had barely been able to get back to her own upper chamber before collapsing with exhaustion. Dael had brought her food to restore her energies, but she had been forced to waste several precious hours resting while she recovered.

Food and sleep however, had restored her energies – up to a point. With Dael's help, she had prepared a camp some distance around the lakeside for the ferals who would soon be arriving, and removed the glamourie from the island in the lake so that, for the first time since its creation, her tower would be visible to approaching strangers. But she knew all too well now that Uriel had been telling the truth. Each time she used her powers here she lost part of them, and the greater the effort she expended – as in transporting all those people and animals to her tower – the greater would be her loss.

Pulling her thoughts back to the business at hand, she turned to the waiting Wizard. 'I'm so sorry, Iriana. There is nothing I can do for him at this time.'

Iriana swung towards her, anger in every line of her body and her lovely face. 'What do you mean, there's nothing you can do? I've seen what you can do, damn it. I've heard you bragging about how powerful you are; how you came here to change the future for us poor, primitive beings. Well, change this, you bitch.' She seized the Cailleach's shoulders and began to shake her. 'Change *this*.' Now that her iron control had finally snapped, her grief was pitiful to see.

'Iriana.' Gently, Athina caught hold of the Wizard's wrists and pulled her hands away. 'Iriana, I have to tell you something that will be very difficult for you to hear.'

Leading the girl to the broad window seat, she sat them both down. There was no easy way to do this. 'There are two reasons why I cannot help your Avithan in the here and now.' Quickly she explained that she should not have been in this world at all, then gave a brief account of Uriel's visit, his dire warnings and the way they were beginning to come true with terrifying rapidity.

'So you see,' she finished, 'I will barely have enough power to help you and your companions accomplish what you must. Healing Avithan would be a long, arduous and difficult task. Even if I survived it, it would be the final drain on my powers, one from which I could not recover. I would perish here, in this world I came to save, and with the death of an Immortal, the entire Universe, in this reality and others, would be thrown out of balance.'

Iriana remained silent for a moment, her face averted, then she turned back to the Cailleach. 'But why? I don't understand this. Even if your powers are so drained, it would only take a little – just a little – to preserve Avithan's life. If you could only heal him enough to keep him from dying, our own Healers could carry on from there.'

This was the part Athina had dreaded most. 'Iriana, I cannot. I'm afraid that the problem is the time spell you and Taine concocted.' She gripped the girl's hands tightly. 'My dear, you must remember that you had no choice. In no way is this your fault. If the two of you had not wrought your spell, Avithan would already be dead, and immolated on that funeral pyre along with Esmon and Seyka. You did the only thing you could to save his life. But neither of you had performed that spell before, especially not on a living body, and the twining of Wizard and Phaeric powers has resulted in a tangle of magic that will take huge amounts of time and effort to unravel – if it can be done at all.'

The tears that began to fall from Iriana's sightless eyes were like a knife in Athina's heart. 'Listen now.' She put all her powers of compulsion into her voice. 'Listen to me carefully. All is not lost. There remains one thing that we can do. When I return to my home beneath the Timeless Lake, I can take Avithan with me. There, where time holds no sway, I will be able to deal with the spells that surround him. Once my powers have restored themselves, I can heal his wounds and make him whole again. But ...' – she lifted a warning hand as she saw the Wizard's face light up with hope – 'I must tell you now that there is no guarantee that I will be able to return your companion to you. My brethren have forbidden me any more direct contact with this world. Once I am safely home, it is almost certain that they will act in concert to block any routes back here, lest I should be tempted to meddle again.'

The joy on Iriana's face froze into a rictus of horror. 'Never?' she said in a small voice. 'Avithan will never come back – ever?'

'I'm sorry, my dear, but I must be truthful, no matter how much it may hurt. There is very little chance that Avithan will be able to return, though I will do my utmost to send him back. But now you, who love him, must make this decision for him, and for his parents. You know him best, Iriana. Would he want to be saved, and live in exile for all eternity? Or would he rather remain here, hovering between two worlds, neither alive nor dead? For I warn you, if I cannot undo the spell, then no one among the Wizards or the Phaerie will be able to do so.'

Iriana was utterly still. Even her tears had stopped falling. 'Will you let me be alone with him for a while?' Her voice seemed to come from very far away.

'Of course.' The Cailleach got to her feet. 'When you're ready, come downstairs and join the rest of us in the kitchen.'

Iriana waited for the sound of the door closing, then walked slowly over to Avithan, looking with Melik's vision at that dear, still face, and wondering what to do. If Athina was wrong, and the Wizardly Healers could save him, then she would be condemning him to an eternal exile for nothing. Yet if she kept him in this world and no one could break the spell, she would have cost him his only chance of life.

Lying there, he was as white and still as a statue carved from alabaster. Was there any spark of consciousness remaining within the prison of the spell? Iriana knew that thoughts seemed to have little connection to time. Could they still exist if time did not? Was Avithan's mind aware of what was going on around him but unable to reach out and communicate? Iriana shuddered. The notion filled her with horror. If she kept Avithan in this world, would she be condemning him to such a fate?

If she were in that position, she would rather be dead.

If only there was some way to reach his parents. She dreaded to think what Cyran and – perish the thought – Sharalind would say when they found out what had happened. She was willing to wager that they, at least, would want to try to save Avithan with Wizardly magic. They had not encountered the Cailleach, or witnessed her powers, nor heard the ring of sincerity in her voice and seen the truth behind her eyes. They would want Iriana to bring their son home to them.

Knowing this, wasn't her decision straightforward? Surely the matter was out of her hands? She only had to get her companion back to Tyrineld – no simple task in itself – and pass the responsibility to the Archwizard and his soulmate. But the thought that somewhere, somehow, Avithan's consciousness might be surviving, trapped and helpless, haunted her. When Athina said that the Wizards and Phaerie lacked the knowledge and power to free him, Iriana believed her. Her head told her to take the easy path, and hand Avithan over to his family as soon as possible. Her heart and gut said otherwise.

Athina had said that she would do her best to return him, and the Wizard trusted her word. Though she would be taking a terrible gamble, and risking Cyran's wrath when he found out, she was sure that Avithan's best chance lay beneath the Timeless Lake.

Iriana laid a hand on his cheek, but felt nothing but the cool, numbing tingle of the time spell. 'Oh, my love,' she murmured. 'I've got to take the risk. I only hope you'll understand.'

Straightening her shoulders, she took a deep breath. For better or worse, her decision was made.

Outside, beyond the tower, the ferals were arriving: hungry and footsore and, in the case of most of them, far from happy to be there. Looking at the lake, Danel was shocked and unnerved by the changes that had been wrought there. An island had suddenly appeared where none had existed before, lush with trees and mature, fruitful gardens. In their midst, a slender, elegant column of stone soared above the treetops, and a graceful bridge connected the island to the shore. The last time Danel had been here, about six months ago, there had been nothing like this; only the empty lake and the green, dark forest all around. Even if the island could have been constructed, even if such a perfect, finished structure as the tower could have been built in that time, where were the ugly scars that would stem from that work?

There was absolutely no disturbance to the land: no sign that both island and tower had not been there since the dawn of time. Danel shivered, and her feet felt rooted to the ground, unwilling and indeed unable to move any closer. She had fled into the forest in the first place to escape from magic and those who wielded it, and now all her instincts warned her that she was walking into a trap.

Yet it had been her own decision to come here: she had persuaded and browbeaten her followers very much against their wills. How could she retreat now? Run away into the forest with her tail between her legs? If she did, she knew that she would lose respect and authority that might never be regained.

Besides, her pride would not allow her to back down.

Curiosity had brought her here – that, and the desperate hope of somehow gaining an advantage for her people. Now she had put her leadership in jeopardy.

Beside her, Kelon stirred uneasily, plainly as reluctant as herself to be there. Suspecting that Taine and Aelwen had been brought here by the mysterious old woman, he had initially refused to come, but eventually Danel had persuaded him that if Athina was plotting something, it was important that the ferals know about it. Though, by his own admission, his powers of magic were slight, she felt a little safer having him along.

The restless fidgeting and muttering that had broken out among her followers jerked Danel out of her ruminations. 'Well,' she heard Evnas say, 'are we going on, or back? Or shall we just stand here until we grow roots?' He was spared the angry reply she was about to spit at him by the emergence of their host, Athina, or the Cailleach as she had also called herself, who emerged from the doorway of the tower and approached them.

She smiled at Danel and Kelon. 'My friends, I bid you all be very welcome here. Though you would be too many for my tower, I have arranged a place for you to stay a little way westwards along the shore. Follow me, and I will show you.'

Danel had to admit that the campsite was very pleasant. A little way back from the water, a stand of young aspens had apparently been persuaded to bend and weave themselves into some half-dozen domed shelters, all roofed by living creeper and vine. Within, the floors were piled high with fragrant bracken, and soft, warm blankets were stacked neatly at the rear. Outside, a cheerful fire blazed, and grouped around it were a whole series of pots and dishes that steamed gently, giving off a savoury smell. Bread and cheese, apples and sweet pastries lay nearby on sparkling platters, and Danel could see that there was more than enough for everyone.

'Rest, eat, refresh yourselves,' the Cailleach said. 'You will find soap and drying cloths within the shelters also, and clean, warm clothing. There are a number of things that must be said and done before the council can begin, but you will be called when it is time. Meanwhile, be at your ease. My magic guards this place, and nothing can harm you here.'

With that, she was gone. The ferals made a rush for the food, and all the grumblings and doubts changed into the clatter of spoon on plate, and muted murmurs of appreciation. Only Danel and Kelon ignored the feast. Both of them were staring at the tower. Seeing the scowl on Kelon's face, Danel guessed that he was thinking about the one he had loved and lost, but her own anger stemmed from a different source. 'Typical,' she muttered. 'The others, you'll notice – all those bloody Wizards and Phaerie – are staying in the tower. But that's too good for the humans. Will there ever come a time when we'll be treated as equals?' She scowled. 'That Cailleach might fool these others,' – she gestured behind her at her followers – 'but I have a feeling that when it comes to using us, she'll be no better than any of the magic-wielders. Well, let me tell you something, Kelon. I won't have us turned into someone else's pawn. If she's expecting us just to roll over for her for the price of a hot meal, then she's in for a surprise.'

After she had left the ferals, Athina talked at length with Corisand, who was resting beneath the trees. The mud had been washed from her legs, the snarls and twigs combed from her mane and her skin was tingling from the thorough rub down and brushing Aelwen had given her. She had enjoyed a hot meal – a warm mash – and was looking a great deal better. The Cailleach spoke to her at length, hearing how she became Windeye, her experiences in the Elsewhere and, most important of all, the history of the Fialan. At Corisand's revelations, Athina felt a thrill of hope and excitement rush through her. No wonder the Windeye of the Xandim would have such an important part to play in the days to come!

Leaving her to rest, Athina went in search of Dael. Before she spoke to the others, she knew that she must no longer put off the thing she had been dreading most. At this point, he did not know that she must return to her own realm, leaving him here, alone and bereft. As soon as Uriel had departed, she had left to find the others in the forest, and when she had returned, exhaustion had claimed her – but not before she had come to a decision.

There was no way that she could leave Dael without a proper farewell, to mourn her as dead. She loved him too much for that. Hard as it would be for both of them, he deserved to know the truth and now, before she began her discussions with her guests, she must tell him. Knowing that he would be avoiding the Phaerie and the Wizards as much as possible, not to mention the feral visitors, she did not look for him inside the tower but rather walked around behind it to the edge of the lake. There, as she had expected, she found him, dangling a fishing line in the water and looking pensive and sad.

'Dael, I—'

'You've come to tell me you're leaving, haven't you?' He got to his feet, his eyes stormy, his expression hard. 'Well, you needn't trouble yourself. I overheard you talking to Iriana. I already know, Athina. I already know – unless you've come to tell me it isn't true, and that you've decided to stay here after all.'

This was worse than she could possibly have imagined. 'Dael, I cannot.'

On hearing her words, he gave a low cry, as if she had dealt him a mortal blow, then sank, ashen-faced, to the ground. Athina, her heart torn and bleeding, sat down beside him, but when she tried to take his hand, he snatched it away.

'You lied to me.' His voice was low and barely under control. 'You said I was like your son. I thought that meant we'd always be together. You gave me love, dignity, a place in the world and a future – and now you're taking them away again.' He turned and fixed his eyes on the silver, wind-whipped waters of the lake. 'I should have known it was too good to be true.'

The Cailleach, weeping now, fought to find her voice. 'In all the endless ages of my existence, I have dwelt beyond the worlds, beyond the boundaries of emotion. My only joy was the clean, pure pleasure of creation; my only sorrow that, once my worlds were complete, I had to release them to their fate. In coming here I broke the fundamental law of my kind – never to enter or interfere with a finished world. I never understood the reason for that law. I always thought it senseless – until now.

'When I came here, everything changed. I became intoxicated with the pleasures of sensation, the quickening of such feelings within me that I had never known before. Then you came along and assuaged a profound loneliness I had always felt, without even knowing I felt it. I loved, and let that love blind me to so many harsh realities. I knew that you were human. That your lifespan was finite and would pass, for me, in the blink of an eye. I knew that as a mortal, without magic, you could never be brought back with me to the Timeless Lake. Yet I could not bear to lose you, and so I began to deceive myself. I would work something out, I thought. Surely, with all my powers, there would be a way to make you immortal, or endow you with some kind of magic, so that you could return with me. No matter that it had never been done before; I was a Creator, was I not? And after all, there would be time enough.'

She shook her head, and sighed bitterly. 'I truly believed that there would be plenty of time. I, a Creator who should have known better, allowed myself to be blinded by love. I did not realise that descending to this lower world and working with its coarser forms of energy would sap my powers so quickly. It took a visit from my sibling to awaken me to the bitter truth. I now realise that the drain is accelerating with every moment. When I first came here, the loss was so insignificant: a mere trickle that I never even noticed. By the time I discovered my true peril, it was already far too late. So now I must return, while I can, or lose everything that I am.'

'So what you're saying is, you've been forced to make a choice,' Dael said harshly, 'and you've chosen your power and immortality over me. I suppose I can understand. I should have expected it all along, knowing the way my life has been so far – but I, too, let myself be blinded by love. Love.' He spat on the ground. 'I ought to know by now that love isn't for the likes of me.'

He turned to face her, his face streaked with tears. 'Lady, you have given me the happiest days of my life. You made me see that there was more to my existence than suffering, enslavement and pain. You gave me dignity and hope, as well as love. It was an inestimable gift. I should not be so churlish as to feel bitter because you have been forced to take it all back – but I do. I do.'

He took a deep breath, and clasped her hands in his own. 'I can only hope that in time, the bitterness and the sense of betrayal will fade away, leaving only the memories of the perfect happiness and love I've known in my time with you. One thing is certain, though. I'll never forget you. I'll never stop loving you. And I'll never cease to miss you, every single day of my life.' He got to his feet and began to walk away, and his voice floated back to her on the cold, empty breeze. 'Maybe we both should have known it was too good to last.'

Athina, Creator, powerful Immortal and the mother of worlds, put her face in her hands and sobbed. She realised that for the first time she was experiencing the negative aspects of these worldly emotions: sorrow and heartbreak; guilt and the pain of loss. How could the people of this mundane realm bear to live with such feelings? It was like being flayed alive. *Perhaps I don't belong here after all*, she thought. *It's time I went home.* She wiped the tears from her eyes and washed her face in the cool, clear waters of the lake. Then, with heavy steps, she made her way back to the tower.

When she left Avithan, Iriana decided that she just had to get away from everyone, if only for a little while. Though the last twenty-four hours had revealed a strength in her she had never suspected she possessed, her decision to let Avithan go had finally been one burden too many. Now she had lost everyone who had come on this ill-fated journey, Wizard and animal companions alike, with the exception of her beloved Melik. Just for a while, she told herself, she needed to let go and grieve. Then she could be strong again.

She snatched up her coat and went downstairs, peering into each room in turn. It became very clear that the tower was no good to her. Avithan was in the bedchamber belonging to Athina's young human companion, and the Cailleach herself might return to her own room at any time. On the next floor down, Aelwen and Taine were asleep on the hearthrug in front of the fire in the main living area, locked in one another's arms, and the other door was mysteriously locked. The kitchen was empty, but was too much of a thoroughfare: anyone might walk in there at any moment.

As Iriana left the tower, she heard a murmur of voices coming from behind the building. That accounted for Athina and Dael. Wanting to get away from the island, she slipped quietly across the bridge. To her right, a little way along the lakeside, she saw the feral camp, and the wind brought the sound of voices and the smell of food from that direction.

Iriana went left.

She walked around the curve of the lake until she found a pretty beach covered in tawny pebbles and screened by alders and a bank of arching

349

fern. Sitting down on the dry shingle with Melik beside her, she looked out over the silvery surface of the lake. From this position the tower was hidden, and she was glad of the privacy. As time crawled past, she sat there as if paralysed, her thoughts a whirl of images of those she'd lost, her emotions a hard, burning core within her that grew ever larger but could find no release.

I could have done more ...
I should have done more ...
Had I been a better fighter or a better Wizard ...
Surely there was some way I could have helped them ...

Feeling her attention slacken, Melik turned away from the water and began some hunting on his own account, nosing curiously among the ferns behind her, while the Wizard remained lost in her dark labyrinth of pain; unable to escape, berating herself for being weak and self-pitying, which only made matters worse.

She never heard the footsteps approaching behind her; knew nothing until a soft nose nudged her shoulder and a voice called her name in mindspeech. She leapt up in panic, suddenly realising that she had carelessly let Melik wander, and her view now consisted of nothing but a tangle of lush green undergrowth and a large, iridescent beetle trundling its way through the miniature jungle. Disorientated, she stumbled, only to fetch up against the soft, warm hide of a horse, which saved her from a fall.

'Dailika?' Her heart leapt.

'No, I'm sorry. It's me, Corisand.'

That sudden leap into hope, only to have her expectations dashed so quickly, was the final blow that cracked the core of emotion she'd been holding in so tightly. Iriana wept at last, sobbing into the velvet comfort of the Xandim's neck.

'You're mistaken, you know.' Corisand's gentle words came directly into her mind.

The Wizard took a deep breath, then another, and another, until she managed to get her tears under control. 'Mistaken? What do you mean?'

'I am the Windeye. I can see the burden of guilt you carry, dark and heavy, pressing down on you with a terrible weight and preventing you from moving through your grief. And you are mistaken, Iriana. Forgive me for prying into your thoughts, but I can also see what troubles you. There was nothing you could have done to help Esmon. On the contrary, he was the leader, and he was also on watch: it was his duty to keep the camp safe, and he failed you.'

'Yes, but—'

'And you could have done nothing to save your owl companion,' Corisand went on relentlessly. 'Your foe had such a power for evil in him – what could you have done? He gave you no chance whatsoever to intervene, so again – not your fault.'

'I could have—'

'Yes? What, exactly, could you have done?'

'If only I had awakened earlier—'

'If only your foe had never been loosed against you by Tiolani, or he had never been born, or you had never been born, or Seyka. Iriana, you cannot alter fate. If you start on "if only", you'll end up blaming yourself for everything that has gone wrong since the dawn of time. In trying to save Seyka, you might well have been killed instead, and then Avithan would most certainly have died.'

'But I didn't save Avithan,' Iriana said miserably. 'I only took him out of time, but Taine and I messed up the spell between us, and now Athina must take him back with her, to her home beyond our world. There is little chance that he will ever be able to return.'

'Had you not taken him out of time, he would most certainly be dead by now, in which case he would definitely be unable to return. You have given him a chance, Iriana, and under the circumstances, a fighting chance is all that any of us can ask for.'

'But I sacrificed poor Dailika in the process.'

'You had to think quickly, and use the only weapon you had to hand. Otherwise you and Avithan would both have been killed. As Windeye of the Xandim, I can sense horses from far off, and I do not believe your mare is dead. I am aware of an equine presence moving away, heading towards Tyrineld; still half-mad with terror, but beginning to calm. Instinct is driving her, and she is making her way home.'

'But there are so many dangers on the way. She might be attacked by wild animals or stolen—'

'Iriana,' Corisand said sternly, 'Dailika has as good a chance as the rest of us to make it home safely. You can ask no more.' She nuzzled into the Wizard's shoulder. 'My friend, all the guilt you are feeling comes down to one root cause: that you survived, intact, while your companions did not. And I believe we already know the reason for that. Athina has told us that we two are pivotal to the future of this world, and—'

'And Tiolani.'

'I do not count Tiolani,' Corisand said severely. 'She is far too un-dependable. When the Cailleach told me of her vision, she said that we would hold the fate of the world in our hands, *to doom or to save*. It may be that Hellorin's daughter will turn out to be our greatest adversary.'

Iriana, much to her own surprise, smiled. 'I notice that you put the two of us on the side of Good and Right.'

'But naturally.' Though the Windeye could not smile, her flash of humour touched Iriana's thoughts, and in that instant they both knew that they were friends. The burden of guilt eased slightly from the Wizard's mind, and she felt a little stronger. They talked on for a while, each telling the other the full tale of how and why they had come to this present moment. Iriana was particularly fascinated by Corisand's account of her journeys to the Elsewhere, and the history of the Fialan, which the Windeye must capture in order to regain her magic and free her people.

'Avithan wanted to create a powerful artefact that would defend us from the evil that both Cyran and Athina have foreseen,' the Wizard mused. 'Crystals are related to Earth magic, and one that could store the magic of many Wizards for one wielder to use might be the saving of us.'

The idea hit them both at the same time.

'Iriana, would you come—'

'Corisand, if Athina can send me through with you—'

'Yes!' they chorused in unison.

'Let's go and talk to Athina,' said Corisand. Iriana called Melik back to her shoulder, and they all moved off together. All her life, the Wizard had longed for adventure. Now, it seemed she might be headed for another world to seek the magic Stone on which the futures of two races could depend.

34
~

MATTERS OF TRUST

The Cailleach paused in the open doorway and looked into the kitchen. What a difference a few simple comforts had made to this strange collection of visitors, who were beginning to blossom under the influence of warm baths, clean garments and a good, hot meal. Now they were all gathered in the cosy room on the ground floor of her tower: Taine and Aelwen sat at the table, still holding hands, while Corisand was wedged into the narrow space between the table and the door.

There was no sign of Dael.

Iriana, sitting at the other side of the table feeding scraps of bacon to the cat on her lap, still looked exhausted, her face pale and taut with worry, black shadows under her eyes. Still, that was only to be expected. Her losses had been the greatest, and she had just been forced to make a terrible decision, the repercussions of which would affect many lives – particularly that of the one she loved.

There was no time for grieving, however. The Cailleach knew that she must leave very soon now, and before she did she must set a number of events in motion. Hiding her worries behind a smile, she called out a greeting to her guests and walked into the kitchen.

'No, stay where you are.' She waved them back to their seats as they all scrambled to their feet. The scepticism she had sensed in the forest seemed to have vanished since she had brought them here to her tower in the blink of an eye. This newfound respect, she noted wryly, did not prevent them all from starting to talk at once, however.

'Stop.' She held up a hand for silence. 'Let us proceed in an orderly fashion.' She sat down and poured herself a cup of fragrant taillin, sweetening it with honey. 'To begin with,' she said, 'I must tell you that I have another visitor here. Hellorin's daughter, Tiolani.'

'No!' Corisand stiffened in shock.

'Tiolani is here?' gasped Aelwen. 'How did you manage that?'

'The same way I brought you and your companions here, of course. I'm surprised that you need to ask,' Athina said dryly. 'When she fell, she was caught by some of her comrades in a net, but they were all slaughtered by ferals, save Tiolani herself. I rescued her from them – but before I could do so, Aelwen, she had her whole life shattered all over again ...'

Quickly, she told them what Tiolani had overheard when Kelon had encountered Ferimon. 'She must now learn to live with her errors, if she can. I think – I hope – she will be ready to atone, if you will all encourage her, and give her the chance. We need her, my friends – especially you, Corisand.' She had seen the Windeye's ears go back and her neck snake out at the mention of the Forest Lord's daughter.

'Then that is unfortunate, for she certainly will not help me. And why should she, when I did my very best to kill her?' Corisand replied. They all could hear her mindspeech now, since the Cailleach had made certain minor adjustments to allow communication to take place.

'You forget that Tiolani has also killed,' Athina said gently. 'She is aware that she must atone, but she does not know how.' She turned to the Horsemistress. 'Aelwen, you must explain to her that the only way she can redeem herself is to throw in her lot with us, and help save the world from disaster.'

'What, *me*?' Aelwen gasped. 'But the last time we spoke she was threatening my life, too.'

'She was grieving and confused; trammelled in a web of lies, deception and plots wrought by the very one she loved and trusted most. Now she has nothing. If you approach her in the right way she will turn back to you, of that I am certain. She needs comfort and understanding now, but also—' The Cailleach's voice turned stern, and a look as implacable as stone came into her eyes. 'You must impress upon her that her only route to hope and redemption lies with us. It is up to you now, Aelwen. We are all depending on you to bring Tiolani back to us, no matter what your own doubts and feelings may be. Go now. She is in the study. Bring her back to us, for all our sakes; her own not least.'

'I'll try,' the Horsemistress said. 'For her mother's sake, I'll try, but—'

'Don't try. Do. Though you may never forgive her deeds, you must find it in your heart to forgive the deceived, confused and grieving child who perpetrated them. That applies to all of you.' Athina's gaze rested on each of them, one by one, and lingered on Corisand. 'Tiolani has not been in her right mind these last few months. It is our task to bring her world back into balance. We must. Whatever she has done in the past, we need her now.'

Aelwen nodded acquiescence, but her eyes were haunted. Without another word she rose, and went upstairs.

Tiolani was walking in the Magic Bazaar, her favourite marketplace in Eliorand. It was a perfect northern summer's day, the sky a bright, translucent blue and the sun high and strong. A heady medley of scents from forest and garden drifted on the breeze, as the entirety of nature strove to make the most of this short growing season.

The clear northern light was like crystal laced with jewels, throwing dazzling hues into objects that had looked so drab and dull in the dark days of winter. The Phaerie relaxed and opened up to one another, blooming like the flowers that cascaded from window boxes, trellises and balconies, and exploded from garden, pot and urn. The air was alive with laughter, talk and song, and in the Bazaar the traders were calling out the merits of their wares in lilting voices. And such wares there were!

Some bright stalls, with their billowing canopies of moonmoth silk, held all manner of paraphernalia for scrying and magical focus: great chunks of rough crystal contrasting with clear, polished spheres in a rainbow of colours; wands and intricately carved staffs, gleaming mirrors in all shapes and sizes, and gem-studded bowls of silver and gold. There were magical robes that changed colour as required, and kept the wearer warm or cool at need, and food that could change its texture and flavour to whatever the palate desired.

Tiolani was relieved and happy to be home. She'd awakened from a dark, dread nightmare, too horrifying to remember, but now she was home and safe, wandering through the delightful Bazaar with Arvain on one arm, and Ferimon on the other. Wanting to share her feelings, she turned to her lover. 'How wonderful home is. I don't think I ever really appreciated it before, but last night I had this hideous, appalling dream—'

'Did you? Did you really?' Ferimon turned to her – and changed. Instead of his beloved face, there was the head of a wolverine, one of the most vicious of all the forest predators. He snarled and bared lethal, pointed fangs. 'Stupid Tiolani. Gullible Tiolani. Your nightmares are only just beginning.' Suddenly he grew, shooting up into the sky until his gigantic form towered over the city. With a snarl he stooped, those fearsome jaws snapped, and Arvain was gone, devoured.

Tiolani screamed and tried to run, but she could not move a muscle. All she could do was look on in horror as Ferimon devoured the market, gnawed the buildings, consumed the shrieking, fleeing people. When he was done, Tiolani stood alone in a wasteland of tumbled ruins.

Ferimon looked down on her and laughed. 'Stupid Tiolani,' he repeated. 'Pathetic, gullible and naïve. You made me what I am. You gave me the permission, the power, the ability. Soon now, you'll lose everything – your father, your realm and your rule – and I'll be laughing from the grave.' He reached up and devoured the sun, and Tiolani was left alone and screaming in the darkness.

'Tiolani, Tiolani, wake up!' The sound of Aelwen's voice catapulted Tiolani out of one nightmare and into another. Details came at her in a flash. She was still tightly bound in the heavy net, though she was no longer in the forest, but lying on a couch in a room filled with racks of crystals, mirrors, books and scrolls. There was no sign of her captors – and what was Aelwen doing here?

'Don't struggle, child. You'll hurt yourself. You're safe. You're safe.' Only when Aelwen spoke again did Tiolani realise that she was still screaming. With an effort, she brought herself under control, but she could not stop shaking. Everything came flooding back as Aelwen began to cut away the net: her fall, her capture, Ferimon's death and the terrible, vicious, unbelievable words he'd uttered before he died.

The blood on her hands.

As the last of her bonds fell away, she flung herself into Aelwen's arms, sobbing. 'Oh, Aelwen, I'm sorry. I'm sorry.'

'It's all right, child; you're safe now. We'll put everything right, you'll see.' Aelwen held and rocked her, as she had done when Tiolani was a little girl, until the sobbing finally faded away. With scalding shame, the girl remembered the way she had treated the Horsemistress, even going so far as to threaten to kill her. She didn't deserve the sympathy and kindness that she had taken for granted her entire life.

After a few moments, Aelwen pulled gently away, her expression grave. 'Tiolani, we must talk. First, you should know that I'm aware of what happened in the forest between Kelon and Ferimon – and that you heard the truth at last. Now, let me tell you where you are, and what has been happening.'

There were so many revelations in Aelwen's narrative that Tiolani found it difficult to comprehend them all, but the most stunning to her was the notion that her father had trapped the Xandim, condemning them to serve the Phaerie all their days, and that Corisand could no longer be considered a mere beast.

How could this be true of her father? Had Hellorin really been so heartless and amoral as to strip another ancient magical race of its powers and its birthright? To destroy their civilisation and turn them into beasts of burden? But there was no denying it. She closed her eyes and shuddered. Had she not planned to rid the world of humankind for good? *Like father, like daughter*, she thought grimly. *Are we really so very different?*

Desperately she tried to find some excuse for her actions. *Humans don't count. They aren't civilised beings, aren't so advanced, have no magic. They're only one step above the beasts.* Her encounter with the ferals, however, had made her see things otherwise.

'Tiolani?' The firm voice of the Horsemistress penetrated the dark whirl of her thoughts. 'Tiolani? Now that you know the truth, will you come back to us? Will you help us?'

Tiolani blinked herself back to reality, and the face she had known since the day she was born. Something in Aelwen's eyes, a look of approval and pride, had changed; had gone, she knew, for ever. But even after everything that had happened, there was kindness, pity – and she hoped with all her heart maybe there was still some love. The sight undid her; shattered the remnants of her stupid pride, dissolved the last dark shadows of her hatred and planted, in their place, a kernel of hope. Was there really a way to atone for her terrible deeds, or wash the blood from her hands?

No. She knew in her heart that she could not undo what she had done, and never would. But atone? Maybe. She could hope for that.

'What do you want me to do?' she asked.

Aelwen, still holding her hands, looked at her gravely. 'I told you about Athina, and what she said. She has foreseen that our world is headed for destruction, and she came to prevent that, if she could. But she is losing her powers here and must return to her home, so the future will be our own responsibility after all. She foresaw three people pivotal to the outcome; three who, in the days to come, will hold the destiny of the world in their hands, to doom or to save. One is Iriana, a remarkable young Wizard whom you will meet; one is Corisand; and the other is—'

'The other is you?'

'No, child. It's you.'

Tiolani was stunned. This was worse than she could ever have imagined, and she quailed from the responsibility. 'How ... how can I possibly put an entire world to rights?' she quavered. 'Look what a mess I made of caring for my own realm.'

Aelwen's eyes burned into her own, such was the intensity of her stare. 'Don't be so spineless, Tiolani.' The words were like a slap. 'You can't afford to be a spoilt little girl any more, whining and wailing when things don't turn out the way you want them to. One thing is not your fault:

Hellorin overprotected and overindulged you. You never had a chance to grow and learn by making your own mistakes, so when you were suddenly catapulted out on your own, with so much power in your hands, your mistakes were catastrophic, and you will have to live with their consequences for the rest of your days.'

Her strong, horsewoman's fingers ground painfully into Tiolani's hand. 'However,' she went on, 'the past is done, and now you must put it away from you – not to forget it, never to forget the lessons you've learned – but so that you can seize the future. You used your power and authority to take innocent lives. Now, instead, you must save them. It's time to grow up, Tiolani. Take responsibility for your deeds, and move on. Don't let those whose lives you ended die in vain. Join us. Help us.'

For the first time since Ferimon's revelations, Tiolani knew hope.

'I will help you, Aelwen,' she said fervently. 'Tell me what I must do.'

Pride shone in the Horsemistress's eyes. 'Come downstairs,' she said. 'Meet the others and hear what they have to say. Then we can work out what we all must do.'

Athina looked around the table at the incongruous group that she had gathered together in her kitchen. Though it seemed a peculiar place to be discussing the fate of the world, she had decided that everyone would feel more relaxed in such homely surroundings – not that the idea seemed to be working so far. She could see that Dael, who had finally returned to the tower, was still angry and upset that she was leaving. Daniel and Kelon, who had also just arrived, distrusted the Wizards and Phaerie; everyone was suspicious of Tiolani; Iriana was still worried about Avithan; and Kelon looked as if he would like to murder Taine.

Well, putting things off wouldn't help. Athina took a deep breath, and began. First, to make sure that everyone had all the available information, she started from the beginning, with her visions of catastrophe and ruin, and her decision to enter this world. She then sketched brief histories of everyone present, ending with Corisand – which gave her a place to launch into the subject of the Fialan, the story of its creation, and its importance to the future of the Xandim. She was glad that Iriana seemed to have formed a close bond with Corisand. They had come to speak to her before this council, asking whether she could send them into the Elsewhere together, and she had been more than happy to agree. It would be a strain for her to send two rather than one, but she was willing to take the risk since she was sure that the Windeye stood a much greater chance of succeeding with the Wizard's help.

'Corisand and Iriana will be sent into the Elsewhere to seek this powerful Stone,' she went on, 'for it can, according to the Evanesar, be used to free the Xandim from their long slavery. Also, it must be prevented at all costs from falling into Hellorin's hands, for he is also in the Elsewhere and will certainly be plotting to retrieve it in order to return to this world. You must understand the danger here. When Hellorin originally formed the portal to bring the Phaerie here, he let a great deal of his power pass into the Stone. He will be looking to regain that lost magic – and that must not be permitted. The intrinsic magic of the Fialan is that it can store and amplify the powers of others – and everything it absorbs is locked within it forever. None of the energies it stores can ever be removed – but they can be utilised. Now—'

'Excuse me, Cailleach.' Aelwen held up a hand. 'What would happen to all the power if the Stone were to be destroyed?'

'You cannot destroy the Stone of Fate. The Fialan was created to absorb the powers of others. Because of the magic it already holds, there is no physical way to destroy it. It will protect itself if anyone tries. Lives – many lives – would be lost, and all for nothing.'

'And we cannot use magic to destroy it, can we?' Iriana asked. 'It would simply absorb everything we threw at it, becoming ever more powerful, better able to protect itself, and more dangerous.'

'Yes.' Athina was pleased with the Wizard's reply. This young blind girl, with her extraordinary mix of all four Magefolk powers, possessed the intelligence and common sense to use them wisely. For now she was still young and lacked confidence, but because of the current crisis, she was learning, developing and growing at an extraordinary rate. The Cailleach was certain that her name would be carved into history as an example and a beacon of hope to all future generations.

Suddenly aware that everyone was looking at her, waiting for her to continue, she gathered her straying thoughts. This tendency to distraction was getting worse all the time. It was as well that she'd be returning home soon.

'Iriana is exactly right,' she continued. 'She has grasped the paradox of the Fialan: the more magic you hurl at it, the stronger it becomes. She leaned forward, her hands on the table, and looked at them with compelling eyes. 'But over the ages, the Stone has absorbed enough power to develop a primitive consciousness. Since the Moldan is no fit guardian, I am hoping that the Fialan can be persuaded to pass willingly to either Iriana or to Corisand, but there is no way of knowing who it will choose, and only one of you will be able to wield it. Accordingly, it is vital that absolute trust exists between you. Whoever gains the Fialan must do everything in her power to use it to help the other. Whoever does not must accept the disappointment. The entire existence of the Stone has been marred by violence, jealousy and greed. That is all it knows. It will be up to you to teach it that there is another way.'

'The Evanesar told Corisand that it could be used to free her people, but how can that be done in practice?' Iriana asked.

'As I said, Hellorin let a great deal of his power pass into the Fialan when it was created. It is that power – the Old Magic, the Phaerie magic – that you must use to break the spell. I do not know how it can be done, but the wielder of the Stone must persuade it to release the Xandim.

'In the meantime, I suggest that you, Tiolani, return to Eliorand to take up the rule of your people once more, with Taine and Aelwen to assist you. It will be your task to support Corisand and Iriana in this world, by giving the Xandim over to them when they return.'

The Phaerie girl turned very pale. 'But ... but my father,' she stammered. 'If I let the Xandim go, he'll kill me.'

'Slay his only daughter? His only remaining child?' Athina said. 'Surely it would not come to that. But I was just coming to the fate of Hellorin.' Her expression turned granite-hard. 'The Phaerie, with their powers of the Old Magic, should never have come to this world. They do not belong here. They are a dangerous, unpredictable force, without conscience, without limits. Hellorin, who brought them here, is the worst example of his kind. His ways are the old ways, and in a sense, he has never truly understood the differences between this reality and the one from which he came. The Elsewhere has great magic of its own. It is able to withstand the strains that the powerful Old Magic can place upon its fabric. Not so this world. When I foresaw the chaos and destruction to come, it was the Phaerie I feared most, for they have the ability to wreak such destruction, and Hellorin has the will to use that ability.'

She paused and looked straight into Tiolani's eyes. 'Under a different ruler, a more understanding and enlightened ruler, the outcome might be otherwise.'

'Me?' Tiolani gasped. 'But that means—'

'That means leaving Hellorin exactly where he is, in the Elsewhere, and making absolutely certain he stays there.' The Cailleach's tone was flat, matter-of-fact and brutal. 'Corisand, Iriana, you must do whatever is necessary to prevent him from following you back. Tiolani, you must ensure that his corporeal form remains fettered by time spells. If he cannot return to his body, then he cannot endanger you here.'

'Exile my own father? Forever?'

'For your sake, it had better be forever,' Taine said harshly. 'Athina seems to think that Hellorin wouldn't kill his own child, but I know from bitter experience that there is no telling what he might do in a fit of rage.'

Aelwen hushed him with her hand on his arm. 'Tiolani, you must listen to Athina. I also find it hard – very hard – to consign the Forest Lord to such a fate. But what is the alternative? The Cailleach is not the only one who has received these premonitions. Iriana tells us that her Archwizard has also seen dread visions of bloodshed and catastrophe. Your father is proud and independent. He would never work with the Wizards and the other Magefolk to find a solution. Under the circumstances, I would be very surprised if he had not experienced similar warnings already, but rather than share the knowledge with the other magical races, I believe he would be plotting ways to take advantage of the coming upheaval.'

'And what about my people?' Corisand added. 'If he were here in this world, do you think he would allow the Xandim to escape his clutches? I agree with Athina. For all our sakes, he must be kept where he is.'

'Can you do it, Tiolani?' the Cailleach asked gently. 'Are you capable of exiling your own father? Because if you are not, you must be honest and tell us now, and we will think of another way; one that does not involve you.'

Tiolani's thoughts were racing. Here was a way to expiate her guilt, a way to help these strangers who had saved her life. A way to give herself another chance to rule the Phaerie, to make herself into a benign, enlightened ruler who would work alongside the Wizards and the Xandim to save the world from disaster. It wasn't as if she would be killing her father, after all. He would still be alive in the Elsewhere.

She must be brave.

She must be strong.

As painful as it was, she must sacrifice Hellorin to the greater good.

'I'll do it.' She lifted her head and her voice gathered strength. 'You can depend on me to do my part – you have my word on it.'

Athina nodded gravely. 'Thank you, Tiolani. Your courage and sacrifice will make all the difference to our success.'

'And what about us?' Danel's voice cut harshly across Athina's melodious tones. 'Now that you great folk have finished deciding everyone's fate between yourselves, what about the poor, ordinary humans? We've been enslaved down the ages too, but because we have no bloody magic, no one gives a damn about us.'

'The world is entering a time of upheaval and change,' the Cailleach replied, looking from face to face. 'This is something that you must all understand. And though we are doing everything in our power to forestall the cataclysm to come, I doubt that we can prevent it completely.

We cannot stop Fate – we can only work within its limitations and try to minimise the damage.'

She turned her attention to the leader of the humans. 'This new era will be your opportunity, Danel. You cannot conquer the magic-using races – you would be mad to try – but you can influence their attitude towards you by helping them in their time of crisis. In other words, this is the perfect opportunity to make yourself some powerful allies, and—'

'*Help* them?' Danel spat. 'I'd rather die.'

'Then die.' Athina shrugged. 'If that is your choice.'

With a sullen glare, Danel lapsed back into silence.

'There are already some independent humans in my realm,' Iriana said. 'The fisherfolk who live up and down the coast near Tyrineld. They started by chartering their boats from the fish merchants in the market-place. A tithe of the catch goes to the merchant, then the remainder is theirs to sell or trade. Now they are beginning to build their own boats, and working to become truly independent. If you'll leave the Phaerie realm and come to us, I'm sure there will be a place for you.'

'I can find a place for them in my own kingdom,' Tiolani snapped.

'Surely – at the end of a spear,' Kelon sneered.

'Enough.' Athina's voice cracked out like a whip. 'It reveals a great deal about the nature of humankind that when everyone else is making great sacrifices to assist this undertaking, you are only concerned with what we can do for you. The decision must be yours, Danel, whether the humans will be part of our company or no. If you think it better to return to grubbing for survival like wild beasts in the forest, constantly look-ing over your shoulders for the Wild Hunt, you can leave immediately. Your people have been well fed and clothed today, so you're ahead of the game. If, on the other hand, you decide to join us, we would expect you to pledge us your loyalty; but we would welcome you gladly, and do our best to render you all the aid we can.'

'Yes, you'll help us if it's to your own advantage,' Danel snarled. 'Where was your help when we were being hunted down by the Phaerie? Where were you in the winter, when we were dying from cold and hun-ger? Where were you when we were betrayed into doing the dirty work of a Phaerie traitor?'

She looked around the table, her eyes bright and fierce with contempt. 'No one helps the humans. As always, you just want to make use of us, for your own convenience. Well, you meddlesome crone, if what you say is true, and this period of chaos and disaster is upon us, there should be plenty of opportunities and rich pickings for us among you high-and-mighty folk with magic in your blood. I hope you'll all kill each other, you Wizards and bastard Phaerie, and when this world is well rid of you, the humans will grow fat upon your leavings, and rule the world at last.'

She got to her feet, pushing her chair back so violently that it overturned, and stormed out, with Kelon, his face pale with dismay, a step behind her. As he reached the door, Aelwen spoke. 'Kelon, please. You don't have to stay with her – with them. Come back to us, I beg you. There will always be a place for you in this company.'

He gave her a chilling look, so bitter, bleak and empty that Aelwen blanched. 'You're wrong,' he said. 'There's no place for me here. *He* took it.' With a last snarl at Taine, he was gone, and the slamming of the door reverberated through the silence he left in his wake.

'My, what a display of intelligence and courtesy we've seen in the last few minutes. It makes me proud to be human.' Everyone looked in surprise at Dael, who had been sitting so quietly throughout the discussion that most folk had forgotten he was there. He crossed the room to Athina, and took her hands. 'At least it made me see sense. I'm sorry I was angry with you earlier. That ignorant human and her Hemifae friend have made me realise that you aren't simply abandoning me without a thought: I can trust these people with my future.' He gestured around the table. 'The Lady Iriana spoke of the free fisherfolk of Tyrineld. Maybe, if she would take me, I could go there when ...' For a moment his voice failed him, and he swallowed hard. 'When you're gone.'

'Of course you can come with me,' Iriana said kindly. 'I was dreading the thought of trying to get home alone, and once we're there, I'm certain that the fisherfolk would welcome you.'

'Thank you, Iriana.' The Cailleach's voice rang with gratitude and relief. Rising to her feet, she took a deep breath. 'I think we have accomplished all we can by talking. Now the time has come for us to act.'

35

THE SEARCH BEYOND

Dawn was breaking when everyone gathered outside the tower to say their farewells. The ferals had decamped already and vanished into the forest. Tiolani, looking pale but resolute, was beside Aelwen, Taine and their mounts. The Horsemistress was mounted on Taryn, her black stallion, and Taine rode Kelon's Alil, while Tiolani had taken the Huntsman's pretty red and white mare. Iriana and Corisand waited together, the Wizard's eyes shining with excitement, while Dael stood wide-eyed at Athina's side.

'Are you ready to perform the flying magic?' the Cailleach asked Tiolani.

'I'm ready.'

'Then farewell, and go with our blessings.'

Iriana hugged Taine. 'Thank you for being such a support that dreadful night.'

He ruffled her hair. 'It was a pleasure, little sister. You helped me too, remember? Good luck to you in your travels, and I hope that one day we will meet again in Tyrineld.'

For the first time since they had been thrown together once more, Corisand addressed Tiolani directly. 'I'm doing my best to trust you, but it's mostly because Aelwen and Athina want me to. Don't prove them wrong.'

Tiolani glared at her. 'You'll never trust me, Corisand, any more than I trust you. I haven't forgotten that you tried to kill me.' With that she lifted her hands, and the pale shimmer of the flying magic curled around the three riders. The horses leapt skywards, then they were gone, vanishing into the clouds above.

Athina turned to Corisand. 'Was that really necessary?'

The Windeye put her ears back. 'It was to me – and I suspect it was to Tiolani. Now at least we both know where we stand. And speaking of standing, it's time Iriana and I were on our way.'

The Cailleach's silver-white hair glimmered like moonlight, and her eyes glowed with the piercing blue of Taku's glacier as she lifted her hands. 'Safe journey, my children, and may good fortune attend you.'

'And you,' Iriana said. 'Please – if you can somehow manage to heal Avithan, will you ... will you tell him I love him?'

'Of course I will. But I suspect he already knows.'

Blushing, Iriana thrust her staff into her belt and turned to Corisand. 'Are you ready?'

The Windeye of the Xandim inclined her beautiful, sculptured head. 'More ready than you'll ever know. Climb onto my back, my friend, and hold on tight.'

Corisand had refused a saddle and bridle, not knowing how they would translate to her alternative form, and now she felt a slight tingle of alien magic as the Wizard used the hint of an apport spell to boost herself up into place. Iriana was light and balanced on her back, but natural horsewoman though the Wizard was, Corisand could feel her tension, communicated through her legs and spine, and the tightly clenched hands that were knotted in her mane. It was understandable. It would be impossible for Melik to pass into the Elsewhere. Dael had promised to take the greatest care of him until Iriana returned, but the blind girl was being hurled into the unknown without any of her companion creatures to act as her eyes.

The Cailleach lifted her hands, and Corisand felt a thrill of immense power pass through her to Iriana, linking the three of them. The Windeye concentrated with all her might on that beautiful other place: the shores of the shimmering lake cradled in the forest's dark embrace, the soaring silver peaks all around. It was so easy, with such otherworldly power behind her. All she had to do was follow the deepest yearnings of her heart. The magical energy filled and filled her, until it was all she could do to contain all that force. Then suddenly there was that odd, sideways shift of reality. Athina, the chamber and the world were all gone.

Corisand went home.

And, in an echo of her first time, fell flat on her face. Her human form was not designed to take a rider on its back. Even as she and Iriana went sprawling, their fall cushioned by soft black moss, the Windeye felt her heart leap as her powers sprang to life within her. She was the first to get to her feet, and saw that she was once again in the area of luminescent amber mist that had been her initial gateway to the Elsewhere. She turned to find Iriana still sitting on the ground, tears streaming down her face.

'What's wrong?' Corisand knelt beside her. 'Have you hurt yourself?'

The Wizard turned a glowing face towards her. 'I can see you,' she whispered. 'For the first time in my life I can truly see.'

Corisand hugged her. 'Oh, Iriana, I'm so glad.'

Iriana wiped the tears away, and her voice steadied as she took a firm grip on her emotions. 'And you! I can't believe it. It *is* you, isn't it? Yes, of course it is,' she amended quickly. 'Somehow I recognise you, though I've never seen this form before.' She grinned, her eyes dancing with laughter. 'You look awfully vulnerable without clothes, though – particularly if you have to fight.'

Only then did the Windeye realise that Iriana was still wearing the travelling garb she had worn in the other world, whereas she herself was naked. Somehow, in the Elsewhere, she had never thought about clothes. Why should she? They had never previously been a part of her life, and in this enchanted place her magic provided any warmth and protection she might need. Nonetheless, she decided to humour Iriana's concerns. Joyously switching to her Othersight, she took a double handful of air and wove a garment of grey shadows that copied Iriana's tunic and breeches. It left her limbs free to move, yet covered her from head to toe. 'There,' she said. 'Is that better?'

Iriana's eyes were huge and round. 'That was Windeye magic? What was that beautiful silvery stuff you were manipulating?'

Now it was Corisand's turn to stare in astonishment. The vision the Wizard had gained was not the normal sight of her birth world, but was clearly very similar to her own Othersight. Did that mean Iriana could also—

Without warning, a bolt of fire struck down from above. Aurora, her great wings with their swirling colours outstretched across the sky, could clearly be identified through swirls of the fog. Diving forward, Iriana shoved a stunned Corisand aside just as another jet of flame shot from the glittering eyes of the eagle to tear a smoking scar in the shrivelled moss, just where they had been standing.

'Aurora, stop,' the Windeye yelled with both her physical and mental voice. 'It's me.'

The only reply was another sizzling zap of flame, close enough to singe their skin and crisp the ends of their hair. 'What's wrong with her?' Corisand panted. 'Taku would—' She was forced to throw herself aside once more as the next lance of fire came down.

'Split up,' Iriana shouted. 'Confuse it.'

'No, don't—' But Iriana had already shot away from the Windeye's side, zigzagging to avoid the incandescent bolts. 'Taku, help us, please.' Corisand jerked out the cry as another fiery missile came down inches away, its hot, concussive blast hurling her backwards. She rolled and scrambled to her feet, her head ringing. Iriana was a shadowy wraith, away in the mist to her right, and Corisand saw a further explosion of flame drive her further away. 'Don't lose sight of me,' she called. 'We'll never find each other again.'

Once more she cried out to Taku – and this time he answered. The spectral head of the great serpent appeared, eyes shimmering intensely blue through the mist. The relief that flooded Corisand curdled into disbelieving horror as a glittering spear of ice hit Iriana, piercing straight through her body. Instantly she was covered in a glistening frozen carapace, transfixed like a ghostly statue, her face contorted in a rictus of agony, her clouded eyes staring open as if beseeching the Windeye for help.

Not Taku! Corisand was stunned by such betrayal – then suddenly everything became clear. The attacker was not the Evanesar but Hellorin. He had ambushed her in the guise of her friends, even as she entered the Elsewhere.

Another fusillade of ice spears came hurtling down to form a glacial palisade that surrounded Windeye and Wizard. Corisand felt the cruel cold beating at her, felt the skin on her face tightening and her limbs growing numb, but the outward pain and peril seemed insignificant, overwhelmed by the colossal surge of anger boiling up within. 'We'll see about this,' she growled. Now that she knew her opponent, she could fight. Using her Othersight, she pulled in warm air from outside the chilling barrier of Hellorin's ice wall and fashioned it into a dome fused with adamantine will, to protect herself and her stricken friend. 'I know you now, slavemaster,' she cried out in challenge.

'Much good will it do you, beast-begotten interloper.' The Forest Lord's voice crashed like thunder against her ears. 'The Fialan is rightfully mine, and I *will* have it back.'

'Oh, will you?' Corisand muttered. Spinning her mirror of Othersight as Taku had taught her, she made a window through the fog and looked upon her foe as he really was.

The images of Taku and Aurora vanished. In their place stood Hellorin, taller than a tree, towering into the cloudy sky above, the crowning antlers a silver shadow above his brow. Quickly, the Windeye wove a net of air and shadow, hurling it at her foe with all her strength. As it flew through the air it expanded to cover the titanic figure, wrapping him in a clinging shroud, finer than cobweb, stronger than adamant. It covered him from head to foot, stifling his missiles of fire and ice.

Hellorin roared with rage as he struggled against his bonds, his face contorted from the strain and his eyes ablaze with hatred. Corisand threw herself into keeping the bonding taut, pitting all her magic against his power. She knew she had little time. Her strength was no match for that of the cunning, ancient Lord of the Forest. Each moment seemed to stretch into hours as she strove to contain him. Pain and exhaustion spasmed through every nerve and muscle, setting her entire body alight as her will was battered over and over by the thrust of Hellorin's mind. Soon it would crumble, she knew, like the walls of a fortress under siege – yet what could she do? He had forced her into a manoeuvre that was essentially defensive, and she dared not relax that defence for a single instant or her imprisoning spell would crumble and all would be lost. Her initial plan had been to keep tightening her net until the physical and psychic pain forced her enemy to flee, but she had overreached herself. Lacking the strength to overcome him entirely, she was now locked in a deadly stalemate from which she could not escape.

Hellorin knew it. A cruel laugh came from within the concealing web as he increased the pressure on her will still further. Corisand could only look on in horror as the meshes slowly began to fray and unravel, loosening their steely grip. He was almost free ...

Once the Windeye had bound Hellorin, he could no longer maintain Iriana's imprisoning carapace. As his concentration wavered and the ice that had held her so remorselessly shattered and fell away, Iriana saw Corisand locked in a desperate battle. Letting her powers sing free within her, she pitched into the fray. Suddenly the land itself rose up against the Phaerie Lord. The ground beneath his feet cracked and crumbled, breaking up into great boulders that she lifted into the air and hurled at him, hammering his tottering form. As she pulled the pressure of his fearsome concentration onto herself, she saw Corisand's net tighten once more, and increased her assault to keep him off balance. A veritable whirlwind of earth and loose stone, called up at her behest, surrounded him in a lethal fusillade.

Her face set with ire and determination, she clasped the end of her rough wooden staff in a white-knuckle grip and fixed her eyes on her foe with deadly concentration. Then she squared her shoulders, lifted the staff and brought the heel down hard upon the ground. The earth gaped open, a great, dark, jagged maw that engulfed the Forest Lord, and closed over him with an echoing boom.

As Hellorin's assault was banished, Corisand staggered from the recoil of her own magic. The remnants of her web tangled into a snarl of silvery filaments that melted back into the air. Iriana sagged against her staff, panting, as her storm of earth and boulders thudded to the ground.

The Windeye was looking at her, her eyes round with awe. 'Is he ... did you destroy him?'

'If only I could.' Iriana abandoned the unequal struggle and sat down abruptly. 'With luck, however, it should take him a good while to find his way out of my spell. I took him by surprise that time, Corisand. Once you bound him, his concentration was on you, and I managed to get loose from that dreadful freezing spell. He won't let it happen again.' She shuddered. 'Now that's an experience I don't want to repeat in a hurry. It bloody *hurt*.'

Even as they were speaking, the mist was starting to fade and clear. The last tatters swirled away to leave them on the beautiful shores of Taku's lake, mysterious in the soft evening light. Iriana gasped at the sight. 'It's amazing. A whole new perspective. All those extra colours ... I never guessed it would be so beautiful. No wonder you fell in love with this place, Corisand. You must—'

Out of nowhere, the Evanesar were suddenly there. Iriana's eyes narrowed. She leapt to her feet, staff in hand, and Corisand acted just in time to stop her flinging another spell at them. 'Wait, Iriana!' She seized the Wizard's hand. 'It's not Hellorin this time.'

Looking up at the towering figure of the great ice-serpent, she cried, 'Taku, we've been attacked. Hellorin nearly killed us.'

Where were you?

Though her accusing question remained unspoken aloud, it hung so palpably between them that it might have been written on the air in fire.

'The Forest Lord had help,' Taku told her gravely. 'We were attacked by the Moldan Aerillia, who prevented us from coming to your aid. You did well in battle.'

'Yes, I suppose you're feeling very pleased with yourself, Windeye.' The form of the massive eagle, its wings rippling with a flood of translucent colours, stretched across the sky. 'But who gave you permission to bring a stranger to this place?'

'And more to the point, *how* did you bring her here?' Taku added, his blue eyes glittering.

'I had some help.' Corisand tried to hide her dismay. She had never expected the Evanesar to be displeased by her autonomous actions. Her explanation of how the Cailleach had come to aid her, however, met with little approval.

'It is forbidden for a Creator to interfere in this place,' Aurora blazed.

'It's forbidden for her to interfere in the mundane world, too,' the

Windeye replied, 'and she knows there will be a price to pay. But she also knows how much is at stake. The various races of our world all stand poised upon the brink of disaster. If there is any way she can avert that, she feels that she must take the risk.'

Taku, always the more temperate of the pair, was more uneasy than angry. 'This intervention is unprecedented,' he said. 'The Elsewhere is an older place. We were here before the upstart Creator race; we remember when they came. I recall that we were concerned about the scope and depth of their powers, but Denali said, "Leave them be. Their work is in a different dimension from ours, and they do not try to interfere with us. These new worlds they like to build are but pale imitations of our own and, unlike the Moldai, who even now are negotiating to obtain some sort of foothold in one of the new realms, we have no wish to be involved. And think on this: it is well that they are a race of artisans, rather than warriors. These Creators are peaceful beings, and for that we must be profoundly thankful. Were such titanic powers as theirs to be turned to war and violence, the destruction would be incalculable. We must not risk pushing their thoughts in that direction by trying to prevent them from doing what they love. Let them be, I say. While they are preoccupied with their playthings, they can do no harm in the Elsewhere."'

He sighed. 'Nevertheless, I think the Cailleach may have sent you at the right time. Hellorin grows bold now. With the help of Aerillia he will take the Fialan, of that I am certain. Once he possesses it, he can conquer both worlds, with disastrous consequences for all of us. He must be stopped.'

Aurora's colours darkened. 'We cannot interfere, fixed as we are in the Elsewhere.' Her piercing gaze transfixed the Wizard and the Windeye. 'Only those with a foothold in both worlds can wield the Stone.'

'There is no time to waste,' Taku said. 'You must go now, with our blessing. You travelled to the ice mountain through your mirror, Windeye. You know the way.'

'But how will I ... Oh, of course.' Corisand, already in her Othersight, spun and twisted the winds to form her bridge of air. But this time, instead of heading for the glacier, it stretched in the opposite direction, towards the foot of the lake, down the seething falls and rapids as the land fell away to the coast, and eventually, to the sea.

She turned to see Iriana gazing at the shining construct, her eyes and mouth round with awe. 'Come on.' She held out a hand to the Wizard. 'It's perfectly safe.'

Iriana jolted out of her trance. 'You made ... You just–' she waved and twirled her hands in the air '–and there it was.' She shook herself as though emerging from deep water and turned to the Windeye, her face alight with a devilish grin. 'By the Light, but I absolutely *love* this place.' She took Corisand's hand and together they stepped out onto the bridge.

'No matter how much you love the Elsewhere,' Taku said in warning, 'never forget for a single instant what a perilous place it is. Enjoy the beauty by all means, but be on your guard at all times. You must be ready to defend yourselves, for Hellorin will most certainly attack again.'

Then Aurora spoke. 'You have confidence in your abilities, Windeye, to think you can construct a bridge that will carry you so far, but it is not necessary. You are still recovering from your battle with Hellorin, though your energies are regenerating very quickly due to the magic of this place. Nonetheless, why tax your powers when there is no need? I can take you a certain distance myself. The Moldai have their own realm here in the Elsewhere, and for one of my kind to cross its boundaries would be an act of open war. But you are small. You do not come from this world, and your powers will be unfamiliar. I hope you will be able to pass unnoticed where I cannot.'

'I did not pass unnoticed last time,' Corisand pointed out.

'So there's still a risk,' Iriana said bluntly. The innate temerity of her race could not help but come to the fore, as did the curiosity. 'What about the others of your race? Should there not be two more of you? Earth and Fire? Could they not help us? Where do they stand?'

Taku sighed. 'Alas, even the Evanesar are divided over this business of the Fialan. So far, the others have refused to become involved. Katmai quarrelled with me bitterly over the need to bring you here at all, and Denali remains isolated in her own domain, the Labyrinth of the Mists.' Love gentled his voice. 'I hope that one day you may see it. Oh, the beauty! The calm, shining ocean; the miles upon miles of convoluted cliffs and islands twisting and twining back upon one another to form bays and deep inlets; the thousands of slender waterfalls cascading down the escarpments in sprays of silver; the mists glowing softly with ever-changing rainbows. Denali, the oldest, the wisest of us all, withdrew there after the terrible events surrounding the Fialan's creation. War and discord are too painful for her gentle nature, and so she waits, lost in a waking dream, for the world to change again.'

For a long, sad moment there was silence, then Aurora broke the spell of Taku's words. 'Well, unlike Denali, at least we are making an effort to bring that change about. Come, little Windeye, little Wizard. Come with me, and I will take you where you need to go.'

Night had fallen. The form of the eagle melted back into the glimmering swathes of Aurora's many colours that stretched across the

371

star-scattered sky in streaming curtains of coruscating light; great looping, twisting ropes of rainbow hues that undulated across the firmament
like smoke. One of these streams of radiance swirled down to where
Corisand and Iriana stood upon the bridge of air, and coiled about them.
Strange buzzes, crackles and a sound like distant thunder reverberated
through them as they were lifted gently into the sky, and they could feel
the tides of energy and power surging through their bodies, linking them
to the Evanesar with bonds of magic.

With Taku's farewells ringing in their ears, they learned what it was
like to fly with Aurora.

As they looked down, the world was tinted with shifting, drifting shades:
red and purple, gold and green and blue. The lakes and mountains passed
beneath them, and they swooped down across the ocean, then turned
northward up the coast with its forested inlets, its clusters of tiny offshore
islands and the glaciers tracing glittering paths from the mountains to the
coast. And all around them, the colours of the world kept shimmering,
flowing, changing. They flew high upon wings of wonder over a land of
heart-wrenching beauty, the memory of which would remain bright and
precious to the ending of their days.

It seemed forever, yet somehow was only an instant, before they found
themselves drifting earthwards once again. In the distance, another range
of mountains descended like a barrier to the coast, and both of them
knew, without being told, that there lay their destination. Aurora set them
gently down, both of them breathless and bright-eyed with the wonder of
it all. 'Farewell,' she said. 'May good fortune attend you. Remember, the
futures of many races, not just your own, hang on what you will do next.'

With that she vanished. The sun lifted its head over the land, turning
the mountains to rose, the sea to burnished copper and the sky to gold.

'Well, thank you for that, Aurora,' Iriana grumbled. 'You've made me
feel *so* much better.'

Corisand smiled. 'We're an unlikely pair to be holding the fates of
entire races in our hands.'

'It's like the stories we used to read when we were children – the
unlikely heroine saves the world,' Iriana replied. 'There are times when I
can scarcely believe we're doing this – I keep thinking that I'll wake up in
my bed in Tyrineld, and everything will have been a dream.' She sighed.
'I only wish a lot of what happened *had* been a dream. Losing Esmon and
Avithan, not to mention my poor, dear animals. All my life I read those old
tales, looking through the eyes of one creature or another, and I longed
for all those amazing things to happen to me. But those stories didn't
say enough about the dark side of adventures: the conflict, privation and

loss. Or maybe they did, and I was so desperate for something exciting to happen in my life that I just wasn't paying enough attention.'

'Well, I don't know about any old stories,' Corisand said stoutly. 'In my childhood I was only a foal among other foals. When the dark things happen, I sometimes wish I had never become the Windeye, with the sheer crushing frustration and responsibility of it all. But then I think about all the wonders I have seen, such as our journey with Aurora; the incredible things I can do, and the friends I've made.' She squeezed Iriana's hand. 'Then I know I could never go back to the old way – and do you know what? Neither could you.'

The Wizard's shoulders straightened. 'In Tyrineld I was caged and thwarted; smothered by the loving care of well-meaning but misguided folk. And you're right. You're absolutely right. No matter what the cost, I couldn't go back to that either.' She took a deep breath. 'So – we'd better go forward.'

She looked at the rugged, rocky coastline stretching far ahead, with the wide river mouths, the tumbled boulders big as houses, the uprooted trees piled haphazardly along the waterline like a giant's game of jackstraws, the glaciers that dropped into the ocean as precipitous cliffs of solid ice, all the coves and firths that would double the distance they had to travel. 'My, but this is going to be interesting.'

Corisand shrugged. 'Well, we're not going to get there just by looking at it.' She strode forward. 'I had better cut myself a staff like yours and—'

'Wait, wait.' Iriana tugged at her arm. 'Maybe there's a better way.'

'What do you mean?'

'You remember how you made that bridge of air, back at the lake?' Iriana spoke quickly, her eyes sparkling with excitement. 'Well, what about building another one that will take us right up the coast, over all these obstacles?'

Corisand thought for a moment. 'There would probably have to be a series of smaller bridges – I don't think my power will stretch all that way in one go – but it should be possible. There's only one thing that worries me: what happens if Hellorin attacks again while we're on the bridge? We'd be fearfully exposed and vulnerable up there. And if he forces me to fight, or even just defend myself, it could shatter my concentration. The bridge will disintegrate and we'll both fall.'

'Plague on it,' Iriana said. 'It was such a *good* idea. But maybe … Wait a minute, let me think.' She turned and stood looking out to sea, while Corisand fidgeted impatiently, anxious to be gone.

Then: 'I know!' the Wizard shouted. She turned back, grinning with excitement and talking very fast. 'Why does it have to be a bridge at all? You could make a boat, couldn't you? I read in my studies at the Academy that the Old Magic cannot cross water, so we'd even be safe from Hellorin …' Her words ran down into silence as she saw the Windeye's face. 'What's wrong, Corisand? Why are you looking at me as if I've gone mad?'

'What's a boat?'

Iriana blinked. 'What do you mean, what's a boat? They float, on the water. They can be big or small and people travel on them. You must know—'

'I grew up as a horse, in a forest, in the mountains far inland,' the Windeye pointed out. 'How the bloody blazes am *I* supposed to know what a boat is?'

The Wizard burst out laughing. 'I never thought of that,' she confessed. 'It already feels as if I've known you forever. It seems incredible that our backgrounds should be so different – and yet before we came here to the Elsewhere, I only knew you in the form of a horse.'

'Trust me – my background is different from anyone you'll ever meet.' Corisand joined in the laughter. 'Now, suppose you explain to me exactly what this boat thing is?'

It took them a while to work it out between them. Iriana, concentrating hard, put the image of a little single-masted sailing boat into the Windeye's mind, and Corisand worked and manipulated the fresh sea breeze to duplicate the design. When it was done, it looked beautiful, glistening like spun silver and riding lightly on the water like a swan.

Nevertheless … 'It's just as well the thing is made from air and magic, and not real wood,' the Wizard said, surveying it critically, 'or it would never float.'

'So long as my magic holds it together, it should be all right.' Corisand sounded doubtful. 'Maybe we'd better try to keep close to the shore, just in case.'

'Good plan. Well, shall we?' Iriana bowed and gestured to the Windeye. 'After you.'

'No, after *you*.'

'Let's go together.'

36
~

ON A KNIFE EDGE

From the air, in the strong noon sunlight, the graceful, soaring towers of Eliorand glittered like a cresting wave that poured down the face of the steep hillside. Notwithstanding the beauty, Aelwen viewed the sight with mixed feelings. Three nights before, when she and Kelon had made their desperate bid to escape, she had never expected to see the city again. On the one hand, it lifted her heart to return to her birthplace, her home and her beloved horses. On the other, she was sick with trepidation. Having finally made the difficult decision to leave, it felt like a mistake to be returning. Everything was different now. Her entire life had been a lie.

She had lain sleepless at Taine's side throughout the previous night. It saddened her that Kelon, who had been her friend for so many years, had parted from her on such bad terms, but that choice had been his to make. Worse was the sick feeling inside her, because now that she knew the Xandim were not mere beasts after all, it cast her own life in a very different light. All the while she had been thinking of herself as their caretaker and nurturer, she had been nothing but a gaoler.

It shook her life right down to the foundations.

The shining city below concealed so many shadows: rivalry, envy, lust and betrayal. Murder. Aelwen had sense enough to know that not all the evil would have vanished with Ferimon's death. How many of his supporters remained down there? How would they react to the news that he was dead? And the Forest Lord still had his realm's loyalty. Now that she herself was returning in a traitor's role, the Horsemistress knew that she would have enemies on every side. Many years ago, Hellorin had put a price on Taine's head, and there were plenty of folk in the city with long memories. Would Tiolani be able to protect him, and was she strong enough to return and take back her rule? More to the point, could she be trusted?

Well, Aelwen thought, as they began their descent into the palace, *we're about to find out.*

Their approach had clearly been spotted. In the absence of Tiolani, the Phaerie were without flying magic, so no one came to meet them, but the wide plaza was thronged with members of the court, and many were still swarming like brightly coloured ants out of the great carved doors. Even at this distance, Aelwen could hear their cries of relief and puzzlement. Among the gay rainbow hues, however, she also saw the shimmer of silver mail, and the bright flashes of sunlight on keen-edged swords, and her stomach clenched in trepidation. As they landed, the Phaerie scattered to give the horses room, and into the resulting gap stepped Cordain, with a troop of soldiers at his back. *You could take them for an honour guard*, Aelwen thought. *If you were that stupid.*

Beside her, she felt Taine stiffen, and from the corner of her eye she registered his hand inching towards his weapon. But her attention was fixed on Cordain's face. Dismay and annoyance, she saw there – and, more significantly, guilt. He'd believed Tiolani to be dead. He had been counting on it. When she first came to power, she had removed him from his exalted position of Chief Counsellor and put Ferimon in his place, so he held a grudge, but it was more than that. The girl had turned out to be an unstable, unpredictable killer. Aelwen understood completely why, as the Forest Lord's oldest friend and most loyal vassal, Cordain had decided that the Phaerie would be better off without her.

Cordain stepped forward, his smile as false as the grinning of a skull. 'My dearest Lady, we had despaired of your life. We are all delighted to welcome you back. You must be exhausted after your terrible ordeal.' He took her arm, to outward appearances all solicitude and courtesy. In reality, his fingers were like bands of steel, grinding flesh into bone. Tiolani, instinctively about to strike back, suddenly found herself surrounded by the putative honour guard. When she saw the drawn weapons and the clear, merciless intent in their eyes, she turned pale, and went very still. Aelwen and Taine found themselves similarly surrounded.

'Come, Lady,' Cordain said again. 'You will want the comfort of your quarters. And I am sure we can also find some comfortable accommodation for your companions.'

Aelwen cursed herself for not having anticipated this. Though she had thought that Hellorin's daughter might experience some resistance to her rule, she had not expected such cold-blooded treachery from Cordain, of all people. But with Ferimon dead, Tiolani was suddenly vulnerable, and the wolves were closing in.

We've failed, she thought. *Even before we've started, we've failed.* Even if, by some miracle, they could turn this disaster around and return Tiolani to power, they would still lose valuable time – maybe even long enough for Hellorin's healers to bring him back from the brink and undo the time spells. Even if Corisand and Iriana succeeded in taking the Fialan, he could follow them back to the mundane world.

The consequences were unthinkable.

Then Cordain noticed Taine, and Aelwen saw cold recognition flash across his face. Her heart began to race with fear.

He was Hellorin's loyal supporter. He would obey the Forest Lord's orders, no matter how many years ago they had been given.

Unless she could think of something fast to get them out of this, Taine was as good as dead already.

When Corisand and Iriana shimmered out of sight, Dael found himself alone with Athina once more. For a precious instant, everything seemed back as it should be – then the Cailleach gave a little gasp and crumpled, grey-faced, to the ground.

'Athina!' Sick with fear, Dael knelt beside her.

'Help me.' Her voice was a thready whisper. 'Get me back to your chamber, Dael. My power is fading fast. I must leave now.'

Though in his head he had known and accepted that this moment must come, his heart felt as if it were being ripped out of his chest.

'Now, Dael. Hurry.' He heard the desperation in her voice, saw the shadow of fear in her eyes – and put his own fear and grief aside.

For her.

She weighed next to nothing as he scooped her up into his arms and ran back to the tower, scrambling and stumbling as fast as he could up the airy spiral of the metal stairs. Shouldering open the door of his chamber, he carried Athina to the bed where Avithan lay and sat her on the edge, with an arm around her shoulders to keep her upright.

She held on to him, dropping her head to his shoulder. 'You've been a son to me.' Her voice was fading now. 'Before you, the only joy I knew was that of creation; the only sorrow that of setting my creations free when I was done. You taught me how to feel. How to love. I love you, my Dael. Down all the endless stretches of eternity, I will always love you.'

Even as his eyes blurred with tears, Athina was gone.

Where she and Avithan had been was just an empty bed in an empty room, in an empty world. Deal buried his face in the coverlet, and wept.

Athina found herself lying on the floor because she was too weak to stand, and blinded by her tears. She needed no vision to tell her that she was back home, in her Tree in the Heart of the Wood. She could feel its life and power pulsating through her in the same way as it pumped in shining streams through the walls of the massive hollow trunk.

Suddenly there was no more urgency. Here beneath the Timeless Lake, she had all the time in the world. Athina simply lay there, letting home restore the power and the energies she had lost, and wept for Dael, the child of her heart that she would see no more.

'Your folly astounds me.' The harsh voice that broke through her weariness and grief belonged to Uriel. Once more he had taken his favourite form, a column of scintillating, multicoloured energy – a beautiful sight, but one that could not have been less welcome to Athina, in that moment. She scrambled to her feet, thankful that she was beginning to regain her strength. She had not yet recovered enough power to withstand Uriel – but did he know that? She took her natural form once more, her face growing leaner and more raptor-like, her eyes taking on the fierce, wild, golden glare of the eagle. 'What do you want now?' she snarled. 'I did as you asked, Uriel. I have returned – and your involvement ends here. Get out of my home.'

The soft hum of Uriel's energy rose to a threatening buzz. 'Oh, you did as I asked, my sister – after you had done as you wished, and only when you finally had no choice. And even now, you persist in this insane involvement with your primitive creation.' He drifted across to the still form of Avithan, who had lain, until this moment, unregarded on the floor. 'What is *this*?'

The Cailleach stepped between her angry sibling and the Wizard's helpless form. 'What I do in my own place is my own affair. I owe you no explanations. As you demanded, I have left the mundane world and my involvement there has ceased. You have triumphed.' She could not keep the bitterness out of her voice. 'Now be content and go.'

'Athina, I am not your enemy.' His voice was edged with frustration, and a rumble of thunder sounded overhead as his temper frayed. With an effort he brought himself back under control. 'My dearest sister, I am simply trying to warn you, and to help you. You, of all our brethren, were always the most prone to being ruled by your emotions. Now they have led you to a forbidden place, and as a result, your perceptions have become skewed. Do you truly not see the danger here? That in acting to prevent your premonitions from coming true, you might have been instrumental in bringing about the dreadful future you foresaw?'

'No! That cannot be. I went to stop it. The Phaerie are the chief danger, but if the Xandim are freed, their power will be cut off at the knees. I needed to warn and help the three who will be pivotal to the fate of the world.'

'And in helping the Wizard and the Windeye, you have risked them bringing an artefact of unspeakable power out of the Elsewhere, where it belonged, and into the mundane world.'

'They will use it to avert the disaster, not to bring it about. With the Fialan gone from the Elsewhere, Hellorin will be imprisoned there for good, and one of the greatest dangers to the world will have been removed.'

'But in bringing the Stone back they will leave a trail of energy, of power, of the Old Magic. If the Forest Lord were to find and follow that trail, it would be possible for him to create a portal. Athina, you know this to be true.'

Despite the strength of her own convictions, a chill of trepidation slithered through her. 'Not alone, he could not,' she argued. 'Only half the power of the Fialan was his to command.'

'And if he allies, once again, with Ghabal?'

'No – that's impossible! After Hellorin betrayed him when the Stone was made, Ghabal would never trust him again. He may be mad, but he is not stupid.'

'Even if it meant that he also could return to the mundane world? Could make an attempt, once there, to regain the Stone? Under those circumstances, *I* would certainly set my enmity aside and form a tempo-rary truce. Imagine both of them, Athina, let loose on your precious, unsuspecting world. Would that not bring about the very catastrophe you were trying to forestall?'

The Cailleach felt the blood drain from her face. 'By the Light,' she whispered. 'What have I done?' Only too well now did she realise her terrible mistake. The mundane world had indeed clouded her percep-tions, preventing her from seeing all aspects of the situation.

She felt the clutch of panic around her heart. 'I have to tell them. Uriel, this is my doing. They must be warned.'

'No.' His voice was gentle but implacable. 'No, Athina, you will not be permitted to meddle this time. What's done is done, and the mundane world must live with the consequences. Our siblings have acted in concert to contain you here. I deeply regret this, but it is necessary. There will be no discussion, no debate and no reprieve. You will not be permitted to leave again.'

'No!' Rage and fear blazed up in the Cailleach's heart. 'You cannot.

You dare not.' But she was speaking to empty air. Uriel had gone, leaving her a prisoner in her little world below the Timeless Lake.

Athina sank to the floor and hid her face in her hands. Her thoughts were clouded by a turmoil of emotions: fury and bitterness at her confinement; horror, remorse and fear for the world of her creation, and for the individuals she had so lately come to know and love. Worst of all was the sickening sense of helplessness. Her own blindness, her misguided attempts to help, had brought them to a perilous pass. How could Uriel and the others be so callous? Surely it could do no harm to warn Corisand and Iriana of the dangers? But imprisoned here as she was, there could be no chance of her doing that.

Or could there?

She looked at Avithan, who lay so pale and still. In this timeless place, the shimmer of the tangled time spells had faded, just as she'd hoped. It should be possible to free him from his bonds and heal the hurts that he had suffered. But why hurry? While his body was out of time, Hellorin's mind and spirit had been able to journey to the Elsewhere. Could she do the same for Avithan? Send him to Iriana with a warning?

As Dael would have said, it was worth a try.

Cyran lay awake all night, worrying about his son and Iriana. Unknown to the two younger Wizards, Esmon had been secretly sending back a report, via scrying-crystal, every night when the others were on watch or asleep. Not many Wizards had this ability, but it was very useful, and one of the many reasons Esmon had been selected as an emissary to the Phaerie realm. To spare the pride of Avithan and Iriana, they had not been told that the Archwizard was keeping such a close eye on them. Cyran had wanted his son to handle the mission on his own, in the hope that a success might go some way towards persuading him that he wanted to be Archwizard, and follow in his father's footsteps after all.

Two nights previously, Esmon had reported in as usual from the forest, while Avithan was sleeping and Iriana was on watch. Two hours later the Warrior was dead: though faint and muted by distance, Cyran had felt the wrenching pang of a Wizard's passing, and known that Esmon breathed no more.

What had happened to him? And what had become of Avithan and Iriana, an inexperienced city-dweller and a blind girl cast adrift in the wilderness? In flat-out panic, Cyran had assembled a troop of veteran Wizards from the Luen of Warriors and had ridden out with them himself: partly because he could not bear to stay at home while his son was in danger, and partly to escape the bitter recriminations of his soulmate Sharalind.

It had been a mistake to come, however. Cyran was city-soft and it had been far too long since he had ridden a horse. Before the end of the first day it had been obvious that he was slowing the Warriors down – much to their ill-concealed annoyance, for they wanted above all things to avenge their leader – and so he had let them go on ahead, taking a short cut that angled across county and reached the forest by a straighter route, keeping only two of them to accompany him. Now he was far behind the main body, and he had stopped for the night with his companions so that he could rest his aching muscles and use a simple healing spell on the bruises that covered his calves and inner thighs.

There was no wood on the moors to keep a campfire burning overnight. The Archwizard's thoughts were as dark as his surroundings; filled with anxiety and self-recrimination. *If only I had sent someone else. Someone more experienced. Someone I loved less. Taine was right, when he thought that the whole idea was insane – but so tactfully didn't say so. I was too worried, too shaken by those accursed visions to be thinking clearly, and now ...*

After what felt like an endless night, eventually the darkness began to lift and an eerie half-light took its place. The two Warriors, Nara and Baxian, were already up, feeding their mounts and rummaging in the saddlebags for their own cold and cheerless breakfast. Cyran was just scrambling out of his blankets when suddenly the horses lifted their heads and whinnied. A moment later, he heard the sound of uneven, stumbling hoofbeats on the road, and a bony old horse stumbled into view over the brow of the hill. When the rider caught sight of the Archwizard, he started waving and shouting, and as he drew closer, his words became clear. 'Cyran? Is that Archwizard Cyran? Thank Providence I've found you.'

He looked so familiar – then, with a start, Cyran remembered. Challan. Zybina's former soulmate and Iriana's foster-father, who had abandoned his family for a human woman and run off to Nexis to hide his shame. Now his eyes were dark voids of exhaustion in a haggard face, and as he dismounted he was shaking with exhaustion. Trepidation curled in Cyran's stomach. This did not bode well.

'Come, sit,' he said, handing the Wizard a leather water-bag and squatting down beside him. 'What has happened? Tell me your tidings.'

Challan rubbed his hands over his weary face. 'Two nights ago – well, three nights now ...' He looked to where the sun was just clearing the horizon in a hectic blaze of gold. 'I was not asleep. We were searching—' He broke off, his eyes narrowing in anxiety and pain, then took a deep breath and started again. 'It could not have been a dream.' He clutched at the Archwizard's arm. 'I felt Esmon's passing, then shortly afterwards

I received a message in mindspeech from Iriana. It was very faint and far away, but it was a cry for help. They had been attacked by Phaerie in the forest. She wanted me to warn you ...'

He shook his head. 'I got the impression that she was fleeing for her life. Avithan had been hurt or captured, I think, because she was alone, blind, without even her animals to help her.' He buried his face in his hands. 'My poor Iriana. The last words we exchanged in Nexis were filled with rancour and bitterness, and then for this to happen on top of ...'

'On top of what?' Cyran asked sharply.

Challan took a deep breath, and with a visible effort brought himself back under control. 'Cyran, I know this is not the time to ask, but have you seen my daughter Chiannala? We had a terrible quarrel the night Iriana came, and she ran away. She stole our horse and I think she might have tried to head for Tyrineld – she seems to have inherited my powers in full, and is desperate to train at the Academy and become a fully fledged Wizard. I told her it was impossible, and that was when she—'

'Your *daughter*?' Cyran turned shocked eyes in his direction. 'You had a daughter with that human—' He broke off in disgust. Yet that look of distress, of misery, of desperation on Challan's face so exactly matched his own state of mind that he could not fail to understand. No matter what her breeding had been, the Wizard had lost a child, too.

'No.' He shook his head. 'My sorrow, Challan, but she never came to the Academy. Our recent intake was small. Only one came from outside Tyrineld – a girl called Brynne whose family have a farm out Dunmore way. But she and her father spoke of finding a strange, lone girl on the road who claimed to be an orphan heading for Tyrineld in hope of attending the Academy. Being decent folk, they took her with them, but I'm afraid there was a terrible accident on the way, and the girl slipped and fell over the cliffs. The fisherfolk began a search of the area at once, but she was never found.'

Challan groaned, and put his head in his hands.

"But wait.' Cyran put a hand on his arm. 'It may be too soon to despair. The image of your daughter I see in your mind does not match the one that Brynne and her father gave me. It's not even close. Also, you said that your daughter had strong Wizardly powers, yet we have felt neither her death nor that of another girl. We still have a mystery on our hands, but it is not yet time to mourn, for either of us. We know that our children are still alive, for we have not felt them passing. At least we have that. But whatever has befallen them, it cannot be good.'

He leapt to his feet, trembling with rage, his fists clenched tight at his sides as he stared helplessly towards the north. 'The Phaerie,' he growled.

'Those treacherous monsters. How *dare* they? They will rue the day they attacked my son.'

Challan also got up, and stood beside him. 'I am sorry I could not reach you sooner. Horses are hoarded like diamonds in Nexis, and this poor lame, broken-winded old creature was all that I could find after Chiannala stole mine.'

The sun had risen fully now, and had vanished just as quickly into a long bank of cloud that lay above the horizon. A cold wind snaked and sneered across the exposed flanks of the moors. The two Wizards and the Warrior escort stood in silence, united by anxiety and sorrow.

Then it happened. They were struck by the wrenching pain, the un-nerving sense of void and absence that marked the passing of a Wizard from the world. 'Iriana,' Challan wailed. 'My little Iriana. No, it cannot be true. She can't have gone.'

Cyran staggered as though he himself had received a mortal wound. 'I sent her,' he whispered. 'Her death is on my hands.'

In the next instant he crumpled to the ground with an anguished wail as the dreadful pang came again. 'Avithan,' he cried. 'No, please – not my son!' For a long moment the Wizards were transfixed in horror, then Challan began to weep. Cyran got to his feet, his face bone-white, his eyes burning with a cold, fell light as he stared into the north. 'All my life I have striven for peace and conciliation with the Phaerie,' he snarled, 'but here it ends. Now I will unleash red war upon them. I will not rest until the last of their infection has been wiped from the face of this world.'

37
~

THE OLD ONE

The boat sailed beautifully, flying along before the wind with the Wizard at the helm. They were making good progress. Already the Windeye could see the tiny island in the distance, with its tall tower of rock that resembled the ravaged stump of an ancient tree. She could make out the fir trees and green bushes that clung miraculously to its near-vertical sides, and the dark triangular opening of the cave mouth at its base.

Corisand's concentration was elsewhere. Before they had left the shore, she had woven a shadow-cloak to hide the little craft and its passengers, and was carefully maintaining it as they surged towards the north. Iriana had been enthralled by this new aspect of her magic, and clearly was still musing on it during the voyage. 'I wonder if I could make something like your cloak,' she said. 'Not in our own world, obviously. But if you're right, and I can see in this realm because I'm using Othersight, I wonder if I could link it in some way with my Air magic—'

'It wouldn't work.' Corisand's voice came out sharper than she'd intended. 'You might be able to see in Othersight, but the manipulation of the air is Windeye magic. You can do a great deal with air, I know, but you can't hold it in your hands.'

'I suppose not.' The Wizard shrugged. 'Pity – I would have liked a shadow-cloak of my own, and it might have come in useful too.'

Haven't you got enough already? Corisand bit back the words before they could come out of her mouth. It shocked her to realise that she was a little jealous of Iriana. The Wizard had such a powerful and unique talent, and had been intensively trained; she'd practised her magic all her life, instead of suddenly discovering it out of the blue – and even then not having it available most of the time. 'You know, I envy you, going to the

Academy; coming from an entire race of Wizards so you were learning your craft from the very beginning, and you never were alone.' It seemed best to get her thoughts out into the open, before the notion started to rankle and sour their friendship.

Iriana thought for a moment. 'You're right, I have been lucky, and I'm especially blessed to have a mixture of powers. There's always a balance, though. It hasn't been easy for you being alone and captive, and it wasn't easy for me being blind. I managed very well with my animals to help me, but until I came here I never really knew what I was missing.'

'You know, you're right. I hadn't thought of that. Things are never as straightforward as they appear, are they?'

While they were talking, they had let their vigilance drop – just a little, but enough.

They didn't notice that the wind was rising until suddenly Corisand found herself unbalanced as the vessel rocked and pitched on a steepening sea, and a massive wave slapped over the bows, soaking her with flying spray. With a curse, she scrambled back to where Iriana was steering the little craft. The Wizard's face was pale and taut, her mouth set in a grim line of concentration. In mindspeech, however, she was swearing with inventiveness and fluency.

'Iriana? What's happening? What's wrong?'

'Some bloody thing is attacking us,' Iriana growled through clenched teeth. 'I can feel their magic, trying to stir up a storm.'

'Hellorin?'

'Don't think so – at least not entirely. There's something new here: something strange and very powerful. Ignore the sea. Search beyond the wind. Can't you feel it?' She swore again. 'Plague take it! I thought this world was the home of the Old Magic. Everybody knows that the Old Magic can't cross water. I thought we'd be safe out here.'

'Maybe it's different in this world, where the whole place is founded on Old Magic.'

Though the sea and wind were growing more turbulent by the moment, the sky had remained blue, and unnaturally clear. But now they saw a great black barrier of cloud bearing down on them from the north, against the wind. Brows drawn down in a scowl of concentration, Iriana was muttering under her breath, reaching for focus. Then suddenly she raised a hand, and Corisand felt the alien, Wizardly magic go streaming past her, and up into the sky. With a jerk, the boat heeled over as the wind veered abruptly, blowing them towards the nearest scrap of land – that peculiar rock formation that the Windeye had seen in her mirror of vision, when it had brought her this way.

Iriana, trembling with the strain of her spell, said, 'Whatever that thing is, we'd best not meet it on the open ocean.'

'But what is it?' the Windeye wondered. 'Somehow this doesn't have the stamp of Hellorin. Could the Moldan threaten us from this distance? Taku said he never left his mountain. Surely his reach, then, could not be so long?'

'Don't forget he has the Fialan.' In this time of crisis, Iriana seemed to be picking up the thoughts directly from her mind.

'Then how will we ever get near him, if his reach is so long and he's already aware that we're coming?' Corisand ducked another wave, and cursed herself for sounding so feeble.

'It's not your fault.' Again, the Wizard was replying to her unspoken thoughts as she drove the boat into the waves. 'You've spent all your life as a horse – a prey animal. You have a naturally ingrained instinct for flight, rather than fight. But you're not equine any more, my friend. Now you can think differently. Once you're aware of the horse, you can override that instinct, and be the Windeye.'

There was no time for a reply. The sinister black barrier was almost upon them, and the gale had increased to screaming pitch. It would be a desperate race to reach the island in time. Suddenly, what looked like a long, black serpent dropped out of the bottom of the cloud bank, twisting and snaking down into the water. It formed a slim, sinister funnel shape that joined the ocean to the sky.

'A waterspout,' Iriana gasped. 'If that thing reaches us we'll be torn to pieces.' With her teeth clenched and fire in her eyes, she steered the boat as straight as she could, up the slopes of the gargantuan green waves, through the welter of white water on the crests and down the other side, heading for the tiny slip of land with its tower of rock. Just before it hit the narrow beach, Corisand dissolved the little craft and formed a gentle ramp of air, down which they rolled and tumbled to dry land.

The waterspout was gaining on them, a ravening black monster that covered half the sky. Fierce winds tore at them, and rocks and gravel flew at them as if propelled by slingshots. 'Quick!' Grabbing hold of Iriana's arm, Corisand pulled her to her feet and they hurried across the shingle towards the cave. As they hurled themselves inside, she felt a slight pressure against her skin, as though she had hit an invisible barrier – then she was through, and safe inside with Iriana at her heels.

The screaming of the tempest diminished. The Windeye, utterly stunned, took in her surroundings at a glance. Instead of the dark, dank sea cave she had expected, she and Iriana stood in a kingly hall. Its walls of dark stone scintillated with a galaxy of tiny specks of mica that caught and reflected the light from numerous floating globes, filled with what appeared to be captive moonlight. A great fire roared and crackled in a circular pit in the centre of the chamber, its smoke lost in the shadows far above.

Suddenly a great voice came rolling and echoing through the hall. 'Well, see what the wind has blown in. It is many a long age since visitors have come here.'

Corisand started. She knew that voice: deep and reverberant enough to make the very bones of the earth vibrate, with a grinding, growling undertone that sounded like the movement of entire mountains. She had heard it when her mirror-borne vision had taken her to this place. 'Basileus?' Her own voice came out like the whistle of a bird in comparison to the ponderous, mighty tones.

'Basileus indeed,' the entity answered. 'So, you have come to me in corporeal form, as I asked when last we met. That was bravely done, O Windeye. As you may have guessed, I am another Moldan. I am this rock, and this rock is me – in this world, at least. I—'

He was interrupted by a howl of rage. From outside, in the wild keening of the storm, another voice was heard: cold as the fierce, white, searing core of winter, and this time, somehow female. 'Give me the Windeye and her Wizard companion. Give them to me now. They shall not have the Fialan – it will be *mine*.'

Basileus ignored the voice; ignored the keening of the gale and the crashing of the mighty waves that shook the tower. 'Ah. Now I understand. You have no need to tell me, my friends, why you seek the Stone of Fate. I can see the reasons written clearly in your minds. You play a dangerous game, in seeking to pit yourselves against both Ghabal and Hellorin – and now my sibling, Aerillia, has decided to interfere on her own behalf.'

'Is that who is outside?' Iriana asked. 'The one who made the storm?'

'It is not only Aerillia, for she has allied herself with Hellorin, the Forest Lord – indeed, it was she who brought him here. She, too, wishes to gain the Fialan, so that the Moldai may once again dwell in both worlds, instead of just the Elsewhere.'

'And you?' Corisand asked quietly. 'Where do you stand, sir? Do you not want the Stone of Fate?'

'I would like to see your world again,' the Moldan mused. 'And had I wished, I could have used your ignorance to my advantage – but that is not my way. For my part, you are more than welcome to take the Fialan from the Elsewhere. Ghabal is a most unsafe guardian, and if it falls into other hands, there will be treachery and warfare here. Your world can have it – and all the problems it will bring in its wake. I know you have your reasons for wanting it. I only hope you know exactly what you are about.

'Be that as it may, I will help you now, my friends. Aerillia and her pawn will learn the penalty for assailing *me*.'

'Aerillia!' His roar was loud enough to bring the companions to their knees. 'The Windeye and the Wizard are mine to protect. Get you gone from here, you and the Phaerie Lord, or woe betide you.'

'My brother.' Aerillia's voice turned sly and cajoling. 'Surely you can see the danger in what they are trying to do? If they try to take the Fialan they are certain to fail, puny creatures that they are, but they will awaken the wrath of our poor, mad sibling. With the power that he wields, who knows what damage he will cause to the fabric of this world?'

'And who knows what damage your Phaerie lapdog might cause if *he* gains the Stone, as you so clearly intend. I say again, Aerillia: get you gone from here and do not interfere with me and mine again, lest it turn to your undoing. You cannot have the Windeye and her friend.'

'Then I will *take* them!' Once more, her voice became the savage snarling of the storm, and Corisand saw, as if through the eyes of Basileus, the havoc that she wrought. Mighty winds smote the pillar of rock like hammer blows, tearing at the shaggy trees and bushes that clung to its steep sides. The sea rose up in mountainous waves that crashed down on the ancient bastion of stone.

Basileus sighed. 'She never learns. She could never best me on her own, but because she has coupled her power with that of Hellorin, she believes herself invincible. She forgets that I can do the same.'

The Windeye felt his attention on her, as though her mind had been illuminated by a beam of brilliant light. A gasp from Iriana at her side told her that the Wizard had been included in the scrutiny.

'Windeye, Wizard,' the Moldan said. 'Will you trust me? Will you link your powers with mine?'

'Without hesitation,' Corisand replied. 'I have not forgotten, Basileus, how you helped me to escape Ghabal's clutches when I travelled to his mountain through my mirror.'

'And what of your companion?'

'My name is Iriana, Sir.' The Wizard stepped forward, even though the voice seemed to come from all around. 'Corisand trusts you, so I do also. I will link my powers with you, if it is your wish.'

'Thank you, Iriana. I think you and the Windeye have chosen well to take each other as companions. And now, both of you: open your thoughts to join with mine.'

By unspoken consent, Corisand and Iriana took each other's hands and linked their minds. Then, with a deep breath, they took the final step together.

The Windeye felt the power of Basileus: as old as time, as strong as the very rock that sheltered her. Iriana's magic had an entirely different energy: the inexorable force of Water, the mother of all life, that could destroy a city or wear a mountain down; the clean, fierce blaze of Fire; elusive, tempestuous Air, as difficult as a wild horse to control and focus; and the strong, solid power of Earth, as quick to heal as to destroy. Corisand felt her companions' magic surging through her, mingling with her own ancestral powers to become a force far greater than the sum of its individual parts.

Then suddenly they were everywhere. A dizzying wave of vertigo swept over the Windeye as the constraints of her body dissolved. She was not only Corisand but Iriana too, with a body that felt completely different. She was part of the gnarled stone pillar of Basileus, and felt the drape of vines and bushes around her shoulders, and the slight pull of the fir trees that leant out over the water. She felt the fury of the other Moldan crashing against her in a black vortex of wind and waves, and she was the wind and waves themselves. Corisand, her consciousness everywhere, was both inside and outside it all, watching from a distance yet playing an active part.

Then Aerillia – she thought of the entity as Aerillia, though she knew that the Moldan was linked to Hellorin in the same way that she was linked to her companions – seemed to see them, and the vortex of the storm became a great white dragon that towered high above the stone pillar, its outstretched wings blotting out half the sky. Corisand, part of the gigantic force that was also Iriana and Basileus, felt her own form changing in response, into another of the mighty beasts, this time with scales of gleaming black. Aerillia reared back and hissed a challenge, and the Basileus-dragon bellowed a response. Then the two titanic figures leapt upon each other in an earth-shaking collision, clawing with their long, sharp talons and snapping with their mighty teeth.

There was no doubt that the struggle was real. Corisand felt the strain in her muscles as the two behemoths grappled, and the pain when the scimitar teeth of the white dragon tore into her hide. Magic kept them on the ocean's surface as they battled back and forth; sometimes on their feet, sometimes rolling over and over, locked in deadly combat.

For a time, neither gained an advantage. The white dragon was faster, but the black was stronger. Both were bleeding – actually bleeding, thought Corisand in shock – from numerous wounds. Clearly the white dragon was tiring: her movements were slower now, and her attacks lacked their former force – but her opponent was suffering too. The Windeye, locked in her strange, three-way partnership within the dragon's body, could feel its great limbs growing heavy with exhaustion.

Then Basileus, controlling the monster, put the last of their combined strength into one final, savage attack. Aerillia, taken unawares, was thrown off balance, and the black dragon's teeth ripped into her unprotected throat. Screeching, she tore herself free and fled, leaving behind her a trail of thick blood that stained the ocean crimson.

The huge black dragon vanished, and Corisand found herself standing back in the hall of stone beside a stunned and bedraggled-looking Iriana.

'Well fought, my friends.' The voice of the Moldan boomed around them. 'Aerillia has gone to lick her wounds; she will trouble you no more.'

'Where are our wounds?' The Windeye was examining her unmarked limbs.

'I took them into myself,' Basileus replied. 'It will be hard enough for you to deal with Ghabal, without the additional handicap of injuries.'

'Thank you,' Iriana said. 'Without your aid, I think our journey would have ended right here.'

'Do not underestimate yourselves.' The Moldan's voice was as kind as sunshine. 'The two of you together are stronger than you know. I would enjoy your company for longer, O Windeye, O Wizard, but time is pass-ing, and while Hellorin and Aerillia are recovering from their wounds, you must strike. I hope that we may meet again some day.'

'I hope so too,' said Iriana.

'And I,' added Corisand. 'Farewell, Basileus. Our thanks go with you.'

'One word of warning before you leave, my friends. If you succeed in your quest, beware the Fialan. Though your intentions are good, such immense power has a way of being unpredictable. Once you have it within your world, who knows what may happen?'

38

BEYOND THE ICE

With a little help from Iriana, Corisand recreated her boat and they set sail again, heading ever northward. For a time they sat in silence, each one wrapped in thoughts of what had happened, and how it might affect the conflict to come. The Wizard felt a little more hopeful, now that Basileus had helped them. 'Now we only have to sneak up on the Moldan,' she said aloud.

Their thoughts had been running along such similar lines that Corisand picked up the thread at once. 'Maybe my shadow-cloak will help.'

'It may help us get close up to the mountain, but how do we get inside? At that point, all subterfuge must be at an end.' Iriana frowned. 'We'll have a battle on our hands.'

They sailed on in sombre silence, watching the mountains drawing ever closer. As the details became more distinct, they saw the great ice peak of Ghabal's fastness, glittering like a colossal diamond in the ocean. 'At least we should be able to sail all the way,' said Iriana. But she was wrong. For some time they had been seeing a streak of white across the skyline far ahead, and had taken it for a trick of the light. But as they approached it rapidly, solid obstacles began to appear in the water: chunks of ice ranging from small, fist-sized lumps to great, flat floes that were wider than a room. So far, the temperature in the Elsewhere had been ambient and comfortable, but now it was as though they had run into a wall of profound and savage cold.

They had hit the first of Ghabal's defences. He had ringed his mountain with sea-ice, and had lowered the temperature with shattering effect. Beyond the bergs and broken floes that formed its margins, the ice stretched solid and unbroken to the north, as far as the eye could see. Their little boat could take them no further.

'Well,' said Iriana with a sigh, 'it looks as though we had better get out and walk.'

'It could work in our favour,' the Windeye replied. 'I think the time has come to shield ourselves, but I was worried about the efficiency of my shadow-cloak while we're moving fast and I'm trying to maintain the structure of the boat at the same time. Aerillia seemed to find us easily enough. I'll do much better on foot.'

'Speaking of shielding,' the Wizard said, 'we're going to need something more than a shadow-cloak at this point. We could be attacked at any time, and the closer we get to Ghabal, the greater the risk will grow. You take care of hiding us with your shadow-cloak, and I'll maintain a shield against a magical strike. How does that sound?'

They clambered out of the boat and onto the dazzling white surface beyond. As soon as their feet touched the ice, the cold smote them, drying and stiffening the skin on their faces and striking at their feet and legs.

'Now what?' Corisand said. 'We won't stand this for very long.'

'Let's shield and conceal ourselves while we're thinking,' Iriana suggested. 'And we'll be warmer if we keep moving.'

The Windeye dissolved her lovely boat, not without a pang of regret, and looked around for shadows with which to weave her cloak. Though the ice appeared to be a smooth, unbroken surface from a distance, in reality it was patched with areas of rubble ice: jumbled labyrinths of furrows and sharp-edged ridges where the ice had cracked and been forced upward, and had then refrozen. The shadows were blue against the pristine white of the ice, and as Corisand called them to her, she discovered that her cloak was a different hue this time, blending neatly into her surroundings. Building it carefully, she extended it to cover the Wizard – and even as she did so, she felt a surge of magic as Iriana constructed her own shield around them.

'When we learned our defensive magic at the Academy, I never really believed that one day I would be using it; that it would make the difference between life and death,' Iriana said. 'I only wish I could have used it when Esmon and Avithan and I were attacked in the forest that night.'

'Why couldn't you?' Since the Wizard herself had brought the subject up, Corisand had no hesitation in asking.

'Because the bastard Phaerie assassin was immune to my magic.' Her face hardened with anger. 'I wish I could have killed him with my bare hands.' She strode ahead, sticking to the smoother areas and avoiding the rubble ice, and Corisand had to rush after her, struggling to keep the cloak in place.

And if her own shield was in danger ...

'Iriana – concentrate!' she snapped as she caught up to the Wizard. 'Focus on your shield, not the accursed Phaerie, or he'll reach out from his grave and kill you yet.'

The Wizard turned on her, wrath flashing in her eyes, then caught herself. 'You're right, you're right.' She rubbed her hands over her face and took a deep breath. 'I'm sorry. Sometimes it all comes flooding back, and I start thinking I should have done this or that. It's hard to accept that he had me bested. That I couldn't save my friends.'

Corisand faced her, clasping her shoulders. 'You did best him, my friend. He's dead now, and you're still alive. And you did save Avithan. Without you he would be dead. At least you've given him a chance. If that assassin was immune to Wizard magic – and that's not a trait common to all Phaerie, as you saw when we fought the Forest Lord – then I doubt that your Archwizard himself could have done more.' She smiled at Iriana. 'Having seen you deal with Hellorin the first time he attacked us makes you warrior enough for me.'

Looking into Corisand's sincere brown eyes, hearing her words of comfort and encouragement, Iriana felt the shadows of pain retreat a little, and the claws of grief slackened their harsh grip on her heart. Corisand had steadied her, and it was time to be moving on.

The cold was attacking them savagely now: it sapped their energy and drained their spirits; it numbed their limbs and slowed their movements; it chilled their blood and clouded their thoughts. Their toes and fingers stung and tingled. How long could they sustain themselves under these conditions?

The further they went, the stronger the wind became and the deeper grew the chill. Iriana, shivering uncontrollably, kept her eyes fixed on the goal, willing herself towards the peak of ice and telling herself that every step was bringing her closer.

Then, in the blink of an eye, it vanished. The horizon turned grey and formless. Before they had time to take another breath, the blizzard was upon them. The air was filled with snow driven into their faces by the screaming wind: tiny knife-edged particles of ice that sliced into their skin, clogged their breathing and drove mercilessly into every chink and crevice in their clothing. With a curse, Iriana flung her powers forward, strengthening her shield in the teeth of the gale.

Silence.

Blessed, blessed stillness.

'You did it, oh, you did it.' The Windeye hugged her, but Iriana shook her head. 'Not for long,' she said grimly. 'The Moldan's power is terrifying. It's taking all my strength to keep the storm at bay, and I've made no impression on the cold. He won't leave his mountain, that much seems clear, but with spells like this, he doesn't need to. I can't maintain my shield for much longer, and when it fails we'll be right back where we started.'

All they could do was make the most of the small respite they had gained, and push on as far as they could while the going was easier. As they trudged and stumbled on stiffening legs across the ice-field, their vision obscured by puffs of their own frozen breath, the strain began to tell on Iriana. It was like trying to hold up a falling tree single-handed. She gritted her teeth and tried to keep going as long as she could, but her mind kept losing focus, drifting to the nature of magic and the manifold forms it could take. She remembered lectures at the Academy, and the more practical information she had gleaned from Esmon, about using magic not just as a shield, but as a weapon too.

It struck her all at once.

As her concentration slackened, the blizzard sprang on them like a ravening beast, but Iriana ignored it. 'Corisand!' She pulled her companion to a halt. 'It's not real cold at all. The Moldan is fighting us with magic – just a different sort, which must be why it's so difficult for me to shield. But if the cold is just another sort of spell, then surely it must be possible to form some sort of defence against it.'

Corisand frowned at her, and the Wizard could see that she was trying her hardest to focus. 'Defence?' Her voice could barely be heard above the keening of the wind. 'Tell me how. Shadow-cloaks and mirrors are all I know.'

'You know bridges and boats too,' the Wizard shouted at her, 'and you spun your own clothes out of air when we came here, remember?'

'I wish I'd made them warmer, then.'

'Could you?' Iriana asked hopefully.

The Windeye simply shook her head. 'I'm a horse, remember? Don't know anything.'

Iriana, worried now, tried desperately to rouse her friend from this hopeless mood brought on by the cold. It might have taken her that way too, had she not realised in time what Ghabal was about. She pulled the Windeye close to her so that they could huddle together and share body heat. 'Just because you missed the years of studying and training at the Academy, it doesn't make you useless. You're just discovering your powers, and you've only scratched the surface of what you can achieve. Between us we can deal with this spell, I know it.'

But if we can't find an answer soon, we won't live long enough.

Firmly, she pushed the insidious notion out of her mind and concentrated hard, turning her thoughts back to a particular talk that Esmon had given on shielding. Hearing in her head the kind, strong voice that had been lost from the world for ever, she repeated his words to Corisand.

'There are three types of shield,' she shouted. 'One for concealment – that's like your shadow-cloak – one for defence, like the shield I'm using now, and one for offence. The latter works like a mirror. It reflects the assailant's magic back upon himself. A really good offensive shield can even magnify the damage.' She swore. 'There's only one problem. Cyran was against the use of offensive magic, and he wouldn't let the students at the Academy learn it. The only way to study it was to join the Luen of Warriors.'

'But it's like a mirror?' Corisand's eyes, dull and vague from the cold, suddenly brightened. 'I told you about my mirror, didn't I? The one I used to go mind-travelling? Maybe if we combine my mirror with your shield—'

'It might work,' Iriana said excitedly. 'Maybe if we link minds very closely, then you spin your mirror and I'll build a shield. If we *push* them at one another, maybe we can get them to fuse.'

A glimmer of hope dawned in Corisand's eyes. 'Let's do it now – before it's too late.'

Iriana had practised working spells in concert with other Wizards, but to do it in conjunction with a completely alien magic – that felt very strange. In the three-way link with Basileus, it had been the Moldan's power that had held the entire construct together, but now they had to manage on their own. The Windeye's magic felt like a stream of silver running through her mind: cool, bright, shining and somehow much more fluid than her own powers.

Corisand, her eyes glowing with her Othersight, gathered in the howling wind to spin her mirror, and cast it in a reflective dome over the adamantine shield into which Iriana was throwing all her power. The two magics met and fused in a flash of dazzling radiance with a satisfying sound like the click of a key turning in a lock. Windeye and Wizard were linked with a bond that neither of their races had known before, and their conjoined abilities blossomed and grew to something puissant and unique.

And it was working. Their shield held firm against the onslaught, and both of them rocked with the punch of power that exploded through their minds and bodies as their attacker was hit by his own reflected malice, magnified many times over.

Once more, the winds ceased abruptly.

The flying snow dropped with a hissing spatter, all at once, and fell no more.

The light grew bright again as visibility returned, the savage cold lost its bite and warmth began to creep back into their frozen limbs.

The two companions leant against one another, getting their breath back; each taking care to keep her mind focused on her own part of the shield. 'We're a lot closer to the mountain,' Corisand said at last.

Iriana looked out across the gleaming ice. 'Maybe that was part of Ghabal's defensive spell, like the cold and the storm,' she said. 'The illusion that the peak was much further away than it is in truth. It had me discouraged, I'll admit.'

The Windeye opened her mouth to answer, but the words were lost. A deafening snap like the cracking of a giant's whip split the air, and a long fissure appeared in the ice a stone's throw in front of them. Corisand spat out a curse she had learned from the Wizard. 'It's breaking up. Now that we've broken the cold spell, the ice is melting.'

'Move!' Iriana roared. Grabbing her companion's hand, she ran forward and leapt the widening gap, with Corisand a breath behind. All around them the ice was breaking up into smaller sheets of different sizes, from a table top to a courtyard, which had one thing in common: every one of them was shrinking, the strips of dark ocean between them growing wider by the minute. The frozen surface split asunder with a fusillade of cracks and booms as Iriana and Corisand dodged and leapt from one disintegrating floe to the next, fighting for balance as the floating ice tilted and rocked beneath them, scrambling and slithering in the deepening slush beneath their feet.

It was a terrifying, exhausting, desperate scramble. Corisand put her foot on a patch of bad ice and was suddenly thigh-deep in icy water. With Iriana's help she extricated herself, but not before her leg was wrenched, her boots were waterlogged and she was thoroughly soaked. Luckily, her clothing had been spun from shadows and air. It would be easy to make more – but right now, she did not dare stop moving.

Iriana was faring even worse. She had led a much less physical life than Corisand, and consequently, even in the Elsewhere, she found herself tiring far more easily. In addition, the Windeye had spent her life running and jumping. Her balance, strength and coordination were all excellent, even though she was now on two legs instead of four. It was not so for the Wizard. She was exhausting herself in her constant fight for balance and finding it far more difficult, both physically and mentally, to leap the widening gaps where the depths of the dark, cold ocean lay in wait. Yet not once, even for an instant, did she think of giving up. Gritting her teeth she floundered on, taking one ghastly leap, one slithering, splashing landing at a time; no longer thinking of the peak that was her goal, of the Moldan, of the Fialan. Those things could wait. Now her priority was pure and simple: just keep going.

It became a desperate race – though Ghabal's fastness was drawing closer with every step, the surface underneath their feet was shrinking all the time. The currents felt stronger the closer they came to the ice peak, and the stretches of water between the Windeye, the Wizard and their goal were growing wider. Ghabal might be insane, but he was old and cunning. He had already learned not to attack these interlopers directly while they had their mirror shield in place, but there were other ways …

With an ear-splitting crack, the ice fractured between Iriana and her friend, and the Wizard found herself teetering on a small, slushy, rapidly vanishing raft that was being swept quickly out to sea. Already the distance was too far to jump. Iriana looked at the dwindling figure of Corisand and knew no help could come from her.

The Windeye thought differently. 'Just hang on,' she yelled. 'I'm making a bridge—'

'No – no!' shrieked Iriana. 'Corisand, don't. The shield will fail – it's what he wants.' But she knew, just knew in her guts, that her friend would try it anyway. Well, she wouldn't get the chance. Without hesitation, Iriana leapt into the water.

The cold was a shocking agony that cramped her limbs and stopped her heart. Her involuntary gasp sent water flooding into her lungs, and she was sinking, choking, drowning … Then her lungs adapted, her heartbeat kicked and she was breathing once more, though the medium was icy water that burned her lungs. Iriana felt like weeping with relief. It was one thing to be taught that Wizards couldn't drown, but another entirely to actually trust her life to it. Besides, she was far from out of trouble yet. Her waterlogged clothing was pulling her down and the frigid water was already causing a deadly drain on her energy. She had to get out – and fast.

There was no point wasting time and energy trying to get to the surface. Fuelled by desperation, she struck out towards her goal: the sheer, submerged face of Ghabal's ice mountain.

Iriana's powers had never been so stretched, even when the camp was attacked and she was trying to save Avithan's life. But she had learned a thing or two since then. She was finding that the more she used her magic, the more powerful it became. Despite her predicament, she still managed to spare enough energy to keep the shield intact around Corisand, and her next thought was to use her Fire magic to warm her own blood, so that her body would keep functioning until she reached land. She knew that she was feeding on her own energy. It was like using healing magic on herself – there was the very real danger of consuming too much of her own power and burning out. Even with care she would pay – oh, how she would pay – in exhaustion when she finally got back to land.

There was far more ice beneath the surface than above. The Wizard threaded her way through the maze of bergs in a blue-green world: had circumstances been less desperate, she would have been enthralled by their fantastically sculpted shapes. But she had no time to marvel at their otherworldly beauty. The goal, and only the goal, mattered now. Weariness was dragging at her limbs by the time she reached the peak of ice, but she had made it in the face of all the odds, and was another step closer to the Fialan.

Suddenly, she realised that she might be even closer than she'd thought. As she approached the cliff, what she'd believed, from a distance, to be a shadowy illusion of the ice formation revealed itself to be a cave.

In her excitement she forgot that her reserves of energy were dwindling. The cave lengthened into a tunnel that sloped upwards into the mountain, and she followed it until she found herself crawling out of a pool into a vast cavern. Looking around, she discovered that another tunnel left it on the opposite side. Iriana lay there for a few moments, gasping and spluttering, until her lungs adjusted back to breathing air.

Though the mountain still appeared to have been carved out of ice, the smooth floor of the cavern was a comfortable temperature beneath her. *Why, it's not ice at all*, she realised. She let her sense sink a little way beneath the surface as she had been taught, searching the underlying structure, and: 'By the light!' she gasped. 'It's diamond.'

Ghabal had made himself an impregnable fortress. Not even another Moldan could destroy diamond.

The floor was almost warm, and Iriana felt like weeping with relief. She was so tired of fighting the merciless, inexorable cold. She lay limply for a while, feeling comfortable and drowsy. *I'll move in a minute*, she thought. *Just need to get a little strength back ...*

Iriana shot up with a guilty start, horrified that she had let herself doze. She felt better for the rest, though she didn't think she'd slept for long, but she was horrified that she had left herself unguarded in the enemy's lair. Ghabal, however, appeared to have no inkling of her presence. *Probably thinks I'm dead*, she thought. *Probably concentrating on Corisand now.*

Corisand!

What was happening to the Windeye? And what about the shield?

While she slept, she had stopped maintaining their defence. Had her friend been captured? Killed? She was afraid to call out in mindspeech lest the Moldan should somehow hear.

The frantic Wizard dived back into the freezing pool and, as soon as her lungs adjusted, swam as hard as she could back down the tunnel to the open sea, surfacing as close to the cliff as she dared. If the Moldan noticed her now she was done. She was surprised at how little remained of the ice field she had crossed, though the fastness itself was undiminished – and now she knew why.

Further along the cliff was a deep bay with a flat beach of sorts, and she swam towards it, anxious to get out of the cold water. So far, there was no sign of Corisand. She swam into the inlet and tried to scramble up onto the level beach, but once again the cold had drained her, and try as she might, she kept losing her grip on the smooth surface and falling back into the sea.

Out of nowhere a hand appeared and seized her wrist in an iron grip. 'Quick,' said a familiar voice. 'Let me get you under my shadow-cloak. Then I'm going to kill you for giving me such a fright.'

With Corisand's help, the Wizard scrambled out of the water and rolled onto her back, an enormous grin on her face. Now that she was under the shadow-cloak herself she could see the Windeye. She staggered upright and hugged her hard.

'Oh, but I'm glad to see you.' Corisand's voice was unsteady and choked. 'When your shield failed, I thought —'

She broke off, pulling back from Iriana and rubbing at her face, then staring in astonishment at the moisture on her fingers. 'What in the world—'

'They're tears,' Iriana explained. 'We get them at times of extreme emotion – either sorrow or joy. I suppose that as a horse you never wept.'

'What an extraordinary thing,' Corisand said – then changed her tone abruptly. 'But we don't have time for such nonsense now.' Impatiently she wiped them away. 'Where have you been? What happened to you? How did you survive? What are we going to do now?'

'First, let's get our shield back up,' Iriana said. 'Then I'll tell you everything.'

'No. Never. Absolutely, positively, categorically not. Not under any circumstances.' Corisand looked down into the water and shivered. 'There is no way in this world or the other that you're going to get me to jump in there.'

'I wasn't asking you to jump,' Iriana said calmly. 'If you jump you'll gasp automatically from the cold, and your lungs will fill with water. Unless there's something you're not telling me, I'm the only one who can breathe underwater. You need to lower yourself in gradually, and—'

'And go diving into caves.' Corisand glared at her. 'Have you completely lost your mind?'

'Can *you* think of another way to get into the fastness? This was always going to be the difficult part.'

'But he's bound to know that tunnel's there,' the Windeye argued. 'What if he's waiting at the far end of it to pounce on us like a cat on a mouse?'

'That is the weak point of my plan, I must admit. I thought that maybe you could think of something.'

'*Me?* Why me?'

The Wizard shrugged. 'Because so far nothing has occurred to me. I'm convinced this is our only chance, Corisand. This whole damned peak is solid diamond. He built it from the most impervious substance possible.'

The Windeye turned away from the sea and stared up at the peak. 'And it's only a matter of time before he finds out where we are. When your part of the shield disappeared I spun the best shadow-cloak of my life to conceal myself, and that was when he lost me, but I can't hide both of us so well. The bigger the cloak, the more difficult it is to maintain. Sooner or later my concentration will slip, and the Moldan will be out of this mountain like a—' She broke off as an extraordinary idea exploded into her brain. 'Iriana, listen. I think I've found a way ...'

It took a while for them to refine their plan and straighten out the details, but at last they felt they had covered all eventualities – at least, as best they could. Windeye and Wizard looked at one another. Corisand thought that Iriana looked pale but determined, and suspected that her friend was seeing a similar expression on her own face. She swallowed hard. 'Are you ready?'

'I don't think I'll ever be ready for something as dangerous as this, but I'm not going to let that stop me.' Briefly, Iriana clasped the Windeye's hand. 'Go on, Corisand – and make it a good one.'

The Windeye concentrated, letting her Othersight flood through her like a wave of cool, liquid silver. When she was ready, she began to gather the winds. More she took, and more: more than she had ever handled before. She took her time – there would be only one chance to get this right – and never for an instant let her concentration waver. Such a huge mass of air was difficult to contain and control, but the challenge filled her with a heady delight. She might not have had the Academy, but even on her own, newly-fledged into her powers, she was *good*.

When she had gathered enough, she began to spin.

Not a shadow-cloak this time; not a mirror of seeing. Instead she spun an illusion, throwing all her heart and soul into the pure joy of creation.

Out of the sea he rose: the gargantuan, fearsome form of the Phaerie Lord, his grey eyes flashing, his dark hair flying wild and his face ablaze with savage purpose. He wielded a gigantic, glittering blade. 'Come out, Ghabal.' The thunder of his voice was deafening. 'Come out and fight. Too long have you skulked and festered like a coward in your diamond fastness. You are sickly, weak and puny, beneath contempt, and no fit guardian of the Fialan. It should belong to me, as it did once before. When I have finished you, it will belong to me again. Come out and fight me if you dare, you craven, grovelling fool.'

An enraged bellow tore the air asunder, and Corisand felt the pain of it pierce her head like knives. Then suddenly Ghabal was there: hulking, titanic, misshapen and dark, his giant body contorted like an ancient oak; his brutish features twisted by madness. He wielded a giant, double-headed axe that was vast enough to sever continents. Its blade left a visible trail of dark power behind it, like oily black smoke, as it clove the air.

'You challenge me? *You*, take the Fialan? Who is the mad one here, Hellorin?' The harsh, atonal cackle of his laugh screeched across the Windeye's nerves. She glanced across at Iriana who stood watching, her face tense with concentration. 'Now,' she urged silently. 'Do it now, Iriana. What are you waiting for?'

The Wizard held up a hand to silence her, still watching Ghabal like a hawk. 'You dare not touch me.' Corisand spat out Hellorin's words with contempt. 'Ugly, foul and craven – the world will be better off without you.' She made her illusion lift his sword, knowing full well that to try to use it would expose the ruse. With another roar of rage the Moldan swung his axe back to strike – and froze there, trapped in a gigantic, glittering crystal that caught the light and splintered it into rainbow sparks.

Iriana staggered and fell to her knees, her forehead beaded with sweat. 'It's amazing what you can do with magic here,' she panted. 'There's so much power available – I could never have done that at home.' She grinned weakly. 'My diamond is much prettier than his, don't you think?'

'Come on.' The Windeye tugged frantically at her arm. 'We've got to hurry. I can see how much it's taking out of you to sustain that barrier. We have to get in there and out again with the Stone before Ghabal escapes.'

'Oh, so you want to jump into the water now?'

'Just get on with it, confound you.' Corisand lowered herself carefully into the sea, cursing roundly in fractured gasps as the cold struck home. As Iriana entered the water, she took a mighty breath and held it as the Wizard pulled her under. It was one of the hardest things she'd ever done, to make herself relax and go limp, and let her companion tow her. Though as a horse she had instinctively known how to swim, and the water held no fears for her, she had no idea how to manage it in this form.

Down, down they went into the frigid blue depths. 'Hurry, hurry,' Corisand chanted over and over in mindspeech, her body filled with the ghastly tension of a desperate need to breathe. Her heart was thundering in her ears and every fibre of her being was urging her to let go and fill her lungs as Iriana pulled her into the tunnel – and just as her tortured body could hold out no longer, they cleared the surface of the water. She took a great, wheezing gasp of air and a little water, and clung to the side of the pool as she spluttered and coughed.

When they had both caught their breath, it was Corisand who emerged first and pulled Iriana out after her. The immense strain of maintaining Ghabal's diamond prison was clearly telling on the Wizard: she looked drawn and exhausted, and her face had a greyish tinge. There was no time to rest, the Windeye knew. No time to delay. 'Come on.' She put a supporting arm around the Wizard and linked minds, trying with all her might to send strength and energy to her friend. 'Lean on your staff, and I'll help you.'

The energy transfer seemed to be working, a little. The horrible grey pallor left Iriana's face as she tugged her roughly carved staff from her belt and took a deep breath. 'Let's go, then.' She grasped the Windeye's arm in silent thanks. Hobbling like two old crones, they crossed the cavern and entered the tunnel on the other side – only to be met by a baffling labyrinth of passages, twisting and crossing and running in all directions.

'Oh, *pox!*' Iriana, her strength worn down by the burden she was carrying, sounded close to tears.

Corisand, on the other hand, suddenly felt deeply calm. Her Othersight, much more advanced than that of the Wizard, could sense the Fialan's energy beating against her like a ray of sunlight. Suddenly everything fell into place. 'These tunnels don't mean anything. The Moldan put them here to baffle intruders. Only one goes anywhere.'

'Yes, but which?'

'I know.' The Windeye smiled. 'I can feel the Fialan calling. It will tell me where to go. Close your eyes, Iriana. Don't look at the tunnels

– they'll only confuse you. Let me guide you and we'll find the way.'

In accordance with these instructions, Corisand closed her own eyes and took a firm grip on the Wizard's arm. The energy trail was clear in her mind's eye, glittering like a million emeralds, leading right back to its source – the Stone of Fate. Confidently, the Windeye took the first step forward.

'Not long now,' the Stone seemed to be singing. 'Not long.'

They groped their way into the heart of the fastness, with the song of the Fialan growing louder with every step, until Iriana could hear it too. But Corisand was worried about her friend. Though faint light filtered through the crystal walls from outside, and the going was smooth and unobstructed, the strain was telling badly on the Wizard. Her breathing sounded laboured, her steps were dragging and her hand on the Windeye's arm had begun to tremble. How much longer would she last? How much longer could her barrier hold? They were caught in a deadly race against time now. Only too well did she recall the Moldan's power from their first encounter. If he should free himself before they took the Stone, they were finished.

'Iriana – can you try to go a little faster? We're almost there. We don't have far to go,' she coaxed. The Wizard nodded – the barest movement of her head – then clenched her jaw and kept on going.

And all the time, the siren lure of the Fialan was growing. Suddenly it soared into a joyous paean as they emerged into a monstrous cavern: the mountain's hollow heart.

This was the lair of Ghabal: empty, vast and soulless. Down through the long ages he had dwelt here, tortured and in agony, lost in a nightmare world of pain and torment since Hellorin's betrayal. Corisand felt a stab of pity, as she had when they first met. Firmly, she forced it down. He was insane, and dangerous, and wielded unthinkable power. Given the fraction of a chance, he would crush her like a fly.

Then she saw the Stone, and all thoughts of the Moldan fell away.

It floated high above them, suspended by some kind of spell: a crystal of brilliant emerald light that shot spars of radiance all around the chamber. It was incredibly small to hold such astonishing power – about the size of a circled finger and thumb – but the magic blazed forth from it, and she could feel it yearning, waiting, wanting to be claimed and freed. Corisand looked at Iriana. The Wizard's eyes were wide and filled with a dazzling joy, and she realised that the same expression of longing must be on her own face.

But only one of them could wield the Stone.

I should have it. I found it. I came to the Elsewhere first – had it not been for me, Iriana would never have been here at all. It'll save my people. I need it. I want it.

It should be mine.

But even as these thoughts streamed through her mind, the truth was staring her in the face. She took a deep breath and turned to Iriana, dragging her eyes from the glorious Stone. 'Take it – it's yours.'

The Wizard gasped. 'But Corisand, you need it—'

'I know I do. I know. But don't you see it has to be this way? When we go back to our world I'll be a horse again. I won't be able to wield it then.'

'But you won't be a horse.' Iriana took hold of her hands. 'Corisand, don't you see? You can use the Fialan to keep your shape when you go back through. Then you'll be back in our world with your powers intact, and we can find a way to free your people.'

The Windeye swallowed hard. 'We?'

'Well, you didn't think I was just going to abandon you when we got back, and go on my merry way? You're my friend, you idiot. We're in this together.'

'And there never was a truer friend.' Corisand's voice was unsteady. 'I'll make you a promise, Iriana, here and now, on the Fialan itself. Once my people have been freed, I'll pass the Stone on to you. It will have done its work for me. You can use it to help your people too.'

'Done.' The Wizard's smile was dazzling. 'Here.' She thrust her staff into the Windeye's unready hands. 'You'll need this to focus your magic when you call the Stone. Its power is so vast, you'll need a conduit to handle all the energy.'

'But – it's *your* staff.'

'I never liked the accursed thing anyway. Unfortunately it's attuned to me, but not too strongly, because I so rarely used it. You should be able to manage.' Iriana gasped and turned pale, as if she had been stabbed. 'Go on, why don't you? Hurry. Ghabal has sensed that the Fialan is under threat. I can't hold him back much longer.'

The Windeye willed herself steady as she grasped the staff in both hands and raised it high to focus on the Fialan. She summoned the Stone: longing, yearning, putting all her power and will and hope into that call. She felt a leap of response in the Fialan, a flare of magic, and—

'Why in Perdition are you giving it to *her*?'

The voice cut across her concentration, severing her link. She heard a strangled cry from Iriana and swung around with an oath on her lips – just in time to see the Wizard, her face transfigured with joy, throw herself into the arms of Avithan.

404

Corisand's first thought was sheer, stunned disbelief; her second was for the Moldan. 'Iriana, your shield!' she cried. 'Don't forget your shield—' But even as the words left her mouth, she felt the earth shake under her feet and knew it was too late.

Whirling, she flung all her energy at the Fialan, willing it to her with every last scrap of her strength. The staff quivered in her hands, then twisted, writhed and changed its form. The rough, uneven shaft became smoothly polished wood, with the sinuous carven shapes of twin serpents twining all around it. The Fialan sprang from its high place and floated down towards the staff, and to Corisand's utter shock, the snakes reared up their heads and caught the crystal between them, in their jaws.

Power smashed down the Windeye's arm like a hammer blow, filling her body with what felt like the heart of the sun. Struggling to contain the energy, she felt herself growing; towering over Avithan and Iriana like a colossus with the magic crackling and sparking around her in an aureole.

Avithan cursed. 'Be careful,' he yelled. 'Athina sent me to warn you—'

Before he could finish, the Moldan stepped through the wall and into the vast chamber. 'No! The Stone is mine. It will be mine FOREVER.' With a roar of rage he turned on Corisand, raising the gargantuan axe – but some power of the Fialan seemed to hold him back. Instead he turned like a striking snake and snatched up Iriana in one massive hand.

Time stuttered to a standstill in an instant of frozen horror ... Then the Moldan laughed. 'Give me back the Stone,' he said. 'Give it to me now – or I will crush your little friend to a bloody pulp.'

'No!' the cry came from Avithan, far below. He unleashed a mighty blast of magic – but to Ghabal, it must have felt like little more than a bee-sting. Contemptuously, he kicked the Wizard aside. Avithan smashed into the wall of the chamber – and vanished.

A wail of anguish came from Iriana, and Corisand felt the burning force of her rage all the way across the cavern as she unleashed her will. The Moldan's hand holding the Wizard burst into flame, and with a cry he dropped her to the ground. She lay, unmoving, but her wildfire was still spreading, devouring his arm and shoulder and gnawing at his body.

Bellowing with pain and anger, he staggered towards Corisand, swinging his burning arm at her like a club. She raised her staff and flung a bolt of energy at him from the Stone, but she had not yet learned how to wield it, and it came out unfocused, and too weak to stop him. He staggered back a step or two, then came at her again, raising the deadly axe.

'Please,' Corisand begged the Stone. 'Please help me.' Another bolt of energy shot forth, but Ghabal was powerful and ancient, and still he kept on coming.

She should go. Escape back to her own world – the Fialan knew the way – but Corisand would not leave Iriana, and the Moldan stood between her and her friend. She dodged aside as the axe came down, missing her by a hair's breadth, but he was inexorably backing her towards the wall, and she was running out of room to escape him. Though he was engulfed in flame now, and shrieking in agony, he showed no sign of stopping. If he struck again—

'Curse you all, the Stone is MINE!' Hellorin, the Forest Lord, stepped through the wall of the fastness as easily as Ghabal had done. He too had grown to a gigantic size, and looked at the Windeye with contempt as he flung a bolt of dark energy at the Moldan that knocked him back against the wall. 'I owe you my thanks, Xandim.' His voice was mocking. 'In taking the Fialan from this fool, you opened the way for me to enter his fastness. You really have done me a great favour. You and your little Wizard friend have weakened him enough to make him easy game. And after I have finished with him, I will deal with *you*.'

He turned back to the screaming fireball that was the Moldan – but in succumbing to the irresistible urge to taunt the Windeye, he had delayed too long. Ghabal launched himself at the Forest Lord, and as the two of them grappled, the fire spread to Hellorin …

Corisand took her chance. Diving past them, she shrank down to her normal size. Darting to where Iriana lay, she grasped the Wizard's hand firmly in her own and called on the powers of the Fialan. 'Now. You know the way. Please take us home.'

She was snatched up in a whirlwind of green power, the energy of the Stone, with Iriana at her side. Suddenly Iriana's hand tightened in hers and her urgent thought filled the Windeye's mind. 'Your shape. Hold on to your human shape.'

It was difficult – she could *feel* her body wanting to morph back into the form of a horse – but Iriana, weak and injured as she was, added power of her own.

The shape held firm.

The spinning vortex set them down.

They were back in their own world, where they had started, on the lakeshore next to Athina's island. And gripped tightly in the Windeye's hand, the Stone of Fate, on its serpent staff, coruscated with a fierce and joyous energy, and sang a song of celebration of its own. Long ages ago it had been imprisoned by the Moldan. Now it was free, with a new keeper in a whole new world. The possibilities were endless.

EPILOGUE

Athina, with the shimmering ghostly shape of Avithan's consciousness by her side, looked into the Timeless Lake and saw the two friends, Windeye and Wizard, sitting in the kitchen of the Cailleach's tower. Dael, his face beaming at their safe return, was cooking them a gargantuan meal. They both looked bedraggled and exhausted, and though Iriana had already worked some healing magic on herself, her bruises would take a while to fade.

Nonetheless, they seemed content. Iriana, blind once more, was cradling Melik on her lap, while Corisand held the precious Fialan and its staff.

'Athina must have snatched him safely back,' Iriana was saying. 'We Wizards can feel the death of another, especially if it's someone we're close to. I know he's still alive. And one day I'm going to find him.' She blushed a little. 'There in the cavern – he said he loved me.'

'I hope she does find a way back to me.' Avithan's ghostly face creased in a smile. 'I do love her, you know.'

'I wouldn't put anything past that one,' the Cailleach replied. 'In the meantime, I will keep working on a way to free your body from the time spell.' She sighed. 'Will I never learn? Every time I try to help, it ruins everything. It was the shock of seeing you that broke Iriana's hold upon the Moldan. Were it not for those two valiant, determined souls, the whole thing would have ended very badly.'

'And now?'

'And now they have the Fialan. Corisand will find a way to free her people, and Iriana's folk will gain the weapon you always wanted them to have. And it is just as well. It will take the Moldan and the Phaerie Lord some time to recover, but I think they will bury their enmity for a time in

407

the interests of regaining the Stone. Despite all our efforts, Corisand and Iriana left a trail. Eventually Ghabal and Hellorin will be coming, and the Windeye and the Wizard had better be ready for them when they do.'

'But you've got to warn them!' Avithan's voice cracked with alarm.

'No.' Athina shook her head. 'I cannot. And even if I could, I would not. I have learned a bitter lesson, my friend, and my days of interference are at an end. Now we can only watch – and fate will have its way.'

Avithan sighed. 'I hope they'll be all right.'

The Cailleach smiled. 'So do I. But do you know, somehow I think they'll manage.'